Robert Ryan was born in Liverpool. He has written for the *Face*, *Arena*, *Condé Nast Traveller*, *Esquire*, *GQ* magazine and *The Sunday Times*. He lives in North London with his wife and three children. He is the author of *Underdogs*, *Nine Mil*, *Trans Am* and the bestsellers *Early One Morning*, *The Blue Noon* and *Night Crossing*.

D0474848

AFTER MIDNIGHT

Robert Ryan

review

First published in 2005
by REVIEW

An imprint of Headline Book Publishing

First published in paperback in 2005

4

ISBN 0 7553 2187 1

Typeset in JansonText by
Letterpart Limited, Reigate, Surrey

Printed and bound in Great Britain by
Clays Ltd, St Ives plc

Headline's policy is to use papers that are natural, renewable and
recyclable products and made from wood grown in sustainable forests.
The logging and manufacturing processes are expected to conform
to the environmental regulations of the country of origin.

HEADLINE BOOK PUBLISHING
A division of Hodder Headline
338 Euston Road
London NW1 3BH

www.reviewbooks.co.uk
www.hodderheadline.com

For Anne Storm and her father Bob Millar, otherwise known as F/O T.R. Millar RAAF Aus 422612 – 104 Squadron RAF and 31 Squadron SAAF. Lost over Italy in 1944 and still missing.

Author's Note

Certain elements of *After Midnight* are based on fact. The near-suicidal supply drops over Warsaw from Foggia in Southern Italy by the RAF and the SAAF (South African Air Force), the loss of Liberator bombers in the Italian mountains – one of them still missing, sixty years later – Mussolini's puppet regime at Saló and Villa Feltrinelli, the Red Stocking missions, the sealed trains at Chiasso and the Republic of Ossola, centred on Domodossola near the Swiss border, are all true.

As is the letter written from Foggia by an Australian airman to the one-year-old daughter he had never seen.

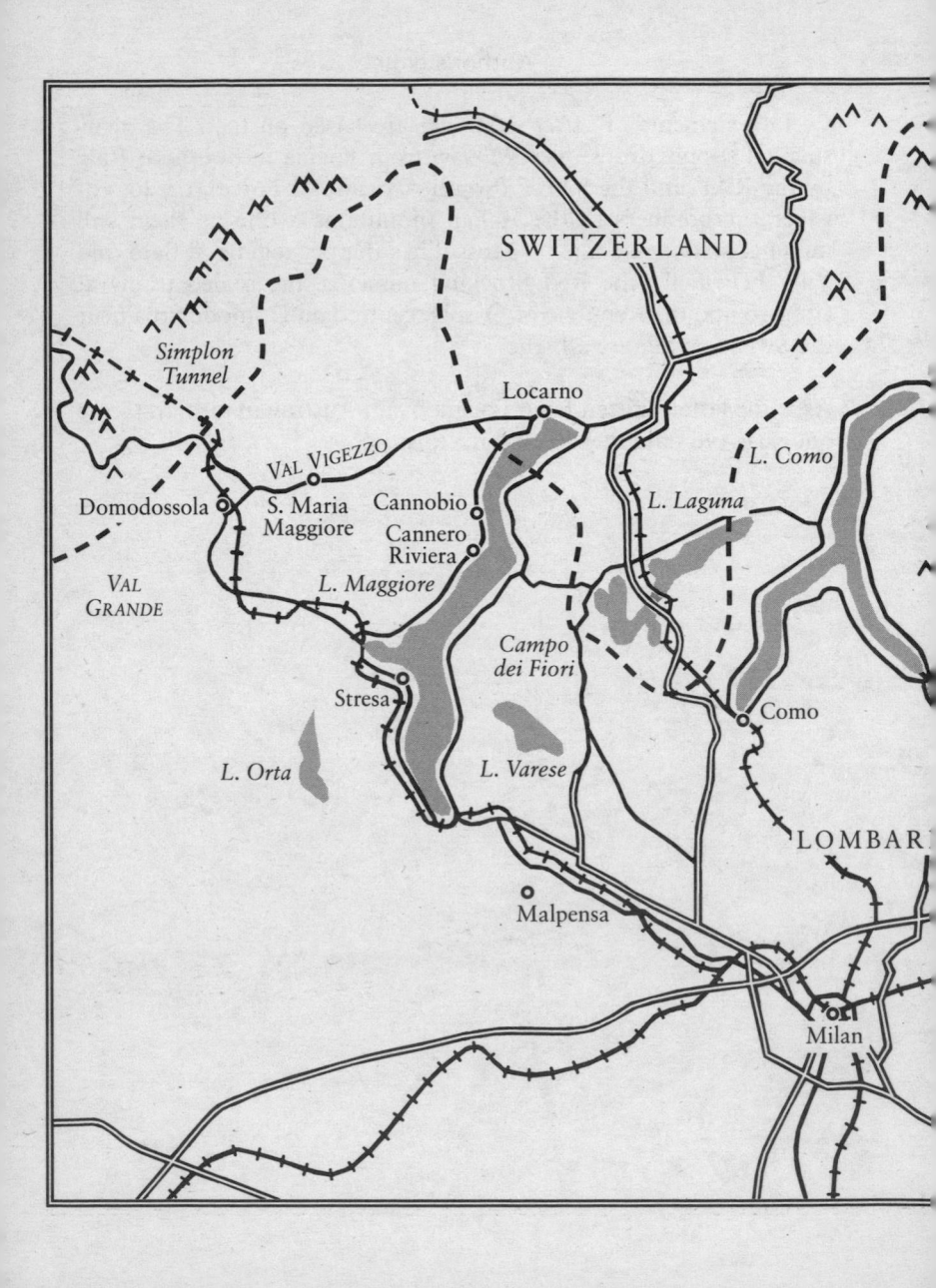

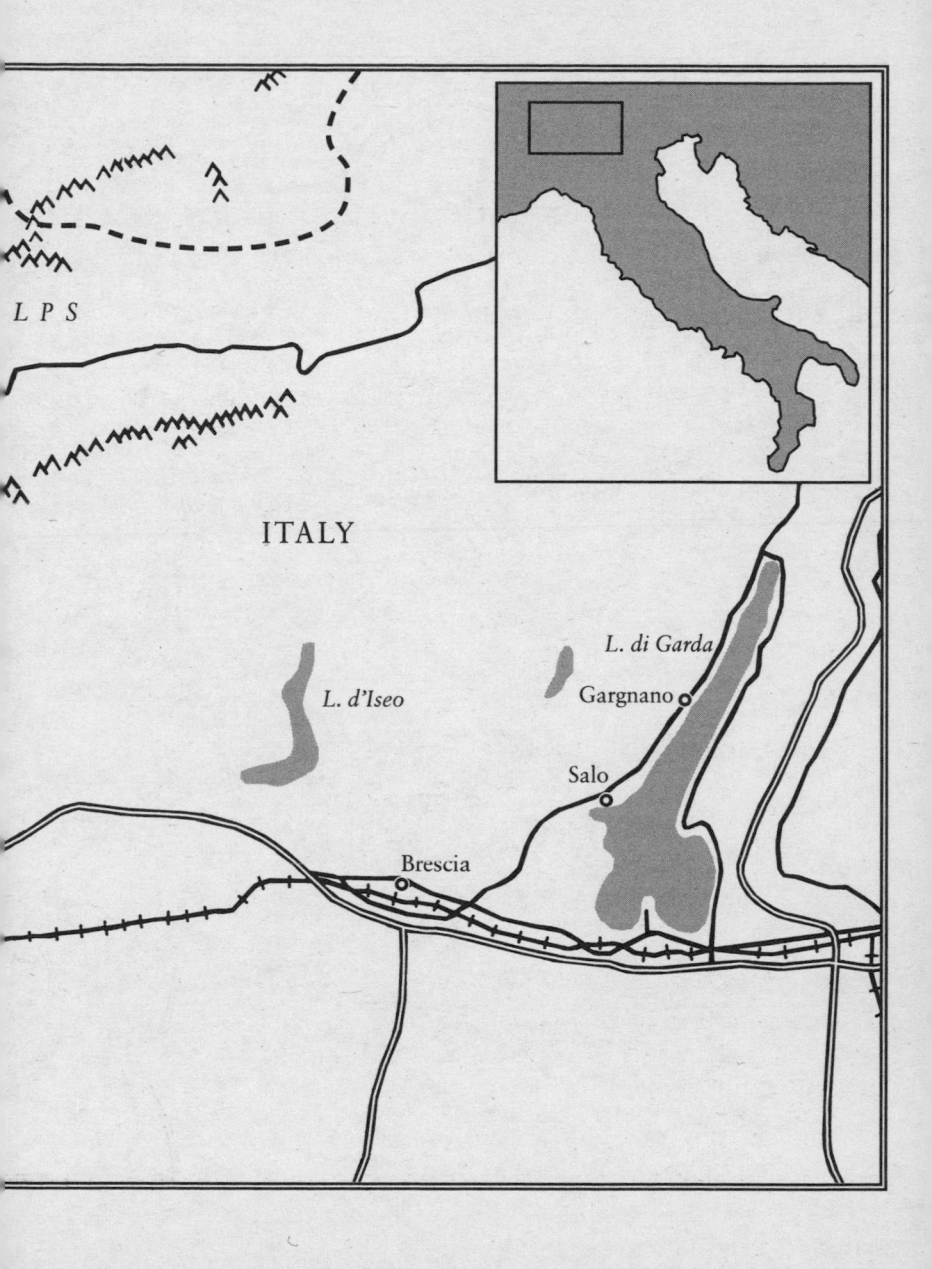

LPS

ITALY

L. di Garda

L. d'Iseo

Gargnano

Salo

Brescia

Prologue

F/O W.L. Carr, RAAF Aus 776557, CMF Italy
Aug 1944

My Dear Daughter,
   This is the first time I have written to you and although you are as yet too young to read it, perhaps Mother will save it up until the time comes when you can read it yourself. In two days' time it will be your first birthday anniversary – a great event for your parents. My regret is that I cannot personally be there to help you blow out your single candle but, believe me, lassie, I will be there in spirit.
   I am writing this from a place called Italy which is far away from our fair land – a place where I would not be by choice so far away separated from a wife and daughter so dear to me. But I am here, precious one, because there is a war on caused by certain people who wished to rule the world harshly and despotically, imperilling an intangible thing called democracy which your mother and I thought all decent people should fight for. You will understand as you grow up what democracy means for us and how it is an ideal way of life which we aspire to put into practice.
   All I ask of you, Lindy dear, is that you stay as sweet as your mother and cling tight to the subtle thing we call Christianity, which has been the core of her way of life and her mother's and mine. I hope that you will love

1

and respect me as I love and respect my father.

That's all, young lady. Have a happy birthday – may they all be happy birthdays. I hope to be home again one fine day. In the meantime, lots of love to you and to Mother.

From Dad,
Bill Carr.

Part One

One

Italy, 1964

For the best part of twenty years he had lain, ready for someone to find him. To begin with, he'd been well hidden in the rear of the mountain hut, with bales of straw, two sheets of canvas, a long-departed *montanaro*'s hoe and half a dozen tree branches piled on top of him. Over time, though, several of the layers had either rotted or been taken.

A few years ago, a group of teenage boys had removed the branches to make a St John's Eve fire in the meadow outside, digging a hole for their pyre with the alp-man's rusty hoe and enjoying themselves under the darkening summer solstice sky by telling ever-scarier stories of the witches and wizards said to inhabit this wild corner of the country, until most of them were too terrified to sleep. In the morning, bleary-eyed and weary, but infused with bravado by the return of the sun, the group had walked down the trail towards the nearest village for breakfast without exploring the hut further.

The brutal winters with their icy winds and heavy snowdrifts had eroded the door of the *baita*, which collapsed off its hinges, permitting various animals to enter, including the last of the wolves still roaming these hills, pulling away corners of the straw and the fabric, their noses twitching as they smelled the decay beneath. Gradually, he was revealed to the world, his right hand still clenched in the fist he had made as he died, containing a last bequest to his discoverers. Except, for the time being, nobody came to claim the piece of metal he held so firmly in his bony grip.

That next winter and summer removed his remaining clothes – his boots had been taken at the time of his death, too warm and comfortable to resist – and what little flesh was left clinging to the bones. His left arm was torn off and carried away by scavengers, which also removed his mandible and several ribs. He lay there now, a yellow-brown collection of bones, slowly collapsing into himself as the rest of his ligaments and cartilage dissolved.

It was this figure that the two giggling honeymooning hikers found when they peered into the hut, his head resting on his chest, as if he had nodded off. The new bride's screams echoed around the granite outcrops which overlooked the ancient alpine meadow and were lost in the mountains, much like the poor dead man's soul two decades ago.

Two

I confirmed that I was, indeed, Jack Kirby, and the Italian operator told me to wait, as she was putting an international call through. As usual, the Italian state telephone company took its time about it. I was standing at the back of the hangar, staring past the dark shape of my plane, out onto the mess of Malpensa airport. They were lengthening the runway so that it could take the next generation of intercontinental jets. Already there were piles of gravel and sand, and bright yellow cement-mixers and Fiat bulldozers eyed us hungrily. We'd been given notice to quit. Kirby & Gabbiano Flight Services were situated right where the smooth, shining new taxiway was to be constructed.

'Sorry, chaps,' they had said. 'We'll try and squeeze you in somewhere, but space is going to be tight.' Well, they had the choice between keeping sweet a seat-of-the-pants outfit whose main client was the University of Milan Parachute Club or preparing for the arrival of hordes of Pan Am air hostesses. I'd tried to blame them for choosing the latter, but my heart wasn't in it.

We'd been living on borrowed time anyway. We had started out in 1962 when an old US TV series called *Ripcord* – about a couple of skydiving troubleshooters – had been dubbed into Italian and had generated a boom in would-be free-fallers. We had what we claimed was a Beechcraft Twin Beech – in reality, its ageing AT-11 variant, an ex-USAAF trainer – which was relatively easy to convert between skydiving and regular passenger use, so it seemed silly not to take advantage of the craze, what with the university jumpers already on the airfield and short of a decent lift vehicle.

Now the boom time might be over, because the same television station was showing *Whirlybirds*, and everyone wanted to be Bell helicopter pilots. TV was doing that to Italy – smoothing out the regional dialects, dictating the latest trends, unifying the nation in a way no politician had managed since you-know-who. Well, I didn't have a chopper, couldn't fly one, didn't want to learn. I didn't trust anything with a glidepath like a housebrick. Or one engine.

Furthermore, Malpensa were suggesting that they didn't really want idiot parachutists dropping in, dodging the new wide-bodied jets, now they were a grown-up international airport. I'd found out that morning that the parachute group had been given its marching orders, too.

On top of that the contract with our main client, Gennaro, the Milanese food conglomerate, looked shaky. During the last run down to Rome, I had overheard two of the buyers talking longingly about the new Learjets. Fast, comfortable, with air hostesses serving drinks and no glass nose to make them look like a retired World War Two bomber. I hadn't figured out how to introduce air hostesses into the jerry-built interior of our six-seat Beechcraft. Besides, I'd have trouble balancing a Scotch, peanuts and the control stick.

There was a hissing noise on the line. '*Pronto?*' I said.

'Mr Kirby?' She sounded like she was calling from the Gobi Desert. But then, I had a grappa hangover, so everyone sounded like they were speaking to me from Mongolia or beyond.

'Mr Kirby?' she repeated from her yurt.

'This is he.'

'My name is Lindy Carr.' I tried to place the accent. It wasn't

English, but then it wasn't Mongolian either.

'Hi. What can I do for you?'

'I got your name from Mr Lang.'

'Did you?' I thought he only said my name when he was in the middle of a satanic mass, performing strange rituals that compelled me to drink far more grappa than was good for my head.

'He's the Special—'

'I know who he is.' And I knew he was queer, which was fine by me, but a bit risky for a man in his position, and I wouldn't repeat that down the line. Archibald Lang was also Special Forces Adviser to the Foreign Office, the official archivist of sabotage and subversion. Which meant his job was to say to historians, journalists and families variations on: 'I'm sorry, we don't have that information' or 'Oh dear, that file seems to have been destroyed by a rather unfortunate fire back in forty-seven' or 'I'm afraid that is covered by the Official Secrets Act.' Why was he giving out my number?

I raised a hand to Furio, my partner, who was dragging his weary carcass into the hangar. A decade younger than me, he was tall, dark, without an ounce of spare flesh on him, and usually fresh-faced, but there were signs of a serious decline this morning. He steadied himself against the glass nose cone and, even in the gloom, I could see the sheen of sweat on his forehead.

Furio had started as a mere dogsbody at the outfit, but I gave him a share of the company and flying lessons after I was short for wages, hangar and landing fees one quarter, and to help me out he had borrowed the cash from his mother, a researcher on *La Stampa* newspaper in Turin. They now owned 24 per cent of the company.

Furio waved back at me but the effort was too much and he tottered out into the fresh air again, bent double, trying to stop himself throwing up. And I thought the young could take their drink. The previous night, we'd been in Milan, drowning our sorrows so comprehensively, we weren't quite sure what they were any more. Oh yes, I reminded myself. They're putting a new runway through our business.

'Mr Kirby?' came the voice in my ear.

'Yes? Sorry.'

'Mr Lang said you know Northern Italy very well.'

I waited while a BEA Viscount chattered its way into the air and flew directly over us, rattling the metal roof. Another threatened species. Turboprop passenger planes were being hunted to extinction by packs of shiny new Boeing jets. I knew how they felt. Old and in the way.

'Most of it. Which part are you interested in?'

'The lakes down to Milan, across to Turin one way, Bergamo the other. North to the Swiss border.'

I'd been there all right. Much of it was my backyard. The glass nose cone of the Beechcraft meant I was the number one choice for flight-seeing up and down the lakes. 'I'm familiar with the region. What do you need?'

'I'd rather show you in person than talk over the telephone.'

'You've been spending too much time with Lang. The only people likely to be tapping my phone are the bank, and only because they are worried about the repayments on the loan for the Twin Beech.'

'I might be able to help with those repayments, Mr Kirby. You see, I want to hire you for a few weeks. A month guaranteed, even if you end up only working a few days. But I'd like to talk about it face-to-face.'

I looked down at myself. Battered leather jacket, a stale shirt, oil-splattered jeans and dusty construction boots. I was thinking it was best to get this done over the phone, not in person. I wouldn't hire me for a month looking like this.

'When are we talking about?' I asked.

'September into October.'

I did some quick calculations. We had to be out of the hangar by

November. We could pretty much guarantee skydiving income throughout the summer, and flying in the mountains in August could be tricky because of the thunderstorms. The two months she mentioned gave us a good window before the snow started. So the timing was good. If she was going to give us four weeks' work in the autumn, it'd certainly help see us through the winter and maybe into a new base.

'Where are you?' I asked, hoping she was closer than the line suggested.

'England at the moment. I will be in Italy at the end of August.'

I didn't want to leave it that long before locking this one down. Anything could happen in a couple of months. She might even find herself a proper outfit to hire. 'As luck would have it, I'll be over there in a few weeks,' I told her. 'You want to give me a number where I can reach you?' It was a London number; I was due to travel to the Isle of Man with my father, but I was certain I could add a meeting with Lindy Carr to my itinerary.

I scribbled the number on the whiteboard with a Chinagraph pencil, right next to the reminder that the plane needed to have the main spar checked for corrosion. Rumours had spread of an imminent airworthiness directive, mandating frequent X-rays of all Twin Beech spars – including any remaining AT-11s – which had sent the value of the aircraft plummeting. That was why I could afford the plane. Mine had had its spar tubes coated with linseed oil from the get-go, and I was confident it was clean, but it was as well to be sure. When I could afford it.

I looked outside again. Furio was talking to Professore Gianlorenzo Borromini, an art historian at the university, who was one of the keenest skydivers and a founder of the club. I could see him windmilling his arms in rage, doubtless cursing the airport and all who worked for it. We'd passed that stage a few days back. All I hoped now was that my partner could resist vomiting on the Professore's well-polished shoes.

I turned my attention back to my potential fairy godmother. 'You sure you won't give me a clue what the job is?'

She said: 'I want to find my father, Mr Kirby.'

'You think he's up there in the mountains?'

'I'm pretty certain.'

'When did you last hear from him?'

'1944, Mr Kirby. He's dead.'

After a few more questions, expertly deflected by Miss Carr, I hung up feeling unsettled, but put that down to the sourness of the grappa in my stomach. Of course, I didn't know then that I was the man who had helped get her father killed in the first place.

Three

A welcoming committee of screeching gulls appeared well before the once-familiar sight of Douglas Harbour on the Isle of Man hove into view. My father and I stood at the rail near the front of the good ship *Mona's Isle*, riding the sickly swell which had been running ever since the ship had left the mouth of the Mersey. Below deck, the air was ripe with a mixture of vomit and diesel. We were better off taking our chances with the voracious sea birds that whirled overhead and the knifing wind from the north that even managed to penetrate our leather jackets. Nobody had told the Irish Sea it was summer and it could calm down a little.

'You all right?'

My father put his hand on my shoulder and squeezed, a rare moment of physical contact. His grey face creased into hundreds of parallel lines as he smiled. A lifetime of building and repairing motorcycles meant that, for as long as I could remember, Dad had always been an unhealthy colour, the result of hours spent over carborundum wheels, lathes, soldering irons, grinders and oil baths. No amount of sun could soften the pallor, and it was as much a part of him as the dirt under his fingernails and the set of Allen keys he always seemed to have about his person. There were more grooves in his face now, and they were deeper than the last time I had seen him, nearly three years ago, but otherwise he was his old self.

'I'm fine,' I replied. 'Thanks for doing this.'

'I didn't have a fatted calf to slaughter to welcome you back. I thought this was the next best thing.'

'You could have done both,' I whined with mock petulance.

'Well, if the Bells in Douglas still does a good meat 'n' potato pie, I might throw that in.'

'It's a start.'

'It's good to have you home, Jack, if only for a couple of weeks.'

Before I could answer, something splattered onto his shoulder and he looked up at the cackling culprit that had defaced his leathers. 'Bloody shite-hawks,' he muttered as he searched for a handkerchief. I unzipped my jacket and passed him mine.

'You hear Winston is ill?' he asked with concern in his voice. My father was one of those Englishmen who treated Churchill with more respect than any monarch.

'No.'

'He was on television last year. Looked bloody awful. Was it shown over there in Italy?'

'I don't watch much TV, Dad. My landlord won't have it in the house. Thinks it poisons the mind.'

'He might just be right.' He pointed across the deck at two giggling girls, trying to hold their miniskirts down in the wind, both clutching the same LP record with a black-and-white picture of four hairy young men on the front. I guessed it was the Beatles. Or maybe the other lot, the Rolling Stones. I had trouble keeping up.

'It's a different world, Dad.'

'What say we skip seeing the course today and leave it until tomorrow?' my father said as he wiped the seagull excrement away.

I had to fight to stop my jaw dropping. Below us in the hold were two Kirby CrossCountry motorcycles, Father's latest project, which had little more than the miles from Brighton to Liverpool we had put on them. The idea was to give them a work-out on the Isle of Man's mountain course – the roads were being closed for two extra days this year because of the introduction of several new categories – and to get some much-needed publicity for the Kirby brand. They were going to need it: the CrossCountrys were odd bikes, higher and less streamlined than the norm, with a bulbous, humped tank and the engine caged in the chassis, which formed a kind of tubular exoskeleton. The look was growing on me, I suppose, albeit slowly. I wasn't certain the public would be so forgiving.

Perhaps the old man was worried about the impact that seeing the course would have on me – the place where I had started out as a bright shining star and fizzled out as a damp squib. Or perhaps he thought I would be rusty – it was a decade since I had ridden a bike in anger. Maybe he was just getting old, and I hadn't noticed. Then I caught his wink and he chortled as he gripped the worn rail and filled his lungs with salty air, as if trying to catch the whiff of motorcycle exhaust that would soon blanket the island.

I punched him on the shoulder. 'Okey-dokey. And I'll make the Horlicks, eh?'

An hour after docking we went across to the pits to have the bikes scrutineered. We weren't here for competition – my father had entered his last works bike thirteen years ago in 1951, the year after I'd quit racing – but any 'specials' which took to the mountain course were still subject to a safety check, apart from those on the free-for-all known as Mad Sunday, when the public got to ride the course. Dad had pulled strings to get us a place on one of the extra official practice days, even though we wouldn't be competing. When I asked how, he came out with some mangled aphorism about packdrills and blind horses. In other words: mind your own business.

It was the usual chaos in the pits, only more so since my day.

There were trailers for the star riders, shiny portable workshops, legions of mechanics swarming over bikes, and plenty of banners bearing names unfamiliar back in the early 1950s – Suzuki, Yamaha, Honda. Unfamiliar and, to be honest, unthinkable back then.

While my father went off to sort out the passes and paperwork, I leaned against my bike, arms crossed, trying to take it all in. There were many new faces, people who had grown into legends in my absence – like Hailwood, who had started here in 1958 when he was just eighteen, before blasting a name for himself three years later, and McIntyre, Hocking and Read. The sights and sounds were much the same, I thought, except for one pungent odour, stronger than the reek of Castrol or REDeX. Money. The quirky little British outfits, once the character of the TT, were few and far between. It was a fierce battle between the big boys and their wallets now.

Some things might have changed but a few go on for ever, I thought, as a mustachioed figure strode towards me, clipboard in one hand, pipe clamped firmly between his teeth, trailing a cloud of Condor.

'Jack Kirby,' the voice cracked out smartly, dragging the facts from the Rolodex that was his brain. 'First competed in 1939 on a single-cylinder Kirby, when you had a little, uh, trouble as I recall.' I nodded. He knew damn well I had been disqualified and banned for two years, by which time there were no more TTs because of the war. 'Raced forty-nine and fifty, RTD in the first, seventh in the second. Gearbox trouble, as I recall. Not been seen here since.' He stuffed the clipboard under his arm and held out a hand which I took. He looked frailer than I remembered but the enthusiasm in his eyes, the sheer pleasure of being among bikes and racers, was undimmed. 'What kept you?'

Geoff Davison was a legend on the island – he'd won TTs back in the 1920s and had since become its unofficial chronicler, writing and editing the *TT Special*.

I smiled. 'You kidding? Geoff Duke. Wasn't worth racing any more, with him around.'

'The Duke?' He plucked the pipe from his mouth. 'I've heard people say you showed more promise than him in thirty-nine.'

I laughed. 'I heard that too.' Of course he neglected to say that the promise was no longer there after the war.

'Course I don't believe it.' He waved his pipe, embers flying from the bowl. 'You were good, but . . . ' He let the rest die. 'I also heard you promised your mother you'd stop?'

It wasn't true. The reality was, the spark had gone. I looked at people like Duke and Bell and Cromie and could see they still had the fire in the belly. For me, something was missing. In 1939, motorcycles were what I lived for. But once the war was over, bike racing seemed nothing much more than going round in circles very fast. Yes, it was dangerous, a test of man and machine, and I respected anyone who went out on that TT course, but hell, I'd attacked flak ships with rockets while skimming the waves at twenty feet, and done Red Stocking missions at thirty thousand. I wasn't the eager boy I'd been in 1939. The thrill had gone. Still, instead of trying to explain this I said: 'Have you met my mother?'

Davison grinned as he recalled the small, dark, fearsome bundle of energy that at one time accompanied my father to the island. She had two pet hates: flying and motorbikes. It was a wonder my parents ever got together, let alone stayed apparently happily married. And she certainly disapproved of my career choices, the unspoken rift between us. 'Fair point. So what are you doing now? Back to Kirby Motorcycles?'

We – well, my father – had a bike dealership just outside Brighton. An excellent location, because it was on the classic bike run to the South Coast, with plenty of passing trade and weekend tyre-kickers who could be converted into paying customers. He sold Triumphs next to Kirby bikes, although not quite enough of them to cover the cost of making his own models. So in a series of sheds out the back, he also produced invalid carriages for the Ministry of Pensions, those flimsy light blue three-wheelers that were given to the disabled. Except Kirby ones weren't flimsy. Dad's were re-engineered so they were safer, more stable, and marginally faster, too. Anyone who was allocated a Kirby-produced carriage was a lucky invalid indeed.

'And maybe race again?' concluded Davison.

I shook my head. 'I'm more of a flyer these days. You know, airplanes.'

'Ah. Shame.'

'Davy.' It was my father, clutching sheafs of paperwork, his face creased with pleasure once more, using the older man's diminutive. 'How are you?' Before Davison could answer, Dad spun round to me and said, 'Over to the scrutineers now. We've got a slot in forty minutes. Pairs at twenty.' Two bikes let onto the course, followed by two others at twenty-second intervals, as opposed to ten seconds in an actual race.

It was then I felt the first flash of fear.

In 1949, I had crashed just after Mountain Mile – which Davison had politely referred to as an RTD, for retired – coming down through the gears for the right-hand sweeps known as the Verandah. I had pranged a valuable fighter-bomber once, a Mosquito, but I could blame that on mechanical failure. The bike crash was all down to me. Trying to take a bend too fast, I caught a wall with the left-hand footrest. I don't remember the actual moment of the bike collapsing beneath me, but my right leg had been trapped under it, dragging me along towards the bridge, where the pair of us smacked into the stonework. I had a long, detailed list at home of the damage that was done. I didn't come out of it too well, either. I spent a few weeks in Nobles Hospital, but I was back the next year. An RTD wasn't the way to bow out, and although seventh place in a field of sixty wasn't glory, it was far from ignominy.

I expected some kind of unease at the memory of the smash fifteen years ago, but on the first lap I flashed by the place of my foul-up, having hit 115 mph on the Mountain Mile, without so much as a shudder. I pushed back up into third as I took the bridge, gave the implacable stone wall a quick glance and brought the revs up before dropping back to second for the Bungalow Bend, cresting the highest point of the course, nudging over 1400 feet, and began the descent down through Windy Corner, ready to take the bike very nearly flat out for the long approach to Keppel Gate.

There, gone, you've passed it. As I crouched low over the bulbous tank – the CrossCountry was not an ideal road-racing bike, but we both knew that – and felt the wind blast press the goggles against my face and sensed my father sucking at my tailpipe behind me, I wondered why I had never come back.

I heard a gear drop and a big Honda flashed by, then Hocking's MV, a Norton and another Honda, leaving me rocking in their wake. *Stay sharp, Kirby*, I scolded myself. *You did this all wrong once before*.

Yes, sir. Brandish Corner, second gear, maximum revs, then third to go through the Cronk-ny-Mona bends, a beautiful sweep, and I began to wish I could do this on something lower and sleeker and faster with better ratios than the hybrid CrossCountry, something I could throw about more. The substantial ground clearance of the frame required for 'trials' riding meant a high centre of gravity.

I gritted my teeth for the jarring ripples of Bedstead Corner which I took at low revs in third, then the sharp right hand of Nook and Governor's Bridge and the first lap was almost over. No record breaker – Hailwood and Duke would be clocking in around twenty-two minutes, while I reckoned we'd be lucky to have done it in twenty-seven or eight – but it was good to be back.

After three laps, my father and I pulled into the pits, both sweating hard in the late afternoon sun, and parked up. Neither of us said anything for a while, just pushed our goggles up and stared at each other. I guessed I looked as much like a panda from all the road grit and oil as he did.

'Well?' he finally asked.

'The seat is too hard, the suspension jars every bone in your body, my neck aches like hell and it handles like a pig,' I said. I thought the Kirby CrossCountry, which was conceived along the same lines as some of the Triumph TR models, was too much of a compromise, likely to excel at neither road races nor trials, although I couldn't argue with its robustness and I had to admit it had done better than I expected. 'Albeit a Gloucester Old Spot.'

'I wasn't talking about the bike.'

I shrugged and told him the truth. 'It felt good. I've missed it.'

He nodded and the grin faded, to be replaced by something more serious, as if the dark cloud of a bad memory had just floated across his clear blue sky. 'Listen, there's something I meant to tell you on the boat over—'

'Jack Kirby, Jack Kirby!' I turned to see a barrel-shaped man dressed in crisp Moto Guzzi team overalls threading through the ranks of bikes towards me. I tried to place him and he must have seen my confusion. He patted his stomach as he cleared the nearby Nortons. 'Jack, so I got fat. But you must remember. It's me. Etienne – Ragno.'

Ragno. Spider. Strip away twenty years and about four stone and there was the skinny kid who got his nickname from the way he scuttled over the mountains, arms and legs going as if he had eight of them. I took off my helmet and goggles and grabbed his hand, pumping it with pleasure. I felt happy to see him. Which was odd, because the last time we'd been together he had been holding a shiny new Sten gun to my head and was threatening to blow my brains out.

★ ★ ★

The Man of Manx was the nearest pub to the pits, and the bar resembled one of those how-many-people-can-you-get-in-a-Mini stunts that the newspapers liked to do in the summer, except every person, man or woman, seemed dressed identically in black leather. However, the respect shown to a pair of Moto Guzzi overalls, and Ragno's bulk and elbows, meant the crush quickly parted and he managed to secure us drinks. It was beer for me, whisky for him, but there was a moment of confusion with his change.

'So if this is half a crown,' Ragno asked, holding up a silver coin, 'what is a whole crown?'

'Five bob. A dollar, as it is sometimes called.'

'Dollar?'

'That's what a dollar used to be worth. Five bob. Four to the pound.'

Ragno took a fistful of money from his overall pocket and examined it as we worked our way through the crowd. 'I have never had a crown.'

'You don't get many of them,' I said.

'What about this?'

'A florin. Two shillings.'

Ragno shook his head in bafflement. 'And people complain about the lira.'

We took our places on the outside wall. While we drank I ticked off the British marques among the herd parked up in the pub car park: Matchless, Ariel, Greaves, Sunbeam, Douglas, Velocette, AJS, Vincent, Excelsior, DMW, Triumph, Royal Enfield. Some were long gone as viable companies, others, as we all knew, were teetering on the brink of bankruptcy. All the machines looked in rude health here, though, their polished tanks and pipes shining proudly in the late afternoon sun.

I'd left my father talking with Geoff Davison and Harold Daniell, a charming, unassuming man with thick spectacles who, if you didn't know, you'd be hard put to guess had been the first man to lap the 37¾-mile mountain course in under twenty-five minutes, at a speed of 91 mph, back in 1938, on an unsupercharged Norton single.

Over our drinks, we gave each other a quick five-minute catch-up, Ragno skipping over the immediate post-war years, simply saying he'd managed to get a job with the Moto Guzzi people on Lake Como and had worked his way up to becoming one of the senior event organisers, helped by his decent English.

'All this is your fault, of course,' he told me. 'That time when we stripped the old bike . . . hooked, I was.'

'I thought Guzzi ditched racing back in fifty-seven. Left it all to MV.' MV was MV Augusta, one of the other great Italian bike companies.

He shrugged. 'Officially, yes. But if a privateer wants to enter a bike we are keen to test and they ask for our help . . . it's pretty low profile. But there is nowhere in the world quite like here to see what a bike can do.'

'You're thinking of coming back officially?'

'Guzzi?' He tapped the side of his nose. 'We'll see. Not for a while, I think. So what about you?'

I kept my synopsis tight, told him about the 'shuftikite' (recce) missions I was sent on after I got back from Italy after the war, didn't even mention the seasons of clear air turbulence chasing, just the few years of racing, and then ferry work on the Sicily–Tunis route and, finally, once I was thrown off the island, my return back north to Malpensa, and the scrag end of flying. It didn't sound like much of a life when you compressed it into three minutes. Maybe because it wasn't.

'So now you are back here, in England?'

'Just a visit. I have some business in London with a young lady.' He started to grin so I added, 'Real business, Ragno. Not that kind.'

'Do you have that kind? Are you married?'

I shook my head. 'Couple of near misses I walked away from, that's all. You?'

He nodded. 'And two kids.'

'Ragno the father? Christ, I still remember when you were a snotty brat with a Sten gun.'

'Yes. I'm sorry about . . . ' He mimed holding a pistol to his own head. 'It was for your own good.'

'I wanted to stay.'

'They'd have shot you. For once, they were OK with the Italians, but English and Americans they thought of as spies. Showed them no mercy.' He pulled the invisible trigger and made a 'boom' noise. 'You know about the anniversary?'

I shook my head.

'The celebrations?'

Again, I had to shrug. 'I've not been counting anniversaries. Not those ones anyway.'

'It's twenty years in September since Domodossola.'

'Right,' I said, taking a gulp of beer. 'Of course, it's the twenty-year anniversary of D-day.' That had been hard to miss, even for me – ceremonies, parades, recreations of the landings, museums opening, Hollywood versions of events in the cinemas.

'D-day. Always D-day,' said Ragno. 'It made a sideshow of us, of Italy. They forgot about us after Normandy.'

I was surprised by the bitterness in his voice after all this time, but I couldn't argue. The day the men and tanks rolled up Juno and Sword beaches and the GIs died in droves at Omaha, what happened on the Italian peninsula was simply a supporting feature. It tied up some German divisions, which was a bonus. Later, it seemed the Allies were more concerned with events in Yugoslavia and Greece than Northern Italy. That's certainly where most of the weapons went. Weapons that could have saved Ragno and his friends. Perhaps.

'Hindsight is a wonderful thing,' I said to both of us.

There was a sharp whistle, and Ragno looked across to the pit entrance. A mechanic in a similar Moto Guzzi outfit to his was waving him over. He slugged back his Scotch. 'There will be a ceremony. Food, drink. You should be there. You played your part.'

As he stood, I shook my head. 'I'll think about it. This job I am going for is in September, so I might be flying.'

Ragno smiled. 'OK. I'll be there. Pavel will make it, I am sure. Rosario for sure. Ennio will also come.' There was a long pause, not quite a silence because the air was quivering with the howl of over-revved engines. There was a name missing, we both knew. Fausto. The best of us. We'd both seen him die the wrong kind of death, out on the streets of a little town called Domodossola.

Perhaps it was just the rays of the lowering sun catching his pupils, but I swear something twinkled in his eye as he finally added: 'Francesca will be there.'

I felt the wound in my chest open. Twenty years and it still hurt like hell. She had been my lover – just once – and men had died because of it.

'I'm not sure, Ragno,' I said gruffly. 'I'm not one for, you know, dwelling on the past.'

He stood and smiled, shook my hand and said, 'Ah, Jack. Men who lived through those times. What else do we have?'

Well, some of us have an appointment in London, I thought, but I just returned the grin and nodded and we both knew I'd be back in Domodossola. How could I stay away? Francesca was going to be there.

Four

From the stern of the Isle of Man steamer back to the Mersey I watched the Dakota climb, imagining the frame juddering as the old girl pulled herself into the sky one more time, a tired old trooper who knew the show had to go on. The youngest Dak flying was getting on for twenty now. I'd flown one for a few brief weeks in Berlin in 1948, when it was all hands to the pumps for the airlift. The one I'd had was creaking arthritically at the joints even back then.

'How is the Twin?' asked my father as he followed my eye. 'Or whatever your plane is called.'

I shrugged. 'She's an AT-11.' I pointed upwards as the DC-3 banked into cloud. 'And she's a damn sight better than that thing.' The AT-11 was virtually identical to the Beechcraft Twins except for her Plexiglas nose. Mine had a chequered history. She was shipped over from the USA in World War Two and used by the US 8th Air Force to train navigators and bomb-aimers. Hence the transparent nose, which housed the trainee, a Norden bombsight, and a bomb-spotting Bell & Howell A4 camera. If you looked carefully you could still see the metal blanking disc on my fuselage where the practice gun turret used to be, because AT-11s were also used for training Flying Fortress and Liberator gunners.

After the war she was given an IRAN (Inspect and Repair As Necessary) then, before I bought her at auction, did a spell as an aerial mapping platform for the Ordnance Survey people. It was a quiet life, so her airframe was only around 1200 hours old. The right engine had 450 hours SMOH (Since Major Overhaul), the left 700. She was fun to fly, reliable and steady as a rock and she was wasted tossing parachutists out into the wide blue yonder on ten-minute jaunts.

I told Dad all this and he said, 'Sounds a bit dull.'

My father thought any plane built after 1930 was too easy to pilot, too much like driving a car. He had been a keen flier in the 1920s, even building his own kit plane. It was his interest in flying and motorcycles – two activities which seem to be inexorably bound together – that fired me up to be a pilot, and it was his tuition and enthusiasm that had enabled me to fly so young. And to ride a bike too young.

'Jack,' my father said solemnly.

'Yes, Dad?' I still hadn't succumbed to the modern trend of using a parent's Christian name.

We were virtually alone on the deck. There was still a full week of racing to go, so the island remained crowded, the ferries back to the mainland half-empty. Even though there was nobody within earshot, he lowered his voice.

'While you've been away, things have changed.'

I watched a girl in a very short skirt totter by, the wind whipping back the dark curtain of her hair to reveal two eyes peering from thick circles of mascara and eye-liner.

'I notice, Dad. Every day.'

His words came quietly. 'I'm going to wrap up the firm.'

It hit me hard. Wrap up? I managed to say: 'What do you mean?'

He tapped his inside pocket. 'I got a letter from Joe Sergeant.'

Sergeant was one of the men in charge of contracts for the Ministry of Pensions.

'Off the record. Personal. You know we go back to . . . '

'The war.' Both had been involved in the design and fabrication of large-scale engineering projects, such as the floating docks used at D-day.

'He says the Ministry are considering proposals to phase out disabled carriages and to offer candidates suitably modified four-wheeled vehicles instead. Mostly Austins and Morrises. Perhaps Minis.' His voice was level and calm, but his eyes were filling up. He blinked the tears back. 'I'm sorry.'

'You've still got the bikes.'

'Honda are opening a dealership in town. Yamaha are looking at sites. Suzuki—'

'Wait. *Wait*.' I took a breath. 'How long have you known all this?'

'Months, I suppose. I wanted us to come away to talk about it.'

'We're on our way back,' I snapped at him.

'There was never a right time.'

'We must be able to fight. Who has the Honda franchise?'

'Steve Riley.'

Riley had worked for my father after the war. While I was off chasing weather on my clear air turbulence sorties, he had wooed and wed Julie, my girlfriend from the age of fifteen. He had even done the TT on a Kirby in 1951, after I quit. 'There's loyalty for you.'

'He told me about it well ahead of time, son. He did the decent thing.'

I laughed. That'd be a first. 'Where is he setting up?'

'Granville Farm, Patcham Road.'

My mouth fell open. It was our address. He was selling out to the competition. 'Dad!'

'I know. It must be a shock. Sorry. It's for the best.'

'It can't be.'

'Not for you, maybe,' he said cruelly and, without waiting for a reply, he went below to the bar, leaving me to curse the gulls.

All the years I'd been kicking around the world, never getting a proper job, a wife, or a decent bank balance, I had always seen Kirby Motorcycles as something strong and lasting. One day, Dad would have had enough and I'd come home and settle down to a comfortable middle age, keeping the line going, us working together again, as we had before the war. I would be disappointed if it all went, but what really concerned me was the thought of my father retiring. It was another sign of his mortality, and I didn't like it. I wanted him to live for ever, and I wanted to be with him while he did.

It turned out nothing was signed so, in a stubborn rearguard action, I spent a week with our longterm accountant Mr Lloyd – nobody ever used, or I suspect even knew, his first name – going over exactly what the financial loss of the invalid carriages would be. We also looked at whether the British bikes, which seemed to be getting more and more troublesome, could compete with the new Japanese models and whether the Kirby marque had any viable future. I even looked at us selling scooters to the Mods who were popping up everywhere, especially in Brighton. I could just see the pitched fights on the forecourt between the two sets of customers, the black leather-jacketed Rockers and the prissy Mods.

At the end of those seven days, I went into town to The Ship pub and got very drunk.

I had accepted that my father was serious, that he intended to retire. He was sixty-six, he kept reminding me, and my mother was looking forward to seeing something of him after all this time. I told him that I thought retirement would kill him. He said that there was always golf. I told him that was the same as death, but with worse clothes.

What there wasn't, he claimed, was a future for the British bike manufacturing industry and for Kirbys in particular.

He showed me a letter from designer Bert Hopwood of BSA: *Management doesn't seem to realise that Continental manufacturers are bearing down on us with models which make ours look pitiful; I also think the Japanese will take advantage of the shambles at the top in the British motorcycle industry. I don't believe they will be content with small and middle-range machines for ever. In my opinion, there is too much consultancy, not enough work to bring our designs up to date.* Perhaps all that was true – Hopwood was famously pessimistic – but it wasn't like Dad to go quietly.

There was a TV in the corner of the public bar in The Ship – something unheard of in my village in Italy at that time unless Inter Milan or Juventus were playing – and the younger crowd were ogling the teenager presenting something called *Ready Steady Go*; who looked remarkably like the girl on the boat. Or probably vice versa.

I wondered if I had been away too long. Since I had been back, I had fought off a strange sense of dislocation, as if my cogs no longer meshed with this particular time or place. I felt like the Triumph Tina, the company's laughable attempt to make a scooter, the one where the transmission seized solid as soon as any human hand touched it. Something that should have been allowed to slope off and die a peaceful death.

I recognised I was reaching the maudlin stage of the evening, and that I shouldn't have any more to drink when, by the happiest of coincidences, Steve Riley walked in.

Five

London, July 1964

I must have winced when Lindy Carr took my hand because she said, 'Are you all right?'

She had nominated Jules Bar on Jermyn Street as a meeting place. It was smarter than anywhere I knew in London, so I was glad I'd made the effort with a jacket, shirt and (borrowed) tie. She probably thought that as an ex-flyer I'd feel at home in the Jules. It was a long, narrow, crowded room, decorated with portraits of famous aces and both RAF and USAAF planes, and during the war it had been a meeting-place for the Allied flyers of both countries, neutral territory where any rivalry was supposed to be forgotten. If the walls could speak, they'd be able to discuss which was superior, the Spit or the Mustang or the Focke-Wulf or the 109 until the Second Coming. I scoured the framed pictures for a Mosquito, but there was none.

A young Irish bartender in a white jacket and bow-tie mixed cocktails for an older affluent crowd, some of whom looked as if they had drunk here in the war. Not me. On the few occasions I was posted close to London, I was more a Bag O' Nails man, sometimes favouring the Tivoli on the Strand with the Antipodean boys. I might have been an officer, but I was hardly a gentleman. Lacking a public-school or university education, and with an engineer for a father, I didn't quite fit in with the Jules crew.

However, that didn't matter too much because, thanks to Dad's enthusiasm for machines, I could fly the arse off a Tiger Moth and pretty much anything else they threw at me. In 1939 or 1940 that would have meant fighter planes but, by the time my number came up, the nature of the engagement had changed, and I got the Mozzies. They might not have had the same hold on the public imagination as Spits had, but I felt I'd been lucky. I sometimes thought of the lives wasted in slow, vulnerable crates like the Blenheim or the Wellington, and thanked the Lord for De Havilland, who had developed the Mosquito as a private enterprise. I was also under no illusion that, had I been flying in Fighter Command in 1940 during the Battle of Britain, the odds were hugely against me being around to meet anyone in Jules Bar.

I looked at Lindy, then at my swollen knuckles and lied. 'I slipped with a spanner.' Hitting Steve Riley had been stupid and juvenile and got me bound over to keep the peace for six months. On balance it was worth it, though. I should have done it when he took my girl.

Lindy Carr already had a table. She ordered a glass of champagne while I went for a Scotch. I looked her up and down while she spoke. She was barely an inch shorter than me, which made her around five nine or ten, with long blonde hair, a glowing healthy face and piercing blue eyes – a world away, and a refreshing change, from all the pale kohl-eyed girls I had seen hiding their features behind their protective veil of hair. Lindy Carr looked like she knew how to get outside and enjoy life, rather than skulk around in darkened basements.

'Say fish and chips,' I requested.

'What?'

'Fish and chips. Humour me.'

'Feesh and cheeps,' she said. Australian. A Kiwi would have said fush and chups.

'Aussie.'

'Yeah. Sydney.'

'Good. OK, carry on.'

She smiled in that way you do when you find yourself sitting next to a madman on the bus, and said slowly, 'I have a picture of him. My father.'

She reached into her bag and presented me with a standard aircrew photograph taken on the ground, a line of young men – kids, like I was – smiling at the camera, only the eyes, dull and lined beyond their years, showing the tremendous strain they were under. Behind them, the deep, corpulent fuselage of a Liberator.

'Here.' She jabbed the front row, indicating a figure slightly older than the others, with an affecting, world-weary grin. The sort of man you'd buy a pint for and listen to his story. 'William Carr. Bill to his friends.'

'Right.' I pretended to examine the picture more intently, but it told me very little other than this was one of many crews who one day never came home. 'And forgive me, you want to find him?'

'His body.'

'Right,' I repeated. 'Which you think is where?'

'I can't be certain, but I have been doing some research.' I had noticed the bulging Gladstone bag on the floor next to her, but had assumed it belonged to one of the men nearby. As she heaved it onto her lap and opened it, I could see it was stuffed with handwritten notes, mimeographed files and books. 'He was based in Southern Italy, with an SAAF squadron, a mixed unit—'

'I know. Mostly South Africans to begin with, but then came Canadians, Australians, Rhodesians and British. But the pilots were usually South African.'

'Yes. Of course they'd had plenty of losses by then. My father was seconded to them from the RAF.' I knew what she was going to say, but I looked down at the eight young men and their aeroplane with new respect as she said it: 'When he arrived, the squadron was about to fly the Warsaw run, out of—'

'Foggia,' I finished.

Foggia sits on the spur of the boot of Italy, inland from the coast. In 1944, it was a bleak place of windswept flatlands; the runway was covered in thick steel plates, to give a firm base for the heavy bombers to land on when the soil turned to thick mud, as it did every winter. The SAAF squadrons flew the big Mk VI Liberators, an American-built four-engined bomber. At sixty feet long, with a wingspan nearly twice that length, they weren't pretty or elegant planes – they lost out in the public popularity stakes to the B-17 Flying Fortresses – but they were tough workhorses. The crew of eight consisted of two pilots, a navigator, a bomb-aimer, three gunners and a wireless operator-gunner. USAAF versions carried ten men, but the RAF and SAAF thought eight was plenty. It had a range of 2,000 miles, which meant that from Italy the bombers could be launched against targets in Eastern Europe previously out of reach – Hungary, Yugoslavia, Romania, Austria.

On 1 August 1944, there was an uprising in Warsaw of the Polish patriots, the Home Army, egged on by Soviet radio which promised the Russian forces would come in and support them. Soldiers and civilians rose up and overran most of Warsaw, taking the Germans by surprise and digging themselves in to hold out until relief came from the east.

But, as everyone soon discovered, the Russians stayed put. Their tanks ground to a halt, their planes stopped flying. The lumbering but lethal Stukas reappeared to bomb and strafe, and the German heavy armour moved in, grinding murderously through the city. The *Armia Krajowa* was abandoned and alone. It transpired that the Russians wanted to make sure they wouldn't face any resistance from a well-armed force of Polish patriots when it was their turn to be occupiers. Why not let the Germans do their dirty work?

The Polish government in exile in London asked for help from Britain, and the RAF tried a re-supply sortie from England. It lost 85 per cent of its aircraft. So it was decided to equip and feed the beleaguered patriots from Foggia.

'You know about that?' Lindy asked.

I nodded. One night in Sicily a bunch of guys in the makeshift bar at an airstrip near Catania, penned in by bad weather, were swapping flying stories. An ex-31 Squadron South African had told his particular war tale, and it had gradually silenced the table.

'We took off at around 19.30,' he began, 'so by the time we crossed the coast of Yugoslavia, it was dark. At Scutari we turned north. Each plane carried twelve canisters, eight feet long, crammed with food and weapons and medical supplies. We went up over Hungary, roughly parallel with the Danube, then right across Czechoslovakia. You had to hop the Carpathians then at fifteen, sixteen thousand. That was where we hit the weather. By then our electronic navigation aids were pretty u/s. So you'd start to come down to eight thousand, then seven, then six, trying to find the Vistula River. Sometimes it was there like a silver band, glinting in the moonlight, ready to lead you in. Other times you'd feel your eyes ready to pop out as you strained to find it through the low cloud. Once you were on it, that's when the flak kicked in – the big guns were waiting for you. Then the searchlights.' He paused and took a gulp of beer.

'As you got closer, the glow from the city itself pulled you in. It was ablaze, you see. There were fires everywhere, orange and red, reflected in the river. You could almost feel the heat of the city coming through the soles of your flying boots. You'd come in at around five hundred feet, half-flap, down to 120 mph, which is just about where a Lib falls out of the sky. Then down, down, three hundred feet, two hundred, skimming the rooftops. You'd be looking for the four bridges, which told you you were in the centre, near the Poles, who were holding out around Krasinski Square. At the fourth bridge, you yanked her round, following the street down to the square itself. Then they'd start firing at you, from each side.' There was complete silence in the room by now, as we all listened intently.

'On half-flap you can't manoeuvre, so you just had to sit there, counting the seconds till the drop, hoping you'd see the letter T or K which told you to let the damn things go. But spotting a letter in a city on fire is no piece of cake. You were so low, they could hit you with small arms and you heard the ping, ping as they went in; sometimes you'd see the engine or prop spark and splutter as a bullet found it. You saw other aircraft go down. Some of them came back round for a second run with one or two engines on fire, just suicide.'

He took another long drink of beer. 'On the first sortie we lost half the aircraft in the attack force.' He shrugged sadly. 'We figured that we would get better at it. But so did they. The flak got more accurate. Every time we went out, half never returned. Eighteen hundred miles – that's if you didn't get lost – twelve and a half hours. If you got back through the nightfighters which were waiting to get you on the return leg, you'd be exhausted. Like death. Yet you couldn't sleep at night because what you'd seen kept playing on your mind. The Liberator that caught the rooftops, cartwheeling into the street below, the aviation fuel flaming in jets or rolling into a fireball, killing God knows how many people on the ground; the ones that exploded in mid-air, those that couldn't find the height to get back over the Carpathians, forced to crash land, those last seen trying to shake off the searchlight beams that had locked onto them. Even if you could blank that out, the bloody Flying Fortresses were taking off, hour after hour, for their daylight raids, so sleep was hard. Then, the next night or the night after, you'd have to do it again. One hundred and eighty sorties in six months were flown from Foggia. Of course, it was all in vain – the

Germans crushed the uprising while the Russians did nothing.'

I handed the photo back, the thick South African accent of that pilot still ringing in my ears, my throat suddenly dry. At some point, I had drunk my whisky so I ordered another and asked Lindy, 'How many missions?'

'Over Warsaw? He went three times. Then there were the oilfields at Ploesti in Romania and bombing the Brennerpass in Austria . . . '

'He survived three passes over Warsaw?'

'Yes. He went down supplying partisans in Northern Italy.'

I felt my heart lurch. 'Did you tell me that? That he was supplying partisans?'

'I thought I had. On the telephone.'

My drink arrived. I reassured myself that it would be too much of a coincidence. How many partisan supply missions did they fly out of Foggia? Fifty? A hundred? Then she said something else.

'Mr Lang said you were up there. Said you had an unusual RAF career.'

'Unusual – yes,' I agreed. 'I'll tell you all about it sometime. So what do you know about his sortie?'

'Ten Liberators went out that night, with drop zones all over the occupied area. A milk run, they said, after Warsaw. Easy peasy. Four came back. I have traced five of the others. My dad's is still missing.'

'Where was your father's DZ?'

I braced myself, but it hit me like a steam train anyway.

'Domodossola. It's a little town—'

'I know where it is.'

'Actually the drop zone proper was to the east of the town. Designated as Plymouth on the mission maps.'

I was having to continually re-evaluate this girl. 'You have the mission maps?'

'Yes. There was a reunion of the squadron in Cape Town I

36

attended where the people were ever so helpful.'

I realised then that I had underestimated her, had thought that because of her age she was just playing at this. There was steel inside, and not too far below the surface. Lindy Carr was serious about finding William Carr, Bill to his friends.

'Why are you doing this?' I asked her.

'I beg you pardon?'

'It's been twenty years. Shouldn't you be at home listening to the Beatles or the Bachelors or some other racket?'

'You probably won't believe this of an Australian, but Bach is more my thing.'

'All right then, tapping your toe to the Toccata and Fugue. What I'm getting at . . . I mean, you can't devote your life to this.'

'I don't intend to, Mr Kirby, just that part of it required to find him.'

'Jack.'

She took a sip of champagne. 'The offer is simple. I want you to help me survey the area. To find EH-148, E for Echo.'

I shook my head. 'You know what you're talking about? Needle in a haystack doesn't even begin to describe it.' I'd done some PR – photo-reconnaissance – in 'shuftikites' in 1945, during the dying days of the war. I knew what an imprecise science it was. 'Then there are the Italians.'

'What about them?'

'They are very security conscious. You want to fly up near the border, photographing the landscape? They arrest you if you turn up with a box Brownie near a military installation.'

She passed me another sheaf of documents. I flicked through them and felt impressed, despite myself.

'You went to the Air Ministry in Rome?'

'My Italian isn't that hot,' she admitted, 'but I got a friend to do it. It's permission—'

'I can see what it is.' A permit to overfly a great swathe of the countryside near the Swiss border. I muttered something about hen's teeth. 'You know how much this is going to cost?'

'You don't look expensive.'

'Don't be cheeky.'

She grinned at me and I found myself returning the smile.

'My plane burns fifty gallons of fuel an hour, wheels up to wheels down. We'll need a camera, a decent one, probably a Wild. Even hiring them doesn't come cheap. Then there's the film. Now I am not up to date, but I soon can be, and I can imagine the developing costs—'

She waved a hand impatiently. 'Look, if you don't want to do it, I have a stand-by pilot who is willing to take my offer.'

'And who would that be?'

'Furio Gabbiano.'

My partner. Make that erstwhile partner, as soon as we'd worked the rest of the summer. Although part of me bristled, the rest wanted to ruffle the conniving bastard's hair. At least Furio had ambition. Mine seemed to have drained away entirely these last few years. 'That was sneaky,' I said at last.

'Sneaky and cheeky, that's me.' She signalled for more champagne. 'And rich. My stepfather gave me a substantial amount of money in a trust, which I came into when I was twenty-one. I could have bought a house, a yacht, some fancy cars. I decided instead to find my father.'

'How did your stepfather react to that news?'

'Like I give a flying fuck.'

The profanity hung in the air, as if it couldn't believe it came from this young woman's mouth, and I found myself laughing, if only at the expressions around us.

'Sorry.'

'I'm sure they've heard worse in here. There's a woman behind you who appears to be having a seizure, but there's always one, isn't there?'

Lindy coloured a little. It was a nice effect. I realised those two whiskies were running round my bloodstream and making mischief. She's just a girl, I reminded my various appetites and imaginations.

'Look, it's your money,' I said at last. 'And I am sure you can find someone to take it if I don't. But not Furio.'

'Why not?'

'He's not as good as he thinks he is.'

'And are you?'

After a moment's hesitation I went for the third Scotch. 'Yes.'

'Lang told me you crashed once.'

I nodded. How come that always popped up? I'd walked away from it. Well, swum. And, just like every pilot claims, it wasn't my fault. Shearing spinners aren't anybody's fault. 'Like I said, I'll tell you about it sometime.'

'Tell me now.'

'I'd rather not. It was a long time ago.'

'But not very far away. Not from where I'll be sitting. I think as a prospective employer I am entitled to know how you came to crash, Mr Kirby.'

The third whisky came with some nuts and crisps. Maybe the barman was worried about my alcohol absorption, too. Even without the booze, I'd have been a little pissed off about being bullied by a girl half my age, just because she had a trust fund burning a hole in the Bank of Sydney's vault. But I went ahead and told her the story all the same.

Six

Over Italy, 1944

Flight Lieutenant Jack Kirby felt the misfire as they approached the Italian coast. It wasn't much, just a skip of a beat from one of the Merlin engines which sent a tiny shiver through the Mosquito's wooden frame. He risked a glance at Sergeant Thornton, sitting to his right, slightly behind him. His navigator was still hunched over the charts, breaking off only to check the luminous green line in the cathode-ray tubes of the AI – the Airborne Interceptor – VHF system, alert for enemy nightfighter activity. He'd sensed nothing amiss with the plane.

Kirby examined each engine in turn, the solid discs of the prop blades spinning just a couple of feet away from where he sat, then scanned the instruments for signs of distress, but all was as it should have been. The blip could have been a supercharger surge, he figured, so he upped the power and boost for thirty seconds as recommended in the manual. There was a slight sense of flexing in the frame as the extra torque kicked in, then the plane settled back down as he reset. It was nothing, Kirby told himself.

They made landfall just to the south of the island of Elba. There had been flak ships moored offshore here until a week ago. Kirby had been part of the group that had fallen on them from a not-so-great height, skimming over the sea so low it felt as if the Merlin's props were shaving the tops of the waves, before launching rockets into the hulks. Most of the enemy guns were designed to aim high, and were unable to crank down to sea level, so they'd got away with one casualty out of six planes. He could still taste the adrenalin and recall the after-shock of fear that chilled him as they landed at Alghero on the west coast of Sardinia. It wasn't like that tonight, though. This was a Red Stocking job, flying high and lonely, six hours in the air for a desperate snatch of conversation with a frightened man at the other end.

Kirby began to climb and adjusted the O_2 supply, feeling the soft flow from the mask against his cheeks. Like most nightflyers, Kirby liked to use the oxygen from the moment of take-off. One less thing to worry about forgetting. As he flew through the ragged clouds with the gentlest of bumps, the heavens were starting to shine brighter. By the time they hit 25,000 feet, the celestial display would be clear and vast.

He checked airspeed. Nudging 250 knots. They were well short of the Mozzie's maximum speed – he had to conserve fuel – but still gobbling up the miles. However, there was nothing to judge their progress by, just the steady, satisfying thrum of the big V12 engines, their noise and vibration filling the cockpit.

He took her higher and the cold began to seep through his heated flight suit as the first ice crystals bloomed on the canopy. He flicked on the airjets that were supposed to keep them from spreading like cancer across the field of vision.

Albie Thornton gave him a new heading and Kirby turned the Mosquito, parallel with the coast now, planning to cut between Pisa and Florence and fly up towards Milan. One last adjustment would take them to the east of the city, well above the marauding nightfighters. Then he would go on to the lakes for the radio run, before making a long loop, crossing back to the Med to the east of Genoa at Portofino, and home.

Kirby pressed the interphone link. 'OK back there?'

'Cold.'

Kirby heard Bishop's teeth chattering.

'You can turn up the heat on the suit. There is a rheostat on the wall.'

'It's on full. Thanks.'

'You put the silk underwear on?'

'Two pairs.'

'Where you from, Bishop?'

The American laughed. 'California. I guess they should've found a Yank from Nebraska for this, huh?'

'Or a Canuck from Saskatchewan. Out.'

Albie Thornton looked at him and rolled his eyes. He was, indeed, a Canadian from cold climes. 'It's crazy enough being up here with you,' Thornton said, shaking his head. He flicked a thumb towards the rear. 'Lock me up if I volunteer for that kind of idiocy.'

Bishop was in a specially constructed cabin that had been shoehorned into the rear of the Mosquito fuselage, between bomb bay and rear wheel. There was no window, just room for one man, his parachute, a radio set, a wire-recording device, and a flask of coffee. Kirby also thought you'd have to be mad to sit folded inside that cramped space for hours on end.

Red Stockings were normally flown by the USAAF using A-26 Invaders out of the UK. However, they'd had trouble getting down into Italy and lost a couple of their planes in the Alps, so 23 Squadron in Sardinia had been given the task of running Italian Red Stockings until the Yanks had a re-think.

A Red Stocking was a covert overfly to intercept and record an Allied spy's transmissions from the ground, an invention of Bishop's outfit, the Office of Strategic Services. The name was a variation on Blue Stocking, the accepted code for a weather observation mission, and it used a system called Eleanor-Joan which operated on 260 MHz, a frequency they were assured the enemy did not monitor. Eleanor, the airborne element of the partnership, was linked to a recording device, which meant the agent on the ground, who used the Joan set, with its range of twenty miles, didn't have to waste time with codes. He spoke his report, it was recorded, and the Intelligence boys played it back at home at their leisure.

Flight Lieutenant Kirby, of course, only knew the time and position at which he had to rendezvous. He had no idea who the agent was, or what he would say. He would not be privy to this. But looking at the flight plans when he was briefed, he couldn't help but notice they would be orbiting at 30,000 feet not far from Saló on the western shore of Lake Garda. Even Kirby knew who was holed up in Saló. *Il Duce*, Benito Mussolini himself.

The second misfire happened as they turned and came in for their run. Thornton felt it this time, and looked across at Kirby, who in turn re-checked his instruments. The needle on the oil-pressure gauge for the starboard engine gave a twitch and dropped slightly. Nothing to worry about, thought Kirby. You could fly one of these beauties home on just one. He held his breath and brought her level.

'Contact.' It was Bishop. He had his man. Kirby put the plane into a shallow bank, looping back round towards the south. Twenty minutes maximum. There were no nightfighters in this area, so it was just a case of passing the time until Bishop said, 'Complete.'

Below he could just make out the lights from a poorly observed blackout and a sudden sparkle of red and white. Fireworks? Unlikely, he thought. Who would be stupid enough to let off fireworks with Allied bombers in the sky?

Eighteen minutes later the needle began to move erratically on the oil gauge. Just above it, the dials indicating oil temperature had started to climb too. Kirby swore to himself. 'Bishop?'

'Not now,' the American snapped back.

Kirby began to lose height. 'Not too much,' advised Thornton as he indicated the altimeter. He, too, could feel a judder in the airframe.

Bishop crackled in Kirby's ear. 'Complete. Everything all right up there?'

'Got a bit of concern over one engine. We're going home.'

'Fine by me.'

The pressure needle on the suspect unit was swinging wildly, the temperature jabbing over into the danger zone. Kirby closed the throttle and pushed in the feathering button to the misbehaving engine so that the blades would turn sideways and reduce drag. It was going to be a long run back, tenser than he had anticipated. Booster pump was off, fuel cock closed, radiator shutter open. That should keep her happy for now.

Wrong. The starboard engine speed shot up into the red. The Mosquito lurched violently and pulled to port. He heard Bishop yell over his headset, and saw Thornton reach for his grab handle, but Kirby heaved her back straight by pulling full port rudder and half aileron. There was a screeching noise and he heard metal hit the fuselage, as if they were taking cannon rounds.

'Are we under attack?' It was Bishop.

Only by the gods, thought Kirby. 'No. Hang on.'

There was another squealing sound that set his teeth on edge and in his headphones he heard Thornton gasp: 'I think the spinner has sheered off.'

'How low dare I go?'

Thornton flicked on his lamp and directed the beam onto the chart. The sudden yawing meant he had lost sense of where they were. 'What are you thinking?'

Kirby looked at him. 'I'm thinking about getting us down. Jesus.'

The oil pressure on the rogue engine was zero, but the prop was windmilling wildly, the drag making the plane buck. Kirby tried to re-feather, but nothing happened. He could hear the grinding of metal on metal. The engine was going to tear itself apart.

'I have peaks at around eleven thousand feet. But they should be to the north of us. Round here, seven thousand.'

Kirby checked the altimeter. They were just falling below twenty. Airspeed at 150 knots. He could taste the tang of adrenalin. The fire warning light on the feathering pushbutton winked on and steadied as metal punched through the cowling, revealing the glow within, soon masked by thick smoke pouring out to merge with the night. Thornton quickly flipped up the lids and hit the extinguisher systems for the engine and the damaged wing's fuel tank bay. The nacelle vanished for a second behind a white mist but, within seconds, puffs of dark smoke started to bleed through again.

Kirby called to Bishop. 'You got that parachute back there?'

'Jesus, you're joking,' said Bishop.

A fresh burst of flame spewed forth. Globs of molten metal spat into the sky. She was still burning all right.

'Kirby?' shouted Bishop, his voice thick with fright.

'Sorry,' said Kirby, 'but I'm afraid I'm not joking. I'll tell you when—'

'Where are we?' asked Bishop.

'West of Brescia,' said Thornton. 'Can't be more precise, I'm afraid.'

An angry shower of sparks spluttered out of the cowling, trailing behind them. The doped fabric of the wing was aflame now. 'Go, Bishop.'

There was a pause and a dry voice said: 'Good luck, Kirby.'

He imagined him taking the wire spool off the machine and destroying it, very much the professional spy. He felt the plane twitch as the rear panel was released and Bishop went out into the night.

'Your turn, Albie.' Thornton hesitated, and Kirby risked letting go of the column with one hand to pat him on the shoulder. 'Don't worry about me.'

'Yeah. See you back home, Jack.'

Thornton struggled into his 'chute, crawled awkwardly through the gap in the control panel and down into the nose, pulled the red handle and kicked out the lower access hatch. Kirby felt the icy air snatching at his legs. Maps and papers swirled in front of him, before they were sucked out into the darkness. Thornton took a deep breath, turned to give a thumbs up and he was gone with a terrifying whoosh. Kirby hoped he'd missed the propeller.

He let the plane ride along for a few minutes, listening to her creak and growl before he undid his harness and let go of the controls to follow Thornton. The moment his hands left the column, the Mosquito spasmed violently and began to roll, throwing him across the cockpit in a tangle. His head smacked onto a sharp corner, and he wiped blood from his eyes. Kirby struggled to the seat, and managed to get one foot onto the rudder bar and a hand on the column, and yanked for all he was worth until he felt her rotate reluctantly back to level flight.

He flopped back into place, his chest heaving from the exertion. As the calm acceptance that he was in serious trouble fell on him, he felt himself relax. This was it then. No need to kick against it. He'd always known this one was on the cards, that sooner or later it would be his name on the board posted as 'overdue'.

Get a grip, he told himself. Get a bloody grip, man. It took a second for him to grasp what the dangling tube flapping on his chest meant. It was his oxygen supply. It had jerked free when he tried to get the 'chute on. He replugged it in, cranked up the flow and felt his head clear.

Right, Kirby you bonehead, *think*. He was going to have to exit through the upper canopy. To do that, the manual said he had to shut down the other engine, the good one. The moment he did that, the windmilling duffer meant the plane would yaw all over the sky, as well as turning topsy-turvy. So he had to go out through the top, which the same manual said wasn't a good idea. He didn't have any better ones though.

As he reached for the upper panel release toggle, Kirby saw the lights below and to his starboard side, and he dipped his wing to get a better look. The lights of Switzerland, perhaps? And could he see them reflecting on water? Was that dark finger an illusion, or could he just make out a lake? Perhaps he'd let Thornton go too soon. No, the man deserved a chance. He had a sweetheart in—

Three deep thuds resounded through the plane, and fresh flames rolled over the wing. 'The Wooden Wonder' they called this crate. Right now, building it out of timber didn't seem such a clever idea.

In the weak starlight, the vague shape down below hardened, until he was certain he was looking at water. Water might be good. There was an L-Type dinghy in the fuselage, which would inflate automatically thanks to an immersion switch, and he had a Mae West. If he survived the landing he'd probably be all right, whereas the chances of walking away from a mountainside impact were slim. If he could turn into the wind and along any swell, he might just be able to drop her down and kiss the surface. The trick was, he knew, to try to avoid digging in the air scoops under the engine nacelles, which would cause the whole plane to flip. Gently does it.

Kirby apologised for the insults he had heaped on her, banked the stricken Mozzie and began to pray like never before as he took her rapidly earthwards.

At first, he thought he was in hell, plunged into a sea of bodies. They writhed around him, arms and legs trying to drag him under the water. Hideous faces leered at him, many of them grinning at his terror and the fate that awaited him.

Then a waxy arm floated past him, severed at the bicep. Kirby kicked back, away from the corpses, and shook his head. The water was cold, but not icy, and his Mae West was inflated. He was alive. He could see the dinghy, on the far side of the corpses, bobbing tantalisingly close.

He couldn't remember getting out of the plane and was only dimly aware of the ditching. He must have hit a boat or a ferry. Why else would there be these bodies? Had he done this? Had he ploughed into these people as he ditched, the props slicing into the poor sods? How many were there? He looked at them again, noted the bloated flesh, and realised that they must have been in the water some time. Dozens at least. But how did they come to be out here in the first place?

There was oil in the water, he could feel it sticking to his skin, so the Mozzie must be somewhere below him. He hoped the lake was deep enough to ensure that nobody could recover the radio gear. He kicked hard for the inflatable, but it seemed to swirl away from him.

After a time he began to shiver violently, his teeth chattering. As this subsided, his lids felt heavy, and he knew he was going to die.

The sound came so faint at first, he thought he was imagining it. Kirby lifted his head from the flotation jacket and cocked an ear. It was a small outboard motor, a two-stroke. Someone was blipping the throttle, trying to stay as quiet as possible. He willed himself to be still. The noise died.

He peered into the night and, a few hundred metres away, a beam of light flared briefly and he heard the ring of voices. German? No, Italian. But what kind of Italian? Friend or foe? Another burst of engine, another flicker of light, and an exclamation of horror. They had found a body part. Then one voice drifted above the others, carried on the breeze, the softer sound of a woman. Perhaps someone searching for a relative.

He heard it again, and he decided it was worth taking a chance. He put his whistle to his numbed lips and began to blow.

Seven

I told the story of ditching my Mosquito in Lake Maggiore in my usual detached way as if it had happened to someone else. As I was talking, Scotch number three drained away, which led nicely into number four, which I always like to have by my side when I answer the question about the bodies in the lake. It came right on cue.

'They were Jews,' I said flatly. 'Italian, a few Serbs. And an Englishman.'

Lindy Carr looked at me with uncomprehending eyes, the way they all did. I didn't blame her. It took some believing. 'What were they doing in the lake?'

'By this point of the war, the Allies were bombing the hell out of the Italian railway system. At the same time, the Germans were trying to get various undesirables north to their extermination camps. One night, a train of cattle cars ground to a halt near Lake Maggiore. The SS men were told they weren't going to move for days, so they unloaded the cargo. They led them down to the shore and shot them in batches, then dumped the bodies in the lake.'

'How horrible.'

'Yeah.' I tried to keep the image of the bloated limbs where it belonged, buried deep.

'What about your crewmen? The ones who jumped.'

I hadn't felt the weight of that for a long time, tugging on my heart. Neither of them had made it. I had.

'What was that about a Red Stocking?' she asked.

'Probably still classified. Don't tell Major Lang I told you or I'll be in the Tower by tomorrow night.'

'*Major* Lang? He called himself Mr.'

I waved my empty glass around, hoping it would thump a passing waiter. 'He was Major when I knew him. Probably a colonel by the time he retired. Anyway, he was a spook. Special Operations Executive in the war, joined SIS – the secret service – afterwards. Never liked him. But then, he was never wild about me.' I finally made contact with a member of staff. 'Ah, there you are. Same again.' We were getting close to the big question now, and I wanted to be comfortably numb when the time came.

'My father's mission was logged as a White Stocking.'

'Right.'

'It means as well as canisters, there was a passenger on board. A VIP.' I knew that, but I just nodded. I even knew who the VIP was.

Go on, ask her now.

'What date was your father's flight?'

'Do we have a deal, Mr Kirby?'

I thought about a Liberator lost somewhere in the mountains, the crew and plane gradually rotting together over the years among the burst canisters, guns, food, medical supplies strewn up the slope like scree. If I'd been lost somewhere in Northern Italy, would I like to think someone, a son or a daughter, would come looking for me? Hell, yes. Course, I'd have to get myself a son or a daughter first.

'We have a deal,' I agreed finally, and she said we should drink to seal the bargain, and I began to like her even more, especially when she wrote me a cheque for £200 to cover initial expenses.

It was only when we left thirty minutes later and I poured myself into a cab to Victoria to catch the last train back to Brighton that I realised she hadn't answered my question. She didn't have to.

I got the train back up from Brighton to London the next morning, splurging some of Lindy Carr's money on first class and the best breakfast British Rail could provide. The grease, and the endless pots of tea a sympathetic steward kept bringing me, did the trick by Clapham. When we reached Victoria, I had managed the evolutionary leap from Australopithecus to Cro-Magnon man. Human was going to take a little longer.

I made some calls from a phone booth at the station, confirmed where my quarry was based these days, and decided to walk to my rendezvous, to try to jump those last few million years in twenty minutes or so. I opted for the long route, up Buckingham Gate, and past the Palace and other arcane institutions for which men like Bill Carr had died.

It seemed remarkable at this remove, that Australians, Kiwis, Canadians, South Africans and Rhodesians had left their homes to come and fly some of the most perilous missions of the war for this nebulous concept of Empire. Bill Carr was the son of sheep farmers in New South Wales who felt the need to give all that up and learn to fly huge, ugly bombers across Europe. He got home only once in four years, just before shipping out of Oz, the result being Lindy, a daughter of whom I suspected he could be very proud.

I struck out along Birdcage Walk, thinking about the Brazilians and the all-black 92nd infantry of the US Army who had liberated large chunks of Italy in World War Two. I guessed there were plenty more anomalies if you dwelt on it. Like the very idea of an Italian SS unit, the one we helped stop in its tracks en route to Chiasso.

I reached Whitehall half an hour early and passed the time watching a march of what my father would call beatniks and lefties heading for Trafalgar Square and the South African Embassy, the banners and chants telling me they were protesting about some black terrorist called Nelson Mandela being sentenced to life imprisonment for treason.

Once that had passed, I played a game where I tried to guess who was in the big ministerial barges – the bulbous black Rover 3.5s – which ferried people to and from the various offices but, of course, my knowledge of British politicians was way out of date.

There was a new government, a man of the people at the top, all beer and sandwiches and promises to go and fetch the white heat of technology. To the civil service mandarins behind the elegant, soot-stained façades surrounding me, it must have seemed as if the Four Horsemen of the Apocalypse were riding into town.

My man appeared right on time, five minutes past one, and he hardly broke stride when he saw me loitering at the entrance to the Foreign Office. He slowed only slightly as he headed towards lunch in St James's, allowing me to fall in at his side.

'Ah, Kirby. Still flying the sartorial flag for pilots, I see.'

I was back in leather jacket, jeans and boots. He was wearing the kind of pin-striped Savile Row suit he might have picked up from his tailor ten days or ten years ago, with shoes so shiny you could signal sputniks with them. On his head was a threatened species – a bowler. Last time I'd been in England, Westminster and the City of London were a sea of bobbing black domes. Now, it seemed, only smooth television spies and Archibald Lang were supporting the likes of James Lock & Co.

'Hello, Major.'

'Oh, just Mr now. I find those people who cling on to their military titles rather sad, don't you?'

He was Special Adviser to the Foreign and Commonwealth Office for Special Forces. The keeper of the keys to all the files, many of which were sealed until 2005 or 2010, when we'd all be gone. Which was the idea, of course. 'Why did you send me Lindy Carr?'

He grinned, but it came out as a leer. 'Charming, isn't she? Have to admire a woman with gumption like that.'

'EH-148. It was my plane, wasn't it? Did you tell her that?'

He stopped suddenly, and I thought I'd shocked him, but he turned and bought an early edition of the *Evening News* from a vendor and tucked it under his arm before continuing. 'No. Did you?'

'She didn't tell me the date.'

'Twenty-eighth of August, 1944.'

My insides gave a little jolt, even though I had known this was coming. 'What are you playing at, Lang?'

'You know, I have to advise on various films and television shows now. *Carve Her Name, Moonstrike, The Guns of* . . . what's that one called?'

'Navarone.'

'That it. All about our wonderful Special Ops men and women. Which they were – mostly. Perhaps it is time someone showed that there were some real shits in the outfit.'

'Meaning me?' I asked, rather redundantly.

He didn't reply. We were almost at Trafalgar Square, where the protesters had halted the traffic, and police horses were wading in to try to move them on. A chant went up about the fascist police and I suppressed a grin. These kids had no idea what real fascism was. Then I groaned inwardly. I was turning into my father.

'Lang, are you playing games with that girl?'

'Did she show you the letter?'

'No. What letter?'

He flashed me his best reptilian smile. 'She's cleverer than I thought. She's holding that back. What arrangements did you make with her?'

'I am to meet her in Domodossola in a few weeks' time.' Once the summer was over, the dense vegetation that covered much of the area would start to thin, which gave us a better chance of spotting something on the ground. That is, if there was anything down there to spot.

'Look, Kirby, it struck me like this. She is clearly obsessed with her father, you don't have to be Roger Corder–' I dimly recalled this was the name of a TV shrink – 'to work that one out. In a way, the war has damaged her as much as anyone who was in it. She isn't going to rest until she finds the plane and Bill Carr. Now, much as I think you were a wash-out as a British Liaison Officer, Kirby, I know you are a good pilot. Maybe you can make amends. How many of us get a chance to do that, eh?'

'Don't the RAF have people to do this sort of thing?'

'The RAF are busy patrolling the airspace over the Atlantic for intrusions by Bears and Bisons.' He was using the NATO code for types of Russian bombers. 'They might not have it in sunny Italy, but we have a bit of a Cold War going on here, Kirby.' He gave a heartfelt sigh. 'There are some organisations trying to locate missing aircrew, but do you know how many aircraft are still unaccounted for, from the last war? Hundreds. They are still finding Spits and 109s and Heinkels in Kent and Essex, Lancasters and Halifaxes in Germany. The SAAF is a long way down their list. But you find that Liberator, the RAF will send a team to collect the bodies, make sure the poor buggers, or what's left of them, get a proper burial. I'll see to that.'

'I'd take your name off the list for the first human heart transplant, Lang. You finally seem to have grown your own.'

He halted again, and for a second I thought he was going to try to slug me, but he merely took off his bowler hat and ran a hand over his lightly oiled hair. We were outside his club, and it didn't look like I was about to be invited in. From the way he was glaring at me, the uniformed commissioner certainly didn't think it would be a good idea. It would take more than a borrowed tie and blazer to make me presentable behind the imposing high gloss and polished brass door.

Lang's tone softened. 'My job now is all about tying up loose ends, Kirby. This is one you can help with. Simple as that. You look after that girl, or you'll have me to answer to.'

With that he bounded up the steps and disappeared, leaving the doorman and me to exchange non-verbal hate signals. I walked off half-wishing Lang had tried to punch me.

I headed up towards Soho. One of the things I missed about Italy was the coffee and, in between the strip clubs and bohemian drinking dens, Soho was the best place for something close to the real thing. As I walked down past the bookshops along Charing Cross Road, I wondered what Lang's game was. It was hard to explain to young people like Lindy the breakdown in Italy in 1944, the shifting boundaries that could turn a downed Mosquito pilot like me into a BLO – a British Liaison Officer.

As soon as I accepted the ad hoc position with a partisan group, Lang, who operated out of Bern, was technically my superior, although at one point he had relieved me of my post. Which was odd, because nobody from the British side had actually appointed me in the first place. I often wondered if he had helped screw up my subsequent career, made it difficult for me to get back into combat flying, and perhaps nixed a move to proper airline pilot. Was he the reason BOAC and the others had scribbled a hasty 'no thanks' to me?

So after the war I had done a couple of years as a CAT hunter, just to try to shake the feeling that I hadn't flown my due. It turned out that, thanks to the debriefing of bomber crews during the war, the Met Office had reams of data on clear air turbulence – CAT for short. With the expansion of airline routes, the Civil Aviation Authority had backed a project to investigate the cause of this phenomenon, which had taken more than one commercial flyer by surprise.

So they looked around for pilots who would go chasing these

atmospheric roller-coasters up near the jet stream and my name had come up, mainly because of the type of plane they had converted for the job. They were Mosquitoes, two of them, with a meteorologist in the right-hand seat and a belly full of instruments, which would go up after any report of treacherous conditions, looking for the kind of sneaky turbulence that might tear the wings off the unwary.

It was fun, in an edgy way, because although I got the Mozzie into some pretty strange positions, it never felt like she was going to come apart on me. I often had trouble conveying that to the Met men, though. They changed with predictable regularity.

We pulled in enough data to keep the boffins going for a decade. It didn't cure me of the bug. I helped out in the Berlin airlift, working for a shrewd businessman called Freddie Laker, then went back to bikes for a while, to the TT; however, while it was OK, it wasn't flying.

I marvelled at the new face of Soho, how the grey seediness of five years ago seemed to have disappeared. There was a current of energy in the streets that even I could pick up on, smart kids with bright faces and knowing smiles outnumbering the shabbier old guard. I bumped into one young man in a startling white suit and hair over his collar who barked at me to watch where I was going, and then inspected his attire to make sure I hadn't sullied it. A faun-eyed girl waiting in a doorway nearby giggled at the boy, who brushed his lapels and winked at her knowingly. Something had happened that I didn't quite catch, a little crackle between them, on a frequency I could no longer receive.

I reached the haven of the Bar Italia, ordered a double espresso and found a spot beneath a signed poster of Sandro Mazzola celebrating a goal. I'd barely sat and slugged the coffee down, before I was back at the counter ordering another, shuddering with pleasure at the caffeine hit.

What was I going to do? I took the second cup back to my table and sat listening to Dino sing 'Volare'. *You know what you are going to do, Kirby?* Yes, I did. I was going to go to the Lakes. I was going to find the plane I betrayed twenty years ago.

Eight

Lake Maggiore, September 1964

The lightning spread across the sky in a complex pattern, illuminating the mountains. A few seconds later, a basso-profundo rumble of thunder was followed by the first hammering of rain on the canopy above my head. It was twenty minutes after twilight, the air thick and warm, but the weather was streaming in fast from across the Swiss border, just like it had that one night twenty years ago. Even as I watched them, the string of lights on the far side of Lake Maggiore began to blur, quickly swallowed by the rolling mist coming down from the hills. The incisor-shaped lumps of granite that formed the backdrop to Lake Maggiore were gone now, refusing to be backlit even by the lightning. The world was closing in.

I was sitting on the verandah of the Hotel Cannero, only yards from the water, sipping a grappa, enjoying the burn in my stomach, feeling remarkably mellow. I had parked my old MV Augusta at the side of the hotel, and the next day I would take myself up to Domodossola, twenty-four hours before the commemoration started, to see if I wanted to get involved with any kind of celebrations, or if I should just move straight on to looking for the

Liberator. In my room were maps of the region and a couple of books on aviation archaeology. They all agreed on one thing: you need a lot of luck to find a downed plane so long after the event.

It had been a busy summer. I'd decided to let Furio's betrayal – or opportunism – lie for the time being. At least I knew where I stood now. With Furio, it was going to be business before pleasure every time. He wasn't the same kind of pilot as me. But then, that was probably a good thing.

In between a few business trips, skydiving and flight-seeing, I had managed to hire a Wild aerial-surveying camera in Zürich. At some point in its history, my Twin Beech had been fitted with one of the US Fairchild photo-recon cameras. It took a few changes to the ring housing, but the Wild was in position now, and it could be operated either by an observer in the nose, or through remote cable by the pilot.

Of course, what I really needed was the big stereoscopic cameras that the RAF used, but they were out of the question, as was getting the loan of a V-Bomber to house one. So, after conversations with Wild and the British Aviation Archaeology Council, I had spent most of my advance on the next best thing: decent film. The only lab capable of processing the Kodak Aerochrome False Colour IR was in Milan, and it was very pricey. I hoped that Lindy Carr had a big vault back in Sydney.

The plan was that when I gave Furio the call that we were on, he would hop the Twin up to the little airfield at Invorio. That strip had been home to a Nachtjagdstaffel squadron back in 1944, German night-hunters, flying Junkers 88s bristling with radar masts and equipped with both forward- and upward-firing cannon. Now it was used by a flying club and a few private planes, but it was perfect for me – as many take-offs and landings as I needed without having to compete with BEA and Alitalia for slots, as I would at Malpensa.

The thunder was overhead, the hotel's windows chattered in

their frames and the lights went out. I heard Maria, the owner's daughter, yell instructions and the waiters began to distribute candles. Another boom and I caught the scrape of a chair to my left, just out of vision. I waited until the heavens provided another episode of unnatural daylight and turned to see her, skin bleached to ivory in the electrical glare.

'Hello, Jack.'

I bit my lower lip. 'Hello, Francesca.'

The glass bowl with its candle was placed between us, and I studied her uplit features in its softer glow. Her face was fuller than I remembered, but there were still those beautiful cheekbones and tantalising lips. When she grinned, there was just the hint of a gap between her two front teeth. Scientists could probably spend millions trying to find out why that eighth of an inch is sexy, but they'd come up with the same answer I always did: because it is, stupid.

'How did you know I was here?'

'Ragno,' she explained.

I had rung the spider boy at the Moto Guzzi factory, told him I was coming up and asked him to recommend a hotel. He had booked me into the Cannero and, it seemed, broadcast that the old BLO was back in town.

'Are you staying here too?' I asked.

She shook her head and, in the candlelight, I caught just a few traces of silver in the black of her hair as it moved across her face. She wore a navy-blue dress with a square-cut neck and a simple brooch that sparkled in the flame. 'We have a villa down at Stresa.'

We. Ragno had told me she was married, but it was still a little twist of a knife. What did you expect, Kirby? That she'd wait for you all these years? It wasn't like there'd been anything there in the first place, was it?

The hotel power spluttered back on and we blinked in its sudden harshness. I could feel her looking at me, and I was suddenly aware that I hadn't shaved. I scratched my cheek and listened to the rasp. 'You look well,' she said. Before I could object, she added: 'A little thin, perhaps.'

'And you look just right.'

She flashed that gap-toothed smile and my heart missed more than one beat. 'Have you eaten?' she asked.

I shook my head.

'The food here is good,' Francesca said, signalling for the menus. 'But there is no mule.'

I laughed at the memory. 'I was getting quite a taste for that, you know.'

'I'm going up to the house tomorrow.'

'San Marco?' That was the name of the hamlet where the safe house was situated; they had taken me there after I'd been pulled from among the dead in the lake.

'Yes.'

'Why?'

'Just for old times' sake. One last look, perhaps. Like to come?'

I hesitated. 'If you want,' I said noncommittally.

'Tell me what you have been up to.'

I shrugged, ready to trot out my thumbnail CV, when she touched my hand.

'All of it, Jack. It's been a long time.'

A wind was getting up, an *inverno*, blowing down from Locarno in the Swiss half of the lake, but rather than move inside we decided to stay put.

While I explained about my father and his ailing company, and taking out my frustrations on Steve Riley's face, Francesca ordered *bresaola*, followed by perch from the lake, and a bottle of *erbaluce* white wine. When the antipasti came, I told her about Lindy Carr.

'You think it is the bomber we were waiting for?'

'Lang told me it is. I think it's his idea of making me suffer after all this time. It's working, too.' I gave a smile that I hoped didn't show too much regret.

Francesca re-filled my glass. 'Twenty years ago. It's hard to imagine all that time has gone. A whole generation.'

I took a heavy slug of my drink. 'So . . .' I shook off the creeping sense of self-pity and asked, 'What about you? Married, I hear. Kids?'

She smiled. 'Yes to married, no to kids.'

'And you live in Stresa?'

'Milan. The villa is a weekend home.'

'You must be doing all right.'

'We are.'

OK, Kirby, play the game, be polite. 'Do I know him? Is he coming to the anniversary ceremony?'

'No, and no. Not his sort of thing.'

'What's his name?' Like I gave a damn.

'Riccardo,' she said slowly. 'Riccardo Conti.'

I squinted at her. The only Conti I had heard of was the one who reputedly organised the reprisals back in 1944. 'Same name as that bastard who did the anti-partisan sweeps.'

She nodded and gave a grim smile, her voice only just rising above the whistle of the wind. 'Same bastard, in fact.'

Part Two

Nine

Saló, Lake Garda, Italy, 1944

The whores arrived on time, at five o'clock, just as the government offices closed for the day. The scruffy convoy of private cars and taxis swept into Saló's Piazza Zanelli and disgorged their occupants. They emerged in a haze of blue cigarette smoke and cheap perfume, many of them already drunk and giggling. Major Riccardo Conti, formerly of the Alpine Rifles, now anti-partisan director of the new Guardia Nazionale Repubblicana, found himself shaking his head. Some of the girls were barely in their teens, their faces plastered with rouge and lipstick, their blouses stuffed with padding to try to emulate their older companions. It was shameful.

Across the square, Adolph, the owner of the Bar Colombara, grinned and waved the new arrivals in. Convention dictated this was the town's premier pick-up point, a convention that arose because Adolph never charged the women for drinks while they waited. Soon the men, German and Italian army officers, members of the *Brigate Nere*, the Black Brigades militia, the SS and the bored sons of diplomats and industrialists who had somehow avoided conscription, would come to select their evening entertainment.

Along the coast at Gargana, in the Villa Feltrinelli, *il Duce* as some still called him – although it was increasingly difficult to see exactly what Mussolini was leader of – would be welcoming Claretta Petacci to the Sala dello Zodiaco, for a session of lovemaking under the stars, albeit only the ones painted on the ceiling. That was, if he had managed to get rid of Rachele, his wife, who was threatening to claw her usurper's eyes out.

New arrivals in a couple of Lancia Aprilia saloons powered past the Hotel Eden and into the square, spraying dust into the Casa del Fascio, the party coffee-house and meeting-place, and took the road towards the *osservatorio*. It no longer did any observing – its antique telescopes had been hidden in caves in the mountains that formed the town's backdrop. As they passed, he saw these cars were packed with handsome young boys, which meant they were due at the Villa Pasolini, current home of a German major and his Swiss lover, on a cul-de-sac off the via del Seminario. Its candlelit terrace at dusk was the accepted meeting-point for those with such tastes.

Conti lit one of the filthy Nazionale cigarettes, grimaced at the taste, and strolled down the hill, across the linked squares that led to the harbour and the lakeside promenade with its once-proud hotels, now mostly billets for officers and hangers-on. He kept a weather eye out for stragglers from the whore convoy, who would rather mow down an Italian officer than be late for the flesh parade at the bar. At the taxi-boat mooring he turned right and thirty metres on slipped into the garden of the Cozzi restaurant, where he selected a seat with a good view of the lake and mountains.

He placed his cap on the table, ordered a carafe of *chiaretto* rosé, which arrived with a few slices of goose salami, courtesy of the kitchen. At least there were few food shortages up north, not compared to the privations of those down south who had been 'liberated'.

He raised his glass to a young lieutenant he recognised, sitting almost lost in the bougainvillaea with one of the Milanese girls. At another table, talking in low voices, were two officers from X-Mas, pronounced Decima-Mas, the marine assault unit headed by Prince Junio Valerio Borghese, which had remained fiercely pro-fascist. The reason they weren't whoring was probably that their commander would have had them publicly castrated. Borghese ran a notoriously tight ship, except when it came to the small matter of his own many adulteries.

There was a hand on Conti's shoulder. He looked up and struggled to get to his feet when he saw the uniform. The palm pressed him down. 'Relax, Major. We're all off-duty now.' The man threw his cap next to Conti's and ordered a *spumante*. 'Major Conti, am I right?'

'Yes.'

'I am SS-Sturmbannführer Karl Knopp.' He was roughly the same rank as Conti, but the SS flashes made the newcomer the senior man. He was in his early thirties, although his hair was mostly grey and his eyes looked tired. There were substantial bags under them, and the skin at the top of his cheeks was thin and bloodshot. Still, ignore those and he was a handsome specimen, not like some of the slugs who picked up women at Adolph's.

'How do you do, Sturmbannführer?' Conti asked.

There was a crackle of gunshots, but nobody took much notice. The little lakeside town transformed into something from the American Wild West as evening descended. Nothing surprised those who had been here with Mussolini for the past nine months. Orgies, drugs, gunfights, murder, sometimes all rolled into a single explosion of passion and death. It was one of the reasons why Conti kept away from the bars. There was a drunken anarchy about it that he didn't like one bit. The wrong word, letting a glance linger too long, and some madman might pull a Beretta or a Luger and end you there and then.

Knopp sipped his drink. 'You are in charge of anti-partisan operations hereabouts, I hear?'

'Mostly,' said Conti. 'But the Black Brigades and other militia are also active in the process.'

Knopp shook his head. The *Brigate Nere* were gaining a reputation for senseless, excessive violence that sometimes even made the Germans recoil. 'Rogues and sadists. I hear you have had much success against the Garibaldi.'

'The Communists? Some, yes.'

Conti knew Knopp would get around to telling him what he was after eventually, so he sipped his rosé and waited.

The German pursed his lips and said quietly, 'I need some help with a partisan sweep. A large one.'

'Has there been more sabotage?'

'No. This is a preventative action.'

Conti signalled for another drink, and asked for a plate of antipasti for them to share. 'You realise I take my orders from Colonel Stoppani of the Esercito Nazionale Repubblicana?' This was the new fascist army set up when Mussolini created his 'Republic' based around Saló in October 1943, almost a year previously. 'Not the Wehrmacht or the SS.'

Knopp laughed. 'And you know better than that.' To prove his point, the SS man took a piece of paper from his tunic and laid it on the table. Conti pulled it towards him. He could see it was full of eagles and stamps and impressive signatures. 'From Berlin?'

'Munich,' said Knopp. 'SS Supreme Command main office. It outranks your Colonel Stoppani by some considerable margin.'

'I suppose it does.' Conti knew that there were SS Supreme Command men attached to the Villa Feltrinelli – laughingly called liaison officers – to keep an eye on Mussolini, and that Hitler had even supplied *il Duce* with a doctor to help with his near-legendary constipation. He assumed his new friend was part of that group.

'I am sure you are aware that units of the 29th SS-Waffen-Grenadiers are regrouping near here,' Knopp explained. This Italienische Number 1, an SS unit of Italians, had fought at Anzio under German control and had then been released to Italian command. Now the Germans wanted them back. 'They are to reinforce the Gothic Line for this winter. They, and some of their armour, will be moving to the railhead at Chiasso in a few weeks' time. I want to make sure that they do not suffer the same fate as Das Reich.'

Conti raised an enquiring eyebrow. He knew that Das Reich was the name of the 2nd SS Panzer Division, but that was all.

'Das Reich tried to reinforce the Normandy beachhead after the Allied landing. They were harried every inch of the way by French partisans. Instead of a few days, it took them more than two weeks to make the trip. Of course, we made the French pay, but that isn't the point. I don't want a repeat of that. Particularly as there is an extra dimension to this journey.'

A firework arced over the lake and exploded, the colours bleached and wasted against the blue sky. Conti popped a piece of prosciutto into his mouth. Knopp was smiling at him, his mouth the shape of a lemon slice. It wasn't a comfortable experience.

'Sturmbannführer,' Conti said slowly. 'Do you want to start from the beginning?'

It was dark by the time Conti and Knopp finished their meal and two bottles of wine. Knopp had done most of the drinking, Conti settling on a modest single glass with each course. As they left, he shook hands with the German, who wobbled off down around the bay to the south, where he had requisitioned a lakeside cottage. Conti lit a cigarette under one of Saló's distinctive horn-shaped streetlights and looked back up at the town, wondering who the hell was supposed to be enforcing the blackout. Light flared from dozens of windows, and a couple of the bars, enough to home in any Allied bomber worth its salt. Then there were the fireworks. They were asking for the town to be flattened.

He began to walk in the opposite direction to the German,

thinking about what the man had said. The Germans were about to present *il Duce* with a very large bill indeed for what they had done – the rescue, the transport to Munich, the setting up and running of the Repubblica Sociale Italiana, the RSI, Mussolini's fiefdom, which more and more resembled the last days of Sodom.

The payment would be taken to the railhead along with the Italian SS, but while the troops headed for Tuscany, the valuables would be put on one of the German trains that ran through Switzerland. The country might be technically neutral but, in exchange for much-needed raw materials such as steel and coal, it was willing to allow German freight to move across its tracks, as long as it was sealed at the borders. What they didn't see, the Swiss didn't care about.

It was just another business arrangement in an increasingly crazy war. Italians at each other's throats, the Americans and British bombing and shelling the hell out of the country, the Germans impervious to what happened to the land, or its treasures, as long as the Americans and British were delayed. The newly formed Royal Army, loyal to the King, was fighting for the Allies, while dozens of units under various names had thrown in their lot with the Nazis. It was civil war.

Many thousands of Italian soldiers languished in German labour camps, treated appallingly; an equal number had been executed to stop them changing sides. Up in the mountains the Garibaldis, the Communist partisans, fought almost as much with the Green Flames, the non-Communists, as they did with the Germans. *Brigate Nere* hunted their fellow countrymen through the north now, executing any partisan found with weapons, by order of Mussolini. His insistence that there be no reprisals against non-partisan civilians was ignored by the fascist militia and Germans.

Opportunity after opportunity to drive out the Nazis with a few bold strokes had been squandered by Allies and Italians alike after the surrender of Italy, and what was left was the worst of all worlds. How would the country rise from this? How could there ever be real peace again?

Conti looked up and saw the faintest streak in the sky, and thought he caught an engine noise, a low whine bouncing between the peaks that ringed the lake. No, it must be a shooting star, he reckoned. He wished on it, hoping it would bring him, and Italy, luck. Because from now on, he had finally realised, it was every man for himself.

Conti knocked on the door of the boathouse and waited. Offshore, somewhere to the south, he could hear the engine of the X-Mas patrol who scoured the waterfront each night, just in case the enemy parachuted in an aircraft-carrier right under their noses. He supposed it helped *il Duce* sleep tighter, but if trouble came, he doubted it would be from the lake.

'Rizalli? It's me.' He hammered again, stopping when he heard the echo of his knocks thrown back at him from the water. There were few houses at this northern end of the town, none within 400 metres, but he reminded himself to take it easy.

Two bolts snicked back inside, and a rifle muzzle appeared in the crack of the door. All was dark within. 'Say it,' said the voice.

'Rizalli—'

'Say it.'

'I am the perfect counterbalance.'

'Then let the punishment fit the crime,' said the voice. The door opened.

The boathouse smelt of rot. A half-submerged wooden lake cruiser lay in the dock, surrounded by an accumulation of detritus and garbage washed under the doors by the sluggish currents. Conti smiled at Rizalli in the weak light of the oil lamp and held up the bottle of wine he had brought with him.

Rizalli was a New Zealander of Italian extraction, one of the

71

Special Forces officers the British had sent to help the partisans. Such was his facility with the language, he had managed, with Conti's help, to get himself right into Saló itself. Rizalli took the Bardolino and indicated that Conti go upstairs, and he followed.

Rizalli spent a few minutes searching for a corkscrew in the mess. Once he had the bottle open, he slopped out two glasses, put the bottle on the warped table and sat on the crate that functioned as the only chair. This wasn't where Rizalli lived, he only came for the so-called Red Stocking transmissions, so the place was short on comforts.

'I thought I heard the plane,' said Conti, taking a sip of the wine. 'A Mosquito perhaps. About fifteen minutes ago. I could have been mistaken.'

Rizalli nodded. 'You weren't. It came. I got the transmission.'

'Did you get an answer?'

More fireworks, this time garish against the night sky, the colours flashing in through the boathouse's single yellow-paned window that faced onto the lake.

'They said no.'

'No?'

Rizalli shook his head. 'Too likely to provoke a reaction, they said.'

Conti found himself spluttering with rage, even though he knew he was angry at the wrong man. 'But the effect on morale, for the whole country! Idiots. Short-sighted idiots.' It was as he thought: every man – and every country – for themselves.

'Furthermore, if we go ahead, they will cut off all supplies. Disown us.' Rizalli's mouth turned down to show he was not pleased at this development either.

'Bastards. Just because they control the purse-strings they think they can treat us like *castrati*.' Conti grabbed his balls in frustration. After a minute of oaths, he took off his cap and brushed his hair back, trying to suppress his irritation. 'What will you do now?'

Rizalli sighed and knocked back his drink. He shuddered. It wasn't the best Bardolino in town, that was for sure. 'I am to inform all British Liaison Officers of the decision.'

'And will you?'

'It's what I have to do. I will send couriers out in the morning.'

The Italian ran through several possibilities in his mind. There was another way to get funds, thanks to Knopp. But he couldn't have the BLOs against him, not all of them. Conti listened to the long string of firecrackers, waited until the sound swelled and drew his gun. Rizalli's eyes widened in shock and he made a leap for the bottle, intent on smashing it into Conti's face. He was dead before his hand reached it, the flat crack of the Beretta lost in the almost continuous explosions of gunpowder overhead.

The next morning, Major Riccardo Conti drove along the lakeside of Maggiore, with the water on his right, towards the Swiss border. Beyond Cannobio, the number of road checks increased, and he had to show his papers half a dozen times before he reached the main crossing point, a ten-foot-high wooden structure, like a proscenium arch, encircled with barbed wire, with a thick, striped pole as a barrier through the centre. A few hundred metres further on there was a similar structure marking the beginning of Switzerland.

How many people would like to take that walk across that no-man's-land? How many had tried and been turned back? It wasn't uncommon for escaped POWs or fleeing Jews to make it within sight of Switzerland only, like Moses, to be denied access to the Promised Land. He himself had received calls from helpful Swiss border guards telling him they had a 'package' of some value to be collected.

Yet he also knew of Swiss citizens who risked the ire of their government by helping Allied soldiers and pilots cross the treacherous passes over the Alps to safety. Once inside, the Swiss had no option but to process them, but Conti was in no doubt they would rather everyone just got on with their war and left them well alone.

There were a mixture of German and Italian guards on duty, but he stepped out of his car and went straight for the former, singling out the lieutenant sitting in the wooden hut to the left of the blockade. He could have arranged this meeting somewhere less obvious, but he was certain that doing it in plain sight was the best way to avoid suspicion.

The lieutenant emerged to greet him, and Conti presented his papers, signed and stamped by Knopp.

'Do you mind if I make a call?' asked the young lieutenant.

'Not at all,' replied Conti, cursing the man under his breath. The German disappeared into the hut, while Conti stood and tapped his foot impatiently, aware of the dozen soldiers watching him. The lieutenant returned, smiling, and handed the papers back. 'All is in order. You must fill in a crossing order, stating your business in Switzerland. And the car stays here, I am afraid.'

Conti nodded and followed the German into the hut for fifteen minutes of rubber stamping and lies.

The café was just inside Switzerland, 200 metres beyond the wire, an Alpine chalet-style establishment, manned by an Italian-Swiss couple who looked perplexed to see a Republican soldier on their premises, worried the war was crossing over to their side.

'How can we help you, sir?' the man had asked unctuously.

'Coffee.'

'Very good.'

'I'm sure it is.'

Conti had told the Germans he was meeting an informer who had information about the smuggling routes the partisans were using over the mountains to re-supply, and about the help the Americans – through the Office of Strategic Services – were giving the rebels. It was rumoured the USA wanted to be as generous as possible to the Italians, regardless of their political persuasions. The British, arguing this was virtually their backyard, were more cautious.

He was twenty minutes late. Conti had finished his first coffee by the time he arrived and was on to his second. He sat down without ceremony, smartly, flashily dressed, with gold rings; a saturnine face with thick black hair and a pencil-thin moustache, carefully sculpted like that of a Hollywood film star. He smelled of citrus fruits from his over-applied cologne. 'Major.'

'Signor Leone.'

'Nino,' he replied. 'How often do I have to tell you? Call me Nino.'

'Nino. Coffee?'

'Please. Your mother sends her regards.'

Conti nodded. He had moved his mother and young brother to Locarno at the beginning of 1940, before Italy had entered the war. Nino Leone had helped her meet the financial requirements for residence by judicious movement of funds and opportunist bribery. 'Is everything all right there?'

'Yes, yes.'

'Monthly payments still coming through?'

'Of course. I would let you know, if . . .'

The coffee arrived and they waited until the owner had retreated behind the counter. The only other customers were two Swiss border guards playing chess, and they were out of earshot.

'Thank you for coming.'

'My pleasure,' said Nino. 'What can I do for you?'

'It's difficult.'

'Oh, don't be so pessimistic, Major. Nothing is difficult. Every problem can be solved. Well, unless you want to save a trainload of Jews.' He gave a little chortle. 'Apart from that . . . fire away.'

'I don't mean that. I mean, if I am to tell you my proposition, you have to say yes. To agree to help me.'

'Before I hear it?'

'Yes.'

Nino took a sip of coffee. 'As you say, that is difficult. What if I hear it and then decide not to be involved?'

'Then, Nino, I will have to have you killed.'

Nino started to laugh again but stifled it when he saw the look on Conti's face. 'Forgive me, but that isn't much of an incentive. What you don't know, doesn't hurt.'

'A million Swiss francs, nearly a quarter of a million US dollars.'

'What is that?'

'Now you know how much you'll be hurt if you don't listen to me. That's your share.'

Conti watched the man's face twitch greedily.

'What do I have to do?' he asked.

Conti leaned back in his chair and ordered a brandy from the owner. While he waited he said softly, 'You sure you want to hear this?'

'For a million francs? I think so.'

The Italian took the brandy and threw back a mouthful. 'We're going to fuck the Germans.'

Nino smiled. He'd heard that promise before. It wasn't proving easy. Still, he had no objection to it in principle. He was pretty untouchable on this side of the border, despite Conti's threats. 'You and whose army?'

'Me and Gruppo Fausto. Although they don't yet know it.'

Ten

Lake Maggiore, 1964

'I suppose you think it is like one of those Hollywood movies. *I Married a Fascist*,' said Francesca.

I didn't answer. It was the day after her revelation about Conti, and I hadn't slept well since Francesca told me of her marriage to the former *Repubblicano*. At least, that was my excuse. I had a feeling it would have been a night of tossing and turning regardless. After all, I'd come face to face with one of the biggest regrets of my life.

Francesca had arrived at nine that morning, dressed in black ski-pants and cream blouse, and she had no objection to riding up the mountain to the old safe house on the back of the MV. As we zig-zagged up over the gorges, past waterfalls and dense stands of moist ferns, it was good to feel her arms round me, no matter how misguided her matrimonial choices were. The roads were perfect for a powerful bike like the MV, which gave the steeper gradients short shrift, and I could lean into the bends, confident there was little other traffic, and feel her grip tighten and her body press harder against me.

I had parked on the edge of the cluster of grey houses that was San Marco, and now we were walking past the *gora*, a stone pergola that formed the communal washing area for the village, towards the house, a big, flat-fronted piece of granite built against the mountainside, with a garden to its left that looked down over the lake. It was in that garden I had found an old neglected 1920s Laverda and spent days stripping it down and cleaning it, while Ragno helped, and eventually got hooked on motorcycles. He was a good kid back then, fearless and eager to fight Germans. I was glad it worked out for him.

As we walked over the crude cobbles, I waited for Francesca to tell me that her husband was really a first-rate chap, to give me all the Mussolini apologia I'd heard over the years – how he'd never wanted to persecute the Jews, how he'd issued orders against reprisals, how he'd tried to make peace with the Allies but Anthony Eden made sure that his overtures were scuppered. About how *il Duce* kept copies of Socrates and Plato to hand, his own notes scribbled in the margins, his love of family, fencing and football, his concern for the environment and education.

I knew all that. I was prepared to accept that Benito Mussolini was not quite the 'complete gangster' and buffoon Eden always portrayed him as, and the rest of the world readily accepted. But then I wanted to remind her that after the partisans had taken the small town of Montefiore in 1944, and then been defeated, the fascist Black Brigades had laid the Garibaldi units, the Communists, in the road, and let the Germans drive their armoured cars over them. True, Mussolini and his *Repubblicani* weren't actually *in* the vehicles, but their bloodstained paw-prints were all over that scene.

Then there was *il Monco*, the Austrian SS Major Walter Reder, alias The Stump, so called because he was missing part of his left arm, who killed 500 civilians in Sant'Anna, near Lucca, for aiding the partisans. Fascist officials had stood by and watched the massacre of their countrymen, approving the action in the name of *il Duce*.

Perhaps, I surmised, she would talk about the need to heal the divisions, to make Italy whole again by burying the past. 'So why come to this commemoration, then?' I would retort. It was bound to open old wounds. But Francesca said nothing else to me except: 'We have to go around the side.'

She let us into the kitchen through the buckled door. Inside, it smelled heavily of damp and mould, but as I stepped into the half-light, I could make out the main features, once so familiar. There was a large fireplace opposite, still stacked with logs, and to the right three *fornelli*, the large charcoal-burners built into the top of a brick oven. This was where Francesca would make her speciality dishes – mule stew and *mondine* – roasted chestnuts – and talk longingly of the *tordelli* or *ballociori* her mother would cook, and of the banquets they would have after the war. Her family had been *contadini* – farmers, but relatively rich ones, owning land on the Lombardy and Piedmonte borders.

The crude wooden table was still there; in the spluttering light of poor-quality candles – the Allies had destroyed all the power plants – Rosario, Ennio, Pavel and Fausto would play *briscola* or *bazzica*, the air thick with the smoke from their tiny but pungent *Toscanelli* cigars.

I had tried to join in, but it takes a while to get used to the Italian forty-card deck: not having an eight, nine or ten was, for someone brought up on gin rummy, disconcerting. It was even harder to stomach the cigars. The home-made grappa though, distilled from the *vinaccia*, the pulp left from pressing the grapes, and running at 70–80 per cent proof, was a revelation. The taste for it had never left me. Ask my liver.

Fausto would only allow everyone to play cards with washers. He told tales about farmers who would gamble for days after the harvest until their little stack of gold Napoleons, their land – even their wives – had gone, and then they would hang themselves the next morning. He said these were stories he had heard, but there was an anger in his voice that suggested it was closer to home.

'It smells the same,' I said.

'I think that's why I don't like to come here very often. Suddenly, I am starving again. Happens every time. I have to smoke a cigarette to kill the hunger pangs.'

She threw back the shutters, letting light flood into the kitchen. I stroked the table-top. I could almost trace the pattern of our evenings from its patina of scratches, wine stains and cigar burns. I asked: 'Who owns the place now?'

'We do – Riccardo and I. We bought it after the war, but never used it. I suppose for a while I couldn't bear to think of anyone else living here, but that passed. I would remember it every six months, and sometimes would come up just to let daylight in. A German is interested in buying it as a holiday home now. For a good price.' I must have made a disapproving noise because she turned to me and snapped: 'What, you think that is sacrilege too?'

'It's just ironic,' I said.

'That I'm not only sleeping with the enemy, but trading with them? Does it make you want to shave my head or tar and feather me?'

Steady on, I thought, where did that one come from? I'd been long gone before such spiteful reprisals against collaborators had kicked in. I had no answer, at least none that wouldn't make matters worse, so I went to the black wooden door that led into the rest of the house from the kitchen and lifted the ancient latch. I stepped into the sunless chill of the circular hallway, the steel crescents on my heels ringing on the terrazzo floor, and felt myself fall through into the past.

Eleven

Lake Maggiore, Italy, 1944

Kirby awoke sticky with sweat, a single sheet over his body. As he tried to throw the cover back, a lance of pain shot up his leg and he froze, holding his breath. What time was it? It was dark, but he could just make out heavy drapes pulled across the window, so that meant nothing. A sense of the scale of the room slowly came. It must be big, because the bed was huge; he could barely touch the edges of the mattress. He reached back above his head and felt a richly carved headboard and could make out ornate plaster-work on the high ceiling. There was a pervading odour of mustiness, of once-rich fabrics decaying.

He raised himself up on one elbow and gingerly pulled off the sheet. The pain again, less sharp this time. There was something seriously wrong with his ankle. He must have snagged it, getting out of the Mosquito.

He thought about the Mozzie, lost in the silty blackness in the depths of the lake. There would be panic by now back at the base in Sardinia. Missing plane, pilot, navigator, OSS man and, more important than all that, the Red Stocking radio gear. Well, they wouldn't have to worry about that. He suspected its final resting-place was too deep for any recovery effort.

Kirby was dressed in a clean singlet and pair of rough trousers with . . . he checked: no underwear. He wondered if his hosts had dried his flying gear. There was silk underwear, an inner flying suit filled with kapok and the sidcot canvas outer layer. He'd ditched the gloves fumbling to get out of the plane, he recalled, so they were lost.

He shuffled across to the side of the mattress, swung his legs off and put his weight down and took two steps, before deciding it was a bad idea. As he slumped back on the bed, he was aware of a movement in the corner. He wasn't alone.

'Hello?' he asked.

In answer, a lighter flared and a cigarette was lit but there was no verbal reply. Kirby pulled himself up once more, staggered to the window and yanked back one of the thick curtains, releasing a puff of dust. A soft grey morning light entered the room, lifting it from dark to merely gloomy. The person sitting in the gilded chair looked to be fourteen or fifteen, at an age, anyway, where he shouldn't be smoking. But then, he was also at an age where he probably shouldn't have a double-barrelled shotgun across his knees either.

As Kirby limped across to the bed and sat once more, the boy got up, broke the shotgun over his arm, and left the room. Kirby hoped he had gone to find a grown-up.

He heard the arguments raging before anyone came to ask his opinion.

'Did he say anything?' A man's voice.

'You told me not to speak to him.' The boy.

'We should move him soon.' A softer voice, a woman.

'Where? He won't make it over the mountains.'

'And if the Black Brigades find him, they'll kill him.'

If the *Brigate Nere* were likely to kill them, this made his saviours the *partigiani*, the partisans.

'Then us,' chimed in the boy.

'We could take him south,' the woman suggested.

'Fausto said to wait here.'

'That was before we got ourselves lumbered with a pilot.'

'If he is a pilot . . . an English pilot, at least.'

'You think . . . ?'

'I don't know. Fausto should decide.'

'He won't be walking for a few days anyway. Not on that ankle,' the woman said.

Kirby listened to a few further exchanges, before he decided to interrupt. 'Hey, hello!' he bellowed. 'Can I just say—'

She appeared in the doorway, a perfectly framed silhouette. As she stepped forward into the shaft of light from the window, he could tell from the way the faded blue dress hung and the angularity of her cheekbones, that she was a good few pounds below her fighting weight, but the sight of her still took his breath away.

'Yes?' she asked.

'Can I just say,' he continued in his halting Italian, 'that I do speak the language.'

She smiled and took her hand from behind her back. It held his Colt automatic, chambered for .38, which was now standard issue on Red Stockings. Nobody ever said anything explicit, but Kirby knew it was meant more for use on pilot and crew than the enemy. Just in case anyone was a bit tardy with their cyanide pill.

'How convenient.' She moved the gun in his direction and he felt a spasm of fright.

'Careful.'

'Safety is on.'

It wasn't reassuring. He'd figured out what was going through her mind. 'You don't think I'm a plant, do you?'

'It happens.'

'Do they normally infiltrate people by crash-landing them in a twin-engined plane on the lake?'

She laughed at this and lowered the gun. 'It was quite an entrance.'

The boy was behind her now, another cigarette in his mouth, leaning against the doorframe, peering over her shoulder like a guardian angel. 'My name is Francesca Lombardi. This is Spider.' The kid nodded. 'The man downstairs is Pavel.'

'I'm—'

'Jack Kirby,' she said. 'We had to go through your belongings.'

'My sidcot?'

'Your what?'

'Flying suit,' he explained.

'It can be repaired. It ripped as you were getting out. All your things are safe. You were lucky to get free, I think.'

He asked about the bodies in the lake, and she explained about the executions and the dumpings. The Germans had also captured their group's BLO during a radio transmission to Switzerland when he had stayed on-air too long. He, too, had been on the train, and had been shot at the lake with the others. Kirby tried to speak but nothing came. There were too many questions he wanted to ask. Such as, what was a BLO?

'How many dead?' he finally asked.

'Three, four hundred I think,' she continued. 'We attacked the garrison on the Cannero island, just a feint, a few well-timed explosions, while we got some of the bodies ashore . . .' So those were the lights he'd seen, the flashes of detonations. 'Then you dropped in.'

'Where am I?'

'In a safe house in San Marco, above Cannero Riviera, on the road to Domodossola.'

He was none the wiser. 'Which lake did I crash in?'

'Maggiore.'

'The one that runs to Switzerland?'

She knew where that thought was going. 'And the one that is well patrolled by the Decima-Mas marines and the Swiss border guards. Yes. Are you hungry?'

'I am,' he admitted. 'You have food?'

Francesca looked at the boy. 'Some stew left,' he said with a shrug that suggested a certain reluctance.

'Just don't ask what the meat is,' she warned.

He didn't care what poor animal the stringy flesh had once belonged to. There was a lump of stale bread which he soaked in the broth and he cleared the bowl, including the chewy lumps of vegetable matter, which appeared to be chestnuts. As he ate she kept up a stream of questions, and he explained that his Italian came from his mother, who was part of the Manzoni family which had ice-cream parlours along the south coast of England, including one in Brighton, where she had met his father.

She told him about the partisan sweeps which were taking place in other parts of the lake district. That he was lucky to be found by their group.

'And your group is?'

A heartbeat of a hesitation. 'Gruppo Fausto.'

That name again. 'What are you? Green Flames? Garibaldis? Christian Democrats?' He reeled off some of the names of the endless partisan groups that the Intelligence Officer had droned on about. It was a fraction of the total running around these hills, he knew. He wished he'd paid more attention to the briefing.

'Just anti-fascist.'

Kirby continued to eat in silence until there was a commotion downstairs in the hallway, and several doors slammed. He heard new voices, raised and angry, faster than his rusty Italian could keep up with.

'Is that Fausto?' he asked.

She frowned. 'Perhaps. Stay here.' Then she slipped out of the room, closing the door behind her.

Kirby counted to ten, put the food tray aside and hopped over after her. He cracked the door and listened. He could hear Francesca's voice to his left, on the stairs, he guessed, from the way it echoed around the big circular hallway below. Directly in front of him was an ornate balustrade that ran around the whole of the level, with a break for the staircase. He could see a series of doors to his left and right, probably other bedrooms.

He dropped down to his hands and knees and slithered forward. There were five strangers downstairs in the hallway, each with a bright red neckerchief which, as the IO had told him, was used to denote one's unit or brigade. The red suggested the Garibaldis – Communists. Facing them were Ragno and an older man, the one she had called Pavel, both with guns levelled at the newcomers. Francesca was on the stairs, with Kirby's Colt aimed straight and true at the man who appeared to be the leader of the group. He saw her thumb ease off the safety. She wasn't bluffing this time.

Kirby examined the figure lying on the floor between the protagonists. From the mass of congealed black across his chest and stomach he had been badly wounded, but it wasn't that which held Kirby's unwilling gaze. It was his face. His ears had gone, and his nose, and both eye-sockets were completely empty. His left leg was kicking, and the low, animal moan Kirby could hear coming from the bloody cave of a mouth meant that this sorry creature was still alive.

'That was uncalled for. The remark about tarring and feathering. I apologise.'

I was back at Lake Maggiore in 1964, with Francesca at my shoulder, breaking into my thoughts, holding a glass for me. I took it and sniffed. It was Scotch, and a single malt at that. 'Jesus, if I'd known this was hidden here . . .'

'I brought it with me,' she said. 'In my bag. I thought we might need a drink after seeing this place.'

I remembered now why she was so easy to fall in love with.

'To Vittorio,' I said, raising the grubby glass.

'To Vittorio.' We both drank.

'There is something else,' she said. 'Something that really has been here all the time.'

I took another hit of the whisky, placed the glass on the floor and took the brown greaseproof-paper parcel from her. The weight and shape gave it away, but I still unwrapped it carefully and held the Colt automatic for the first time in twenty years. Before being stored, it had been oiled and greased, and it looked just as it did the last time I handled it, moments before tossing it to Francesca and telling her to keep it. I looked at her, then across the curve of the stairs, and knew she was remembering the same scene as me.

Lying on the dirty, cracked marble of the mezzanine, Kirby held his breath, straining to follow the debate raging below between the newcomers and his saviours. The problem was, this was conducted in some local dialect. He could pick out names – Fausto, more than once, Udone, Invernicci, Giuliano, Rosario – and the initials of some partisan groups, but the main thrust of the argument kept slipping away.

If these people weren't welcome, he thought, how come they hadn't been stopped down the road? Surely Gruppo Fausto posted guards. If not, what was to stop the Germans?

Then a machine pistol crackled from above him and he felt the cartridge cases bounce off his back. He covered his ears and squeezed his eyes shut, but not fast enough to escape the image of the poor eyeless wretch on the floor dancing spasmodically as rounds slammed into his already ruined body. Another gun opened up, across the way, also firing down into the hallway, the bright muzzle flashes burning through Kirby's closed lids.

From below, there was the boom of a shotgun, the more feeble crack of a handgun – possibly his Colt – and then a long burst from one of the machine pistols nearby, followed by the hollow ring of a brass case rolling lazily across the marble and falling through the rails to bounce on the hall floor. Kirby tensed as he waited for the bullet in the back of his head.

'Who the hell is this?' demanded a voice from behind.

Kirby opened his eyes. The hallway floor was covered in bodies, the terrazzo slick with their blood. Standing among the carnage were Ragno and Francesca, while Pavel was going through the pockets of the dead leader. Kirby looked across to the other side of the mezzanine and there was a short man with a shaved head, a stubble of beard, and a smile on his face, dressed in black jacket and trousers. A partisan, not a German.

Kirby rolled over and looked up at the character who had spoken behind him. This man was fair, with a rough but handsome face, piercing grey eyes, also dressed in black well-worn clothes, with a blue-and-white kerchief around his neck. So it had come to this. The feuds between the various factions had turned into the sort of gangsterism you expected in Prohibition Chicago.

'Who are you?' the man barked.

'He's a British pilot,' said Francesca, coming up the stairs, apparently unfazed by the mass murder in which she had partici-pated. The beauty that Kirby had admired suddenly seemed tainted and brittle. 'We pulled him out of the lake.'

'Ha!' shouted Pavel from below. 'Look.' He was holding up a sheaf of papers. 'Not Garibaldis, *Banda Carità*. *Repubblicani* assassins.'

Kirby looked up at the figure looming over him, still wreathed in smoke from the Labora machine pistol he held. 'You are English?' asked the man.

Kirby nodded.

The man cleared his throat as if he were going to spit on him, but instead he held out his hand. Kirby raised his to meet it and felt hard fingers wrap around his wrist; he was jerked to his feet. An arm steadied him as his ankle gave way.

'Pavel!' the man shouted down. 'Get rid of the bodies!'

'The valley?'

'The valley.' After a moment's hesitation the man pointed to the twisted form of the torture victim and added, 'But leave Vittorio. We will bury him.' He turned back to Kirby and put an arm around him, supporting him under the armpit. 'Come on. We must talk. My name is Fausto.' But Kirby already knew that.

Kirby, Francesca, Rosario – the little shaven-haired partisan – and Ragno sat around the table in the heavily beamed kitchen. It was dominated by a vast blackened range, and one wall and much of the ceiling were festooned with ancient pots and pans. There was little evidence of food to put in them, however. Kirby slowly pieced together some of what had happened.

The *Banda Carità* was an offshoot of the *Brigate Nere*. Vittorio, the savagely mutilated man, had been a member of Gruppo Fausto; the *Banda* had tortured him to find out the location of the safe house, then made out that they had liberated him from the Villa Trentino, the main fascist headquarters in the area, to get past the guards placed on the approaches. Fortunately, Fausto and Rosario had seen them donning the phoney Garibaldi kerchiefs.

'Did you mean to shoot Vittorio?' asked Francesca.

Kirby's appreciation of her beauty was somewhat restored now he knew the truth.

Fausto held out his hands and shrugged. 'You think he'd want to have lived like that? It was a mercy.'

Francesca nodded, her eyes closed. 'I shall have to tell Rosa.'

'Can we eat?' asked Rosario. 'I am famished.'

Francesca and Ragno exchanged glances and Kirby said hesitantly, 'Oh dear, I think I might have finished off lunch.'

'You English. You even take the food off our plates.' Then Rosario grinned, reached into his inside pocket and pulled out a string of fat, marbled sausages, followed by a brown paper bag which he rattled. 'Rice.'

Fausto said: 'There might be a bottle of wine left in the cellar, Ragno.'

The boy scuttled off as Fausto produced a large onion with a triumphant flourish. Francesca rose to her feet, but Rosario snatched it from Fausto's outstretched hand. 'I'll cook it. My risotto is better than yours.' He turned to Kirby and made a face. 'Too dry. It should be a wave. *All'onda.*' He made a flowing motion with his hand.

'He means soggy,' countered Francesca.

'You be the judge,' said Rosario to Kirby, who instantly knew he was about to win one friend and alienate another, no matter which way the contest went. As Rosario fetched down the pans he needed and sharpened a knife to cut the onion, and Francesca worked the bellows to heat the charcoal, Kirby tried to block out the noises he could hear from beyond the door as bodies were dragged across the terrazzo.

Ragno reappeared with an unlabelled bottle of red wine, some of which Rosario decanted into a pan, and each of them received a tumbler full. Kirby sipped and suppressed a cough. It tasted like vinegar, but nobody else seemed to mind.

Fausto had been studying him for some time. Finally, he asked, 'How do you know Italian?'

Kirby explained about his mother.

'You are young for a pilot. What are you? Nineteen – twenty?'

Kirby felt himself bristle. This man couldn't be thirty, yet he was treating him like a junior clerk. He could tell from the way the others behaved around him, from the way they spoke his name, that they thought Fausto was something special. Well, not to him. 'It isn't about years, is it?' he said carefully. 'It's about what you can do.'

Fausto smiled. 'Are you a good pilot?'

'Yes,' he replied with conviction. 'Very good.'

'Yet you crashed.'

Kirby suppressed the urge to explain about the self-immolating engine. 'It happens.'

'You know we lost our BLO? Got himself arrested.' Before he could answer, Fausto added, 'Not that we'll miss him. He didn't speak the language and he was like a damned parrot. Sabotage and subversion, sabotage and subversion. You know, if the English worried a little less about the politics and government of Italy after all this is over – as if it is any of your business – then we might get somewhere, instead of facing another winter with the fascists breathing down our necks.'

'You made it our business,' Kirby said softly.

'What?'

He spoke up. 'By siding with Hitler, you made it our business.'

Fausto grabbed his wrist and yanked him across the table. 'You know less than the last bastard.'

Kirby pulled his hand back. 'We risk our lives to drop you supplies – weapons, medicine, food. You think flying through these mountains is a piece of cake?'

'Oh yes. Sten guns. Pistols. Explosives disguised as mule shit. Very useful. And they always come with a price tag. Here's the guns, now do as we tell you.'

'What do you expect?'

'Mortars. Light artillery. Heavy machine guns. Grenade launchers. Something to fight a proper war with. No strings attached.'

'Perhaps it is not practicable.'

'Ask Pavel. He is from Yugoslavia. They get ten times what we do.'

'What is he doing here?' Kirby asked. 'He's a long way from home.'

Francesca answered. 'A lot of Jews moved west, across the

border, because of the more lenient treatment in Italy. At least, that's how it used to be. You saw last night what is happening now. Pavel joined us six months ago, when the round-ups began in earnest.' She lowered her voice. 'We were out on the lake looking for his family among the dead.'

'Did you find them?'

'We found you. He said the living were more important than the dead.'

'I'm sorry.'

She shrugged. 'Apologise to him.'

'All right, it is settled then,' snapped Fausto. 'I will get a message to your special forces. Tell them the news.'

'What news?' Kirby asked wearily.

'That you are our new BLO.'

Kirby didn't say anything. It probably wasn't a good start to admit he had no idea who or what a BLO was.

'What are you thinking?' asked Francesca.

I had finished the whisky, and she topped me up. 'That it seemed to have happened to someone else. A young lad. I didn't even know what a British Liaison Officer was.'

'We knew you didn't know.'

'So why give me the job?'

'You know why.'

Fausto wanted someone not in thrall to men like Lang. Someone whose only agenda was getting weapons and killing Germans, not playing Whitehall or Washington politics with the future of Italy. I wasn't the first downed pilot to join the partisans, not the last. By the time the Italian campaign drew to its messy close in April 1945, there were Americans, Canadians, Australians, South Africans and Kiwis, mostly aircrew, who had thrown their lot in with the Resistance.

'How did you meet Conti?'

'After the war. I couldn't spend my life mourning Fausto.'

'I didn't say you should.'

'Listen, you have to understand what I mean when I say this, but you British had it easy.' She raised a hand to stop my protests. 'Not in the war, the battles, I know. You were bombed, the Blitz, V-weapons. I have read about it. But after the war, you all shared one thing.'

'What?'

'Being on the same side. Oh, there were a few traitors, but you hanged them, didn't you? You were never on the wrong side, never invaded, never starved the way we were. Here, the unspoken question for men and women of a certain age is – what did you do in the war? Fascist? Collaborator? Partisan? It is a stain we cannot remove. So, I stopped asking people, a long time ago.'

'So you don't think individuals should pay for what they did then? People like Eichmann?' It was only two years since Israel had kidnapped the cultivated monster, put him on trial and then executed him for his part in devising the Final Solution.

She turned on me, her face clouded. 'Riccardo was no Eichmann.'

I realised I had overstepped the mark. Adolf Eichmann had been party to the murder of six million. 'No. I'm sure. I didn't mean to suggest . . .'

She folded her arms and turned her head away to indicate the discussion was over. I walked across the hallway, over the scarred terrazzo, still pocked from the bullets twenty years previously, and into the *salotto*. The window was sealed by rusted *serrande* – metal roller-blinds, which moved reluctantly as I turned the handle. The map was still on the wall, mildewed with age, torn at one corner, but showing the traces of Fausto's tactical marks from when they had raided the Italian SS division en route to Chiasso. We didn't destroy the division, far from it, but Gruppo Fausto got themselves enough weapons to arm a large band of partisans to help in the liberation of Domodossola.

Fausto had fought fascism for a decade; he had been in Spain – which is why he used a Labora, his souvenir of that conflict – and at one time he had been a Communist, but the Soviet-German pact of 1940 had disillusioned him. Even when the Second Front opened and Stalin claimed it had all been a bluff, he stayed away from the official Communist forces. In fact, he hated his former colleagues as much as he despised the fascists.

'Seen enough?' asked Francesca.

I turned and found myself within inches of her. 'I'm sorry I was so tetchy.'

'It is difficult after all this time.' Francesca gave her best forgiving smile. 'You should have come back sooner,' she said softly.

The kiss didn't last anywhere long enough for my liking before she started to close up the house again.

While she was doing that I cleaned out my gun and walked up the hill to shoot some perfectly innocent trees, just for the hell of it, just as I had all those years ago.

Jack Kirby followed Fausto up the hill from the house, looking back as the lake shrank to the size of a large puddle, his breath hurting his throat. Ahead of him, the dirty-blond head of Fausto bobbed from side to side as he tackled the stony path like a goat. Slung over his shoulder was a large black bag, the contents of which were clinking enough to let Kirby know it must be heavy. It didn't show.

After thirty minutes, they reached a small rock-strewn plateau where the trees had retreated and left fat, grey-green grass. Fausto threw down the bag, and Kirby was pleased to see a slight flush on his cheeks. He was not superhuman after all.

'OK, Jaaack?' He protracted the vowel, as he imagined an American would. Kirby suspected there was something sardonic about it, but he couldn't put his finger on why.

'Yes,' he gasped.

'Ankle OK?'

Kirby nodded. It was indeed all right now. Three days previously he couldn't have done that climb. Now it only protested with a dull ache.

'Good. Walk with me, Jaaack.'

They started to circle the clearing. Above them was a saw-toothed mountain range and below a forty-five-degree slope to a few houses, and beyond them the serenity of the lake. The summer sun lit up the whole scene.

'So. How do you like Francesca, eh? How do you like my woman? You want to fuck her?'

Kirby turned and as he did so he felt Fausto's leg scythe into the back of his calves, whipping them from under him. He went down, air blasting from his lungs, his spine bruised by a large stone.

'Shit!' he managed to yell. 'What the hell?' A boot landed on his chest. Fausto was over him, and he had a Luger pistol in his hand. Kirby swallowed hard as it was pointed at his face.

'Stupid,' said the partisan slowly. 'So stupid.'

Kirby shut his eyes. He knew that Italian men, as a race, tended towards jealousy – his mother had told him as much – but this was ridiculous. It wasn't as if the man was clairvoyant. Was he? 'I haven't done anything. I didn't touch her.'

'No. I know.' He pulled Kirby to his feet and dusted him down. 'That was too easy.'

'What was?'

'Catching you off guard.'

'Off guard?' he blustered. 'I thought you were my friend. Why should I be on guard against some ludicrous accusation?' Kirby put genuine rage in his voice, careful not to betray the fact that, for a few seconds, he thought Fausto had been reading his mind.

Fausto produced a cigarette and lit it. 'There were lots of Italians I thought were my friends who pulled worse than that. I surprise you a little by saying something about Francesca and there you are, off balance.'

'*I thought I was among friends.*'

Fausto grabbed Kirby's cheeks and squeezed. 'Then stop thinking that, Jaaaack.' He stretched the name even longer. 'We can't treat you as a friend.' He let go, but Kirby could feel the imprint of the fingertips on his face. 'You represent the British. But BLOs are a fact of life. No BLO, no drops. And I want you to stay alive, not like the last fool. So, I must train you. That was your first lesson. Trust nobody.'

He walked over to the black bag and unzipped it. As he did so Kirby noticed the knots of muscles in his forearms. He up-ended the holdall and a variety of weapons – French, Italian, British and German – fell out onto the grass. 'Nobody will hear us up here. We must teach you to shoot with something other than an airplane.'

'Has confirmation of my role come through yet?'

'Well, we had a message from Bern saying they would prefer to send their own man.'

'What did you say?'

Fausto gave a lopsided grin. 'I told them to go fuck their mothers.' Kirby hoped Bern were as conversant with the cut and thrust of Italian conversation as he was becoming. 'We got you, we're keeping you. Right, pay attention. Sten gun. A piece of shit, but a useful piece of shit, if you know how to get the best from it.'

He let off a short burst of fire that shredded the bark of the nearest tree, making Kirby jump. The clearing filled with the smell of cordite.

'The best way to take the Germans is from the high ground – shooting down on them. A man having to fire up . . .' he raised the still smoking Sten '. . . his arms get tired, his accuracy goes. You must be up the slope in this country, never at the bottom of it. Understand?'

'Surely you can be more exposed on higher ground.'

He snorted dismissively. 'Bullets coming from above always disorientate. Now that was the Sten on automatic fire. Better to use it on single shot. You select like this . . .'

Kirby wondered what Fausto had meant about Francesca, and why he had chosen her to distract him, but after a while it faded from his mind, chased away by the hammer of firing pins on cartridges.

She was waiting for me as I came down the track. I could see the cigarette smoke curling from behind the corner of the house. I slowed, padding as softly as I could on the first fall of crisp autumn leaves. She was leaning against the brick, face turned upwards to catch the sun, her neck long and inviting.

'Can you still shoot straight, Jack?' she asked, without moving.

'I was just seeing if I remembered what Fausto taught me.'

She turned her head. 'He said you didn't need much teaching. Said you were good.'

'He never told me that,' I said.

'Well, he wouldn't, would he?'

'No, I suppose that wasn't his way.'

She looked at me as she took another drag on the cigarette. I liked to watch her smoke. Unlike many of my compatriots in the war, I never really picked up the habit. Just now and then, when the moment demanded it or it seemed churlish to refuse.

'Want one?'

I hesitated and nodded and then we were both against the wall, letting the rays warm us while we inhaled tobacco and watched the beams slice through the curls of smoke.

'Don't judge me too hard, Jack.'

'I'm not.'

'Let me tell you a couple of things. After what happened at Domodossola I felt sure you'd come back. Write. Call. You didn't.'

'I sent a message.'

'Not a message, Jaaack.' She let my name stretch out the way Fausto used to, and we both smiled at the memory. 'I'm not talking about messages through official channels. "Are you OK? Stop. Me fine. Stop." I am talking about proper letters. I was sure you'd come back.'

'So was I,' I said, truthfully. 'But somehow, it all slipped away. I wasn't sure what was between us. If anything.'

'An Italian man would have come to find out.'

'You loved Fausto.' I tried to give it a finality, but there was a ghost of a question mark at the end of the sentence.

She took out a pair of thick black sunglasses and slipped them on.

'At my age I have to watch the sun. On my eyes. You know what he was like. Fausto consumed you, you couldn't help yourself. Like a whirlpool, you circled round him until you were pulled in. It made knowing your true feelings difficult. You were sure I loved Fausto, were you? Even then? If so, you knew more than me.'

I shook my head, wondering if the hollow in the pit of my stomach was simply hunger, or something much worse. 'I wasn't sure of anything,' I said quietly.

A silence settled over us, as we both thought back to our messy parting, and before I could ask about the aftermath, she volunteered: 'After he was gone, what could we do but surrender? We released Riccardo Conti and before the Germans could institute reprisals, he allowed most of us to slip away. There were some examples made, but not many; a few to save face. Mostly Communists. It could have been like Val Grande.' This was a complete rout of partisan forces in the mountains in June 1944. Most of those captured had been tortured and executed in hideous ways, even the *alpigiani*, the mountain men, just because the partisans used their meadows and forests for shelter and rest.

I knew all this, but I couldn't resist saying: 'So they didn't matter, the Garibaldis.'

'I didn't say that.'

'Sorry.'

'After the war, I ran into him again in Milan. Riccardo. This was after 1946, when there was an amnesty for all fascist actions, except the most extreme cases. I see him coming towards me. Well dressed, prosperous, handsome. Still, I cross the road to avoid him, but he crosses as well. He insists on coffee. For some reason I say yes. And that afternoon, Riccardo, he tells me about how he plans to make amends. The Hope Foundation – you know it?'

I shook my head.

'It's a little like your Cheshire Homes. Care for servicemen, no matter which side they fought on. That was the important part. Then the Hope Houses, for orphans, something like your . . . er . . .'

'Dr Barnados?' I offered.

'Yes. They were also his idea. Part of the rebuilding, the healing process. Riccardo asked for my help, fund-raising and so on. He himself put in a lot of money.' Now she turned to face me to emphasise the point and I watched her mouth work, hardly hearing the words. 'A lot of money, Jack. Like I said before, you British don't understand that part. It was like trying to heal a family after a bitter feud. Resentment flares up all the time. Riccardo managed to work through all that. He was a good man. *Is* a good man.'

'And he was here.'

'It's always an advantage.' She stubbed out her cigarette and stepped away from the wall.

'I'm here now,' I said, rather feebly.

She laughed and shook her head, arching her eyebrows in surprise. 'Twenty years too late, Jack.'

'Story of my life, Francesca.'

I felt a deep sadness in my bones, a sense of promises not kept, hands not played, of missed opportunities. It didn't lift when she slid her arm through mine and walked me back towards the bike, hair brushing my shoulder, our time alone clearly over.

Twelve

Once I had dropped Francesca back at her car, I returned to the hotel where there was a message from Lindy Carr saying she would meet me after the ceremony in Domodossola. It came with a parcel, which I took up to my room. I ordered lunch from room service – a bottle of wine, bread and cheese – and sat at the metal table on the small balcony overlooking the steamer jetty and studied the documents she had sent across. It was all that she knew about the crew of EH-148.

After a few hours in their company, learning about them from their official files, and their letters to and from relatives, wives, children and lovers, they were no longer just eight anonymous men who got caught by the capricious mountain weather.

Bill Carr himself may have been the son of farmers, but he was university educated in economics. He had had job offers from several public utilities in Australia, when he decided that his career could be put on hold while he went off to fight. Before he did so he married the woman the newspaper clipping called his childhood sweetheart. He trained with the Australian Air Force and came to England via Canada, eventually ending up attached to an SAAF squadron at Foggia.

At twenty-six, Carr was considered an old man by his seven

comrades. Also on board were Flight Sergeant Reginald Lisle, the co-pilot, a South African from Durban aged twenty-two and bomb-aimer Michael Leonhart, also twenty-two, another South African from Cape Town. Sergeant Air Gunner Donald McRae, from Nevis in the West Indies, was just twenty. Two other Sergeant Air Gunners, David Herrington, twenty-one, and Ron Walters, twenty, were Australian and South African respectively. Nineteen-year-old Derek Dawson was an anomaly: the radio man and air gunner, he came from Chorley in Lancashire. An Englishman. The observer/navigator was Jon DeWitt, a Rhodesian, the only son of a tobacco farmer. The letter from his father told how the twenty-two-year-old was meant to come back from the war and carry on the farm. Now there was no one, the father was ill, and it was to be sold.

Every single man left a story of a calling missed, a girl never married, a son or daughter never seen. When those eight went down on EH-148, it broke the lives of many more people across the globe. Lindy was just trying her best to put the pieces back together. Yes, it was crazy and probably doomed to failure but, after reading the documents, I had a sense of what was driving her. Not least, the seven other families who had offered money, best wishes and assistance in the quest. They wanted to know, too.

There was one other document listing the eight men. It was a page from a pre-flight log, outlining the mission, the crew and the scribbled addition: *plus SN*. Supernumerary. There was a passenger on board that night. I leafed through the documents again, but found no mention of his name, no letters from friends or families. Just *SN*. It was this man who made it a White Stocking, a drop of personnel into enemy territory. Ah well, it didn't matter. I already knew who had been in that plane, squeezed between the Liberator's waist gunners, ready to make the jump. It was Jimmy Morris. On his way to relieve me of my post.

★ ★ ★

I had dinner in the hotel, alone, mulling over the mess I had got myself into. Employed by a young girl to find the remnants of a plane which could be anywhere in an area the size of Wales. Then there was Francesca. So much was left unsaid there. Why hadn't I come back sooner? Because falling in love with her had cost too many lives last time.

I always had trouble reading her signals, then and now, and I wasn't sure whether she was basking in warm memories or inviting me to . . . no. That was just a fantasy on my part. It was over as clearly as the war was. Closed. Nice to see her and all that, but it was time to move on.

By the time I finished eating, my head was pounding and I needed some air. I fetched my jacket from the room and turned right out of the hotel, walking past the restaurants with their terraces packed with loud German tourists and over the rickety bridge spanning the river to where they were building a new Swiss-financed holiday complex, complete with marina.

The sun was behind the mountains, streaking the sky with its dying rays, and the lights on the waterfront at Luino across the lake shimmered on the water. I walked down the stony beach to the edge and tossed a pebble out into the gathering darkness, waiting for the plop.

Jimmy Morris. His legend was well known now, but the name meant little to me back then. I hadn't heard that he had a record stretching back to France, Crete, Yugoslavia and mainland Greece. That he was the man you sent in when the Resistance had fractured into a dozen warring factions. Jimmy was the man to bang heads together, to get them all pulling in the same direction. Lang and the others thought I was too soft, not able to impose the will of Britain on the partisans. That might have been the case, but there was another factor. Sometimes, Whitehall's agenda and the partisans' aims didn't match because the Italians were right.

Jimmy never made it, of course, so we never got to see the clash of the Titans that would have been Morris versus Fausto. He was out there along with eight brave crewmen, lost in the mountains and valleys. It was possible that he'd turn up alongside Bill Carr. Or maybe not, because there was still a chance that the Liberator was elsewhere or entombed in a glacier and we would never find it.

I heard footsteps behind me, but I didn't turn, not wanting to speak to anyone right now. It was a mistake, because I was unprepared for the pain that exploded in my kidneys as a fist drove itself home and I staggered into the water up to my ankles.

There were three of them, facing me in a rough semi-circle, none of them kids. I sized them up as quickly as I dared. The man in the middle was dark and bulky, with a heavy monobrow that gave him the look of a primate. The one on his left was blond and lithe, the other stockier, with the beginnings of a gut, but that was also dangerous because he would have some weight behind him.

I should have gone down immediately, of course, and stayed down, but my thick leather jacket had helped deaden the blow, and when you've been riding bikes as long as I have, you get used to pains in the kidneys. In fact, you get used to pain. So I heaved myself up and let my anger burn bright and hard.

These guys clearly hadn't seen enough movies, because they were supposed to come for me one at a time so I could dispatch each of them in turn. Instead, ungallantly, they all rushed me at once.

I got a solid and satisfying blow into the throat of Blondie, but something hard cracked across my temple and the stars came down to earth. I managed a stiff finger in the eye of the Gutbucket, an elbow on his nose, a hefty kick to the knee, the steel plate on my heel making a good connection, and he was down in the water, out of it.

As I turned to the Monkey Man, I felt the weight in my jacket. I still had the Colt. I reached for it, but the Primate caught me with a short, sharp punch, right up into the solar plexus, that lifted me out of the six inches of water. Then he backhanded me with the short length of wood that had clipped my temple moments before, and I was staggering.

I managed to clear the weapon from my jacket, but the blond one, recovered from my earlier punch, kicked me in the ribs. I lost count of the hits they got in. My head was in the water, my face being pushed into the silt, the air from my lungs bursting from the corners of my mouth. I felt the Colt torn from my grasp.

A hand grabbed my hair and pulled me free and I rolled onto my back, holding myself clear of the water with my elbows as my chest heaved. The three were on their feet, staring at me, and at least they were breathing hard. I'd made them work for this.

Monkeyman had my gun, levelled at my head. How many shots had I used on those trees? Six? Seven? The .38 carried nine rounds, one more than the standard .45 auto. So they had either two or three bullets left. At this range, though, he would only need a single shot.

Gutbucket was the first to turn and leave, followed by Blondie. Now there was just the gunman, arm outstretched, showing me the business end of my own weapon. I thought about closing my eyes, but I had a feeling that was all he would need to pull the trigger, a sign of acquiescence, and I kept staring at that simian brow until he bent over and smacked me across the face with the barrel, spinning me into the deeper water, where I lay, listening to him splash off and into the night with my gun, until the only sound was the wheeze of my lungs and the lapping of waves against my side.

Thirteen

Italy, 1944

Major Riccardo Conti stood in the marshalling yards at Brescia and stared across at the locomotive which had been flung across the tracks by the Allied raids as if it were a child's toy. Elsewhere he could see huge craters, with the rails either thrown up towards the sky by the blasts, or pummelled into the earth. It was the same story right across the massive complex: more and more damage. No trains were going to be moving in or out of Brescia for weeks.

It was mid-morning now and still there was chaos. When Knopp had told him that 'units' of the 29th Waffen-SS Division were re-fitting and moving out, he had imagined the usual slick German war machine. Not so. A full division should have around 200 tanks, 150 heavy guns, 300 half-tracks, 60 armoured cars, and hundreds of trucks. Instead, he doubted there were ninety vehicles in all. There were barely a dozen tanks, mostly Panzer IIIs, all on ugly low-loader transporters, perhaps nineteen armoured cars, ten *Kettenkrads*, the tracked motorcycles, and a motley assortment of lorries, mainly requisitioned Italian models. It looked as if the 29th – or this brigade of it at least – was down to using the dregs of the motor pool. He hoped that the armoured units already in place to the east of Pisa, dug in for the winter, and the *Nachschub*, the supply regiment, which had gone on ahead by road, were better equipped.

The men, too, were far from the finest SS tradition. They looked tired and ill-motivated or young and very frightened. Nor were the Grenadiers before him all Italian, as they had once been – heavy losses had been made up with Croatians and Romanians.

Conti looked at his watch. The 29th should have pulled out by now, but there were still clumps of soldiers standing near their trucks, waiting for fuel, and frantic activity around the radio truck. An Opel lorry arrived, towing a trailer full of fuel canisters, and the sullen troops snapped into life, grinding out cigarettes before jostling for the cans to strap to their vehicles.

Almost unnoticed by the others, three Henschel trucks pulled into the yard and parked some distance away. Each of them had a Grenadier on the running board, who stepped down smartly and took up a position at the rear of the soft-sided lorry. Sturmbann-führer Karl Knopp stepped down from the lead Henschel, spotted Conti and walked over.

'Ah, Major. You have my report?'

Conti handed over the morning's summary of partisan activity along the 29th's proposed route. Motorcyclists had run down it at first light, checking for the kind of roadblocks partisans liked to leave overnight. An engineer unit had followed, sweeping for mines at potential flashpoints.

'Nothing,' said Conti. 'I personally organised an *Alpini* sweep last night, fifteen kilometres either side.' He smiled. 'A few strays were taken care of. Nothing substantial.'

'Good.' Knopp quickly flicked through the pages and then pointed at Conti's staff car. 'Tell your driver to meet us at Chiasso.'

'I'm sorry?'

'You are coming with us, Major. You tell me there are no partisans, I want you to put your arse where your mouth is.'

Conti tried not to look too concerned. 'I have other duties—'

'You have a duty to the Reich.'

This is for the Reich? he thought, but said: 'Sturmbannführer, you have my word—'

'You can ride with me in the first truck, Major.' Knopp indicated two of the armoured cars. 'We shall get those KFZs to flank us. Just in case your word isn't good enough.'

Knopp walked away to arrange his protection and Conti removed his cap and scratched his head. This wasn't going the way he expected at all. He walked over to his staff sergeant to tell him there had been a change of plan.

As Jack Kirby set up the Bren gun on the ridge, looking down at the road below, he heard a movement behind him and Rosario dropped a bag of ammunition next to him. 'Don't worry, tomorrow you will have an MG42,' he said.

The German gun was acknowledged to be better than the slow-firing Bren. 'Is it heavier?' asked Kirby, rubbing his bruised shoulder, and Rosario laughed.

The sun was setting now, the light fading to a soft dusk, and he could only just make out the shadowy figures on the opposite side of the road; like him, positioned high above it. Fausto's maxim was being employed to full effect – always fire from the high ground.

'Where's the Boss?' asked Kirby.

Rosario pointed down towards the road to the south of their position, where he could just make out some activity at the verge. 'He's setting the charges over there. Take out the armour. Timing is everything.'

Kirby turned and watched Francesca struggle up the hill behind them, carrying a sack of grenades and a Mauser rifle. He raised a hand and she smiled before nestling down 300 yards away in her designated spot, as dictated by the map on the salon wall where they had been briefed the previous night by Fausto. Jack wished the leader was up with them rather than planting bombs in the culverts. The group felt directionless when he wasn't around.

'You know what to do?' asked Rosario, as if he had read his mind.

Kirby nodded. 'I wait for the flare.'

'Right. No matter what happens, *you wait for my flare*. Good luck, eh?'

Kirby watched him go and shivered. It was much easier playing at war from 30,000 feet.

It was early afternoon by the time the convoy had formed up and left the yards at Brescia, heading north-east for the rail terminal at Chiasso. Progress was slow. The tank transporters were lumbering, temperamental beasts, and there were frequent stops for repairs. Those in open-topped half-tracks scanned the sky nervously, waiting for Allied planes to find them. Rocket attacks on convoys by marauding RAF Typhoons were not unheard of. However, the only plane they saw was a tri-engined Sparviero, re-painted in Luftwaffe colours.

Conti was sitting on the passenger side of the lead Henschel truck, with Knopp between him and the driver. He followed the route on the map, ticking off the villages, noting the high degree of damage inflicted by the nightly bombing raids. Whole hamlets had disappeared, leaving only the church, perhaps, or a schoolhouse intact. They skirted Bergamo, a town also scarred by bombing, and with a large partisan population, and carried on north-east. The countryside was now dissected by a succession of long low ridges. At first the roads, which only dated back to the 1920s, went over them, straining the transporters, but after a while the construction crews had decided to cut through the hillsides.

There were fluffy vapour trails high in the darkening sky and, far to the south, a smudge of smoke on the horizon. Another daylight raid on Milan.

At around six o'clock, they pulled to a halt outside Calco and Conti got out to stretch his legs.

Ahead, one of the tanks was being rolled off its crippled transporter. It was going to have to make it under its own steam. It would bring up the rear, because its tracks would chew up any road surface, and there was no time for the engineering corps to make running repairs.

Conti walked around to the rear of the truck and lifted the canvas flap. He jumped as a face peered out at him. 'Yes, Major?' It was a Feldwebel, toting one of the MP40 machine pistols that people mistakenly called Schmeissers. In fact they were made by Erma, Steyr or Haenel. They were good weapons, reliable, accurate and well made. The partisans prized them highly, because they enabled them to ditch their crude Stens.

Knopp appeared on the far side of the lorry. 'Nothing to see, Major. Just crates. Lots of crates.' He offered Conti a cigarette, which he took.

'We won't make Chiasso by dark at this rate.' It was perhaps forty kilometres, but progress was desperately slow.

'No,' said Knopp. 'But there is a garrison at Bebbio where we can spend the night if need be. The trains don't depart until mid-morning tomorrow.'

Conti looked up at the dispersing streaks in the sky left by the bombers. If the trains run at all, he thought. The raids were becoming more accurate, more destructive, and it wouldn't be long before there was no rail network left. 'Why don't we just go on ahead. These trucks are faster than some of this shit.' He indicated the crippled transporter.

'Safety in numbers, Conti.'

There was yelling from up ahead and a variety of barks and coughs as engines were re-started and the trucks juddered into life.

They drove past the tank, which waited until the last vehicle had gone before taking up its position at the rear of the convoy. Conti watched in the mirror as it slid further and further behind.

Darkness began to shroud them as they passed through the deserted village of Anzano. A lone dog snarled at them, but there was no sign of inhabitants, hostile or otherwise. The houses shook as the machinery rolled by.

A motorcyclist began weaving down the line issuing instructions for the overnight stop at Bebbio. The road was running through a series of rocky hills, and again it had been carved through them, rather than going over. The cliff faces sloped up at forty-five degrees, and were topped by sparse tree cover.

'Hungry, Major?' Knopp asked.

Before Conti could answer, there was a detonation behind, then the screech of metal and, in the mirror, he saw a stream of red flame across the road. The driver stamped on the brakes. Ahead, a triple flare – red, silver and blue – arced into the night and began its lazy descent to earth. There came the crackle of machine guns, and three, four, five more explosions. Hand grenades.

'Don't stop!' yelled Knopp at the driver. 'We'll be a sitting duck here. Keep moving.'

Guns chattered nearby, and muzzle flashes dotted the hillside around them. Knopp turned to Conti, his face twisted in fury.

'You stupid bastard! You told me this was clear.'

The truck rocked from the impact of an explosion on the road beside it. Careful, Conti thought, or we'll all go up. A column of orange flame punched into the sky ahead. He'd thought those twenty-gallon petrol drums strapped to the armoured cars looked vulnerable. Another went up, and another, spewing black smoke into the twilight sky.

The cab of their truck was illuminated by the sparking of an MG42, raking the hillsides from the back of the half-track ahead. They felt the concussion of a grenade and the glass in the windscreen split with a sharp crack. The gun fell silent.

'I lied,' said Conti. He shot Knopp and the driver in the head in quick succession, wincing as a cloud of blood and bone washed over him. He clambered across the bodies, ignoring the rattle of air from dead lungs, and pushed the driver out of the door. He looked for the guards who had been on the running boards, but they were nowhere to be seen. Ahead, someone was yelling at him. A stray bullet splintered another part of the windshield, causing him to jump back in the seat. This was too close for comfort. But then, he wasn't meant to be here in the first place.

There was the deep boom of an 88mm from one of the tanks, but he knew the Panzers wouldn't be able to elevate their guns high enough to be a danger to the attackers, and the majority of them were trapped where they were stopped, still clamped to their transporters. The convoy was doomed.

Conti decided he'd worry about the sergeant in the rear of the truck later. He revved the engine and crunched into reverse, backing away from the beleaguered column. He wiped the blood from his face with his sleeve, then tore at his jacket buttons with his free hand as he skirted a disabled armoured car. He hoped his men had managed to take the other trucks, too, otherwise all this was a waste of time and lives.

Fourteen

The Italians don't like drunks. It isn't easy to cut a *bella figura* when your system is overloaded with booze, so they tend to drink moderately, at least in public places. Which explained the look I got when I staggered back to the hotel wet, bleeding and dishevelled. Fortunately, Maria, the daughter of the owner, knew I'd imbibed a very modest half bottle at dinner not an hour before, and she guessed that it took more than that to reduce me to this state.

I supported myself against the wall, leaving a dank stain on their gold wallpaper and a dark puddle on their marble floor, and explained in a loud voice that I had walked into a construction piling at the building site down by the shore and, concussed, had staggered into the water.

Maria tutted and took me through into the kitchen, where she sat me down next to a free sink and carefully sponged away the blood with a cloth among the clatter of dishes and pans as the washing-up brigade, composed of a variety of young cousins – *cugini* – earning pocket-money, finished their shift.

'You want me to call a doctor?' she asked as I winced at her dabbings.

'No.'

'The police?'

I raised a painful eyebrow at the question. 'I walked into a piling.'

She touched my cheek. 'A piling that was wearing rings, perhaps?'

'Maria.'

'Signor Kirby.'

There was a *questura*, a police station, in town, but I didn't want some young bumbling *polizia* coming across to ask dumb questions and deciding I had beaten myself up. If I were to report the attack it would be to the *Carabinieri* who, despite the jokes about their intelligence, were better trained than the regular force and less corrupt. But the nearest *caserma*, barracks, was in Stresa. Besides, I'd have to spend hours filling in forms, producing my *permesso di lavoro* and passport and pilot's licence and generally adopting the subservient, forelock-tugging tone – there is even a word for it, *ruffiano* – Italian cops expect, even when you are the victim. No, thanks.

'Let's skip the police. Please.'

She nodded reluctantly. 'Your shirt is ruined but the jacket will dry, I think. You should see a doctor.'

'I'll be OK,' I tried to reassure her from behind the dull thud in my head.

She disappeared and returned with a large glass of clear liquid. I took it and smiled. Doctor Grappa would do nicely.

He was waiting for me at breakfast, out on the terrace, sipping an espresso and looking smart in a lightweight grey suit, cut sharp. He had a big square jaw and smile which showed American-style glistening white teeth. I didn't like him. But then, I didn't like anyone that morning. My face looked like I'd been sprayed by the DDT fly powder still popular in Italy – all yellow splodges – with one swollen eye Charles Laughton would be proud of and several crusty gashes, including a very nasty one from the track of my gun barrel along my forehead. My ribs ached so much that I was skipping every other breath, which made speaking difficult. I sounded like I'd just gone up against Roger Bannister on the track and then been passed across to Henry Cooper for a couple of rounds in the ring.

He stood up and we shook hands. He told me his name was Giovanni Gronchi and before things got too formal he said: '*Diamoci del tu*' – let's use the familiar form of address – meaning he wanted to be my friend. I didn't need any more friends. Then again, I certainly didn't need any more enemies, so I nodded.

'Are you all right?' he asked with what seemed like genuine solicitousness. 'The lady at the desk warned me that you had had an accident.'

'I should buy myself a torch.'

'You didn't do it flying?'

I would have bristled, but bristling was going to hurt, so I sneered a little. 'No, I did it walking into a steel-reinforced post.' Well, best get the practice in early. I was going to spend the whole day denying I'd been beaten up by three guys, one of them Mighty Joe Young's second cousin, who stole my gun.

'I hope you don't mind me coming to see you, but my employers called you at the airfield and we were told you were here, and it's only a forty-five-minute drive from Milan, so . . . here I am.'

'Here you are.'

Maria brought me a coffee, examined her handiwork on my face, shook her head, and left. 'Your employer being?' I prompted.

'Your employer, too. Gennaro.' The dairy, food and produce conglomerate I flew for.

Forty-five minutes is a long way to come, to tell me I am fired, I thought. 'I don't think I have anything on the books with them at the moment,' I said.

'No. But we would like you to have – flying to Rome, then Naples. We are doing some business with the farmers. But as you know, down there everything has,' he wrinkled his nose, '*odore di mafia*.'

'The smell of mafia,' I repeated. You don't work out of Sicily, as I once did, without knowing something about organised crime, even if I'd been too small – and poor – for them to bother with. 'Someone should bottle it and sell it. They'd make a killing.'

He frowned at the poor attempt at humour, but it was the best he was going to get.

'I thought it was the *Camorra* who controlled all the fruit and vegetables down there,' I said.

'In Naples itself, yes, but we wish to visit several places in the south. Calabria, for instance.'

I smiled, but didn't mention that then he would have to deal with *La 'Ndrangheta*, the most brutal of Italy's crime organisations. I was sure he knew about those blokes. Many of them had been put back in business in 1944 by the Allies, who figured anyone banged up by Mussolini was a good guy, thus returning power and control to some of the most evil and violent gangsters the country had ever seen.

Of course, as a northerner Gronchi would expect corruption to be endemic down south. Up here, went the reasoning, the Austro-Hungarian Empire at least imposed order and honesty and a decent work ethic that dissipated as you went further south. To men like Gronchi, anywhere beyond Rome was bandit country.

'So you think you might need a quick getaway?'

'No, just flexibility of movement,' Gronchi said. 'The passengers will be two buyers and myself.'

'When?'

'Starting now, for six weeks.'

'Six weeks?' I dropped a sugar in my coffee and watched the colour bleed into the cube. 'How much?'

I am used to the fact that any quantity of lire sounds a lot even when it is only enough to buy a pack of cigarettes, but the figure he named had enough noughts behind it to start the greed centres in my brain tingling. New car, new bike, down payment on a new plane . . .

'I am here for a commemoration,' I said flatly, trying to keep the avarice from my voice. 'At Domodossola.'

'Your partner told me. It lasts, what – two days?'

'Then I have a month's work up here,' my mouth said without being told. Must be the blows to the head.

'Perhaps you could sub-contract that to others?'

'Nobody that I know of.'

'Your partner?'

'We only have one plane.'

'You could hire one, perhaps.'

'Difficult.' There weren't dozens of planes for hire by the day in Northern Italy. You had to lease them, which meant tying yourself in for a twelve-month contract. And, anyway, you mostly hired pilots, not their aircraft. They just got thrown in with the bargain.

I stirred my coffee and looked at the crowd waiting for the steamer to take them across to the market at Luino. A ripple of expectation went through them as they spotted the boat leaving the far shore, and the crush at the gate tightened.

'I appreciate Gennaro's offer. I really do.'

'A generous offer.' Too much for scum like me, suggested his new tone. I was clearly supposed to be grateful.

'Can't argue with that, Signor Gronchi. Nor can I accept a job then cut and run as soon as a better offer comes along, especially as I have spent my client's money on cameras and film. I mean, what would that do to my standing in the industry?'

At least he was polite enough not to burst out laughing at the thought of me having any standing. Instead he grimaced. 'You know, turning this trip down will not reflect well on your suitability for future assignments.'

'Big stick?'

'I beg your pardon?'

'I've had the carrot, fat and juicy, now here comes the big stick. "You'll never work in this town again." Is that it?'

'I'm sorry you see it that way.'

'What way am I meant to see it?' I realised I was shouting, trying to drown out the racket in my skull, so I switched to soft and serious. 'I am already contracted until the first week of October. So, much as I would like to fly you between meetings with the fruit and veg branch of the mafia, I can't oblige. Give my apologies to your employer.'

Gronchi stood so quickly it took me by surprise. He didn't offer his hand, or wait for me to get up. He simply said, 'I will report your decision,' and left. He didn't even pay for his coffee.

I asked the kitchen to rustle me up a four-egg omelette – the Italian habit of skimping on breakfast has never appealed to me – then went back to the room to tackle the vagaries of SIP, the phone system. It and the PTT, the post office, were two of the big downsides to living in the country. That and a chaotic political system which had never recovered from the factionism of World War Two.

I managed to contact Furio, told him I had just declined the chance of us getting rich, and that the economic situation was so dire that people were trying to rob the likes of me now. He laughed at the futility of that before remembering to ask how I was. I requested he get his beautiful, talented and endlessly kind mother to pull a few strings for me at her newspaper, although maybe he could skip telling her about the company's missing mafia payday. Then, tomorrow, to get his arse and the Beech up to the airfield at Invorio.

Involving Furio's mother was probably pointless, but the more I thought about being worked over by the three guys, the less I was convinced it was a straightforward robbery. They were too old for casual street crime and, if not the best that money could buy, they'd used their fists before. Furthermore, how did they know to ignore my wallet, which only had a few thousand lire in it? No, I wasn't some simple crime statistic. I had a hunch I might be dealing with a jealous husband.

Fifteen

I don't know what I expected when I arrived at the piazza in front of Domodossola's grandiose railway station. It was mostly car park now, and I left the MV in front of the soulless cafeteria selling what they called 'hamburglars' where formerly there had been two bars and the Casa del Fascio, destroyed in the fighting.

I examined the walls and pavements, thinking there might be some sort of plaque or memorial stone where Fausto fell. There was nothing. Perhaps it wasn't a sufficiently heroic death. Strange, he'd come close to going out in a blaze of both glory and gunfire several times but, in the end, in the dying moments of his great adventure, some slimy little nobody got to murder him.

I looked back at the station forecourt, where it was once shrouded by the sandbag barricade we'd put up as the Germans got closer and closer to us. Two sets of rail tracks left the town, one heading north for the Simplon Tunnel, the awesome engineering feat that put this nondescript town on the map the first time round, and a second which crawled along the valley floor before rising into the mountains and switchbacking its way up, then down, into Locarno.

It was along the former route that Major Archibald Lang had come, from Special Forces HQ Number 2 in Bern; it was the latter route I had reluctantly taken to freedom. Back then, in 1944, you could see the whole square from the blue, narrow-gauge tramlike Locarno trains as they pulled out of the station. Now the line had been sunk and covered over, with access to the tracks down a subway to the side of the main building.

I walked around the piazza, stopping before a poster reminding the inhabitants of Domodossola that it hadn't been alone. In 1944, the CLN – the *Comitato di Liberazione Nationale* – an organisation that tried, with varying success, to impose order and discipline on the disparate groups fighting the Germans – had proposed a series of free republics, where partisans would drive out the enemy and wait for the Allies to arrive. Those that were not liberated by winter would be supplied by air drops. The poster listed them all:

Alto Monferrato (Sep–2 Dec), Alto Tortonese4 (Sep–Dec), Bobbio e Torriglia4 (7 Jul–27 Aug), Cansiglio (Jul–Sep), Carnia (Jul–Oct), Friuli Orientale (30 Jun–Sep), Imperia (Aug–Oct), Langhe (Sep–Nov), Montefiorino (17 Jun–1 Aug), Ossola (10 Sep–13 Oct), Val Ceno (10 Jun–11 Jul), Val d'Enza e Val Parma (Jun–Jul), Val Maira e Val Varaita (Jun–21 Aug), Val Taro (15 Jun–24 Jul), Valli di Lanzo (25 Jun–Sep), Valsesia (11 Jun–10 Jul), and Varzi4 (Sep–29 Nov).

Underneath each one was a single word: *tradimento*. Betrayed.

The Ossola Republic was centred on Domodossola, and it was the only one to receive official recognition from Switzerland. Like the others, it was woefully undersupplied and it waited in vain for the Allied forces to break through. It was probably hopeless optimism to expect the latter to divert divisions from France and Arnhem, but it didn't feel like that at the time. It felt like abandonment.

This republic lasted just thirty-four days before Germans, supported by Italian fascists of X-Mas, the SS Italienische, parachutists of the Guardia Nazionale Repubblicana, and the *Brigate Nere* 'Christina', overwhelmed it once more. It was that fleeting month of freedom, and the men and women who achieved it, that we were here to celebrate. I locked the bike and began to walk up the street named after Paolo Ferraris, one of the heroes of those few short weeks, wondering why Fausto never got a commemorative road named after him.

The celebration for the twentieth anniversary of the *Repubblica dell'Ossola* began in the square outside the *municipio*, the Town Hall, the site of so many ideological battles between Communists and non-Communists, where agendas and proclamations were drawn up and issued. I still remembered finding Fausto sitting beneath the statue in the centre of the piazza, cigarette in his mouth, Spanish machine pistol across his knees.

'What are you doing?' I had asked.

'They've been in there six hours,' he replied wearily, 'and they've finally decided on a name for the Republic. I'm going back to defending the approaches.'

Maybe that was why there was no commemoration of him. Fausto never believed in taking part in the political battles. Spain and Stalin had cured him of that. By 1944, he just wanted to blow the heads off any Germans who came up his road.

By the time I reached the piazza, the crowd was thirty deep surrounding a stage set up outside the *municipio*. Around the edges were a few groups of *vitelloni*, Italy's own brand of disaffected youth, the boys aping Adriano Celentano or James Dean, smoking, laughing, apparently indifferent to the proceedings, but also curious enough not to move on.

As I manoeuvred myself for a decent view, I felt hard arms fly round me and squeeze me so tight that I gave a yell which made the speaker look my way with a frown.

It was Rosario, still small, powerfully built and bald, now with a

Zapata-style moustache and an embroidered shirt that made him look like a beatnik. 'Jack – good to see you! Shit – what happened to your face?'

'I fell.'

He squinted at me. 'Yes?'

'Yes.'

'You see a doctor about this falling?'

'I don't make a habit of it. How are you?'

'Good, good.'

There was a moment's awkward pause and I asked: 'What are you doing now?'

'I play jazz.' He mimed what I guessed was a saxophone. 'Rome, Positano, Montreux, Corsica, Nice, all over.'

Rosario had been a musician before he became Fausto's right-hand man. I had never asked him what kind. It was difficult to equate the hard-as-nails partisan I had known with cabarets and concerts. Rosario had always made me a little nervous. Fausto I think I understood – he was a natural leader – while Pavel was fighting the people who had destroyed his family and country. Ragno was in awe of Fausto, a puppy dog, but Rosario was his own man. I came to the conclusion that Rosario liked nothing more than a scrap; he enjoyed killing Germans.

'I have my own club, too. You should come.'

'I will.' I didn't like jazz, at least not the modern kind, but even I knew for any jazzman to have his own club was quite a coup. He handed me a card, stylishly embossed with a figure playing saxophone and the name: *Rosa's*. The address was in Milan, not far from the Duomo.

'*Rosa's*? Why not *Rosario's*?'

'Don't worry,' he laughed. 'I haven't gone queer. I don't know why, but people go to a club named after a woman more than a man. So I shortened my name. Still me up there. In trousers. What about you?' he asked. 'What are you up to?'

'Still flying.'

'Still crashing?' He pointed at my scratches.

'That's not how I got the face, Rosario.'

He laughed and slapped my back. 'Dinner, tonight, on the square,' he said. 'Will you be there?'

'Yes. Will you play?'

He nodded. 'It's how I started. When the circus or fair came to town, I played clarinet for the acrobats for a few lire. Then weddings, funerals, processions . . .' I could see his mind drift to the time before the war, when he was a scruffy kid with a useful talent to entertain. 'So tonight, I go back to my roots.'

'Just don't expect any acrobatics from me.'

'On that ankle?' He kicked me playfully. 'I still remember the football match—'

'OK, OK, that's enough. Tonight.'

'See you then. I have to find Pavel.' He took my hand and stared into my eyes the way Italians do when they want to convey their absolute sincerity. 'Good to see you, Jack Kirby.'

As Rosario slipped away, I turned back to pay my attention to the proceedings. The current mayor was reciting a roll call of those who took the time and the trouble to hammer out the fine details of the *zona liberata*. Filippo Beltrami, Antonio Di Dio, Ettore Tibaldi, Gisella Floreanini, Giacomo Roberti, Giorgio Ballarini – the Communists, lawyers, doctors, priests, teachers, veteran anti-fascists who, even if they didn't bury their differences, had managed to come to some agreement. If only the *commandanti* of the *partigiani* had managed to do the same.

The list went on, each person receiving a glowing eulogy. Some of them were there to receive them with blushes, others earning a moment's silence and a mass making of the sign of the cross. I had forgotten how long-winded Italian ceremonies can be and started to skirt the crowd in search of caffeine and a grappa when Francesca spotted me at about the same time I saw her.

She was up on the stage, at the edge of all the suits, sashes and brocaded uniforms, a sheaf of notes held tightly in her hand, dressed in a sombre black suit that made her look like a sexy widow. She was to say a few words about Fausto, following on from similar praise for the Beltrami, Piave, Valtoce, and Perotti partisan divisions.

Even from this distance, she could see my face wasn't what I like to think of as the worn but handsome visage she had kissed at the house, and I made a complex charade about falling over. She signalled she would see me later at the dinner. I nodded, knowing from the length of the introductory speech that it was going to be much, much later.

As I turned I saw him at the edge of the crowd. Nino: *il Giurista*. Nino, the lawyer. He was older, of course, and stockier; he had grown a beard and was wearing heavy black sunglasses and the collar on his jacket was turned up. But, hell, I'd know the man who killed Fausto anywhere.

I felt the loss of the Colt doubly now, but I sidled up behind him as quietly as I could. He muttered as I jostled him, figuring it was just another eager member of the crowd. I pushed a knuckle into his back and whispered into his ear, 'You know that Marshall Industries of Kentucky make the finest silencers in the world. As used by the CIA. There would be a very soft plop and your spine will sever. You'll collapse in agony. I'll be gone. Do you believe me, Nino? Nod if you do.'

He nodded. It was rubbish, of course, but I said it with the conviction of a hired assassin. I was banking on him not knowing a silencer from a cigarette. If he did, he'd know I'd forgotten that the pros called them suppressors – there is no such thing as a fully silent pistol, unless you are using one of the big single-shot Welrods or its derivatives.

'Walk ahead of me to the café on the left of the market square. I'll be two paces behind. Don't do anything stupid. That big fat head of yours is too tempting a target. OK?'

Another nod and he turned from the fringes of the gathering and walked up the cobbled street into the old town, which had more or less survived the bombardment intact. There has been a market every Saturday in this square since Roman times, and where there are markets there are always cafés. In this case, four of them. He chose the correct one and walked inside, waiting at the counter.

I joined him and ordered two coffees. 'Kirby,' he said.

'Hello, Nino.'

Nino Leone was a Swiss-Italian who appeared in Domodossola hours after the free republic was declared, offering to bring in food, medical supplies and even weapons from the Swiss side. He kept some of those promises, but not the one that Fausto wanted the most: anti-tank weapons. There had been an argument. Only one of them walked away.

'You have some nerve coming here,' I said.

'It's a free country.'

'It was then. I'm not sure about now. Not for you.'

He narrowed his eyes. 'It was self-defence.'

I wanted to punch him, but I accepted that he was partially right. Fausto probably shouldn't have shoved the Labora under his chin. You shouldn't spook a man like Nino. And when an 88 shell explodes fifty yards away, it's liable to make you all the more jumpy. 'You think that would stand up in court?'

He made a noise that could have been a laugh. 'You think it would even get there? Something that happened in that chaos? Jesus, if they tried every man who killed an Italian between forty-three and forty-five . . .'

'I saw it happen.'

He nodded. 'I know.'

I gripped his arm. '*Why* did it happen?'

'It just did.' He looked at me and realisation dawned. 'You don't have a gun, do you?'

'No,' I admitted, 'but there are people here who have, who would kill you if I told them you were here. You aren't liked.'

He sipped his coffee and indicated my injuries. 'You don't look like you are winning too many popularity contests.'

I had to smile at that. 'No.'

'If you have no gun, then I'll be going.'

'Why did you come back, Nino?'

'Why did you, Kirby? I was part of this, too. I know you would like to think the Republic was about Fausto and Rosario and Francesca and maybe even you . . . but it wasn't. It was lots of people, a collective, a very special moment. And I did my part – which is more than the British did.' I made to speak, to tell him that at the time we felt abandoned, but we now knew that the supplies didn't come because of Arnhem, of Warsaw, of Yugoslavia, that the air-drop resources were stretched too thin, but he kept going. 'You know nothing of what really went on here, Kirby. They simply used you to keep Bern happy. Their little SOE mascot. They laughed behind your back. A flyer playing at being a partisan, making those big puppy eyes at Francesca.' Now I really wanted to punch him, but he was just goading me, I knew, because he thought he was safe. My fists were clenching and unclenching. 'You were an outsider then. You are an outsider now.'

'So were you. Just a middle man. Out to make a quick buck, like the rest of your nation.'

I was trying to needle him in turn, but he laughed in my face. 'As I said, you know nothing.'

'I know that if I were you I'd make myself scarce.'

'I don't have to skulk in the shadows, Kirby. For you or anyone.'

Nino strode off and I didn't try to stop him. The sound of distant applause echoing round the arcades told me the mayor's speech was over. I realised it was the second time that day someone had walked out on me and stuck me with the bill. Maybe the scars and scabs spelt 'sucker'. I threw down some coins and left.

★ ★ ★

I took my time strolling back to the *municipio*. I was half-hoping that Nino had run into Rosario and that the little guy had snapped the lawyer's neck, but no such luck. I worked my way into the mass of people, jostling until I had a good view of the stage.

There were two surprisingly brief and affectingly modest addresses by ex-partisans, one of whom I knew had held a bridge against armoured cars for six precious hours, and then a commotion as someone climbed up out of the crush and was ushered to the front of the stage, looking young and nervous in that venerable company. However, Lindy Carr took a deep breath and began to speak into the microphone.

'Thank you for letting my voice be heard on this important day. You may wonder what I am doing here, because I was hardly born when you were fighting for your freedom.' She paused, and the mayor stepped forward and gave a rapid translation before she continued. 'My father was a man called Bill Carr. He was a pilot. He flew out of a place called Foggia, in the south. I'd like to tell you about him, and then read something.' She tapped her jacket pocket. 'In here is my dad's last letter, and he wrote it to me from Foggia.'

Sixteen

Foggia, Italy, 1944

Bill Carr tramped through mud towards the broken-backed barn which served as the squadron headquarters; it was time for the day's operational briefing. The weather had been atrocious for the past five days, and the airstrip was a quagmire. The perforated steel plates that formed the runway had sunk into the mud, which at least helped muffle the noise of aircraft tyres as the bombers rumbled into position.

Right now though, it was just after lunchtime and unnaturally quiet. The last of the USAAF B-17 Flying Fortresses had departed on their day raids, and the ground crew had yet to start the engines of the South African Air Force's Liberators. Carr moved aside as a car drove by and stopped outside the barn. From it stepped Captain Elwyn Davies, the squadron's Intelligence Officer, and another man Carr didn't recognise, who was wearing civilian clothes. They had disappeared into the ops HQ before Carr reached it.

'OK, Bill?' There was a slap on the back from Kier, one of the South African pilots. There had been some resentment at an Aussie, on secondment from the RAAF, getting the pilot's seat a few months ago, but that had all disappeared after the first of the 'gardening' raids in Romania, when the squadron had mined the Danube. Carr had nursed his plane back on three engines with a fuselage full of holes, leaking oil and gasoline, with a wounded tail gunner. Nobody suggested a South African could do any better after that.

'Fine. You?'

'Tired,' yawned Kier. 'I'm gonna move into town. Can't sleep here.' He pointed to the line of tents where many of the officers were billeted.

'You can't sleep there either,' Carr told him. He too had tried living in Foggia itself for a while. It was a bleak posting, the city wrecked by Allied bombers, the people reduced to living in hovels without sanitation. There was no sign of a cat or a dog – they were either dead or eaten. In their place were hordes of dirty kids, many with disfiguring sores, all of them lousy, begging for cigarettes and chocolate, their older sisters offering to make even more desperate trades. The parents were sullen, treating the flyers not as saviours, but simply another set of conquerors. The city was never peaceful; there was always someone scavenging among the ruins, arguments over scraps of food, people hustling at all hours.

After two weeks, Carr had had enough and had moved into a pigeon loft on the edge of the base. For a while the birds kept him awake with their constant shuffling and cooing, but soon there wasn't a single one left. They had all gone into pies.

Inside the converted barn, which smelled of a mixture of old animal manure, cigarettes and pipe tobacco, Bill Carr took his place at the rear of the congregation and lit his own pipe. At the front sat Brigadier Jimmy Durrant, the group's commanding officer, Lieutenant Colonel Johnson, the Air Staff Officer, Captain Elwyn Davies and the unknown civilian.

Carr turned as his co-pilot, Flight Sergeant Reg Lisle, came and sat beside him. They exchanged brief smiles. Lisle had originally found it hard to hide his resentment at not getting the pilot's seat. Now he too accepted that the best man had been chosen to fly EH-148.

The noise was growing as more crew arrived, joshing with each other, trading wisecracks and insults. Each pilot or co-pilot had their own way of dealing with their apprehension while trying to ignore the map hidden behind a sheet on the wall which would tell them their destination for that night. Carr and Lisle preferred to keep still and quiet.

'Right, gentlemen, if you will, please.' It was Elwyn Davies, the IO. He glared at a latecomer. 'I'll recommend the Pig and Whistle close during the day if you can't drag yourself away,' he said, to laughter. The tardy pilot was one of the few teetotallers on base. The Pig and Whistle was a remarkably authentic version of an English pub built by the British anti-aircraft unit in their spare time.

The gathering settled down after a few coughs, their minds working overtime. Where would it be tonight? Warsaw? Romania and the oil-fields again? Up to bomb the Gothic Line?

'Now. Before we discuss your designated target . . . a few words about Romania. Reports suggest that the mines you laid have sunk . . .' Elwyn Davies consulted his notes '. . . sixty tugs and two hundred barges.' A half-hearted cheer went up. They all knew what those raids had cost them. 'And that the journey-time from the oil-fields to Vienna has now trebled. So well done, all. I know it wasn't easy.'

There had been murderous ground fire from the banks of the Danube on every occasion, getting worse as the weeks went on and the Germans got wise to the approach runs. They had lost some good men to claim those tugs. Bill Carr had almost been one of them. Still, that was nothing compared to Warsaw, but he preferred not to even think about that.

'Which brings me to tonight.' Elwyn Davies pulled down the

sheet, revealing the large map of Europe. In the north of Italy was a small parachute symbol, and another and another. There was a collective sigh. Not Romania or Hungary then, but a supply drop to the partisans.

A babble of relieved conversation broke out while Elwyn Davies handed out the charts and the drop-zone photos from the 'shufti-kites', as they called the reconnaissance planes. Reg Lisle turned and winked at Bill Carr. A partisan supply drop, more than likely in remote countryside. Which meant no murderous flak towers, few nightfighters, drop runs at a decent height. It was almost like a night off.

After the briefing, which went over the partisan locations, ground signals and the weather en route and at the Incipient Point, where they should see the flares shaped into a T, the normal routine was tea and snacks in the mess. This was usually followed by a run-through for the rest of the Liberators' crews and ground support as to the target and types of bombs they would be carrying. This time there were no bombs to worry about, just the enormous supply cylinders which had been broken out of the stores. These would be packed with weapons, medicines and food. Bill Carr asked Lisle to take care of the second briefing because he had something to attend to, but as he was about to leave, Elwyn Davies called him over.

'Bill, I'd like you to meet Jimmy Morris. Jimmy, Bill Carr who, despite being an Australian, is a damn fine pilot. There had to be one, I suppose.'

The man in the civilian suit gave Carr a vigorous handshake and said he was pleased to meet him. He was close to forty, Carr reckoned, but there was an energy force exuding from him all the same. He had a sallow face, black hair and a moustache. His eyes were pale green, with the most unnerving direct stare.

'Bill, Jimmy here is going SN on your flight.' This meant super-numerary, an extra body, not expected to pull his weight.

'Right-oh,' was all Carr could think of saying.

'A White Stocking run. I'm going out with your canisters,' Morris beamed, as if he was looking forward to being turfed out over the mountains.

'I hope not,' said Carr. 'Be bloody cold in that bomb bay.' Morris could exit either from the rear hatch or through the open apertures where the tail gunners stood. And it would be a good idea for him to go well before the canisters, or he would risk tangling with them. 'Have you jumped before?'

Both Elwyn Davies and Morris laughed. 'Yes, but not from a Liberator. Think you can show me the ropes?'

Carr felt he was being patronised, but he nodded. 'We'll get you down in one piece.'

Carr cadged a lift back to the *fattoria* that served as the officers' mess and found himself a corner with a mug of tea, a ginger snap biscuit and a pad. Foggia reverberated with noise once more. Ground crews were running the big Pratt & Whitney engines to test them, as the twelve huge supply containers were loaded into the Liberator's cavernous belly and the great snakes of ammunition fed to the guns. Coffee, tea and sandwiches were being stowed, mostly to be saved for the return run. Only a very few had the stomach to eat on the way to a drop.

Canisters of chaff, the aluminium foil used to confuse enemy nightfighter radar, were placed in the waist, where the gunners would hurl it out into the night if necessary. Already, DeWitt, the young Rhodesian navigator, would have plotted a course and be checking and re-checking it until he could get them there and back blindfolded, with or without the electronic navigation beams. Carr approved of that.

Soon the Liberators' pilots would walk around the deep fuselages and under the high wings, looking for leaks or damage. Then, once inside, after completing an instrument check, they would start the warm-up. Master switch to battery, set mixture controls, throttles cracked, superchargers zero boost, master ignition on, fuel booster pump on; wait for the hum and set starter switch to mesh. Ignition. Repeat until all four engines are running. Boost to 48 inches, release brakes and the stomach unknots as finally they are on their way, eight men, off on a mission to help save the lives of freedom fighters they have never met and never will.

But, before all that, Bill Carr had two tasks to perform. One was his customary prayer for himself and the crew, a very personal and private ritual that only Lisle knew about. The second was to write a letter on the tiny sheets of paper onto which someone had stamped the squadron logo, issued to aircrew for personal correspondence. So prior to his milk run to the Lakes, Bill Carr composed a letter to the daughter he had never seen, the very letter that, twenty years later, Lindy Carr would read out to a hushed crowd in Domodossola.

Has she shown you the letter? Lang had asked me back in Whitehall. No, I had replied. Clever girl, he had said.

Lindy Carr, having given the onlookers a thumbnail biography of her father, produced a piece of card from her jacket, no more than five inches by three, dark with tiny writing. To conserve paper, she explained. This was the letter Bill Carr wrote to her from Foggia, no doubt in some ops room with the deep thrum of Liberator engines warming up in the distance. Pausing every so often for the mayor's translation, Lindy read in an increasingly confident voice.

'*My Dear Daughter,*

This is the first time I have written to you and although you are as yet too young to read it, perhaps Mother will save it up until the time comes when you can read it yourself. In two days' time it will be your first birthday anniversary – a great event for your parents. My regret is that I cannot personally be there to help you blow out your single candle but, believe me, lassie, I will be there in spirit.

I am writing this from a place called Italy which is far away from our fair land – a place where I would not be by choice so far away separated from a wife and daughter so dear to me. But I am here, precious one, because there is a war on caused by certain people who wished to rule the world harshly and despotically, imperilling an intangible thing called democracy which your mother and I thought all decent people should fight for. You will understand as you grow up what democracy means for us and how it is an ideal way of life which we aspire to put into practice.

All I ask of you, Lindy dear, is that you stay as sweet as your mother and cling tight to the subtle thing we call Christianity, which has been the core of her way of life and her mother's and mine. I hope that you will love and respect me as I love and respect my father.

That's all, young lady. Have a happy birthday – may they all be happy birthdays. I hope to be home again one fine day. In the meantime, lots of love to you and to Mother.

From Dad,

Bill Carr.'

Lindy paused and wiped away a tear. 'My father posted that letter as he went off on the mission to Domodossola,' she told us. 'He never came back, and the plane has never been found. My dad is somewhere up in those mountains, and if anyone knows anything about EH-148, I would be very grateful for any information you have. Thank you for listening.'

As the translator finished his version, the crowd broke into applause and I joined in, clapping until my hands stung. When I had agreed to take on the search, I did it for two reasons, one of them commercial – I needed the money – one of them sentimental – finding a fellow war-time pilot. Now, hearing his words from twenty years ago, I realised that there was an element I had overlooked. Bill Carr was not just a brave pilot, he was a good, honest man and a father who never got a chance to raise his daughter, yet he had managed to leave her a memento that crackled with the warmth of his humanity. I was now more determined than ever to find Bill Carr, no matter what it cost me. I'd like to think I would have felt the same, even if I had known at that precise moment just how high the price would be.

Seventeen

I skipped the dinner in the piazza. Listening to Lindy reading her letter, on top of meeting Nino the Lawyer, had sapped my enthusiasm for eating and drinking in celebration of Domodossola. It was, after all, a doomed effort that had cost many lives, Bill Carr's included, those thirty-four days of stubborn optimism, most of us believing until the first shells fell that we could hold back the opposition with sheer willpower.

There were a number of Communist protesters circulating in the town. I never quite grasped the difference between Italian Reds and the regular Marxist-Leninist issue, except that the ones hereabouts seemed more down to earth than ideological. They had recently fomented large-scale strikes in Turin at the Fiat factories, claiming industry and government were keeping wages artificially low. From what I knew about Italian big business – not much, admittedly – I reckoned they were right. Perhaps that made me a fellow traveller, one of my father's dreaded 'pinkos'.

The groups of young long-haired Commies here were pussy cats compared to some of the Turin strikers, and all meekly stepped aside for a battered old man like me trawling through the bars and cafés. I eventually tracked Ragno to a counter where he was arguing politics with a small cluster of the Reds and asked him a favour, which he readily agreed to, using the good graces of Moto Guzzi. Unfortunately, he sealed the deal with a hug.

I also located Lindy Carr, tear-stained but relieved that her public speaking was over, at the centre of a group of well-wishers, and I arranged to meet her at the Cannero the next morning to go over our arrangements. When I got back to the hotel, I couldn't even face a drink, so I went to bed and dreamed of dark mountain ridges looming up out of the night at me.

I was up at seven, hardly rested, so I showered and re-read some of the documents from the crew of EH-148. It didn't help lift my mood much. Lindy turned up at ten, and Maria gave us the use of the small salon off the main dining room, where I spread out the large-scale maps of the area, hoping to give Lindy some idea of what to expect. I also went over what I had extracted from the squadron reports.

'It was a warm front,' I explained, 'which came over the mountains much quicker than expected. With it came high cirrus clouds, which blanked out the stars, and the winds were gusting fifty knots instead of the expected five. That was before the electrical storms. All the Liberators had GEE fitted. You know what that is?'

'I do,' she said. 'Electronic navigation.'

'Yes, using beams. But up here, in the mountains, with a storm brewing, it was useless. So they needed to fly by dead reckoning. For which—'

'They needed the stars.'

'And a reliable met forecast. Now, every one of those ten planes was affected,' I said, 'but your father's was the northernmost drop. He had the highest mountains to contend with, the worst shears and vortices. You have to understand that the air around the sides of the Alps gets bloody rough.'

Clear air turbulence, on which I was something of an expert. 'It clings to the sides like a whirlpool. Hit that unexpectedly and . . .' I rammed a fist into my palm.

I noticed her eyes were moist. 'Sorry. I didn't mean to be insensitive.'

'No, it's OK.' But she didn't look it.

'Shall I get some coffee?' I offered.

'Yes, please. Can I smoke in here, do you think?'

I nodded and she put a cigarette to her lips with shaking hands.

'You were very brave yesterday,' I told her.

She lit the cigarette and sucked hard, the tip glowing bright red, then let out a long stream of smoke. 'I just remembered how brave my father must have been, and it was easy.' She sighed and looked down at the map, then pointed a finger at its western extremity. 'You know, one of the planes almost made it to France. He missed clearing the Alps by twenty feet. Two of the engines made it over the border, but not the rest of the Liberator.'

'I've been thinking about this. Your father would have known they were in trouble. He would have had a choice – try for Switzerland or France, and get interned, or keep going, try and get out of the muck and get home.'

She thought for a while, contemplating the motivations of a man she had never met. 'He'd have tried to get home.'

'I think so too,' I said. I had nothing but that letter and some personal history to go on, but I felt it very strongly: Bill Carr would have wanted to get his crew back, to carry on the war for as long as necessary. 'He'd be trying to turn south for Foggia, running down over to the east of Genoa. All he'd need was a rip in the sky for his man DeWitt, the Rhodesian, to get his bearings. He was a good navigator, apparently, who had graduated top in his intake. He had already refused an offer to be an instructor. And he was still only in his early twenties.'

'You've been doing your homework.'

I nodded. I'd been trying to imagine myself in that plane for weeks now, switching my mental image of warfare from the sleek handsome Mosquito and the exhilarating roar of its twin Merlins, replacing it with the bulbous bruiser and its quartet of dull thudding Pratt & Whitneys. To feel the weight of being responsible for seven other men, hearing the cacophony of combat when they engaged, a babble of voices in the ear, a plane filling with cordite from the relentless hammering of the .50 calibres, wallowing through the sky, trying to dodge the lights and the flak, a sitting duck for any German nightfighter worth its salt. Not on the partisan drops, but Yugoslavia, Romania, Poland, they all would have been like running gauntlets of firestorms. Some nights I awoke bathed in sweat, grateful my war hadn't been like that.

'One other thing,' I said. 'I think your father came round twice. I think the clouds obscured the drop zone, but instead of aborting and getting out before the worst of the weather hit, the mad bastard looped around and flew back down the valley.'

Lindy looked puzzled. 'How can you know that?'

I licked my lips and took a deep breath. 'Because I heard it. Because I was on the ground that night. I was one of the reception committee. I lit the flares he never saw.'

It was a T for that particular drop. The Germans and anti-partisan Italian units had got wise to Xs; they often covered dozens of square miles with them, to confuse the aircrews. So we changed the signals regularly, according to instructions from Bern. I was at the very base of the T with my three flares. Fausto, Rosario and Pavel were in different hollows, a good mile away, to form the rest of the letter. I couldn't see them, but I knew they were there.

I still recall looking up at the sky, ears straining for the sound of those engines, waiting for the moment to light my flares.

'You were there?' Lindy asked.

'Lang didn't tell you?' He had said he hadn't, but I would always double-check anything that man said.

She shook her head. 'No. I . . . that's strange. A strange coincidence.'

She lit another cigarette and the coffee arrived and we passed some time in silence.

'Did you hear it crash?' she asked eventually.

'No.'

'You must have.'

'We each had three flares. The rule was you only lit two. The third was if one of the others didn't function.'

'But you lit three,' she guessed. 'And you stayed on longer than you should have?'

It made me sound noble, which was far from the truth. 'Yes. You are out there with a big light blazing away, which gives you a good chance of getting spotted. As the third flare burned, we came under fire from an *Alpini* night patrol. We had to run, with gunfire chasing us down the hill. The Americans could have tested their nuclear bomb up there that night and I'd have missed it. Being under fire does that. I'm sorry.'

After a while she said: 'It's not your fault. Whether you were on the ground or not, you couldn't control the weather.'

No, I almost said, but I could have controlled myself.

Eighteen

Italy, 1944

'You can't come.'

'What do you mean?' Kirby shouted at Fausto across the kitchen of the safe house.

'Someone has to stay here.'

'Leave Ragno.'

'He's only a boy.'

'It's my replacement. I should be part of the reception committee.'

Fausto slung his gun onto his shoulder. 'They shouldn't replace you.'

'I'll tell him that. Look, I'll have a better chance of convincing him than you will. I should start as soon as he lands.'

The message had come from Bern that Kirby was to be relieved of his post as a priority. Someone 'properly trained and briefed' would be parachuted in to take over. This person would also decide 'appropriate long-term strategy for the partisan groups operating around Domodossola'. The instruction was signed by a Major Lang.

Rosario tapped his watch. 'We have to go. It'll start getting dark soon. The planes could even have taken off by now.'

'Please, Fausto? You know I should be there.'

Fausto shook his head but threw Kirby a haversack anyway. 'Three flares. You only use two. Francesca will show you where and how. You wait till you hear the engines, eh?'

He walked over and nuzzled Francesca's ear affectionately before walking out.

Francesca shrugged. 'I'll get the bikes.'

They cycled uphill, slowly, for three miles from the house, and then struck out on foot to the east, through a stand of ash trees. Using gauze-shrouded flashlights, Francesca led Kirby over old shepherd's trails, and across icy rivers, still climbing until the trees thinned and the earth flattened out. They were between the rolling hills and pine forests of Val Vigezzo and the Val Grande, reputed to be the wildest part of Italy, home to bears, boar and, it was rumoured, the occasional wolf.

Still visible in the fading light were the sharp-faced mountains which fringed the whole region and which made flying through the valley so tricky.

Eventually, the terrain became rougher, and Kirby and Francesca had to scramble over fields of scree. After an hour, the ground became flatter and softer underfoot once more and Francesca slumped down, pointing to a shallow depression in the earth, lined with moss and ferns. 'This is it.'

'What now?'

'We wait.' She shrugged off her backpack and produced a lump of coarse bread and some cheese. 'And we eat.'

Kirby sat on the ferns, flattening them out around him into a soft cushion. They were still warm from the day's sun. He suppressed a desire to roll over and sleep. They told tales of witches and spells in these mountains, and as the last of the daylight went from the sky and the world was reduced to inky shadows, he could see why. He began to whistle to himself.

143

'Ssshh!' Francesca hissed. 'Keep quiet.'

Kirby took some of the food and munched as quietly as he could, looking up at the silent heavens now and then.

'Why are the British so opposed to us liberating Domodossola?' she whispered.

Kirby shook his head. He had sent reports via couriers to Special Forces HQ Number 2 in Bern, requesting full support for the liberation and holding of the town. Fausto was convinced it was an important blow against the occupiers, and the kind of morale boost which could cause all of Northern Italy to rise up as one, finishing the war this year rather than next.

The message came back: *Stop all but essential sabotage. Do not attempt to liberate any areas of the north.* Followed by the news that Kirby was to be replaced as soon as possible. In Bern, they didn't like what he was saying.

Gruppo Fausto had raided the SS Italienische Number 1 for weapons and Bern blamed Kirby for this breach of standing orders. As a matter of urgency, he was about to be relieved of his role as BLO by the man in the Liberator winging its way up the coast of Italy, a man who, Bern no doubt believed, would stop such privateer actions. Bern, however, didn't take into account Fausto's intractable nature.

'I don't know,' said Kirby, not wanting to be drawn.

'Fausto says it's because they are frightened of Italians controlling their own destiny again. They want to impose their rule.'

'Perhaps.'

'Do you agree with them?'

Kirby shook his head. 'No, but you can see their point.'

'Ah, Mr Reasonable.'

'Am I?'

'I think so.'

He watched a hawk circling, hunting the first of the nocturnal animals. After a minute, it collapsed its wings and dived headlong, disappearing into the long grass. 'What were you going to do?' he asked her. 'Before all this happened?'

Francesca shrugged. 'I wanted to go to business school. I know, shocking for a woman.'

'I don't think so.'

'See? How reasonable. Here, it is shocking. Everyone says "Get married, have kids, learn to cook".'

'You can cook.'

She giggled. 'Rosario is right: his risotto *is* better than mine. But if you tell him so, I will cut your throat while you sleep.'

He cocked his head, thinking he had heard something.

'Owl,' she said. 'Don't be jumpy. You'll hear the bombers all right when they come.'

'Why business school?'

'To run the family estates. To sell our wine and olive oil elsewhere. There are lots of Italians in America. Big market. But . . . we'll see. Fausto says we shall see once all this is over.'

'You'll do what he says.'

She chewed on the bread for a while before she answered. 'In some things, yes. In war, definitely. He has been doing this longer than any of us. In peace, I don't know.'

'You should do whatever you want to do with your life.'

'Like now? You think I want to be sitting out here with you?' Francesca laughed. 'I didn't mean that. I like sitting here with you. Under other circumstances, it would be very pleasant. But not waiting for guns and men to fall from the sky, for a patrol to find us.'

'I like being here too. Despite the risk. Maybe because of it.' Kirby felt himself blush as her dark eyes turned to him.

'Do you like Fausto?' she asked.

He tore off a large fern and began to shred it, still alert for noises from the sky. 'I admire him,' he said truthfully. 'The way he can pull men together. He has a strength. I wish I had that.'

'Are you jealous?'

'Of the way he can command men? I think I probably am.'

Francesca moved across towards him, rustling the ferns. 'That's not what I meant. You will have that one day. He is almost thirty. An old man.'

'Do you love him?' Kirby asked.

'Many men love him. Don't you?'

Kirby gave an embarrassed laugh, feeling very English. 'Well, no, but as I said, I respect him.' He threw a large frond into the night and repeated his question: 'Do you love him?'

He was surprised to see her hesitate before she nodded. 'But sometimes, I feel . . .' He let her search for the word. 'Suffocated. He is a forceful man, with a strong personality and sometimes, sometimes I want to break away.'

The first chill of night caught them and she moved closer.

'How do you break away?' he asked.

He felt her mouth on his, and she pushed him back into the grass. There were voices protesting in his head, but he ignored them. As he fumbled with the buttons of her blouse, over her shoulder he noticed the stars going out one by one, but by then she was working at his belt, and the only sound in his ears was the pounding of his heart.

Nineteen

'I didn't hear the Liberator crash,' was what I said to Lindy, but I could feel the sweat of shame prickling on my forehead. 'We were attacked by fascists. *Alpini* – mountain troops – the only ones who'd be up there. They must have seen our flare . . .' I let it fade, unable to elaborate, and I switched tack, back to business. 'So, if we conclude that Bill Carr didn't cut and run for the Swiss border, we still have . . .' I waved my hand over the map to indicate the expanse.

'Not quite,' said Lindy, digging in her bag. 'I have this. These are the searches that were made after the war, by the South African War Graves people and by members of the SAAF Service Society.'

She spread out a map with several hundred square miles of Italy and Switzerland cross-hatched in red. 'Where did you get this?' I asked.

'From my father's squadron. You see, they didn't just abandon them. They made an effort in forty-six and again in forty-seven.'

I pointed to the thick black line marking the border, with crimson shading on either side. 'They searched the Swiss Alps too?'

'No, but these sections here and here are well climbed and skied. Zermatt. Cervinia. Mont Blanc. Any plane that went down there would have been found by now.'

I studied the map for a long time, subtracting the populated areas and those now being overrun by tourists, such as the Aosta Valley, and those that would have displayed any wreckage to an overflying plane. EH-148 must have been well hidden to keep itself secret for twenty years.

'If we assume he crashed near here, and didn't try to get into Switzerland, it leaves us with this.' I pointed at the Val Grande, an oval-shaped space guarded by the peaks of Mount Zeda, Togano, Rossola. Averaging around 2,000 metres, they weren't the big boys of the area – there were mountains that soared to twice that, especially the gloomy Mount Rosa just to the west – but they still commanded respect. 'It's the most likely area. Plenty of tree cover and fast-growing vegetation in some parts to swallow even a Liberator. Remote and wild enough for it to be missed in others. There is talk of turning it into a national park, but as far as I know there have been no complete surveys.'

I followed the Liberator's probable flight path with my finger, hugging the rail lines to Barese, then turning to port as the Swiss border loomed, over the lake at Luino on the eastern side, then a dog-leg up the valley, towards Santa Maria Maggiore, losing height all the time for maximum drop accuracy of the human and canister cargo he was carrying. Then another correction to head for the dropping zone just to the south of the Val Vigezzo. Once they got hit by weather, Carr and his navigator would realise if they went straight on they would have to tangle with the Alps, and even if they cleared them in atrocious weather, the war was over for them, assuming they did manage to land in one piece.

Carr needed a course heading to the east of Turin, but away from the big flak towers that protected the railyards and factories there. If he got a bearing, he could well have turned towards the Val Grande, pulling on all the power to gain the height back. Even so, one of those great granite mountains might have got him. It was certainly feasible.

'It's as good a place as any to start,' Lindy said.

Fine. That only left us with about five thousand square miles to cover.

'I didn't ask you about your face.'

'I thought you were being polite.'

'Does it hurt?'

'No. It's my ribs that hurt.' I pointed to the scabs on my forehead. 'These just frighten dogs and young children.'

We had moved on to lunch, both of us exhausted by the emotional effort of attempting to find Bill Carr on that map, and of trying not to relive the last terrifying minutes in that plane. Lost, alone in the sky, buffeted by unpredictable winds, searching for a tear in the cloud cover, or lights on the ground, and the difficult decision made by Carr to come back round again. I thought of that night in my stricken Mozzie, and across twenty years, my heart went out to them all.

I hadn't lied about the *Alpini* attack. As soon as I heard the plane, I rolled out from under Francesca, lit the first flare and waited. What I didn't know was how long the plane had been up there, hoping for a complete ground signal. It was unforgivable because it only needed one missing light for them to abort the mission: faulty signals often meant enemy decoys. I couldn't shake the feeling that Carr had come round for a second look because of my tardiness, hoping he would get a full set of the lights.

It was when I lit the third flare that we were shot at, machine-gun fire; Francesca grabbed my arm and we stumbled down the track in the dark, voices and flashlights behind us, back through the forest to the bicycles. 'Ah well,' said Fausto, when we finally gathered back at the house. 'Look on the bright side – you're still our BLO.'

To me, there was no bright side, and the attraction I had felt for Francesca since I first set eyes on her was soured for ever. I had chosen it over my duty. After that night, I never so much as touched her again, until that kiss twenty years later. After all, I was just a little light relief from her relationship with Fausto. The knowledge of what I had caused was the reason I had never returned. It was as simple as that.

Lindy stared at me as she shovelled big forkfuls of spaghetti into her mouth. No sparrow-like portions for her.

'What?' I asked after five minutes.

'It kind of suits you, that beaten-about look.'

'Thanks.'

'No, really. You get a decent haircut and shave, you'd shine up quite nicely, for—'

'An old man.'

'A pom, I was about to say.'

'A pom? You know, I'd almost forgotten you were a colonial for a minute.' I watched her bristle, with some satisfaction. 'Tell me about Australia.'

'Nothing to tell. Big. Beautiful. Friendly. But a long way from anywhere. Or, at least, it thinks it is. Which is why our young men and women keep coming to miserable old London. My stepfather is not a bad man, but deadly dull.'

'And your mother?'

'Would like to know the truth as much as I would.'

'The truth?'

'About where my real father died.'

'Jack.'

I looked up and it was Furio, waiting for an introduction to a woman he clearly considered too attractive to be wasted on me. He'd always liked blondes, Furio.

'Ah. Furio Gabbiano, Lindy Carr, our employer. I believe you spoke on the telephone.'

'Yes. How do you do. Pardon my English,' he said.

'But you know an offer of work when you hear it, eh?' I said.

Lindy put her fork down and wiped her mouth. 'Jack—'

'It's OK. I wanted to wait until you two were together to sort this one out.'

'Jack—'

I was ready to let rip. I'd been saving this. 'Furio, when we are negotiating a contract, it isn't quite the done thing, old boy, to say you'll—'

'Jack, I lied.'

'What?'

'About Furio saying he'd fly me. I lied.'

'Oh.' My sails drooped alarmingly as the wind was taken out of them.

'It was just a cheap ploy. Sorry. I thought you'd take the job if you believed someone else might. I'd spoken to Furio on the phone . . . Sorry. I meant to tell you it was a bluff. I forgot.'

Furio smiled like an idiot throughout this exchange, not following a word.

'You brought the plane up to Invorio?' I asked him.

'Sí.'

'Good. We can get started tomorrow, weather permitting. Looking good though.' I made a play of scanning the sky like a great sage of meteorology. I'd already checked with the office at Milan airport and it was going to be fine flying weather, but I wanted Lindy to think she was getting value for money.

I also wanted to tell her how time-consuming and debilitating an air search can be. We'd be doing a photo run, infra-red and black and white, and visual searches, the sort that make you feel you are going to wear your eyes out before their time. Then we'd have to go over the photographs with magnifying glasses. Come to think of it, she *was* getting value for money. I still felt sore about her cheap trick with Furio, though – I'd been festering on that all summer. Nothing galls me more than a wasted fester.

'Furio, get a chair, get a fork, get some food inside you.' I signalled to Maria that we had company for *i secondi*. 'And Miss Carr is paying.'

Invorio airfield looked a little like me – past its best and knocked around. There was a collection of pre-war hangars, a couple of prefabs housing offices and café, and an ugly square concrete block of a tower which still bore the faded markings of the Luftwaffe group that used to operate from it. It was fine for what I wanted, though.

I had done this by the book – filed flight plans with air-traffic control, although I was going to be well away from any commercial corridors, and double-checked Lindy's clearance with the military. We had the camera, film, the plane, a line of fuel credit, and a couple of pilots. It was time to begin.

As with all aircraft, the Beechcraft came with a long preliminary checklist before take-off and, like most pilots, I was sometimes tempted to skip the more mundane parts of it, but I never did. So I sent Furio and Lindy off to rustle up something to drink from the scruffy café and got to work. I had also asked Furio to brief Lindy on the *regali* that would appear on our expenses – the little gifts to various people at the airstrip that would help lubricate our stay. It was the Italian way.

I checked the cowl-flaps were open and then the oil-cooler duct for debris and birds' nests. I had welded a dipstick onto the inside of the filler cap, so it was easy to confirm the oil level in each engine. Then I ran a hand along the leading edges and inspected the condition of the two-bladed props, which had now done 400 hours apiece since their last major overhaul. I did the visuals on the tail fin, rudder and elevators and checked the radio aerials were secure.

The Beech was a big plane, thirty-eight feet long with a wing-span of forty-seven feet, and you can't rush the procedure on an aircraft coming up for its twenty-first birthday. Its Perspex was starting to turn milky like a cataract in places, and the aluminium was showing age-blooms of oxidisation but, by the time I was back where I had started, all looked hunky-dory.

I was ready to move inside and start with the checklist there, making sure we had enough fuel, that the controls were working, the gyros caged, the throttle friction set for take-off. There was no just leaping in, pumping the primers and engaging starters with this baby.

When I snapped open the fuselage door and poked my head into the gloom of the interior, I came across one preliminary that wasn't in the *Pilot's Notes*. Perhaps it should be. *Check behind pilot's seat for dead body. Remove if necessary.*

It was Nino Leone the Lawyer, and judging by the congealed mess where his left eye should have been, I guessed he had been shot.

Part Three

Twenty

I knew enough about the Italian police and justice system to want to avoid all contact with them. I particularly wanted to avoid anything to do with a *Pubblico Ministero*, an examining magistrate, who had the power of arrest, investigation and interrogation as well as deciding on a verdict. They were a one-man legal system, and there were rumours that it had turned some of their heads. I can't think why.

The police who came to the airfield were a couple of wary members of La Polizia *in borghese* – plainclothes – along with three of the uniformed branch. They examined the body, declared the man dead, called for a pathologist and told the three of us we were under arrest. I wanted to ask what the charge was, but kept my mouth shut. You don't jib the cops here. The new *leggi Cossiga*, the anti-terrorism laws, allowed detention without charge for forty-eight hours. If they decided to prosecute you, you could wait three years before your number came up at the courthouse. Smile. Be nice. Say 'sir' a lot. These were the best options.

We were taken to the *questura* at Arona. They decided this was too big a case and we were moved, in separate Fiats with flashing lights – just to let everyone know that dangerous criminals were on board – south to the station at Novara. I was put in a holding room which smelled of fresh paint. It was furnished with a desk and two chairs and a window that only a giraffe could see out of. Someone gave me a lukewarm cup of instant coffee, which I suspect was part of the grinding-down process. Nothing would make a Milanese talk faster than the threat of powdery Nescafé. We English are made of stronger stuff and the guard watched in horror as I drank it without wincing.

Inside, I was wondering who the hell had bumped off Nino, and why. Furthermore, and rather more importantly, why choose my plane as his next-to-final resting place? Was this connected with three men taking a strong dislike to me down at the lakeshore? I also wondered if anyone had overheard me talking to Nino in the market café. Could anything I said have been misconstrued as a threat? Well, only most of it.

A *Commissario*, a man half-excited and half-appalled by having a murder on his patch, came in for the *preliminari* questions, as he called them, and I went over the same story I was sure Furio and Lindy were trotting out. The previous day we had had lunch, discussed the search until late afternoon, when Furio went off to Turin to visit his mother, dropping Lindy at Bavenno, where she was staying, on the way. Furio was the last to see the plane, having flown it in from Malpensa and secured it. No, I didn't think Furio or Lindy had met Nino. In fact, I was certain of it.

The *Commissario* by now reckoned I had no friends in high places – otherwise I would have dropped them into my first three answers – and became more aggressive in his line of enquiry, especially when I admitted seeing Nino at the ceremony and to speaking with him afterwards. I figured to hide that would invite trouble later on, but I could tell that my cop scented blood.

I refrained from asking the obvious question. If I'd killed Nino, wouldn't I have stashed the body somewhere else, other than my own plane? But I knew what he would answer to that. What better *depistaggio*, red herring, than discovering the body myself?

A telephone call deprived me of the *Commissario*'s company and they racked up the torture with another cup of dishwater coffee. Again, it hardly touched the sides. People would be coming to watch this crazy bravado soon.

With a display of great sadness the *Commissario* told me my *caso* was being handed over to a 'higher authority' and that I would have to wait for two hours or so to be interviewed again. Which meant I might end up facing one of those *Pubblico Ministero* megalomaniacs. Furio and Lindy, the *Commissario* added, had been released. I tried to recall if I had met any friendly, and cheap, lawyers recently. It looked like the higher authorities had narrowed their suspects down to me.

Before he left, I had asked my interrogator about my plane, and was told it was a crime scene and had been impounded by the state. I began to wish I had kissed it goodbye. Not all the claims about the speed of Italian bureaucracy are true, but that is because most of them underestimate just how bad it is. People were still getting call-up papers for World War One, there were still 20,000 pension claims before La Corte dei Conti for that very war, and it took an average of six years to get a tax rebate. So I could reckon on ten before I saw my Beech again. I made a mental note to tell them that you have to turn the prop regularly to stop the bottom cylinders filling with oil.

I was tired of the coffee, and of having to use the primitive lavatory because of it, by the time the *Pubblico Ministero* came. He was fifty, with a shock of silver hair, and a suit fashionably cut in what the Italians think is the English style. His brogues were wonderfully shiny, he had long black socks that showed no leg, and beautifully manicured hands. He was no provincial policeman, that was for sure.

The guard let him into my cell and was told to leave. The newcomer cleverly refused the offer of refreshment, turned and fixed me with clear unblinking blue eyes. He took out a small moleskin notebook and turned over a few pages.

'Mr Jack Kirby,' he began.

'Well, they got my name right. It's a start.' It was, too. Once your name was entered incorrectly on any form, as far as the state was concerned, that was your moniker for life.

'My name is Dottore Giorgio Zopatti.'

I didn't ask him what he was a doctor of: I doubted he was there to take my blood pressure. 'From?'

He took a slim wallet from his suit – nothing bulky enough to ruin the line of the jacket – flipped it open and slid it across the table. If he had taken my blood pressure the mercury would have popped out of the tube, but I tried to stay calm. 'The SISDe.'

The Servizio Informazioni per la Sicurezza Democratica is roughly the equivalent of MI5. Except the SISDe, like its foreign espionage counterpart SISMI, was well known to be the old fascist Intelligence Service, re-branded and re-launched, but with the same personnel. I had spent part of the war trying to kill these blokes.

'I don't see there is anything to do with national security here. It's a murder case.'

'Your face is quite damaged.' Clearly he wasn't going to discuss jurisdiction with the likes of me.

'You should see the other fella.' He leaned forward and I raised my palms and said quickly, 'I'm joking. I went stumbling around in the dark by Lake Maggiore, near my hotel. Walked into a concrete piling. Accident.' I turned my head to show him the marks on my temple. 'Look, they are several days old.'

He examined my wounds for a couple of seconds. 'How many times did you walk into this piling, Mr Kirby?'

'I fell over. I was concussed.'

'And you saw a doctor?'

'No. But the hotel will confirm what happened.'

He looked up at the ceiling, just a glance, but I knew then we were being taped, possibly filmed. I tried to keep calm, but my hands felt clammy. *La Polizia* occasionally bent the rules; the security services didn't have a rulebook to bend.

'How well did you know the victim?'

'Not well enough to let him in my plane without permission.'

'He could fly?'

'I don't know.' I realised I had to keep the answers straight. It wouldn't pay to be clever. 'He was a lawyer.'

'A lawyer? What gave you that idea?'

I shrugged. 'When I met him in 1944 he said he was a lawyer.'

'He was *faccendiere*, perhaps, but no lawyer.'

A Mr Fixit, not always a complimentary term. 'Well, it doesn't surprise me.'

'Officially, according to his documents, he was a *Treuhänder*.'

I shook my head at the German term to show he would have to explain.

'A fiduciary agent. A trustee. A go-between, you might say. A cog in financial transactions.'

'I never had any dealings with him.'

'You met him in 1944?'

'In Domodossola.'

'Ah.' His mouth twitched, but he managed to refrain from spitting on the floor. Old fascists didn't like to be reminded about any of the free republics they helped put down. 'How did you meet?'

I gave him the short version, which was much the same as the long version. Nino dealt directly with Fausto, not the minions and certainly not with the BLOs. We British, in particular, were kept out of discussions with the Swiss, because we had failed the Republic.

'Leone was supplying materiel to the partisan forces from Switzerland?'

'Yes.'

'A violation of their neutrality, surely.'

What, I almost said – like Switzerland buying four hundred million pounds' worth of Nazi gold to help finance the war, much of it looted from the vaults of conquered states? The complicity between the two nations went all the way down to one of its big coffee and confectionery companies supplying the Wehrmacht with chocolate. I didn't think I should start down that road, so I said, 'No, since Bern had recognised the Republic.'

'So he supplied arms?'

'I think he arranged for their purchase. And for food and medicine.'

'In exchange for?'

'I don't know.' Time off in Purgatory? 'Maybe he wanted to see Domodossola succeed.'

'Maybe.' He said it as if I had told him that a squadron of airborne pigs were circling Mount Rosa. 'You have been involved with guns.'

'No,' I said.

'Sicily?'

'You can't pull Sicily on me. The most lethal thing I flew was bad red wine.' Most of us freelancers had been chucked off the island when it emerged that it was a major supply route for weapons used in the Algerian insurrection against the French: down to Palermo, across to Tunis, then either overland or by boat to the rebels. I kept well clear of it, not least because the French had put an SDECE team onto it, and they weren't fussy about how they stopped the trade. Eventually, worried that de Gaulle's secret service might start assassinating pilots, Italy had stepped in and imposed flying restrictions from the island, which put us all out of business. Which was how I ended up at Malpensa flinging skydivers at wide-bodied jets. I told him this, as forcefully as I could. I didn't want him to think Nino and I had fallen out over a shipment of carbines to Algiers.

'Are you glad he is dead?'

'Glad is too strong a word. It suggests I care.' I cared he might have bled on my floor, though.

'Do you own a gun?' he snapped.

'No.' I did, but someone took it off me. Shit, what if . . . no, that was too ridiculous. And how could they connect any gun to me anyway? But suddenly I was scared. Here I was mouthing off at some unreconstituted fascist who very likely thought the Domodossola Republic was an aberration that fully deserved to be crushed, not a blow for Italian freedom. My ribs began to throb.

'He was definitely shot, then?'

'We'll know when we get the pathologist's report. But you saw his face?' I nodded. 'You are familiar with gunshot wounds?' I had to agree I had seen one or two in the past. 'Is it true that the victim killed a friend of yours?'

I didn't answer.

'The partisan leader Fausto,' he pressed.

'You are well informed.'

He smiled at me.

'Nino said it was in self-defence,' I told him.

'Was it?'

'I don't know.'

'Did you see it?'

'Yes.'

'Then tell me—'

'I don't know what it has to do—'

He thumped the table hard and I jumped, despite myself. '*Tell me!*'

'Can I get a glass of water?'

'After you tell me.'

'I need the water. My throat is dry.'

He relented and asked the guard in the corridor to fetch a drink. While he stood scowling and tapping his well-buffed toe, I had a

163

feeling it was the last victory I was going to enjoy for a while.

I sipped the medicinal-tasting water as I told Zopatti the story. 'It was a sight I will never forget. Nobody who was there will. We had been fighting for two weeks. We had the railway, we had the hills, we controlled the power and the border crossings. There were 3,000 partisans in the hills, and Fausto had 400 of them loyal to him. We were well armed, mainly with Italian and German weapons from the raid on the SS convoy, we were well motivated and the opposition knew it.

'Priests were sent in to negotiate an armistice with the Germans, if they wanted it, and we were surprised when they agreed. There were five hundred of them, German and fascist, and we gave them safe conduct out of the town. Some people told me it was raining that day, but I just remember bright sunshine. The Germans assembled in front of the railway station, while we stood on the steps, roofs, at windows, and watched them go. There was no cheering, not at first. Just the crunch of their damned hobnailed boots as they marched to their vehicles.

'The party started the next day – dancing in the streets while the council read out the manifesto.

'So we had what we wanted: we had a whole free section of Italy. We arrested what fascists were left and locked them in one of the railway stores. Treated them well, mind. The schools were re-opened, but the fascist curriculum was torn up, trains started running with partisan guards on them, right up into Switzerland.

'Money was short, food was short, but the Red Cross sent supplies. The Italian military attaché in Bern, loyal to the King, sent commanders to unify us. Huh. Like that worked. Then the British Special Operations people arrived to tell us how stupid we had been . . .'

Major Archibald Lang found Kirby with Fausto, trying to organise an effective defence of the town around the football stadium to the east. He had a face like thunder. Apparently, he was the same with all the BLOs – there were six at that point, all attached to different partisan bands. He reserved his greatest wrath for Kirby, though. He dragged him back into town to the hotel where the Special Forces had set up their HQ. The two of them sat on a torn and dusty sofa in the tatty remnants of what had once been the lobby, amid half a dozen other people who studiously ignored them.

A lame child, thin and rickety from eating nothing but chickpeas and polenta for too long, came in to beg but was quickly hustled out. The joy of freedom was being replaced by the reality of being isolated and surrounded by hostility.

'You know who was on that Liberator?' asked Lang.

Kirby slumped back into the sofa, and felt the springs shift. One of them dug into his leg, but he stayed put. It might keep him alert. 'No.'

'Jimmy Morris.'

Kirby shook his head to show the name didn't mean much.

'You know who he was?'

'My replacement.'

'Your replacement. He'd never have let this shambles happen. He was worth twenty of you.'

Not dead he wasn't, Kirby wanted to say. He had a feeling Lang would argue even that point. His voice was quivering with barely controlled rage as it was.

'Who is in overall command of the military defence?' Lang asked.

'We don't know yet.'

'You don't know? It is five days in, man. Who is co-ordinating everything?'

Kirby was dog tired. Nobody was in overall control, because nobody could agree who it should be. The Communists – irritated at being excluded from the original surrender negotiations – thought that Fausto was a British agent. He thought the Communists were no better than bandits, mainly because in the past they had re-supplied themselves by raiding other partisans. The constant bickering by men with loaded guns was very hard on the nerves.

'I want you to come back to Bern with me.'

'No.'

'I'm not asking, Kirby.'

'He can't go with you.' They both looked up. It was Francesca, cigarette in her mouth, face looking every bit as drawn as Kirby's, dressed in green overalls three sizes too big, cinched in at the waist with a leather belt from the German stores. She crunched over the broken glass towards them and stood at Kirby's shoulder.

'And you are?' asked Lang.

'I am a lieutenant with Gruppo Fausto. As you know, Fausto doesn't speak English. We need Kirby.'

'I can get you another Italian speaker.'

'Fausto wants *him*. The men trust him now. He has killed Germans with them.' Mainly by firing down at a helpless convoy in the dark, but it was a start. 'You want to do something useful, Major, get us an airborne division to help defend the town.'

Kirby thought Lang was going to explode. 'You think we've got an airborne division to spare on you people?'

'We people,' she said with beautiful, drawn-out sarcasm, 'have expelled the Germans. If we keep them out, Italians will know it can be done.'

Lang took a deep breath. 'And if your town here and its post-liberation organisation' – his turn to lay on the scorn – 'is a paradigm for what will happen after the Germans have gone, I would say you can expect civil war and chaos for Italy, my dear.'

'Lieutenant My Dear,' she corrected. 'And he comes with me.' She grabbed Kirby by the shoulders, hauled him to his feet and ushered him outside. The last thing Kirby heard was Lang yelling about putting him on a charge.

'You're a bunch of clowns,' came the drawl from behind them as they walked down the street. Kirby turned. It was Hirschfield, an Office of Strategic Services man who had been another of the motley chorus advising against liberating the town. He fell in next to them. Kirby noticed he had an overnight bag in his hand. 'I told you, if you don't succeed, they'll hang you out to dry.' He veered off towards the station.

'Where are you going, Captain Hirschfield?' called out Francesca.

'Back to Switzerland, to tell Dulles you've got a circus here. Regular Barnum and Bailey.'

'Maybe,' she spat after him. 'But at least it's our circus.'

Hirschfield was still laughing when he disappeared from view.

Zopatti listened intently as I recounted the whole episode.

'He was right,' I said, much as I hated to admit it. 'Lang was right. The OSS guy was right. The Communists and the non-Communists could never agree. There was no single central command. Meanwhile, infuriated by the temerity of the partisans in taking a whole swathe of the country, the local German commander based here, at Novara, ordered Domodossola to be re-taken. It was – by armoured cars, tanks, mortars and artillery. We held out the perimeter as long as we could, but there was no way of moving men or supplies to where they were needed most. There were shells exploding over their heads and *still* the commanders were arguing about rank and authority! Anyway, the Germans were on the outskirts, moving into the town when we were at the railway station, ready for some sort of Alamo last stand. It was then I saw Nino Leone kill Fausto.'

Twenty-One

Italy, 1944

Kirby felt the air judder as it compressed even before he heard the whistle of the artillery round. 'Get down!' he yelled. A dozen men and women fell to the earth as one, hands over their heads. The 88 shell landed in the centre of the string of cafés on the far end of the railway piazza, sending glass, tables and chairs spiralling into the air, then crashing around them. When the smoke cleared, there was no front to the building that had housed the cafés. Kirby could see a body on the upper floor, gun still in his hand.

'Back to work!' yelled Fausto. He had sandbagged a crescent in front of the station and lined up his only field gun at the main street leading north. The air was full of the crackle of small-arms fire, with the occasional thump of a mortar round. On the outskirts were German armoured cars and half-tracks, picking their way through the defences. The main railway line had been cut at Varzo by *Alpini*. The only way out of Domodossola now was to Ascona, just outside Locarno, so a column of wounded were being loaded onto the small, blue electric train that ran through the mountains to the lakeside towns. Soon the power to that line would be gone.

Already scores of civilians had left for Switzerland, women and children mostly, with partisan escorts, trying to make it up hills hit by squalls of icy rain, then over passes filling with early snow. Kirby wondered how many of them would reach the border.

Pavel, Ragno, Francesca, Rosario and the others each chose a spot from which to make their final stand, positioning their weapons in a hollow at the top of the sandbags. Kirby looked up as he heard an aero-engine. A little Fieseler Storch spotter plane wobbled its way over town.

Fausto examined the defences and nodded, as if satisfied.

'One tank will blow this all away,' Kirby said.

'If we had anti-tank weapons . . .' Fausto began.

'Well, we haven't,' Kirby snapped back, tired of this constant refrain. 'And if someone had co-ordinated blowing all the bridges, they wouldn't have got tanks and armoured cars up here!'

'You are beginning to sound like your Major Lang.' Most of the outsiders, including Lang and his team, had pulled back out to Bern days previously, feeling fully justified that their dire warnings had come to pass. The Germans and fascists couldn't leave Domodossola free. It had to be destroyed, as an example.

Francesca came over and spoke in Fausto's ear, and he nodded. 'She is right. You must go.'

'What?' Kirby retorted.

'We will fight until we get an armistice like the Germans did. An honourable surrender. But you, you are a foreign spy. They will shoot you. Prefect Vezzalini has warned there will be reprisals.'

Another shell landed up by the *municipio*, its spot marked by a twisting column of smoke. 'I'll take my chances.'

Kirby felt the gun on the back of his neck. He could smell the oil. It was Ragno, with his brand new Sten.

'Get on the train to Ascona,' said Fausto. He pointed at the blue carriages. Its klaxon sounded as if in encouragement. 'We don't want to have to worry about you.'

'So you'll shoot me?' Kirby asked Fausto, brushing away the barrel of the boy's Sten.

'You are not wanted. It's our fight now. The British let us down. Everyone let us down.'

Kirby shook his head at the naivety of this. 'They were never going to send an airborne division—'

Fausto's face twisted into hatred. He made an effort to calm himself. He had honestly believed there would be an airdrop. 'Go. Leave this to Italians.'

Kirby looked at Francesca, but she lowered her eyes and nodded.

'Come with me,' he said to her suddenly and Fausto snorted. Now she shook her head. 'You said yourself the fascists have promised reprisals. This is madness,' Kirby pleaded.

The Excelsior Hotel seemed to shudder as an artillery round went in through the roof. There was a pause before the centre floors dissolved into a flower of masonry dust. The heat of the blast swept over them. The little Storch came back and Kirby raised his pistol and fired three ineffectual shots. He, more than anyone there, knew just what a waste of time and ammunition it all was.

'Get on the train, Kirby,' said Fausto. 'I have business. I can't waste any more time with you.'

He made a signal and Ragno grabbed his sleeve and pulled Kirby down the platform towards the train. As he went, he saw the figure of Nino emerge from the smoke drifting along the avenue to the north. Fausto hopped over the barrier of sandbags to meet him.

'Hear that?' asked Ragno, a tremor of fear in his voice.

Kirby stopped and listened. There was a faint squeak of tank treads, just audible above the whine of rifle shots. Rosario and Francesca came across to make sure Kirby didn't do anything stupid and helped usher him down the platform. 'This isn't fair,' he said to them.

'It's very fair, Jack Kirby,' said Rosario. 'You did your part.'

Reluctantly he stepped into the first carriage, finding a place among the outstretched legs of the wounded, his eyes drawn back to the town, now wreathed in a haze. Up in the hills, he could see muzzle flashes. Mortars were falling on the football stadium now, and fires had started. He heard the deep *whumpf* of an 88 shell nearby. The tank was firing.

'Come with me,' he said again to Francesca, but again she shook her head. 'You don't want to die. He's a fool.'

'He's my fool.'

'You said this was your circus – look how it's ending.'

She stared at her feet, and he couldn't see the expression on her face.

'Come with me.'

'Her place is here,' said Rosario irritably. 'And nobody is going to die.'

Kirby took out his Colt, checked the safety was on and tossed it to her. She caught it with her right hand and smiled her thanks. 'Good luck, Kirby,' she said.

'You too, Lieutenant.'

'Come back.'

Before he could answer he heard the sound of shouting, just as the little train jerked into motion. The partisans turned and watched the same scene as Kirby did, except his view was receding rapidly.

Out on the square Fausto had Nino by the lapel, his Labora machine pistol under the lawyer's chin. He was yelling in his face, and Kirby imagined he could see the angry spittle flying from Fausto's mouth. He pushed the barrel up into the fleshy folds of Nino's throat.

The shot was lost in the noise of the train and the detonations of ordnance, but just before they rounded the first bend into the railway yards, where the fascists had broken free from their sheds and were jeering the trainload of fleeing partisans, Kirby saw Fausto stagger back, clutching the stomach wound from Nino's pistol, and fall into the gutter.

Twenty-Two

'But your friends survived,' said Zopatti when I had finished.

'With Fausto gone, the fight went out of them. As you know, Domodossola was unusual in that there weren't wholesale reprisals. In other places, thousands of partisans and civilians were executed. Not there.'

'And you?'

'When we arrived at Locarno, everyone was interned except Swiss citizens. After a few weeks, I was transferred to Basle and debriefed. I got back to Britain eventually.' I never flew serious combat after that, though. They had me ferrying replacement aircraft around Europe, doing the odd high-altitude photo-recce. Nobody ever shot at me again in anger. I sort of missed it.

'Why didn't they kill Nino?' asked Zopatti. 'Your friends at the railway station?'

'I don't know. I was too far away. Fausto had a gut wound, they were trying to save him. More shells fell. It was just chaos. Nino slipped away.'

'Or perhaps they did kill him for Fausto after all.'

'What?'

'Perhaps they did take revenge for the death of this Fausto, but twenty years later. They see him at the commemoration, they follow him, bang. Is that possible?'

'It is possible.' I could imagine Rosario or Pavel doing it. The loyalty they felt towards their leader made it believable that, even after two decades, they wouldn't blink at murder. 'Although why they'd put him in my plane is anybody's guess.'

'Why would he take the risk of coming back at all?' mused Zopatti.

'Beats the shit out of me,' I said.

One of the guards arrived with a note and Zopatti frowned at it before he screwed it into a ball. 'Your lawyer is here.'

'He took his time,' I said as casually as I could. I didn't have a lawyer, as far as I was aware.

'Yes. It was probably the sex change that did it. They take a while.'

It was a she, then. 'Am I free to go?'

'After you have signed a statement, yes. But you are not free to leave Italy.'

'No. Of course.'

The chair scraped along the concrete floor as Zopatti rose, but something occurred to him that made him sit back down. 'You know, even though we were on opposite sides, I always thought the partisans who took Domodossola were very brave.' From his inside pocket, he produced an envelope and threw it on the table. 'And, it transpired, very resourceful.'

I didn't open the envelope there and then, I was too wary about it being a stunt for the cameras. An hour later, I was presented with a transcript of my conversation with the Dottore, which I read carefully to make sure they hadn't inserted the line: *Then I killed Nino and hid him in my plane and forgot all about him until I opened the door*, but I couldn't find it anywhere so I scribbled my initials on each page and left.

Francesca was waiting at the front desk. She had clearly been giving the clerk a hard time, because he seemed more pleased to see me than she was. 'Mr Kirby, at last,' she said. 'Shall we go?'

I leered at the clerk. 'I need a decent cup of coffee.' That told him.

As we walked to her Alfa, she asked: 'How are you?'

'Spooked.'

'You stood me up the other night. I thought you were coming to the dinner.'

'I wasn't in the mood.'

'Me neither. I left early.'

'How did you know where—'

'I called your hotel, then the airfield, who put me through to Furio, who told me about the body in the plane and the arrests. They treat you OK?'

'As well as the Secret Service can treat you.'

'Secret . . . ? What the hell were they doing here?'

'You're the lawyer, so it seems. You never mentioned that in your curriculum vitae.'

She climbed behind the wheel while I folded myself stiffly into the passenger side. She gunned the engine in the way that is hard to resist in an Alfa sports and spun out of the *questura* car park, heading north.

'Things happened while you were away. I became an advocate. I am mostly corporate, not criminal. I work for the Hope Foundation as well. Most of what I did back there,' she indicated the police station with her thumb, 'was bluster and the name-dropping of Riccardo's more influential friends. But I am qualified. You thought I had become a little housewife with a rich husband? All tennis and tanning?' She raised an eyebrow and one corner of her mouth, which dimpled her cheek in a way that melted my heart.

'I never thought you were a little anything, Lieutenant.'

She gave me a cold look. Nobody had called her that in quite some time, and maybe it no longer sat comfortably, but I still remembered her getting ready to die behind a line of sandbags, Stens, Colts and Berettas against tanks. In the end, it didn't come to that. Once again, the priests went to work and the survivors of Gruppo Fausto had negotiated a safe passage to Lake Orta and avoided imprisonment and execution. The fascists, with the eyes of the Swiss Red Cross on them, had kept to their word for once.

We skirted the lake, its water glistening in the late-afternoon sunshine, the nearby islands with their vast terraced gardens and opulent palaces looking serene and peaceful. The Borromeans. The islands were named after the wealthy Milanese dynasty which had owned the fishing rights in the lake for four centuries. They still did, providing a nice steady family income.

'You look worried.'

'Well, it's not every day you find a corpse in your plane. Especially one you thought deserved to die anyway.'

'Nino? It was a long time ago, Jack.'

Maybe, but the man had killed her lover. I would be surprised if she could dismiss it like that. A thought came to mind – maybe she was part of a Gruppo Fausto revenge pact – but I quickly dismissed it. Instead, I repeated what Lindy had said. 'But not that far away.'

'No. Not far away at all.'

She squealed the tyres on a hairpin, and I felt the back of the car break away and fishtail. I held the dash as surreptitiously as I could. As she caught the drift with a flick of the polished wooden steering wheel, she noticed and smiled. 'Relax.' We drove through Stresa, its piazzas now full of tourist cafés and Coca Cola hoardings and handwritten *Wir sprechen Deutsch* signs dangling on door-handles. Some people could forgive and forget, especially when the customer was paying with Deutschmarks. Perhaps, like them, Francesca had successfully consigned Fausto and his war to the distant past. Maybe Lindy and I should take a leaf from that book and walk away.

'Where's your villa?'

'Back there.' She indicated the shoreline to the south. 'Riccardo is at home, otherwise . . .'

'Sure.' I was still fairly certain that the three who beat me up had been Riccardo's lads, and the incident was a response to my few hours alone with Mrs Conti at San Marco. It was a nice kiss, but the final bill was a little hefty. Still, that seemed par for the course with Francesca.

We crossed the bridge over the eastern reaches of the lake and turned left towards Domodossola. 'I'm that way,' I said, pointing to the right.

'Like I said, relax.'

The wheels locked as she braked hard and spun us onto a small side turning between a couple of neglected vineyards, kicking up stones and a spray of grit. 'Oops, nearly missed it.' We began to climb through a series of switchbacks, past flinty rockfaces covered in moss, a spring gushing out of the earth every ten yards or so. The air was dank and refreshing against my face, the sky occasionally shrinking to a long gash high above us as we plunged into a gorge. I did as she suggested and tried to enjoy the ride without thinking too much.

'Plant pots,' she said after a while.

'Sorry?'

She indicated the shape of Mount Rosa over to the west. 'Look at the sides.'

There were several big scars disfiguring its slopes, what must be massive scoops close up, although from a distance they looked like the fingermarks on the side of a kid's sandcastle. 'They take out the granite to make plant pots and chopping boards and what do you call them . . . kitchen worktops. They think the mountain is infinite. Already it is changing profile. In thirty years, it will look like an apple core.'

'Who does it?'

She smiled, full of sadness. 'Oh, one of my husband's subsidiaries.'

There was little traffic and she danced the car through the turns and over the bridges that spanned the deep crevices sliced into the mountainsides. I couldn't help thinking how much more fun it would be on a good racing motorcycle.

There were villages huddled around their belltowers every few kilometres, but they seemed moribund, with all the gaiety of the graveyard. Not so much as a café was open. There was the occasional black-clad crone sitting in a doorway, who either stared at us impassively or raised a hand in silent welcome, albeit without much enthusiasm. Dogs yapped at us or hurled themselves through the air until caught short by their wire, snarling after us as if their tethering was our doing. The few men we saw were chopping wood, stacking willow branches ready for drying, digging drainage ditches, all too busy to pay us much attention. It didn't look like I was going to get my coffee. I doubted we were going to come across many *Wir sprechen Deutsch* signs in this neck of the woods.

Ahead of us, I could see the tooth-like guardians of the Val Grande, getting closer. We were on the opposite side of the area from where we had laid out the drop zone for EH-148. This was the scrubbier end of the region, where the trees barely covered the lower slopes of the mountains. Only walkers and naturalists came up here. What were we doing here, apart from admiring the view?

A thought suddenly occurred to me. Perhaps Francesca knew where the Liberator was.

We pulled over onto a rough verge dotted with stunted olive and fig trees, the remnants of an attempt to make this land productive. We were within walking distance of the ridge called the Corni di Nibbio, marking the place where two glaciers had collided and created a long knife-edge from the earth. Over the aeons, wind and rain had flattened the top, leaving a long, natural viewing platform. As I stretched my limbs, grateful for fresh clean air, not to mention freedom, Francesca swapped her lawyer's shoes for something more sturdy, took a small pack from the boot of the Alfa, slung it over her shoulder and signalled we climb, following a zig-zag stone path up towards the ledge. She moved with a confident grace, her feet finding solid ground each time. I simply followed in her footsteps. At the top, she indicated a rocky outcrop and sat, cross-legged.

The shadows were lengthening, and much of the vista below us was in shade from the mountains. I could see the rapids and waterfalls of the Val Grande River quite clearly; some of the upper alpine meadows, dotted with dilapidated *baiti* and *rifugi* – wooden cabins and stone huts – were still glowing in the afternoon sunshine. Immediately below us were overgrown stone ramparts, one of the chain of forts built across this wilderness in World War One, in anticipation of an Austro-German attack on Italy through Switzerland which never came; the Austrians had struck further east. There had been dozens of these strongholds, some high on vantage-points, other cleverly carved from the rock and moulded into the cliff, hard to spot until you stumbled on them. These latter were now slowly crumbling back into the landscape, and were even more difficult to locate.

From her pack, Francesca took a silver screw-top flask and poured me a cup of inky black coffee. Still standing, I reached down, took it and sipped. 'Thanks. I needed that.'

She poured herself one and gripped it two-handed as she gazed into the distance. From somewhere far away came the faint sounds of an Italian autumn, the flat crack of a shotgun, the snapping of a pruning hook on wood. This was the time of grape-picking, vine-stripping, fruit-squeezing, hare-hunting, mushroom-gathering and olive-pressing, and even up here, the air held the tang of woodsmoke. Like everywhere else in Europe, Italy was losing its seasonal rhythms to the artificiality of modern life, but the battle was not yet lost.

'You think the plane is out there?' she asked.

'I was hoping you would tell me,' I said.

She did a good imitation, if that's what it was, of surprise. 'I have no idea. Why should I know?'

'I'm clutching at straws.'

'So is your friend. That poor girl. So much riding on the search.'

'You think I shouldn't do it?'

'Unless you can guarantee results.'

'That's going to be difficult without my Beech.' She looked up quizzically. 'It's a murder scene. Or at least a crime scene – Nino was probably killed elsewhere.'

'How can you know that?'

'The plane's cabin interior is pretty clean. If they'd shot him in there . . . well, you know.'

She nodded to show I didn't have to paint a picture of splatter marks, and poured herself a second cup from the flask. She knew exactly how much mess a gunshot wound to the head can make. 'Can you get another plane?'

'I could,' I said without much enthusiasm. If I was going to fly between those peaks, skimming the vegetation, and riding the eddies and vortices that played like mischievous sprites across the Alps and their foothills, I wanted to be in a plane I knew instinctively, one I felt at home in, a ride that was good and steady like the Beech. 'Francesca, why are we here? It's a nice view, good coffee, fine company but—' I plucked at my shirt and wrinkled my nose. 'A shower would have been nice first.'

'I need you to listen to me.'

I crouched down on my haunches, finished the coffee, threw the dregs into the grass, and handed the cup back for a refill. 'I'm all ears.'

She pointed north-west, beyond the mountain known as Pedun. 'When we were out there that night, you didn't miss the plane.'

I shook my head in sadness. She was trying to assuage my guilt. A kind but misguided gesture. 'No matter how you look at it, I was somewhat distracted.'

'Maybe. But I didn't have your full attention.'

'It felt like it.'

'You think I don't know if a man is fully engaged with me?' She handed the full cup back. 'You picked up the first sounds of the engine, I am certain.'

'Are you trying to make me feel better after all this time?'

'If you'd come back earlier, I might have told you the truth.'

I wasn't certain what she was talking about, so I said: 'Why didn't you tell me the truth back then?'

'During the war? Orders. I was a lieutenant, remember? Fausto's lieutenant.'

I suddenly felt cold. A wind had appeared, blowing from the north, off the glaciers we could see as white waves over the Swiss border. I zipped up my jacket. 'What *is* the truth of it, Francesca?'

She reached up and pulled her hair back, expertly knotting it, a little distraction so she didn't have to look me in the eye. 'That it wasn't your fault. Fausto and the others . . . they never lit their beacons at all. You were the only one who did. If the plane crashed because of anyone, it was because of Fausto.'

Twenty-Three

I wasn't sure where the next few hours went after Francesca took me to that ridge and kicked the ground from beneath me. I couldn't recall being dropped off by her at the Hotel Cannero, nor saying goodbye to her. I lay on my bed in shock for what seemed like five minutes, but was probably much longer.

From the hotel, I made calls to check that Furio and Lindy were OK, and I explained why we couldn't fly, and wouldn't be able to for the foreseeable future. I offered to return Lindy her money, to call the whole thing off, but she refused, which was good, because I no longer had it. I even suggested she find herself another pilot, but she gave me a 'we're all in this together' speech and suggested she come over and get me drunk.

It was tempting, but I was a grown-up now, and I told her I could manage that part all by myself.

I didn't. I went down to the bar and shocked Maria by ordering a Coca Cola and asking for a pen and paper. I doodled for half an hour, writing down names, putting a line through them, or question marks.

Why would Fausto sabotage the drop of supplies? I had asked Francesca that question.

He wanted the supplies, she had answered, but he didn't want the man. He was gambling that, without flares, they would drop the canisters blind; it wouldn't be the first time. He'd take a chance on finding them. Supplies were one thing, but the Liberator crew would never turf out a senior BLO into a dark and stormy night with no DZ. There was a good chance, then, that Fausto and his group would get a result – the ordnance they wanted, without the interfering Englishman. If someone tried to infiltrate him over the Alps later, well, they'd deal with that at the time.

That was why they hadn't wanted me along that night, but I'd insisted. So they did the next best thing – put me to the south with Francesca, where I couldn't see that their flares weren't lit.

Here was the big question, the one I was too cowardly to ask. Was that whole business out in the ferns with Francesca her way of distracting me, of trying to stop me lighting my flare? If it was, it didn't succeed. I'd snapped out of it in time to get my signal going. In a way, though, it would have been better if her ploy had worked – the one single source had obviously confused the pilot enough for him to come round for a second view. If it had been all dark, he might well have dumped the canisters and headed on back. Whichever way you added it up, it was my stupid fault that those men on the Liberator had died. I drew nine little black crosses along the bottom of the sheet.

When I ran out of paper and searched my jacket pockets, I found the envelope Zopatti had given me. Before opening it I looked around, unable to shake the feeling of being watched. All I could see close by were the two ancient women who apparently came every season, wrinkled biddies sipping *negronis*. I somehow doubted they were SISDe plants.

I slit open the envelope and took out the three pages within. They had been torn from catalogues, one of them French, one English, the other, with prices quoted in dollars, probably American. I'd like to pretend I recognised the items that were circled in red pen right away, but I had to read the inscriptions.

A rock-crystal flask, with gold crucifix, a reliquary which, the description said, was inlaid with precious stones and enamels, and a liturgical ivory comb. The reserves on all three were in the thousands of dollars, pounds and francs. What was a reliquary? I had no idea. I folded the pages and put them away, and helped myself to a Scotch from behind the bar. I might not have a clue, but I knew a skydiver who did.

For someone like me, who was used to the dark satanic motorcycle factories of the British Midlands, Moto Guzzi came as something of a shock. Situated at Mandello del Lario in a series of tall, mustard-coloured, flat-fronted buildings, it backed onto a huge concourse which overlooked Lake Como, a place even more breathtaking than Maggiore. This was a part of the earth where, it seemed, God got the combination of water, mountains and sky just right.

Before going to Milan, I took a very expensive cab across to see Ragno at MG. He was on the third floor, a big empty space with makeshift offices around two walls; there was a gleaming red Stornello bike at one end and a gold Falcon at the other, both in Perspex cases. In the centre of the room stood a wooden packing crate, bound with wire stays, and next to it, a machine under a thick green shroud.

Ragno was sipping coffee, looking out of the window; he was dressed in his best overalls, a variety of tools in the top pocket. When I stepped from the freight elevator, he threw his arms open and walked towards me, ready for a hug.

'Ribs still not good,' I warned him.

He settled for shaking my hand. 'Nino?'

I sighed. 'It wasn't me.'

'It wasn't me either.' He laughed. 'But part of me wishes—'

'Don't even think it. There's the cold clammy hand of SISDe on this.'

He blanched. 'Shit. Why?'

'I don't know. That's the problem with the Secret Service. They don't like sharing information.'

'You enjoy the ceremony?'

I made a non-committal gesture. 'Enjoy? Can you enjoy such a thing?'

'I still miss him.'

'Fausto?'

A nod. 'You know my father had been shot by the fascists. I was an orphan. Fausto took me in, trained me, gave me a gun. Everyone else said I was too young, couldn't be trusted. And I was just a kid. But I would have died for that man.'

In the absence of anything to say, I put a hand on his shoulder and squeezed it. Then I changed the subject, like an emotionally stunted Englishman should. 'Is this it?'

I pointed at the crate and he beamed. 'Yes.'

Ragno pulled out wire-cutters, clipped the stays, and yanked away the wooden sides and the big foam slabs of packing. Underneath was a Kirby CrossCountry, the motorbike I had ridden round the IOM mountain course. Apart from a thin tear of oil from the crankcase, it was as good as new. Ragno had arranged for the Moto Guzzi delivery people to pick it up on a run to the UK. I pulled away some more packing material. Spare tyres, big diamond-studded Avons for off-road work. Thanks, Dad.

'Looks better than I remembered,' he said.

'Yes,' I agreed. 'It'll be perfect. Thank you, Ragno, I appreciate it.'

'*No problema*. At least this looks like a real bike.'

I saw him glance at the shrouded motorcycle and asked, 'What is that?'

His mouth crumpled. 'That is the future.' He jerked at a corner of the material and the sheet snapped off. I didn't say anything. 'Go on,' he prompted. 'Say what you are thinking.'

'That's a Guzzi?'

He let out a long heartfelt sigh. 'It's called the Dingo. Appropriate, eh?'

It was some sort of scooter/light bike hybrid, and next to it, the CrossCountry glowed like the statue of *David* or the *Mona Lisa*.

'But,' I spluttered, 'what about the Vs?' The big V engine was what you bought a Guzzi for. Anything else, you might as well get a Vespa or Lambretta.

Ragno shrugged. 'Same thing is happening here as in England.'

'The Japanese?'

He shook his head. 'Well, we have to blame someone. Tell me – why do people buy motorbikes?'

I shrugged. 'Freedom, speed, excitement . . .'

'No. No, we think that because that is what *we* like, but really it's because they're cheap. People buy them because they are cheap to buy and cheap to run. So, now they have money, they want cars. A little Fiat Topolino perhaps, to take the family, or perhaps a Ford. So much better, easier than a sidecar.'

I nodded. It made sense. 'So we are blaming our bikes, when—'

'The market will shrink. Bound to. Those who love bikes will always buy bikes. Those who have them because they can't afford anything else . . . Tell your father – get into cars.'

'But this?' I indicated the Dingo.

He winked. 'Oh, don't worry. Guzzi will make big bikes again. Just not as many as we have in the past. This is like Rolls-Royce making a Mini. Stupid. I can't look at it.' He pulled the cover over the scooter again. 'So shall we put some petrol in your steel beauty and see where that oil is coming from and get you on your way?'

'Thanks, Ragno.'

He slapped me on the back. 'Always a pleasure to help Jack Kirby.' There was a pause and I considered asking him about that night when the Lib went down, but I knew what he would say – that he was just a kid who knew nothing. I let the moment pass.

Ragno fetched a drip tray and a box of tools and hunched down beside the CrossCountry. 'Tell me something, Jack.'

'If I can.'

'After we spoke at the TT, I heard people say you had raced there before the war.'

'Yes.'

'You never told me.'

'I told you I had raced.'

'But the TT . . .'

I didn't bother mentioning that when I met him, he didn't know a TT from a tea dance. He can only have discovered the mythology surrounding the event after the war.

'I looked you up,' he went on. 'I found your post-war races, but nothing before.'

'I was there, Ragno. I'm your original Ghost Rider.'

He stopped undoing a hexagonal bolt. 'You want to explain that?'

I didn't. I was impatient to get away, but it seemed rude not to, so I told him.

Twenty-Four

I told Ragno about the race, but I found it hard, at first, to recapture the feeling, to get inside the skin of the young lad who was hammering round the mountain course of the Isle of Man in 1939. Yet as I spoke, the words slowly led me back there, until I could feel the wind on my face, the tightness of the goggles.

My voice fell into the rhythm of the road, and I was back accelerating down the dip of Bray Hill for the fifth time, feeling the front wheel go light on the bumps where the road junctions meet the course, my teeth chattering from the vibration. Then I was up the incline to the brow, where I opened the throttle and felt the bike hang in the air.

I leaned forward as the motorcycle thumped down then gripped the tarred road surface, and accelerated towards the left-hander at Selborne. It was a messy execution, and butterflies flooded my stomach.

The field had thinned by this time – accidents, refuelling cock-ups, mechanical failure. *Settle down*, I told myself. It was the next to last lap, fuel load well down – the bike must have shed 50 pounds in weight since the pit stop. I knew this was my best chance at getting into the record books.

I took her down to the right-hander, making sure the bike didn't drift to the left too much, where the wheels could be snatched from under me by the camber and the ruts. I remember, sometimes I wished I carried a little more weight, more bulk on my skinny young body, to help heave the machine. 'It'll come,' my father used to say, 'all too quickly, and then you'll wish you had a little less of it. For the moment,' he said, 'you'll just have to make do with ordinary, everyday skill.'

Full throttle, holding on as the bike juddered over the uneven road surface. Just a touch of adverse camber, correct for it, and past 80 mph. Hedges, the odd road sign, manhole covers, gutter gratings, access roads, sandbags, hay bales, all zipped by, only half-registered at that speed.

And then we were at Quarterbridge, one of the worst bends on the circuit. If a rider wasn't careful here, he'd end up sliding through on his arse. Down to first, then up and out, pouring the power back on. I felt the back wheel struggle for traction, find it, and then I was ready for the change down for Braddan Bridge, all the way to second.

I was at Union Mills and there was a rider behind me, at my shoulder, but I wasn't worried about that. I was alone out there, just me and the machine and a road that was trying to kill me. It had claimed many others in the past; there would be more in the future.

Away from the Railway Inn, accelerating again, smiling as the engine revved smoothly, and I could sense I was drawing away from the challenger, pulling up the long climb to Ballahutchin. Perfect. *Don't get cocky*, I reminded myself.

Greeba Bridge – brake, brake, change down, two gears, then back on the gas before another rapid deceleration down to second for Ballacraine. I was sweating now, steaming in the leathers. *Bang.* A crash as the suspension bottomed on Doran's and the pipes sparked in protest as they were dragged along the blacktop. Damn. Fortunately, the lack of fuel on board meant it was just a glancing blow. I was lucky that time.

Laurel Bank loomed, the raw rockface waiting to take the head off any careless rider. Down to second, then ready for the left and right. Throw the bike, but not too much. My dad always said it was the kind of feel pilots had to have when they were juddering on the edge of a stall, acutely aware of where that fine line was. I could certainly do that in the cockpit. I just hoped I could here. Nine miles gone of the fifth lap.

As I talked through the race to Ragno, a quarter of a century later I could still feel the glow of pleasure at the delicate waltz I took at Black Dub before the swing into Glen Helen, and the fluttering in the stomach as I crossed the thin trickle of a stream and opened her up at Barregarrow, the spectators flashing by inches from me, a blur of smiles and cheers and waves. Then I was at the Mitre Hotel and there was another knot of onlookers, and the bike was flowing now through the bends, but I knew I would have to drop anchor for Ballaugh Bridge. Keep her straight and true for the jump.

Into Quarry Bends and Sulby Bridge, both of which have proved disastrous for many a rider. I cranked the bike over, getting my knee down, the unforgiving road surface humming a grain of sand's thickness from flesh and bone; the nervousness was there again, but fleeting, and it disappeared as I straightened. Seventeen miles had gone.

Now I was ready for Ramsey. I took the School House in third and remembered to breathe, to calm everything down. You took this section slow, watching for the town's lethal gutters and gratings. I picked up a signal from the team at Ramsey – a large W-8, showing that Woods was in the lead by eight seconds. I wasn't racing against Woods, though. I was racing against myself.

Now the Gooseneck, and Jesus that was a sly one, a hairpin going uphill; you had to come right down to first, and make sure you kept the line. There was Julie at the bend, where it was slow enough for her to be seen, holding up my unofficial time for the previous lap. Twenty-five minutes and three seconds. Not good enough, boy. Ever since Daniell bust the twenty-five-minute barrier, it had become the marker, the line you had to cross to be taken seriously as a contender. Julie looked magnificent, the breeze tugging at her floral dress, the blonde hair coaxed into cascading curls.

There was no mist hanging around, clear skies and no excuse for not going for it. More power on the Mountain Mile, where I got a chance to let my aching arms relax. Too much, perhaps. The wind caught me just as I came up for Mountain Box. I was already nearly on the grass, lining up for the turn, when I felt the big gust buffet me, pushing me across towards the fence. I cursed in language that would have earned me a clip round the ear from Dad, but I got her back on line.

I twisted on the power and risked a glance down at the speedo needle, swinging over to one-fifteen, one-twenty as I streaked on down towards Craig-Ny-Baa, my cheeks and lips stretched backwards by the slipstream. Twenty-five minutes or bust, I told myself over and over again.

It'd be sub twenty-five, or I'd die trying.

Ragno, satisfied he had found the leak from an ill-seated gasket, straightened it and applied a dob of sealant to be on the safe side, before reassembling the crankcase. He looked up and said: 'Did you make it?'

I nodded. 'Yes. I broke it, came in under twenty-five minutes by half a second.'

'But?'

'But I was too young.' Impatient to do the race, not willing to wait another year, I'd persuaded Dad to enter me when I was still seventeen. Or as I told him, seventeen and almost three-quarters.

'The age limit was?'

'Eighteen.' How they found out, I never knew, but my effort was scrubbed from the rolls. Even then, the TT was getting a reputation as a fast way to a coffin. They knew if it was discovered they were letting in under-age riders, there would be an outcry. So my time was buried, struck from the books. I was banned for a couple of years, and Kirby Motorcycles was fined. Only people like Geoff Davison remembered it now. And my father. But, by God, I'd done it.

'So as far as the official history is concerned, it never happened?'

'That's right.'

'Tough. An unsung hero – is that what you say?'

'Yes. Story of my life. By the time my ban was lifted, the war was here.'

'I know that part,' he said with a grin. He stood and wiped his hands as he indicated the CrossCountry. 'That should be fine. Ready to ride. Where are you taking her?'

'Milan,' I said. 'See a man about a dog.'

Ragno looked puzzled. 'What kind of dog?'

'That,' I assured him, 'will be my first question.'

'A reliquary is a receptacle for keeping religious relics in. The bones of saints, the hair of Christ, that sort of thing.'

Professor Gianlorenzo Borromini was examining the three torn pages that the SISDe man had given me. He was head of Art History at Catholic University in Milan and also one of the founders of the skydiving club. He was around my age, but athletic and dynamic. He worked from the Palazzo Lanzone, just south of the Museo Archeologico. His office, which I expected to be overflowing with dusty tomes and unattributed El Grecos, was clean, simple and furnished with sleek modern furniture in light wood and steel, with modern art – well, blocks of solid colour that I guessed would pass as modern art – rather than Old Masters on the walls. I had trouble taking my eyes off a sculpture next to his desk, an assemblage of mirrors that reflected themselves.

'Michelangelo Pistoletto,' he explained, catching my glance. '*A Structure for Measuring Infinity*. You know his work?'

'No.'

'You will,' he said with absolute certainty.

I switched back to the matters at hand. 'And the comb?'

'Used to prepare the priest for Mass. Combing the priest's hair became common in the fourth century, and stayed that way for a thousand years or more. The Greeks still do it, I believe. The flask may well have held the wine. Except it is a very beautiful example, because it still has this gold cross, like a necklace, around it. Usually they were separated a long time ago.'

He turned over the pages I had given him. 'So, these are three small auction houses. London, Zürich and New York. Not your Sotheby's.'

'You can tell?'

He waved an arm, indicating down the hall. 'I can show you hundreds of similar catalogues in the archives, Jack. The thing is, although not top-flight houses, this is where the real bargain-hunter would go.'

'Or the man trying to keep a low profile.'

He pursed his lips. 'Perhaps. Is this a new sideline now we are to lose our club?'

'No. Someone gave them to me, with no explanation.'

'All three items are medieval. And they are generic, rather than specific. You know what I am saying?'

'That nobody could prove you didn't own them?'

'Precisely. You try and sell a Rembrandt, or a Bellini, the chances are someone will know its provenance, its history: when it last came on the market, where it has been for the last hundred years, or at least when it was last seen. But these, the chances of them being previously catalogued specifically are slim. Of course, there are forgeries of such things, but given the reserves, I suspect the sellers sincerely believe them to be genuine.'

'Is there anything else you can tell me?'

'Without seeing the actual pieces? Not really.'

I got up and shook his hand. 'Thank you, Professor.'

'Any time, Jack. We should talk about a new airfield.'

'We will. For next year. I promise.'

I turned to go and he said, 'I . . . well, there is one thing. So obvious to me, but . . .' He put his fingers together in a pyramid.

'What?'

'Well, the enamel on the reliquary suggests it was made in Ravenna. Perhaps the twelfth century. The scene carved onto the ivory of the liturgical comb is the martyrdom of Saint Justina of Padua. Justina was a Christian martyr who died under the persecutions of the Roman Emperor Maximian. The shape of the cross around the flask is also distinctive. All three, they are Italian artefacts, Jack, taken from Italian churches.'

I smiled. 'Yes. Thanks, Professor. I think I had guessed that.'

I walked down the steps of the Istituto d'Arte and hesitated for a few moments before putting my helmet on. I wore it in the cities even though it wasn't yet the law. I'd been in the country long enough to know it wasn't worth the risk of getting brain damage from some driver who was too busy checking that his new sunglasses looked cool to notice a mere bike rider. As I fastened the chinstrap, I went over what I had discovered. So what did we have? Three pictures of medieval works of art that Zopatti had suggested were somehow tied in with the partisans. Very resourceful, he had said.

Europe was still awash with stolen and confiscated artworks, even ones from looted churches, although their routing was usually through Switzerland or Spain or Portugal – the big repositories where the Nazis shipped their booty.

Zopatti was suggesting that it wasn't only the Germans who had their hands in the collection box. Well, he certainly had my attention, which is what he intended. The bastard also had my plane, so I was going to have to talk to him and find out what garden path he was leading me up.

I had just checked the oil leak had stopped, kicked the Cross-Country into life and moved into the traffic when, with a backward glance – the bike had no mirrors – I spotted Gutbucket stepping out of a black Lancia and heading for the Palazzo I had just left. The Lancia pulled away from the kerb and took a position fifteen feet to the rear of me. I could guess who was behind the wheel; I'd been followed by the men who stole my pistol.

Twenty-Five

I headed north, the National Science Museum on my left, the castle ahead, a Lancia Flaminia with tinted windows some way behind. It was a big car, hard to manoeuvre in the swarms of buzzing scooters, but I didn't try anything stupid like attempting to outrun it as the road curved right and opened out into the Piazza Sant' Ambrogio with its beautiful church and the monastery that housed the archaeological museum just ahead to the right. They hardly registered; I was in no mood for sightseeing. I had to make a decision, and fast.

Why were they following me? If they wanted another slice of me, they knew where I was staying. No, they had to be interested in where I was going. Which meant they either wanted my new bike, or the pages I had shown to the Prof. I didn't want them to have either.

The traffic on the Corso Magenta would be heavy – coaches and hire cars and taxis, all trying to get close to the re-built Santa Maria delle Grazie for a glimpse of Leonardo da Vinci's *The Last Supper* which had, fortunately, been painted in the only part of the church to survive an Allied bomb in 1943.

I revved the bike and weaved into the scooter pack, wondering whether I should make a left or a right, when the lights changed to red. I was too far away to jump them, so I made do with looping around the outside of the other riders and between two saloons to get near the front for a decent getaway.

I leaned over and checked the situation behind in the wing mirror of one of the cars bracketing me. The Lancia Flaminia isn't an easy car to miss, but even so, it seemed inordinately large in the frame. It was close.

Ahead of me, there was the usual parp of impatient horns at those who hadn't roared away from the lights as if they were in a time trial. I watched the twin streams approach each other from left and right and clicked down on the gear lever into first. My left hand holding the clutch began to ache. I took the revs up and let my fingers open.

The power snatched in and I caught it and let it drive the back wheel. No spin, no wheelies, just a nice smooth curve of torque. I felt my elbow clip a mirror as it pulled me forward, but ignored it. I was committed now. Horns started bleating at me even before I had made it onto the junction. I was about to give them something worthwhile to protest at.

I reached the traffic coming from the left first, a line of scooters, and I took them in two easy swings, shifting this way and that, dodging a little Fiat. I felt the bike judder as my knee caught the side of a Beetle. I rattled across the tramlines, around the rear of a tram, a line of appalled faces peering down at me from the windows, slowed for an Alfetta that hadn't even seen me and I was gone, heading up towards the station and the Parco Sempione, where I'd make some cut-throughs that no bulbous Lancia could follow.

I could feel air flapping into my jeans from a rip, thanks to the VW, and now my elbow hurt from clipping the mirror. I risked a backward glance towards the fading sounds of angry horns. There were no cops in hot pursuit, and no sign of the Lancia. I revved the bike and bumped down four steps onto a gravel path and swung into the park. Even as I felt a twinge in my spine from the jolts, I allowed myself the hint of a smile.

I called the Professor from the phone box at the café at the little airport of Bresso, which is actually within Milan's city limits, to the north of Ospedale Maggiore Niguarda. I had logged in at the reception desk when I visited him at the Scuola; Gutbucket would have been able to read the entry after slipping the security guard a *bustarella*, a little packet. So I had to warn him that they would know who I had seen.

'Listen, I'm sorry, you may get a visitor.'

'I have already,' he chuckled. 'Very interesting.'

'You OK?'

'Me? Of course. And you?'

'I think I broke every traffic law in the city.'

Another chuckle. I had to admire his composure when someone had been to his office to lean on him. 'Which makes you an honorary Milanese.'

'What did he want?'

'Your portly friend? To know what we were discussing.'

'And?'

'And I told him to go to hell.'

'Thanks, Professor.'

'Oh, it was a pleasure. You know —' He named a prominent media figure in the town, one who was reputed to be as ruthless in private life as he was in his professional dealing.

'Not personally. But, yeah.'

'I advise on his art collection now and then. Left to his own devices, he has appalling taste, but I quite like him. I told my visitor I was a friend of the family. A close friend. He got the point.'

Very Italian. If you don't have a big stick, then make sure the other guy knows you know someone who has. And the Prof knew someone who carried a telegraph pole.

197

'Thanks,' I said again, meaning it.

'Don't mention it.'

'Oh, and Professor . . .'

'Yes?'

'The first half-dozen jumps at the new airfield are on me.'

He was still cooing when I put the phone down and headed back for Maggiore. I stopped at a motorcycle repair shop en route and bought a big ugly rear-view mirror on a stalk which I bolted onto the left handlebar. Anyone planned to pull alongside me, I wanted to see them coming.

The Cannero was going up in the world, so it seemed. Parked next to the entrance, near the ferry terminal, was a large silver Mercedes. The driver, in a grey double-breasted suit, was polishing the bonnet, even though the whole car already gleamed like the Queen's best cutlery drawer.

I parked the bike round the back where it wouldn't lower the tone, and slipped into the hotel via the side entrance. He must have been expecting that, because he was sitting in the chair near the elevator, where he could keep an eye on both entrances.

He stood as he saw me and nodded a greeting. 'Dottore,' I said. 'Come to arrest me?'

I held out my hands for cuffs and Zopatti shook his head. 'Alas, no.' He looked down at my knee, where a flap of denim had peeled back to show the raw graze underneath. 'In trouble again?'

'All part of the joy of bike riding,' I assured him.

'You looked at the envelope I gave you?'

'You know I did.'

He ignored that. 'I want you to come with me to Lake Garda.'

I sighed. 'I've just been to Como. But you know that, too.'

'Why do you suppose I know anything?' As he said it, he managed a convincing shrug of bafflement.

'Look, I'm hungry. I can't argue with cops on an empty stomach.'

'We can get something to eat in the car.'

I swivelled my head. 'That's your Merc? Very nice.' A Mercedes that size meant he was more than a foot soldier in the SISDe. 'But can we stop pretending you didn't have me followed this morning.'

He frowned. 'I didn't have you followed.'

'No? Big Lancia? I clocked it in Milan.'

A shake of the head. 'I assure you, if I had wished to have you followed, you wouldn't have noticed.'

I accepted that. His people would have done a better job than the jokers who tailed me. They'd have more than one car for a start, maybe even a couple of guys on motorbikes, too, a dozen people in all. 'What's at Garda that is so urgent?'

'I want to explain about the items in the auctions.'

'Has it got anything to do with me and my plane?'

'It might have. And the death of Signor Nino Leone.'

'You could tell me now,' I protested, 'while I eat.'

'I could. But context is all, don't you think?'

'Are you sure you aren't arresting me?' I asked again.

'As I said, no. I hope there is no need. But if you come with me voluntarily, I'll make sure you get your plane back, Mr Kirby.'

I nodded my agreement, pretty sure I wasn't going to get a better offer all day. I was wrong, of course.

Twenty-Six

'The Sala dello Zodiaco,' said Zopatti, waving his arm wide around the room. 'Here, every evening, Mussolini and Claretta Petacci would meet for a session of lovemaking.'

I looked up at the faded stars on the peeling ceiling, which seemed to have reacted to the thought much as I had, with something close to disgust. Pieces of it were floating down towards us in a steady shower, like celestial dandruff. 'At least, that is the legend. Those with their ear to the door claimed they mainly argued about favours for Claretta's family. That was when Mussolini's wife wasn't trying to scratch her eyes out.'

I was getting the guided tour of Villa Feltrinelli, an elaborate pink-ish wedding-cake confection on the shores of Garda. Except the wedding cake had collapsed a little and someone had eaten the icing, as well as shooting the bride and groom and hanging their bodies upside down from a petrol station at Piazzale Loreto in Milan. Even the pink stone was tainted here and there by drab olive camouflage paint which had been inexpertly removed.

'They weren't executed here?' I asked, trying to get clear the hazy details of Mussolini's demise.

Zopatti didn't answer immediately, but led me through to another first-floor room, its wood panelling warped, with fading cherubs staring down at us from the water-stained fresco. Two tall glass doors, several panes shy of a full set, looked over the lake, where the mountains descended to the water. Beyond them was a limitless horizon, suggesting we were looking at the sea, rather than a lake.

'No. They were shot at the Villa Belmonte on the shores of Como.' He gestured to the west of where we stood. 'In one version they were shot elsewhere, with *il Duce* bravely trying to stop their captors abusing his mistress. The execution we all know about was then faked for posterity.' His smile was mirthless.

'You don't believe that?' I asked.

'It smacks of convenient fable,' he said, flinging open one of the doors, provoking a small avalanche of glass shards. 'Come.'

We moved downstairs, passing towering panels of stained glass of cathedral quality, taking steps which he told me were not marble, but polished plaster over wood. Fausto Feltrinelli, the timber magnate who built this place as a summer home, had considered marble far too commonplace to use, Zopatti explained.

On the ground floor we passed through a salon, its yellow and gold striped banquettes torn and stained, and stepped outside onto a stone terrace dotted with clumps of weeds and slick with moss. Uneven steps led down to a once formal garden, shaded by unruly olives. To our left was a dying rhododendron tree – not bush – the largest I had ever seen. My tour guide indicated we walk along the waterfront to the small pier.

'You know,' Zopatti said, 'a strange thing happened one day. We found a dead man in a boathouse.' He pointed at the brick structure next to the jetty. 'Not this one. Some way to the south.' We both watched a steamer ploughing across the water, heading in the direction of Sirmione, a tiny sailboat racing in its shadow. I envied the people on board that sailboat, their heads full of nothing more than the whip of taut sails, the war something they barely, if ever, thought about.

'Recently?' I asked eventually.

'Forty-four,' said the Dottore. 'He had been shot with a Beretta. The strange thing was, he had been broadcasting.'

I walked across and sat on one of the low lichen-covered colonnaded walls. I knew he wouldn't do likewise, for fear of staining his suit. 'You found a radio?'

'An aerial. No radio. Whoever killed him disposed of it. I don't understand why we didn't detect a radio so close to our centre.'

'Because it was a Red Stocking set,' I said, and explained the system designed for communicating right under the enemy's noses. I talked about the Mosquito's high, fast flights. Aware that we had been on opposite sides in the conflict, I again kept my tone neutral. It wouldn't do to gloat.

'Ingenious.'

'Not so ingenious – you caught one of them. Poor guy.'

'I said he was shot. Not by us, though.'

'How do you know that?'

'Because it would have been big news. Whoever made the discovery would have made a . . . what do you say? A song and a dance about it. Citations. Promotions. And they would have turned over the radio set. There was a reward for radio sets.'

'Do you mind me asking what you were doing here back then?'

'Not at all.' There was defiant pride in his voice. 'I was a junior Intelligence Officer with Decima-Mas. You know of it?'

'I know it earned a lot of respect,' I said carefully.

'Later on it was wrongly used, but to begin with, I think we were the equal of your Special Boat Service.'

That was quite a claim, but I didn't want to disabuse him. He might even be right. The first chill wind of night was getting up, and the villa suddenly felt oppressive and gloomy. 'You patrolled the lakes?'

He nodded. 'And the shoreline. One of my colleagues discovered the body.'

'Forgive me if I don't see—' I began.

'Let me finish,' he said firmly. 'I think the man was murdered by a compatriot of his. A partisan.'

'Your point being?'

'For the past twenty years, we have listened to the same story. Patriots good, fascists bad.'

I grinned at him as if this were a self-evident truth and I got a look in return that threatened to freeze the lake behind me. 'Tell me, Mr Kirby, do you think it is possible to be a good man in a bad place?'

'I can't give you absolution, Dottore.'

He took out a pack of cigarettes and offered me one. I shook my head. After he had lit up, he said: 'I don't want your or anyone else's absolution. I am not ashamed of what I did in the war.'

The irony wasn't lost on me. 'I wish I could say the same.' To answer his querying expression, I said: 'I made some mistakes, made decisions I am not proud of.'

Zopatti came close to me. 'I didn't say I didn't make mistakes. The problem is, we make a mistake in peace, it costs someone their career, their happiness, their freedom, perhaps. Back then, it costs them their life. I am not here to defend *il Duce*, Kirby, I know what I think about him, I know how I wish it had turned out differently. But I don't think he deserved to be displayed like that. Humiliated. My God, even Hitler was spared that.'

'I thought Stalin used Adolf's skull as an ashtray?' I had heard it had been recovered from the charred remains outside the bunker and found its way to Uncle Joe.

'Another convenient fable.'

The breeze began to whistle through the garden, a mournful sound that did nothing to lift my mood. I didn't feel up to this discussion. Mussolini, who might have begun his career with noble ideals, ended up costing the lives of 400,000 Italians, blighted many, many more, had left the entire nation with a heritage that still wasn't resolved. I could accept that Zopatti thought he was doing the right thing back then; we all did. He had to accept that time had spun a different tale.

'My point is this,' he went on. 'The partisans contained both good and bad. They raided each other for weapons, argued about who got the most supplies—'

'I was there, Zopatti. I saw all that.'

'Maybe you missed some things. Follow me.' He began to walk through the olive grove, away from the lake, towards the cliffs at the rear of the property. I limped after him. My knee was aching. I badly needed a good, long soak in a steaming hot bath with a cold beer in my hand. On our right were a series of concrete pilings, and in between them the shattered remains of huge panes of glass. It was an old lemon-house, now derelict, the trees within it unkempt and dying.

'I will tell you something interesting, Mr Kirby.'

'There's a Hilton next door with limitless hot water?'

He laughed. 'Not yet. I was due to meet up with Nino Leone on the day his body was discovered.'

It wasn't quite as good as having a decent hotel within limping distance, but it got my attention. 'How come?'

'I had traced him in Switzerland. He was in a little legal trouble. I said if he talked to me, maybe I could help. Unofficially.'

'What were you going to talk to him about?'

'I will show you.'

We reached the cliff where he indicated a stone arch, an entrance of some kind, blocked by a slatted wooden fence. He pulled at the barrier and it swung aside easily. I felt a breath of stale air on my face. A tunnel led into the hillside. Zopatti produced a small flashlight and stepped in. I again took up the rear, brushing cobwebs from my face as I went. I could smell mould and damp, and hoped I was only imagining the scuttle of rodents.

Judging from the way the beam petered out into blackness, and the dull echo of our footsteps, it was an enormous space. 'The Germans built these tunnels,' said Zopatti's hollow voice. 'When Mussolini was rescued by Otto Skorzeny in 1943 and brought here to set up the Republic, you know there were rumours that Skorzeny also took *il Duce*'s personal bullion hoard during the raid, which never surfaced.'

We moved deeper into the complex, the ground sloping down, and I kept glancing over my shoulder to make sure there was still daylight back there.

'I heard Skorzeny ran an underground railroad for Nazis from Spain,' I said. '*Die Spinne*. The Spider. That he was rich.'

'Not from the bullion, though. Firstly he set up the Perons' secret police in Argentina. A very brutal secret police, so I heard. He did the same for Nasser in Egypt, often using SS men. Then, Skorzeny helped move Nazi diamonds and war criminals out of Europe, and for all I know still does. That's how he got rich.'

'He's alive?'

'In Spain. A good place for an old fascist hero.' He sneezed and took out a handkerchief. The dust and spores in the air were getting to him. 'No, Hitler did not get reparations for the rescue in gold. It was from what was stored in here: Mussolini's war chest. Billions of lire worth of artefacts, stolen from churches and art galleries and museums across Italy. Some of it was still here in these caves at the end of the war, the dregs. However, in August 1944, a certain Sturmbannführer Knopp came with a bill for the Skorzeny rescue. Three truckloads of art and artefacts were to be given to him from these storage areas. It was to be taken to the railhead of Chiasso, under guard by the 29th SS Division. The SS were to head south. The art was to be put on a sealed train through Switzerland.'

I got his drift now. 'The 29th SS Division was attacked by partisans en route.'

'Yes. They were mauled, not destroyed.'

'But—'

'But in the confusion of battle, the three trucks disappeared.' He coughed. 'Shall we get out of here?'

I nodded. I wondered if he realised I knew the next part. That the 29th SS Division had been attacked by Gruppo Fausto. That I had been there.

The sun was kissing the mountains goodnight by the time we re-emerged into the garden, and Zopatti was still sneezing from the dust and dirt. I sucked in the fresh air to try to shift the smells that had lodged in my nostrils. I finally turned to him. 'You know I took part in that raid?'

'No, I did not.'

I wasn't sure I believed him. 'You think I had something to do with the missing loot?'

He laughed. 'If you got rich on stolen Italian art, Mr Kirby, you have done a fantastic job of hiding it.'

I looked down at myself. I should have been offended, but I joined in with his laughter. Then, slowly, as the shadows overtook us and I began to shiver – not only from the cold – I told him what I remembered about that night.

All we did – Francesca, Pavel, Rosario, Ragno and I – was provide covering fire from high up on the hillside, concentrating on the tank transporters. Once we had blown the tyres of those, then we knew the column would grind to a halt. I could still smell the stench of cordite, fuel and flesh, feel the judder of the Bren against my shoulder, the ache of the bruises for weeks afterwards. I remembered Francesca's elated face, lit devilish red in the burning oil drums.

It was too easy. Even as I watched tracers pour into them, saw the flash of grenades hurl body parts into the air, I knew we weren't fighting front-line troops. They would have hit back. These men were slaughtered, until two of the half-tracks broke a path through for them to cut and run, leaving us to collect a handsome stash of weapons from the dead. There were no wounded. Fausto saw to that. It was a cruel night. I remembered the bark of his Labora, over and over again as he stepped among the fallen.

What I didn't remember was anyone running up the hillside with the contents of several churches under his arm.

'Of course, we only suspect those three items I showed you were from the haul. With medieval religious artefacts . . .'

'It's hard to prove provenance.'

'Yes. We imagine anything more high profile than, say, a liturgical comb or a reliquary would have been fenced a long time ago, when things were more fluid.'

'Through Switzerland.' It wasn't a question. It was the obvious route. 'And Nino? You think he was the conduit?'

'I suspected so. Now, unfortunately, he is going to be difficult to question.'

'Why are you talking to me about this?'

'Because, Mr Kirby, everywhere else is obfuscation and friends in high places. You know the term *muro di gomma*?'

'The rubber wall? Yes.' It was a phrase used to describe police investigations that got nowhere, that were continually rebuffed.

'It is what I keep hitting. I think if you discover the truth, you will tell me, without lies. You were, I believe, a good man in a bad place.'

I was a little taken aback. I guessed it was as close as I was going to get to a compliment, and I almost regretted I couldn't help him.

On the way back in the Mercedes, we sat mostly in silence, feeling the night close in around us, lost in our thoughts. Eventually, I explained to Zopatti about the three men who beat me up, and being followed in Milan. He swore again it was nothing to do with him. I thought it best to leave the Colt out of the story. I may have softened towards him, but I wasn't that stupid.

'So you really didn't follow me?'

'I said I didn't. I wish I had. Whoever is following you must be interested in the artefacts. Could you give me a description?'

I gave him a quick thumbnail sketch of the trio and he switched on a reading light and scribbled some notes. 'It really has nothing to do with me. It seems there are others interested in you.'

'Typical. You wait twenty years . . .'

His puzzled smile told me he didn't know the old joke about London buses. 'About the missing artefacts,' I said with all the sincerity I could muster. 'I never saw anything like those items, you know. Not in the safe house, not in the mountain huts we sometimes used. Or the trucks.'

'Would you have noticed if they had taken them that night?'

'Yes. Fausto, Rosario, all the others, we left the scene together. No candlesticks or what have you.'

'Ah. Maybe it was what you call an inside job. Some other people took the trucks, some people who were already with the convoy, perhaps.'

'Germans?'

'Or Italians.'

'Maybe,' I said. I suppressed a yawn. 'I am surprised you are still interested. Why?'

'I hate loose ends,' he replied.

'If Nino was in charge of the loot, it was a good reason for him to kill Fausto. He'd get to keep the rest then.'

'Perhaps.'

'Or?'

'Or maybe the articles have been in Italy all this time. Perhaps Nino came back to collect a new item every so often. Perhaps, while he was collecting one – and waiting to see me – curiosity got the better of him and he went to Domodossola. Someone saw him, and . . . bang. Vengeance is his.'

Or hers, I thought. 'Who or where would he collect it from?'

'You tell me, Mr Kirby.' He spread his arms out. 'It would be nice to know, wouldn't it?'

Wouldn't it just.

As we neared Maggiore, he said: 'This plane you are looking for.'

'The Liberator.'

'You think you will find it?'

'I don't know. We've convinced ourselves we know where it is. It might be another convenient fable.' He laughed. 'If it got out of the area, it could well have flown south to Genoa and crashed in the sea. Then we'll never find it. All I did was promise to look. Now, all this happens. Believe me, I didn't want to get tangled up with SISDe.'

'Few people do, Mr Kirby,' he said. He stroked his chin for a moment. 'It is not healthy for that young woman, this search. An attractive girl like that.'

'I've told her. She's missing out on pop music and pep pills, or whatever it is young people do today. And you are right, she is easy on the eye.'

'Is that why you are doing this?'

I tried to act shocked. 'Because she is attractive? I thought I was a good man back there?'

'But still a man.'

'No, Dottore, that's not why I am doing it.' I could feel anger invade my voice. 'Too many flyers never got a decent burial. If I can help add eight more to the total who have, and earn some money into the bargain, I'm happy.'

He looked out of the window for a few moments. 'I have had them turning the propeller. I believe you have to on radial engines, to prevent the lower cylinders oiling up.'

Only about once a week, but I was almost touched by his concern and impressed by his knowledge. 'You are full of surprises,' I said.

'That's my job, Mr Kirby. Come to the airfield tomorrow. You can have your plane back.'

'Thanks. I appreciate it.' We pulled up near my hotel, and I climbed out and slammed the door. I leaned back in through the open window and said, 'And if I come across any lost Caravaggios, I'll be sure to give you a call.'

Twenty-Seven

I didn't need or want to see anybody else. It had been a long day. My knee hurt and my head throbbed. I was tired. In fact, I was getting the kind of ache deep in the bones I recalled from twenty years previously, after too many missions and not enough sleep. Now the burden of history, the slagheap of the past, was piling on top of me until I felt I could barely breathe.

So I was not overjoyed to see Furio's Fiat parked up. Too many people knew where to find me, friends and enemies alike, and for a moment I considered booking in down the road for a quiet night, but went through to the bar instead. I'd move hotels the next day, even though I'd be sorry to see the back of Maria and her first-aid skills.

Furio was sitting with Lindy. He was on Coca Cola, she was tugging on a Cinzano.

'Hi,' I said, without much enthusiasm.

'Oh Jesus Christ, it's not that bad, is it?' said Lindy. 'What happened to your knee?'

I didn't bother answering. Furio motioned that she had been boozing with a quick flick of the wrist, winked at me and handed over a brown A3 envelope. 'Sit down. You look like you need a drink.'

I did as instructed. 'Long day,' I explained. I ripped open the envelope and pulled out the clippings from inside. They were from Furio's mother, copies of articles taken from the newspaper files. 'Thanks. I'll get her some flowers.'

'You'll get her fired if anyone sees those. Read and then eat them or whatever it is you old spies do.'

'I was never a spy,' I corrected him. 'More like a spy's oily rag.'

I raised my glass of Scotch at them and sipped while I read. It was dull stuff, mostly from the business pages. Every piece used the same head and shoulders picture of Conti, serious-looking, greying at the temples, in his early fifties, but still bloody handsome. He looked like an Italian film star, not yet over the hill, but with the summit in sight.

'Look at the last one,' suggested Furio. 'The name of the company.'

I scanned the columns. The article was saying something about share trading and flotations and bearer bonds, the kind of thing I have trouble with in English. Four paras from the end, I hit it, and couldn't help but laugh. It seemed that Riccardo Conti, Francesca's husband, was a major investor in Gennaro, our former employer.

'What do you make of that?' asked Furio, when I had stopped chortling.

'I think it answers all my questions. Francesca, through her hubby, has been giving us work all these months as an act of charity. Riccardo here,' I flicked the picture, making a satisfying hollow noise, 'goes along with it. But when I come up here to his little lake, and start seeing his missus more regularly, he has me worked over and then offers me a job down south. A double incentive to move along.'

'And then puts a body in your plane?' asked Lindy.

'Well . . .' I hesitated. Italian businessmen can be ruthless, husbands jealous, but it seemed a little extreme. I thought they just left dead fish on your doorstep as a warning, rather than real people. 'I think that it is tied in with the war. Don't ask me how, it's too long a story.'

'Another?' asked Lindy, pointing at my glass. I hesitated but then acquiesced. One more, I promised myself, then bed.

Furio paid for the drinks. I promised I would dispose of the Conti files and he said he was going. 'Get a good night's sleep,' I advised. 'If Zopatti is as good as his word, we get the plane back tomorrow. We can make a start.'

Lindy let out a whoop and slapped my back with an enthusiasm that set the other patrons staring. 'Well done, mate,' she said, the Aussie accent thicker than ever.

Furio offered her a lift and she declined, so I walked him out to the car. 'How long has she been hitting the bottle?' I asked. I had the impression it would take a fait bit to dent Lindy, but dented she most certainly was.

'Since we found the body, I think.'

Shit, I should have thought of that. A dead man in a plane. She's going to be bracing herself for what is left of her father, making herself nice and numb. 'OK. I'll call last orders and pour her into a cab. See you at the strip.'

I went back in and sat down to do some gentle nursemaiding. Lindy shifted position to sit next to me and patted my arm. 'How'd you get the plane back?'

'Usual mix of charm, humour and threats,' I lied. 'And then I let an old fascist tell me fairy stories.'

'Were they good ones?'

'Not for me they weren't.' Truth was, I still hadn't digested it all. I needed some time alone to go over everything Zopatti had told me, to see where and how it applied to me.

'What are you doing, speaking to fascists?'

'Good question. One I would have asked a few days ago. Now I am not so sure it is quite so cut and dried. This guy was on the other side. It doesn't make him bad or even wrong about

213

everything.' I thought about what Francesca had said. 'Damn, that's me being reasonable again.'

'I think you are a nice man.'

'Thanks. But I'm not. Not particularly.'

She put a hand on my shoulder, leaned closer. Her voice was slurred; I realised the fact that she could still speak was a small miracle. 'Do you want to fuck me?'

Now, there is a loaded question, I thought, as I felt myself blush. I guessed it was a generational thing but, even in the war, when morals were meant to be a lot laxer, I had never had quite such a direct approach. Well, not from an amateur. I stalled by hitting the whisky, but it burned my throat like battery acid.

'There is no easy way to answer that.'

'You can do it anywhere you like.' I was about to say that, apart from the odd roll in the ferns, beds were usually my location of choice, when I realised I'd misunderstood. I was so red by now, Milan air-traffic control were probably diverting traffic away from me.

She stood up, grabbed my hand and started pulling me to my feet. Unless I wanted a tug of war with a formidable and very drunk woman, I'd have to come quietly. I scooped up the Conti material as she whisked me off.

I sobered up with each step on the stairs. At least, most of me did. There was that little voice saying: Why not? Go on, my son. You're a man, she's a woman. *Barely*, replied my sensible half. *She's a girl. Young enough to be your daughter.*

You stupid English prig, came the retort. I ignored it.

I let her into my room and she crossed to the bed. There was a little stagger, and I knew that her view of the world was beginning to rotate. She started to unbutton her blouse, and I could see she had nothing on beneath it, and I knew I had to do something before the situation got out of hand. Before *I* got out of hand. I threw the newspaper clippings on the bottom of the bed, sat next to her, and held her wrists.

'Whoa,' I said gently.

'Sorry. Do you like the "I'll-just-slip-into-something-more-comfortable" routine? Shall I go to the bathroom?'

'Lindy.

'Uh-oh.' Her mouth turned down. 'You aren't happy, are you?'

'Look, you are a very attractive woman—'

A big sigh. 'But you're queer, is that it?'

'No!' I almost yelled, before I realised it was a ploy to make me disprove her. For a moment, I thought of agreeing with her, but something – the voice of my father perhaps – stopped me going down that route. 'No. It's just—'

'You want to let go of my hands?' she said with a sudden hardness in her voice.

I did so, but she didn't do the buttons up. I made sure I kept eye-contact. 'It's more like a professional thing. Employer and employee. We pilots are like . . . lawyers, or doctors. We have codes of conduct.'

'Really?' She hiccuped, her self-esteem seeing a glimmer of light at the end of the dark, spinning tunnel. 'I've never heard of that.'

'I know it's hard to believe, looking at me.'

Her eyes were cloudy and hooded. I was losing her, and myself. She was going to need another drink soon to keep her momentum going. Right on cue, she asked: 'You got any booze up here?'

I shook my head.

'What about room service?'

'No, Lindy. We've got a big day tomorrow. That's the other thing about survey pilots. Like footballers or boxers, no sex before a big game.' I began to clutch at straws. 'Did you know Japanese swordmakers had to abstain for three days before they started a new blade?'

'You're shittin' me.'

The drink certainly seemed to have released a florid turn of phrase. 'Ask Furio.'

'I wish I had,' she said in a quick rabbit-punch to my ego. It wasn't Kirby she was after, not a father figure after all, just a compliant man. Maybe she figured I was the more desperate of the Kirby and Gabbiano partnership. She was probably right. 'I need something to drink.'

'I'll get some water,' I said as brightly as I could.

She sneered at me as I went to the bathroom and splashed water on my face and peered at myself in the mirror, while I wondered what the hell was wrong with me. When I eventually came out with a tumbler of water the girl was asleep, knees curled up to her chest. I was thinking how to throw blankets over her without waking her and whether there was a spare room in the hotel when there was a knock at the door.

Maria, I figured, either watching my back or protecting Lindy's honour. I opened the door, and there was Francesca, her smile fading as she looked over my shoulder into the room. I wasn't too sure which was causing her more surprise – the half-naked girl on my bed, or the pictures of her husband lying discarded at Lindy's feet.

Part Four

Twenty-Eight

I peeled the police tape off the door of the Beech and nobody shot me or clapped me in chains, so I guessed Zopatti had been as good as his word. A diamond-bright day had dawned only about forty minutes ago, but I knew I had a lot to do. When anyone has been in your aircraft without you present – anyone at all, but especially cops – you need to go through everything from the tyres up. You don't want to find out that one of them has bent the caging mechanism for the gyro or trodden on a control surface while clambering over the wing when you are up at 20,000 feet.

I heaved myself into the fuselage and worked up to the pilot's seat, slipping myself in and tapping the instrument panel. 'You OK, girl?' I asked my plane softly.

'Fine, thanks for asking.'

I turned. It was Lindy, her head in the doorway.

'Hi,' she said.

'Hi. There's coffee on across the way.' I pointed to the little café. 'Put it on my tab. Well, your tab.'

'I will.'

I had caught up with Francesca before she had time to drive off and had jumped into the passenger seat. It had taken me an hour to calm her enough to explain what had been going on. She was vehement in her defence of her husband, suspicious about the girl, disbelieving about what Zopatti claimed, but she finally accepted I had had a rough day.

She promised she would confront her husband when the opportunity arose, but she was sure I would have no more trouble from that direction – if it *had* come from that direction at all. I got the impression the first opportunity was going to arise over breakfast that very morning. And had she found out I was at Malpenso and put work my way? No, she said, but I wasn't sure I believed her. She probably thought she was saving my pride. It was pretty much past saving, but I let it go.

When I got back to the room, Lindy had gone. After five minutes' panic, Maria told me she had called her a cab, which came to the other side of the hotel, which was why I hadn't seen it. I stopped worrying, except for a moment's concern about the cabbie's safety, but then I remembered it would be Giorgio at that time of night. Sixty with one tooth. Even less of a proposition than me.

Furio appeared at the airstrip five minutes after the girl, and we agreed I would do the interior checks while he went over the outside. Lindy sat in the rear seat, drinking coffee noisily.

'Rudder movement?' I yelled.

'Full. Fine,' came the reply from Furio.

'I'm sorry,' said Lindy quietly.

'Flaps?'

'Yeah, good.'

'Jack.'

'I know. Forget about it.'

'I'm so embarrassed.'

'Trim tabs?'

'Free and easy.'

I turned. 'Hey, it's me who should be embarrassed. Look, it wasn't that you aren't—'

'Don't. Please. I'm not that sort of girl. I don't even . . . I was pretending to be someone else – one of my friends back home, who seems to take life a lot easier than I do. She treats men like tissues.'

'Just call me Handy Andy,' I said with as much mocking self-pity as I could muster. I busied myself with the magnetos and the fuel gauges.

'Don't make it worse.'

Furio's head came through the door. 'I think they managed to leave it in one piece,' he grinned.

'Yeah,' I said. I switched the fuel cocks to the front tanks and pumped the primer for the starboard engine six times, just like the manual said. Everything by the book today. I looked at Lindy. 'You want to forget all that crap and do some flying?'

A smile of relief split her face. 'You betcha.'

The AT-11 had never needed much of a run at a rotation and we quickly cleared the airfield and were climbing over the southern stretches of the lake. I scanned the instruments rapidly. You can do all the checks you want, parked on the apron, but up here is when the aircraft tells you the truth. Oil pressure was 80 lbs starboard, slightly less port, but that was fine, and the cylinder heads were warming up nicely. The Beech was telling me she was OK, thanks. I turned the heating on.

Lindy shouted: 'Can you copy his flightpath?' I gave her a thumbs-up. I had been intending to do that. I indicated she should put the headphones on. Soundproofing in World War Two planes wasn't a high priority, and I didn't want to spend the next few hours yelling myself hoarse.

Furio was down in the nose, loading the Kodak film. Infra-red film had been in use since the mid-1950s, and it was getting better all the time. The principle we were working on was very simple, if you stripped away all the Kodak-speak in the manual. Old and young, or indeed diseased, leaves absorb different wavelengths at the infra-red end of the spectrum. So patches of fresh growth should show up as different coloured clumps on the film.

Sometimes you didn't even need an IR to see it. You can virtually re-create the German barrage in the Ardennes forest in Belgium from the vantage-point of the US monument at Bastogne, especially in autumn when the older trees turn first, leaving the hillsides with perfect dark green circles marking the explosion of 88s. It is a sight as sobering as anything in the many museums in that part of the world.

The Liberator was a big, heavy bruiser of a plane, a Sonny Liston rather than a Cassius Clay: wingspan 110 feet, close to 70 feet long, weighing in at around 50,000 pounds, including the 1,000 gallons of aviation gasoline EH-148 probably still had on board when it went in. Because of its high wing, it could carry more load and more fuel than any comparable plane. It was one of the unsung heroes of the aerial conflict.

If that monster hit a wooded area, the sheer bulk of metal, ploughing into the earth at maybe 200 mph, would cut a mighty swathe through the treetops and then the trunks and the undergrowth. Even after twenty years, we – or our Kodak film – should still be able to pick out the scar. That was the hope, anyway. I had checked with the Italian Forestry Department about logging and forest fires which might give us a false positive and, apart from a small blaze in 1960, we were in the clear.

I kept the Beech climbing as we passed over Arona. Ahead, so close it looked like we could touch it, was Campo dei Fiori – the access road to the mountain's summit a thin ribbon of black etched in its side. We were already higher than its peak. To the west we could see right over to Como and Garda; south the ugly sprawl of Milan, with the Pirelli tower rising from it like a beacon, but north were the pavlova-like peaks of Switzerland. I hoped Bill Carr wasn't sitting on one of those, because we were all wasting our time then. The Lib would only appear when the glacier decided to spit him and the plane out, and that could take decades.

I turned the glass nose towards the Alps, heading up the lake, the Borromean Islands already featureless specks, although the wake of the steamers shuttling to and from them could be seen quite clearly. I felt a shudder go through me. I could easily have hit one of the islands when I ditched the Mozzie.

'He'd be losing height about now,' I said, as I picked up the road leading from Cannobia towards the Val Vigezzo.

She peered at the tight switchbacks coiling up the hillsides, the new concrete bridges spanning ragged gorges and the tiny clusters of grey houses, seemingly carved directly from the stone. 'It's beautiful.'

I looked at the rolling hills ahead and the great swatches of pine and, lower down, oak and chestnut, and squinted my way back twenty years. Not when you are flying blind with a storm coming it isn't, I thought, but I just nodded. 'You know that traditionally this place produced chimney sweeps.'

'Really? Why?'

'I don't know. But if you met a travelling sweep anywhere in Europe any time in the last few hundred years, chances are they came from Santa Maria Maggiore or thereabouts. The locals also claim to have invented eau-de-Cologne.'

'Are the two facts related?'

'Probably. The wives most likely doused themselves and the sweeps when they got back from their rounds. I don't know whether eau-de-Val-Vigezzo is quite as snappy, though. Whoa.'

We were at fifteen thousand and something swiped us, a rolling parcel of air, causing the Beech to buck fiercely. I glanced at Lindy. Her smile was uncharacteristically thin.

'Clear air turbulence,' I said. 'Nothing to worry about.'

'What causes it?'

'Air of different densities.' We juddered over a light chop. 'You usually get it higher than this, up around twenty-five, thirty thousand. Except around mountains.' There were plenty of theories about CAT. I gave her the straightforward one. 'Around places like the Alps, with extreme temperature gradients, the air moves like waves, rolling over each other. Sometimes you go through a big roller.'

'Like that?'

'That was a wavelet,' I said.

'I don't want to meet a wave then, thanks.'

And you don't want to be caught in the vortices created by a storm. Thunderclouds act like a brick wall to the wind – it has to go round, under or over them. Flying a Liberator low in the mountains, you only have to hit one of those downdraughts, and you can lose enough height to start shredding trees with your props. Or to go right into them.

We were over Domodossola now, the unassuming town sitting on its flat valley floor, the main rail line showing clear until it was swallowed by the Simplon Tunnel which cut through the heart of glacier-topped mountains, soaring to more than 12,000 feet. I kept my distance. I could see clouds of mist and ice at the summits, sometimes blown into long streaks of spindrift. Besides, the border was down there somewhere, wiggling its way along the passes and over the icy wastes. I didn't want to cause an international incident by flying into Swiss air space. I turned south.

'Pass me the chart,' I said. Lindy did so and I clipped it into its holder. I had overlaid the clear sheet with the first search run. I clicked my mike. 'Furio?'

'Yes?'

'All OK?'

'Ready when you are.'

'Starting our approach now. Don't waste film on the bare mountainsides. Not unless you spot anything.'

'OK.'

I told him our position and he checked it on his own chart. The

Beech carried 206 gallons in front and rear tanks, and averaged around 50 gallons an hour, which gave us an operation window of about three and a bit hours, with fuel to spare in case of problems.

I kept her as steady as I could until we crossed the Corni di Nibbio ridge where Francesca and I had sat a few days previously, then told Furio I was looping her about. 'How's it looking?'

'Green,' he said, 'with some nice touches of red and orange. Autumn is here.'

'Ha ha.' We bumped over Mount Massone and I turned the Beech once more. 'We'll go down and do a visual on the same patch,' I assured Lindy. 'Just in case.'

'Are they inhabited?' She pointed to one of the *rifugi*, the stone huts on the high, sloped Alpine meadows.

'Not now. Up until around forty-three, when the Germans did their big sweeps, you had some *montanari*, the men who looked after the pastures, perhaps the odd group of smugglers. The Germans took the cattle, ate them and shipped off any men they found for forced labour in Germany. Nobody ever re-populated it. There are plans to re-build them for walkers. For now there are mostly wild animals up here.' And maybe eight dead airmen; and Jimmy Morris.

We didn't find anything that day. Nor the next, although we were due to pick up the film from the first day, which held out some hope. Lindy kept smiling, but I could tell she was disappointed. We'd rehearsed the very small chance of finding anything over and over again, but I knew that some part of her had been expecting that we'd pop over the Val Grande and see the distinctive twin tail of a Lib sticking up out of the undergrowth.

When we landed after the second day's grid run, Dottore Zopatti was waiting at our parking spot, along with the airport manager, who quickly made himself scarce. As I shut the systems down, the SISDe man lit a cigarette. I took my time making sure

the fuel cocks were shut and the magnetos off before I went out
to see him.

'Mr Kirby.'

'Dottore. Changed your mind about the plane?'

He laughed. 'No, I haven't. But someone has.'

Furio chocked the wheels and came over to see if he could help.
I waved him away and suggested he should just get on down to the
lab with Lindy to pick up the previous day's shots.

'What do you mean?'

'The military have requested the airport withdraw your permission to overfly Val Grande.'

'Why?' I spluttered.

'National security. There is a border.'

'It's hardly the most militarised one in the world.'

'No. But a border is a border. However, you're a lucky man.'

'Yeah?'

'Because you know me.' He smiled what I am sure he thought
was a winning smile.

'Well, that is a bonus,' I said, trying to keep the sarcasm below
his radar.

'And because my department is also concerned with national
security. We have objected to the objection.'

'Meaning?'

'Meaning you probably have two or three weeks before someone
in Rome makes a decision. Is that enough?'

I had no idea, but I said: 'Should be.'

'Good.'

He turned on his heel and, even though it almost stuck in my
throat, I said it anyway. 'Dottore.' He hesitated and glanced over
his shoulder. 'Thanks.'

'Don't mention it.'

That was the second time he had been nice to me. I didn't like it.
Zopatti wasn't really an accommodating kind of guy. Not unless

there was something in it for him, and for the life of me I couldn't think what. And were the military just being jumpy or had someone – and I could guess who – tried to put an end to my gainful employment? Well, sod 'em. Looked like I had friends in high places too. I walked around the Beech one last time, patted the warm engine cowling to thank her for another good flight, and went to find a cold beer.

It wasn't difficult to locate the villa at Stresa. I mentioned Riccardo Conti in the local bar and they pointed me to a grand ochre building behind high walls, right on the shore. Keeps himself to himself, they told me. Doesn't like unannounced visitors. I promised I wouldn't let on who told me how to find him.

It was a nice, expensive-looking house, well kept, with a red-tiled roof, its parapets lined with urns and classical statues. I rang the bell on the column outside and peered through the bars of the gate. The little speaker box remained mute. The house looked firmly shuttered.

Then it dawned on me. They would have gone back to the city. Summer was over, as Furio said, and come autumn the migrants fly back to Milan. I wasn't sure what I had intended to say to Riccardo, the jealous husband, anyway. I could hardly tell him that I had no interest in his wife, because that wasn't true. Also, I might have ended up punching him, and that didn't seem to have got me very far lately. Maybe I just wanted him to know that I knew who was trying to run me out of town, and why.

Once I was sure nobody was coming, I walked away from the gate, kicked the bike into life and headed off for an evening poring over strange photographs of trees.

By day five, it had become a routine. The early-morning inspection, the coffee, the route planning, the buzz of expectation, the dull ache of disappointment at the end of the day, then the optimism miraculously renewed at dawn. It was like playing the Italian lottery every day, but I wondered how we would feel after a month of it.

Today, it was a run up and down an area known as *vaso da notte* – the chamber pot – a large natural bowl backed by cliffs on one side, with a series of Alpine meadows beneath them. It was a beautiful flying day, clear skies, no wind, not too hot, so there were no thermals or shears off the cliff-face.

'What are you going to do, once you find him?' I asked Lindy.

'I'll contact his old squadron—' she began.

'No. After that. When it is all over.'

'I haven't really thought about it.' Her pretty face was creased by uncertainty.

'You should.'

Furio came over the phones. 'Keep her steady, Jack.'

'Sorry.'

'You know, I thought I'd wait. Something will come along.'

'It doesn't, not really. That's what I thought. Look where it got me.'

She flicked her hair and pouted. 'Flying beautiful women around Italy?' she laughed.

Looking for dead men, I almost added.

'You could do worse,' she said.

'Yeah, I could do worse.' I would remember those words when, indeed, things did get very much worse.

Twenty-Nine

The ball hung in the sky, allowing Jack Kirby enough time to get under it. As the crude leather football plummeted towards him, he thought better of heading it. Instead, he stepped back and took it on the chest, the impact almost winding him, and trapped the ball dead under his right foot.

He looked ahead at the makeshift goal at the end of the field where they were playing. Ragno was in between the pair of tree branches forced into the grass. In front of him were Pavel and a couple of partisans he hardly knew. Behind him, he could hear Rosario shouting for the ball, but he kicked off and began a sprint for goal, flicking the misshapen sphere from one foot to the other as he went, happy with his turn of speed. Ragno crouched down, anticipating the attack.

He sensed someone at his shoulder. Ignoring him, he swept round a clumsy Pavel, then stopped suddenly, letting his follower run on, ready to feint past him. But Fausto turned with him and barrelled through to take the ball, using his weight to push Kirby aside.

Kirby stumbled backwards, felt his ankle go once more, then he hit the rough grass hard. 'Foul!' he cried. He looked up in time to see Fausto score at the other end with a strong left foot.

Kirby limped over to the edge of the meadow.

'OK?' shouted Fausto.

'Bloody foul that was,' he said and the others laughed.

'You run like a girl.' Fausto mimed legs flailing to the side. 'It was a fair tackle.'

'Yeah, right. I'd hate to see an Italian foul then.'

Kirby sat down near the treeline and helped himself to some water. It was early morning, not yet seven, and they felt safe enough at this time to come out and play a game of soccer. It was letting off steam. In three days, Fausto claimed, they would move against Domodossola, starting the dominoes falling that would result in the liberation of all of Italy.

He squinted in the harsh light at the two figures approaching from the hamlet. One was Francesca, he would know that swing and stride anywhere. The other was taller, a willowy man in civilian clothes. Francesca led him around the edge of the game until they were walking towards him, and Kirby struggled to his feet. The football match stuttered to a halt as the partisans became aware they had an unexpected visitor. Kirby noticed Rosario walk over to where he had laid his machine pistol.

Francesca said: 'This is Flight Lieutenant Kirby. Our BLO.'

The newcomer smiled. He wore rimless glasses, had a face so thin you could imagine the skull under it, and a floppy fringe of blond hair. 'Captain John Hirschfield. Office of Strategic Services.' OSS, the American Special Operations people. 'How do you do?'

'Fine, apart from the ankle. Still gives out.'

'Glad to see you guys can find time for football. Aren't you a little, uh, exposed out here?'

'The Captain is with the Green Flames south of here,' explained Francesca.

'You have more Germans down there,' Kirby said. 'Football might be trickier.'

'So it would seem.'

Kirby looked for evidence of the disapproval he was sure the man intended, but the tone was flat and neutral. Still, he suspected the Captain thought that soccer and war didn't mix: if you had time for one, you couldn't be pursuing the other properly.

'Can I have a word?' he said to Kirby. 'In private?'

Kirby nodded and the pair of them walked away from Francesca.

'You all right?' the American asked as he noticed Kirby's limp.

'Yeah, it'll be OK soon.'

'Is that why you never went over the mountains?'

'That and the fact they needed a BLO who spoke Italian.'

'Maybe. They didn't need you, Kirby. An *ingenuita*.'

Kirby stopped in his tracks. 'What?' The term was an insult, implying gullibility.

'This is a job for professionals now. Advisers who can advise.'

'Or instruct?'

'If need be. This hare-brained scheme—'

'Look, Captain, I think they are a little browned off about being told by people like you that their ideas are hare-brained.'

The American hesitated. 'My outfit and your boys are concerned.'

'My boys being Lang?' Kirby knew someone must have briefed the OSS man.

'Lang is mighty pissed at you. He put his best man on that plane you missed.'

'I *missed*?' spluttered Kirby. 'There was a storm, for God's sake!'

'Not as big as the one at Bern when the news came through. I think Jimmy was special to Lang, if you get my—'

'*Get down.*'

Kirby pulled him to the ground as fast as he could, yelling the same warning to the others. All did as they were told, and there was silence, just a few early cicadas, then the others heard the buzzing. The skeletal German spotter plane was to the south of them, its wings wagging in the first of the morning thermals as it flew over the ridge, apparently without a glance in their direction.

The Captain raised his head. 'You have good hearing, at least.'

'What are you here to do?'

'Have a last crack at persuading these idiots to hold off till next spring.'

They got to their feet and brushed themselves down.

'Good luck,' Kirby said.

'Which one is Fausto?' the Captain asked.

Kirby pointed him out and gave a thumbnail sketch of him to Hirschfield. 'What if you can't persuade him?'

'If he goes ahead and it fails, I'll have him strung up by his balls.'

'And if he succeeds?'

He had the decency to smirk. 'We'll say he couldn't have done it without us and take all the credit.'

While Hirshfield and Fausto argued, Kirby trudged down the hill with Francesca, towards the Captain's Green Flames escort, a surly couple armed with American burp guns. He stepped as gingerly as he could over the stone path, favouring his stronger ankle.

'Are you avoiding me?' Francesca asked.

'Should I be?'

'No.'

Kirby stopped well short of the pair. 'We shouldn't have done what we did. It was wrong.'

'Why?' She fixed him with her eyes. 'Because of Fausto?'

'Partly. But because of the plane, too. It was dereliction of duty.'

She took his hand and they headed off at an angle, deeper into the tree-cover. 'You know Fausto was a bastard?'

'Seems a bit harsh.'

'No, literally. A foundling – abandoned by his mother. What happens then is that the orphanage pays a poor family to take him in.'

Kirby leaned against a rock next to a small stream, took off his boot and sock and dipped his throbbing foot into the icy water. It felt better instantly. 'So?'

'Everything about Fausto stems from that. The way he likes to have this family around him, his need to be liked, admired, the fact that he finds it difficult to show his emotions.'

The flat rattle of machine-gun fire came through the trees and Kirby struggled to get his boot on. As he did so he could hear raised voices, aggressive and unyielding on both sides.

'Oh shit,' said Francesca.

Kirby ran as best he could back towards the main path down, just in time to meet the Captain, who was now flanked by his two guards, steaming past, an expression of disgust souring his face.

'What happened?' Kirby panted.

'That little idiot threatened to kill me. Then he fired over my head,' yelled the OSS man over his shoulder.

'Fausto?'

'No, his pet dog.' That'd be Rosario.

'Why?'

He stopped and said quietly, 'Because Fausto wants to get you all killed, Kirby. And the asshole has my best wishes for carrying it out.'

Hirschfield pushed on without a backward glance, although his minders kept their weapons aimed back up the hill until they disappeared into a bank of hazel trees. A moment later, Kirby heard a car start and screech away. So much for the Secret Service, he thought. Driving around in daylight was hardly clandestine activity.

Fausto and the others appeared moments later, their faces no less dark than the American's. It looked as if the negotiations hadn't gone well.

Kirby waited until they had moved past and turned to Francesca. 'Tell me again how Fausto just wants to be loved?'

She shrugged. 'He doesn't like being told what to do either.'

'Yes, I noticed.'

★ ★ ★

'Penny for them?'

I looked up at Lindy, who had placed a hand on my shoulder. I was sitting on an oil drum on the edge of the airfield, watching an assortment of mechanics and pilots playing a scratch game of football twenty years after my game with Fausto. There was lots of fancy footwork, and hysterical clutching of heads, but one of the kids was really rather impressive. He looked like he might be wasted as a grease monkey. As he leaped above a taller opponent and headed the ball in a flurry of swirling black hair I realised it was Diego, whom my partner Furio was paying to sleep with the plane, just in case anyone else thought it might double as a morgue. He was wasted doing that, too. He had *furbizia* – the kind of unpredictable cunning with a ball – and gamesmanship when that skill failed, which could thwart any defence. Fausto had it, too – *furbo*, the art of dodging, of bending the rules, that Italians admire so much.

'I was just thinking about another game.' I didn't bother explaining about Fausto and his reaction to being leaned on by the OSS. 'You know my team, Brighton and Hove Albion, was once beaten eighteen–nil by Norwich?'

'They still your team?'

'Yes. Extenuating circumstances. It was Christmas 1940 and the Albion had to appeal to the crowd for volunteers to make up the numbers.'

'And you volunteered?'

'I did.'

'And they lost eighteen–nil?'

'Yes. I was a better TT rider than a footballer,' I explained.

'I should hope so.'

It also showed me the difference between a professional footballer and an enthusiastic amateur who had mainly played in parks and pits. Norwich had a full, fit pro squad that day and ran us ragged. I should have applied that lesson to Italy, perhaps, and realised I was out of my depth with Fausto.

'Furio says he's ready when you are.'

I threw away the last of the coffee which had turned cold in my cup. 'Right.' I stood up stiffly and began to walk across to the Beech, watching the sun flare off its fuselage.

'You OK?' Lindy asked.

'Yeah, why?'

'You're limping.'

I laughed. 'It's an old war wound. It hurts sometimes.' But I walked the next 200 yards just fine.

Thirty

I had undone the fasteners on the cowl of the Beech's port engine, trying to locate a tiny oil leak that had spotted the apron overnight, when I was called to the hangar to take a call. It was the Professor, phoning from Milan.

'How are you, Jack?'

I ignored the odd tone and second-guessed what he was calling about. 'I'm OK, thanks. Look, I talked to them about using this field for the club. It's a bit of a longer drive—'

'That is not why I am telephoning.' This time, there was something in his voice that made the hairs on my neck prickle.

'Right. How can I help?'

'Have you upset anyone lately? I mean, anyone important?' Fear, that's what I could hear.

'My bank manager, mostly. Although even he is smiling at the moment. Why?'

'You remember I told you about my family connections?'

'I do.'

'Well, my friend called me and told me not to advise you on any more relics.'

'Ah. And you said?'

'I'm sorry, Jack. He isn't the kind of man you argue with.' There was a pause. 'I had to promise him.'

'Fine. I won't trouble you again about any of that stuff,' I said, trying to sound as reasonable and unpissed off as possible. 'Thanks for your help.'

'Sorry, Jack,' he repeated.

'Forget it, Professor. And the skydiving offer still stands.'

I hung up and walked back to the plane. Someone was leaning on the Professor? I made a mental note to tell Zopatti we had tickled some nerves somewhere along the line, and that by backtracking from the Prof – as long as the Dottore's balls were big enough to take on his 'friend' – he might find out who it was.

When I reached the Twin, Furio was twisting the Dzus cowl fasteners shut. 'Got it,' he said. 'Clip by the screen.'

There was no oil filter as such on the engine, just a mesh screen, awkwardly placed round in front of the carb. 'Good.'

While we waited for Lindy, we drank coffee and did a leisurely external inspection. 'Jack, what do we do once we find the plane?'

'The champagne's on you.'

'No, I mean longterm. We can't carry on like we did. I know this plane is good, but skydiving at her age . . .' He shook his head. 'One day she'll come in heavy and you will crack that spar.'

'Not me. I don't do heavy,' I countered.

'Me then. One of us. You miss my point. This is a dead end, Jack. My mother says we should have a plan. A proper future for the business.'

I winced as I hit coffee dregs and threw the sludge away. He was right. At one time I would have flown the Wright Brothers' Flyer just to get in the air, moved dead sheep or grommets to pay the fuel bill, it was all the same to me. The game had changed now. Furio liked to fly, for sure, but he wanted the columns at the bottom of the page to add up at the end of the day. Me, I'd never even bothered filling in the pounds, shillings and pence.

'You must not say anything, but my mother has found something out.'

'That I'm a has-been who is ruining her son's life?'

'Jack, be serious for once,' he said, with a sudden intensity.

I leaned against the fuselage. 'Fire away.'

'The Aga Khan is building on Sardinia. In the north. Luxury hotels, apartments, villas . . . Millions and millions of lire. The first thing to go in is . . .'

'An airstrip,' I said.

'How do you know?'

'An airstrip and docking facilities for all his pals with their floating gin palaces. Whisk them in, show them a piece of scrub, whisper in their ears about gold taps and tennis courts and swimming pools, take a deposit.'

'Well, not the Aga Khan personally perhaps.'

'No, but his minions. It'll probably work. The rich like being among their own kind. They're the only ones who understand them. So what's Mummy thinking of?'

'That they will be flying in investors from the mainland. Nice, Cannes, Corsica, Rome . . . some of them will have their own planes, but others . . .'

'But others will be just dying to get in an old broken-down bomb-training crate.'

He winced, as if the Beech could understand me.

I tapped the hot aluminium behind my head. 'Sorry – we love her, but love is blind. These guys are used to shiny new Pipers and Cessnas and Learjets, the Sophia Lorens and Gina Lollobrigidas and Monica Vittis of aircraft. They'll think they aren't being taken seriously if we turn up with our overmade-up sister who's a little long in the tooth.'

Furio became more animated. 'My mother has a cousin who is a manager on the project. He says that we could arrange a loan through the holding company to buy something a little smarter. All right, a lot smarter. Maybe just a single, but new or nearly new. The development is going to take ten, twelve years, Jack. If we can get in as a favoured air carrier—'

'Taxi service,' I corrected, wondering why I was getting so irritated. Perhaps it was the thought of flying a single-engined job.

'Jack—'

I shook my head. 'You know what the problem will be?'

'No.'

'I'll listen to those pricks gabbling away about whether to have marble or granite in the kitchen and I'll want to open the door and fling them out into the sea. That's the problem.'

I walked off to get some more coffee, confused as to why I was being so aggressive. It was a reasonable plan, and being a glorified air taxi was a lot better than being a skydiving shuttle-bus and we both knew it.

I turned and shouted: 'Hey, Furio!'

'Yes?' he replied sullenly.

'I'll think about it. OK?'

He beamed back at me.

I'd think about it and reject it, I knew. Because part of me was feeling it was time to go back home, sort out what was left of Kirby Motorcycles, make sure my father was all right. Just like Lindy was doing, in one sense. But it was right for Furio, he was young and unattached and I'd help him as much as I could, making sure he didn't get stiffed on a plane and the like. It looked like Kirby & Gabbiano was about to run out of runway. Still, I'd known it would happen one day. After all, he had a life ahead of him, and mine was all in the rear-view mirror.

Lindy was already at the counter getting a coffee and she bought me one. As we walked back, I said: 'I think Furio is trying to make a businessman out of me.'

She cocked an eyebrow. 'Kinda late, isn't he?'

I had to laugh. 'Yeah. That's what I think.'

★ ★ ★

Our first potential sighting of Bill Carr's Liberator came that evening, after another long but seemingly futile day's flying. We were in my room at my new hotel on Lake Orta, which was handier for the airstrip, when we found it on the photographs taken on day four. When I say we, it was Furio who spotted the oval. It was there all right, and the more you stared at it, the more pronounced it became. I checked the frame number and consulted the map.

'What do you think?' asked Lindy.

I thought it was the wrong shape, but it was probably best not to speculate at this stage. 'Could be.'

'But not the right shape,' she said.

'No,' I laughed. 'But I wasn't going to mention that. We are looking for something long and wide. It wouldn't have made this pattern. Not unless it nose-dived in. And I don't have Bill Carr down as a nose-diving kind of fellow.'

'No. Not deliberately. But then, I figure he wouldn't have chosen to go in at all if he had had any say in the matter.'

'There's that,' I conceded. 'He might have had no choice.'

Furio looked at the map and back at the photographs. 'Look, this track here. It is only about a few hundred metres from the site.' He traced it with his finger. It was wider than most of the trails that criss-crossed the area; more likely to be an old drover's road or a fire break. You could access it from the small town of Vogogna at the west of the park without too much difficulty.

'I could get us in there,' I said. 'We could take a look on the ground and settle it.'

'I'll take the plane up,' chipped in Furio. 'If it's nothing I'll do the next sector with the remote. So we won't have wasted a whole day.'

'I'll get us an air-ground radio link organised.' I looked at Lindy and offered her a choice of going with me or Furio. 'Plane or bike?'

She hesitated. 'I want to see what's on the ground.'

'You sure? Because . . .' I was about to warn her about the state of any bodies we might find, but she was way ahead of me.

'I know what you are going to say. I don't expect to find him in the cockpit smoking a cigarette, asking what took us so long.' The words were hard, but there was a glint of tears. 'I'll come with you, if that's OK.'

'Yeah. Let's get some sleep,' I said. I touched her arm. 'Stay here tonight. In another room,' I added hastily as Furio looked up. 'We'll go on the CrossCountry. It was built for this kind of thing.'

'Sure.'

'You certain you are OK?'

'Certain. Scared, that's all.'

I turned to my partner. 'Look after her.'

As they left, I saw his hand hover over her back, just at the base of the spine, and squeeze. I laughed to myself as the door clicked shut. I should have seen that coming. Not once did Furio object to driving into Milan with her to get the films. Normally he would have insisted on turn and turn about, or at least have suggested it. Ah well, he was closer to her own age.

'You are a difficult man to track down.'

I shook my head to clear it of sleep, then wedged the phone under my chin and looked at my watch. It was just after midnight. 'Shit, Francesca. You found me, though.'

'A friend in the Polizia checked the registration cards for the last few days. Not as nice as the Cannero, eh?'

'Less of a commute to the airfield.'

There was silence while I blinked away my tiredness. 'I came out to see you at the villa,' I told her.

'I heard.'

'How?'

'Nosy neighbours. They called me, told me a man so scruffy he could only be an Englishman had called round. He was riding a motorcycle. Well, you don't have to be Tenente Ezechiele Sheridan to work that one out.' Sheridan was their version of Sherlock Holmes or Gideon of the Yard. 'Why did you come out?'

'To tell Riccardo he is being ridiculous.'

'Is he?'

'So it *is* him trying to screw me up at every turn.'

'Don't put words in my mouth, Jack.'

'Someone is making waves for me.'

'He says not him. And anyway, what would you have done if he had been there?'

'I thought I could convince him I am here for a plane. Not you.'

'Is that right?'

'Yes.'

'Oh.'

I sat up and switched on the bedside light. I wasn't going to get to sleep again in a hurry. 'Why did you call?'

'To see why you came to the villa. To hear you say you aren't interested in me.'

'Sorry.'

'I've had a wasted journey then.'

'Where are you?'

'Downstairs.'

I let this sink in. I was an adolescent again, my imagination running away with me. Or perhaps the disappointment I thought I detected was real. I said: 'You want to come up?'

But the line was already dead.

Thirty-One

It was hard to know which of us looked worst over what was a very late breakfast. Furio kept yawning, and I swear Lindy nodded off into her coffee at one point. I felt like I'd been through the wringer, but I also had to curb a desire to whistle, very loudly and cheerfully. I hadn't thought that the registration cards would include the room number. Francesca had been tapping on the door before the phone was back in the cradle. She'd stayed until past dawn. We didn't mention Riccardo Conti at all, even though we both knew he shared the bed that night.

Lindy stretched her arms out and made a sound of contentment.

'So much for you two getting—' My own yawn truncated my sentence and the pair of them collapsed into giggles. 'Jesus. I think maybe we could skip the search today.'

Furio slugged back a double espresso and signalled for another. 'No, I'll be fine.'

'Lindy? Just Furio and I could go up to the site.'

'Nah. It's probably nothing anyway, but I want to be there. What's your excuse?'

'For what?'

'Well, you can guess why we look like this. What about you?'

243

I smiled at her. 'I think it was those mussels for dinner. You wouldn't believe—'

'No, right, thanks,' Lindy said quickly. 'I get the picture.' She stood up. 'Let's go and see if we can find my father. I mean, it's not like we got a Samurai sword to make or anything, is it?' She finished with a wink and I had to smile. I had a feeling she could see right through the shellfish story.

'See you outside in five minutes,' I said.

I waited until she had gone and said to Furio: 'You OK?'

'Sure.' He seemed surprised I'd asked.

'You and Lindy. How did that happen?'

'It just happened. I like her.'

'Did she tell you . . . ?' I began, then bit my tongue. It would do nobody any good. 'Did she tell you about her stepfather?'

'Yes, of course. Why?'

'No reason.' I drained my coffee, and pushed a piece of bread into my mouth. 'Don't hurt her, Furio.'

He looked pained at the very thought, but when he saw the expression on my face, he took it the wrong way. 'Ah. Not until she writes the last cheque, eh?'

I shook my head. It wasn't my job to sort out their love life. I had my own to try to make sense of. I reached over and ruffled his hair. 'Not until we've cashed it, idiot.'

They were building a new Autostrada that year, and the traffic was slow up the side of Lake Orta and to what would become the junction at Gravellona. Things improved when we picked up the 33 and followed the river that feeds the lakes, north to Vogogna. I'd changed the bike's tyres to the big studded Avons, which were going to be good for off-road, but were skittish on asphalt. I kept the speed down.

The weather was cooler than it had been, and we both wore thick sweaters under our jackets and scarves round our necks. The sun had lost its focus, hidden behind a thin streak of cloud, and was past its zenith already. We had left it very late. Perhaps I should have gone with my instinct and called it off for the day.

At Vogogna, I found a wide stony track heading up into the hills that I was certain led to the site. I checked the map and scanned the sky. No sign of Furio. 'Ready?' I asked Lindy. 'It gets bumpy. Hold on tight.'

Before I could start off, she said, 'He's not second-best, you know. I didn't just do it on the rebound, if that's what you think.' Her voice was muffled from inside the helmet.

'Lindy, I am not thinking about it at all. If I did, I'd be pleased for you. You make a nice couple. He likes you.'

'He said that?'

I caught the tone and said: 'Oh no, I'm not playing that game. Hold on.' I revved the bike and felt her arms slide around my waist. Even over the engine noise I heard her whoop as we started uphill, the bike making short work of the surface. Whether her exclamation of joy was because of my riding or the idea that Furio talked about her, I didn't know.

It was surprisingly wide for one of the Val Grande paths, cutting between chestnut, alder and sycamore trees. It took us over a series of ridges, where the deciduous trees slowly gave rise to a dense stand of pines that stretched for miles in either direction. The road carried on into it, picking its way between the trunks in slow, lazy curves, climbing all the while. I stopped before an ancient fallen pine bristling with sprouting etiolated greenery seeking the light, and consulted the map, photograph and compass.

I looked up once more, wishing I had some of that secret military technology they talked about on science programmes – as seen in spy movies – where you could use satellites to locate yourself anywhere on earth. It was hard to imagine the little Sputniks being able to do that, but I was sure they could and more. My generation and my war made people terrified of looking up into the sky for fear of what might come down on them; the current crop of boffins had turned space into the stuff of nightmares.

'Found it?' Lindy asked.

I manoeuvred the bike around the trunk. 'Up ahead a way,' I shouted.

The propwash from the plane made us jump as the Beech roared over the ridge behind us and up into the sky, wings rocking. Stupid bugger, I thought, showing off to his girlfriend.

I pulled over, made Lindy get off the bike and took my radio out from under the seat. Another thing I'd like to see from spy movies – a communications system smaller than a suitcase. The speaker crackled. Through the trees, I could hear him turning.

'Ground Force to Eagle Eye. Can you hear me?'

Lindy looked hard at me. 'Ground Force? Eagle Eye?'

'Old habits die hard. Do you copy me, Eagle Eye? Over.'

Lindy took off her helmet, shook her hair out and unzipped her jacket, even though the air was crisp up here.

'Ground Force, this is Eagle Eye. I copy and see you. Over.'

'Good. How far do we have to go? Over.'

'About a kilometre and a half up the track. Over.'

As the Beech came overhead, still low, I saw a hint of a slipstream from the port engine. 'You are all right up there? Over.'

He was turning again, banking the Beech just beyond the rise. Now I was sure I could see something. Suddenly, I was sweating.

'Furio. Port engine. What's the temperature and oil pressure? Over.'

Nothing but static. He was concentrating on the turn, watching the airspeed, so as not to stall.

'Jack?'

'Yeah. Go ahead. Over.'

'Oil pressure is five pounds . . . no, ten . . . back to five. Over.' The minimum was fifty. I recognised the panic in his voice from other planes and other pilots, a long time ago. It was a tone I had hoped never to hear again. 'Christ, the cylinder head is cooking.'

I watched him come round. 'Furio, Furio, concentrate on the height. Keep the height and airspeed up. OK?'

'Jack—' The fire alarm, a modification I'd insisted on fitting, filled the cockpit, screeching over the radio.

Now there was smoke leaching out of the bad engine, a knotted rope of black and white against the sky. 'Extinguisher. Hit the extinguisher button.' I fought to keep my own voice reasonable, calm. It was what you wanted from a ground controller. 'Over.'

Carbon-dioxide mist spewed out of the nacelle and over the wing, and vanished. I could see that he was losing height now. He had to work hard to compensate for the bad engine. You can't feather a prop on a Twin Beech, and the drag of a windmilling one was serious. 'Furio, get her up.'

'Jack!'

The plane made it over our heads, but one wing dipped and a trail of branches and leaves began to arc skywards, marking his passage through the treetops.

'Furio.' I closed my eyes and prayed. This was where the ground controller starts hoping there is after all a God, or at least a patron saint of pilots.

The tip of the wing dug into something harder, and I didn't see it, but I heard him shout, followed by the screech of folding and ripping aluminium, and I imagined the plane flipping, smashing down into the pines, rolling and disintegrating as it went, the wood punching through the thin fuselage and Plexiglas.

The explosion was scarlet and black, and the noise boomed through the forest, sending scores of panicking birds skywards. There was another noise, more constant. Lindy, screaming.

I indicated she get on the bike and I kicked it into life, my brain running over the whole sequence, analysing what he did wrong. Lindy threw her leg over behind me.

I tore the bike up the path, over-revving it, forcing my way through the brambles and ferns that had colonised parts of it. Their tendrils whipped at my face, and I could taste blood but it hardly registered.

The air became full of tiny flecks of glowing carbon, like fireflies zipping around us, smashing into my goggles. Ahead, there was a white glow like a pathfinding flare, burning my eyes. I ticked off parts of the plane as we got close, mostly sections of wing. Then the heat hit us, and we could feel the oxygen being sucked out of the air so I stopped the CrossCountry and dismounted. I helped Lindy off. She had trouble standing and I slipped my arm round her and took her weight.

Just visible through the burning pines was the shape of the fuselage, on its nose, incandescent as the aluminium burned and threw out a toxic cloud that rose high above the canopy. It was more or less intact apart from the wings. I had no doubt Furio was in there, already incinerated.

I looked at Lindy, her face bright from heat and horror, and pulled her closer. I knew what she was thinking. This must have been how it ended for her father. It's a pilot's nightmare. I've been in that cockpit, on the ground and in the air, hundreds of times and I've woken up trying to bat the flames away with hands that are already melting.

I moved Lindy well back and propped her against a tree, explaining that there was still fuel that could go up; I made sure she understood she had to stay put. She still hadn't said a word. She reached up and wiped a tear from my eye and all I could do was nod my understanding. I picked my way through the trees and skirted around the perimeter of the site.

Branches were burning now, dropping fiery embers and resin onto me. I traipsed through the thick pine needles, unable to keep my eyes off the wreckage, hoping a figure would stagger out, knowing he was probably killed the instant he hit the ground, praying that his neck had snapped to save him from burning to death.

I felt the air move around me in waves, and a sudden downdraught of rotor-wash. It was a helicopter. I looked up but couldn't see it through the smoke drifting across the sky at treetop-level. Probably the mountain rescue team. They'd got here fast.

My lungs began to hurt and I wrapped a handkerchief around my lower face. All sorts of dangerous materials – plastics, rubber, metal – were burning in there, and I started to cough. My throat was already seared and raw, and I had to make my circle wider to avoid choking. I moved deeper into the woods. It was then I saw the skeletons.

There were three of them and they had been there a long time. Trees had grown up around and through them, so they were now almost a part of the forest itself, barely illuminated in the fractured light that penetrated their protective canopy. If it hadn't been for the flames glinting off the browned metal ribs, I wouldn't have noticed them at all.

I pulled the undergrowth aside and forced my way through. I was no expert, but I reckoned they were the bare bones of German trucks, Henschels or Büssings. The canvas had all gone, exposing the rusted supporting hoops I had seen in the flames, and the metal elsewhere was thin and papery. The wooden sides and running boards had mostly crumbled to dust.

I bent down and picked up one of the remaining slats. It was singed, but from a long time ago. Someone had burned out three trucks. It was what we had seen on the IR map. Not Bill Carr's plane at all, but new growth where this trio had been driven up the wide path and torched in the woods, twenty years previously.

The door of the lorry came off in my hand, and fell to earth with a muffled thud. The body that was in there was barely recognisable as such, charred down to a blackened, shrunken simulacrum of a human. There was another in the rear flatbed section. I picked up the shreds of uniform as carefully as I could. The belt buckle was scorched but intact, the words *Ehre Heisst Treue* just visible around the eagle. One of the alloy buttons had a faint SS-BW stamped on the rear, which meant the uniform was manufactured at the SS clothing works at either Dachau or Ravensbruck. I threw them both back and didn't bother examining the other two vehicles. It would be more of the same.

I trudged back towards my own tragedy, a small part of my brain nagging me that I had probably found Zopatti's stolen art. Three trucks, he said, had been taken from the convoy. I ignored it. I had bigger worries than some ancient piece of looting. Like finding out who had killed my friend.

The heat was still lashing out from the trees, although the fire seemed to be moving slowly. I knew we needed to get out, because if a wind got up that could penetrate this forest, we could easily be outrun by flames. And there were too many corpses in this place already.

'Lindy!' I shouted.

There was a splitting and cracking noise and a blazing sapling keeled over, coming to rest in a shower of sparks. Another tree spluttered and gave birth to flames.

'Lindy!'

She was more or less where I had left her by the bike, her face streaked with tears. I stood for a second and held her once more. 'I'm sorry. There us nothing we can do. If the fire really takes, the Rangers will come and douse it with water from the lake. We don't want to be here then. You hear their chopper?'

She shook her head. I went over to the bike and touched the tank. It burned my hand. I was about to put my helmet on when I felt something cold against my neck.

'Kirby.'

I turned slowly. There was a tone to her voice I didn't like. And what had happened to Jack, exactly?

Lindy Carr had stepped back away from me in case I tried to jump her. She now stood five yards from me, gripping a gun in a two-fisted stance that was good enough to make my stomach flip. Not just any old gun, either. She was holding my old Colt .38.

Part Five

Thirty-Two

It was the wild look in her red-rimmed eyes, along with the clenched jaw and the muscle twitch in one upper arm that kept the gun moving jerkily, that frightened me. Plus the increasing discomfort from the flames scaling the trees behind me. The back of my head was almost burning now. I'd smell hair singeing soon.

I managed to say: 'Lindy? What the hell are you doing?'

'This wasn't meant to happen.' Her face crumpled, but I still wasn't sure I could make that distance between us before one of the Colt's slugs hit me. How on earth did she get hold of my gun? It was last seen in the presence of Monkeyman and Co. 'It wasn't . . . wasn't meant to be like *this*!' She shouted the last word and it echoed through the woods.

I heard more foliage crackle and fall. The air was thick with smoke, coiling around us like fingers of swamp mist.

'Lindy, we have to get out of here.' There were flames visible from the corner of my eye. The fire had crept round to my peripheral vision, sneaking like a thief in the night.

'*Lindy*.' I took a step forward. The gun flashed and I felt the percussive thud of the round zing by my ear. 'We're going to die here. Look, the fire is coming round us. We will shortly be cut off. We have to go.'

'Maybe.'

'No, not maybe – for sure. Whatever this is, we can sort it out later. That's Furio in there—'

'I know who is in there! I know.' She began sobbing, but not hard enough to affect her aim.

I tried to keep my voice level. 'It won't do us any good to join him. Not now.'

She nodded and took a piece of paper from her pocket and handed it over, keeping the gun well back, away from my grip, as if she'd been trained in this. 'These are the coordinates. Can you find it?'

'I'll have to check on the map.'

'Don't do anything stupid.'

'I get the feeling I've been nothing but stupid for the last few weeks.'

'You started well before that, Kirby.'

A little bulb went on. Who would have told her about my wartime career, even before I got a chance to? One man. 'Lang blamed me, didn't he? For your father?'

'Just check the map.'

I did as I was told. It was one of the high meadows, to the east, with another track running to it from where we were, smaller, just a series of dashes on my map. I nodded. 'I can get us there. But—'

The explosion caused me to stagger forward into the bike, knocking it off its stand. I felt vegetation and metal fall on me, burning my exposed skin. I waited five seconds, holding my breath, and looked up. Flames were ahead of us now. The circle was closing.

I rolled over, and felt my ribs protest again. It hadn't done them much good, throwing them onto the cooling fins of a Cross-Country, but I was more or less in one piece. Which was more than I could say for Lindy.

I left the bike where it was and crossed to her. She was lying on her back, and there was a sliver of metal jutting out from her upper right arm. A chunk of fuselage, I thought. Blood had welled around it, onto the leather of her sleeve, but seemed to have stopped flowing. A second piece had nicked her neck, and thin rivulets ran down into her sweater. Her face was blackened down one side, with steel or carbon particles. A fuel tank must have gone up.

I was sweating now and I took off my leather jacket, pulled off my jumper, threw it away and put the jacket back on over my T-shirt. Lindy had managed to sit up and had transferred the gun to her left hand. It was still pointing at me. Christ, she was good, I had to give her that.

'You need a doctor,' I said.

'Take me to the coordinates.'

I shook my head.

'Take me.'

She fired again, but I didn't flinch this time. 'You re-load that, or is that your lot?' I had only left a couple of rounds in there after my tree shooting.

'Re-loaded,' she said.

'I don't believe you.'

The third shot threw up debris around my boots. I believed her.

'I should look at that wound.'

'Yeah. Let's finish this first.'

Another detonation, low and dull, and now I could feel a wind coming through the trees, and like charcoal under a bellows the fire swelled and flared, radiating heat and light. The remaining aluminium became a white sun in the woods. Lindy got to her feet.

'Get on the bike,' I said, as I walked over and yanked it up. 'But you can't threaten to shoot me and hold on tight at the same time.'

She grimaced and I knew that arm must be hurting like a bastard. 'Truce?'

A curtain of fire descended across the pathway ahead. This was no time for negotiations. 'Truce,' I answered. She nodded and shoved the Colt into her jacket pocket. 'Now get on. And put the helmet on.'

It took a minute before we were both ready and the curtain of fire before us was even fiercer. I licked my lips and they were as dry as the forest floor. I kicked the bike and she stuttered and I found myself saying: 'Not now, baby. Not now.' I kicked again; she turned and gave me a half-hearted huff.

'Fuel?' shouted Lindy.

'What?'

'You opened the fuel valve?'

Instinct had made me flick it off when we had halted. I reached down and turned it on, kicked and the CrossCountry burbled into life.

'Thanks. You know bikes?'

'Used to ride them on Grandad's farm.'

I put her in first and rode for the fire, head down, feeling Lindy do the same across my back.

As we neared I felt my cheeks start to crisp. If the conflagration was deeper than a foot or two, this was going to end here, with no answers, no valediction, just two charred corpses.

Lindy screamed as we went in, the fire spitting at us with jets of resin-fuelled fire. I closed my eyes. Despite the gloves, my hands felt like they'd been put in an oven. '*Shiiiitttt!*' I shouted at the top of my voice as an arc of flame shot across my face.

Then the bike misfired.

I twisted the grip once more, praying a vapour lock or oxygen starvation wasn't going to kill the engine and us with it, but it picked up and we were through, into a stand of tall thin pine trees, the shimmering orange wall behind us.

I took us past them, to where the cool air felt like balm on my skin, and stopped. The crash site looked as if hell had come to earth. The wind was taking the fire slightly to the south, away from us now. It was possible the gap between the deciduous trees and the pines might act as a fire break. I heard the Rangers' chopper again. They'd know whether to let it burn or not.

'You OK?' I looked at the arm with its inch of protruding metal. It didn't seem to have got any worse, but her hand was clenched in a tight fist, the knuckles white.

'Yeah.' She sat up and looked at me. 'Jesus.'

I pulled up my goggles and felt the sting of raw, blistered skin. I looked in the mirror. There were two crescents across my cheek, flecked with burned rubber, my top lip had swollen and my eyes were crimson from the toxic smoke from the plane. Now I felt cold, and I regretted leaving the jumper behind.

'I think we both need a doctor,' she said.

'You were going to shoot me a minute ago,' I complained.

'That was before you saved my life.'

In a movement that made me wince, she reached up and pulled out the metal from her arm, gasping as she did so. I saw her eyes roll in pain, and thought she was about to faint, but she sucked air in through her teeth and then smiled. She flung the jagged triangle into the undergrowth, and flexed the bicep several times. 'Ow.'

'Lindy,' I asked slowly, 'who is waiting for us at the meadow?'

She blinked her reddened eyes and said: 'Just an old friend.'

Thirty-Three

I knew where they would be waiting for me. The glimpses I saw as the track twisted through the greenery told me that the field that was our destination sloped up to a thick wall of pines and, just where grass met tree, there was an old *rifugio*, a mountain shelter, still relatively intact. They'd be in there. As I climbed the bike up the hillside, I took deep breaths to try to ease my scorched lungs. I looked back at the plume of smoke still spiralling from the crash site. The helicopter was a mere speck to the south, on the far side, probably calling in a water dump.

I reached the edge of the field, which was covered in a thick mat of coarse knee-high grass and nettles, dotted with late wildflowers. I stopped the bike at the bottom of the meadow, killed the engine, and we dismounted. The hut was around 400 yards away up the slope, and approaching it gave me precious little cover. I held out my hand to Lindy.

'What?'

'The gun.' I pointed to her jacket pocket.

'No.'

'You told me this wasn't meant to happen. Furio wasn't meant to die. Well, he did. I don't want to join him.'

'That was an accident.'

No, it wasn't. Engines don't spontaneously combust. Not those old Pratt & Whitneys. The oil pressure fluctuating suggested something else, maybe torn-up rags in the oil tank, an old trick. It meant they would have had to take care of Diego, the nightwatchman, but that was easily done, either by money or force. I put as much iron in my voice as I could manage. 'I am not walking out there without the gun. Now shoot me or give it to me.'

I looked into her eyes. They were glazing. She was going into shock. I'd have to worry about that later. She didn't stop me when I stepped forward and removed the gun from the jacket. I checked the action and said, 'Wait here.'

I started tramping into the clearing, kicking up clouds of seeds from the thistles and dandelions, all the time feeling eyes, and maybe even telescopic sights, on me. Part of me wanted to sit down and weep for poor Furio, but I knew that had to wait, too. He'd understand. I had to use the anger at his death to keep me going. I was huffing and sweating again by the time I was a third of the way up the hill. That's when I stood and shouted.

'This is it. No further. Show yourself.' I waited. My voice sounded tiny in the mountains. There was no reply, just the ticking of my heart. I was sure I was right though, so I said his name. 'Come on, Lang. I haven't got all day.'

He stepped out from the dilapidated hut, looking incongruous in that remote setting. He was dressed in a three-piece suit, a tailored black coat with velvet collar over the top. In his hand was a walking stick, probably from Swaine Adeney Brigg or some other fancy purveyor of country accoutrements to the Duke of Edinburgh. On either side of him were two of my robbers, Monkeyman and Gutbucket.

'Hello, Kirby.'

The minders flanking him had weapons, modern small submachine guns. I was within range of them, I reckoned, if they knew what they were about. 'What the bloody hell have you done, Lang?

What have you done?' I pointed behind me to where the remains of the Beech lay. 'A man is dead.'

'That wasn't my doing.'

'No? I would bet every last cent that somehow, in some way, this one lands at your door.'

'Look, I can't stand here shouting, Kirby. The old throat isn't up to it. Come closer.'

'And get cut in half by those two?'

'They won't do that.'

The movement to my left caused me to spin and I fired two shots at the shadow in the trees. I didn't think I'd hit him, but you never knew your luck. I swivelled back. 'Tell him to stay away.' It had to be Blondie, the third of the trio that had jumped me that night. 'I'm staying put. You'll just have to go hoarse, Lang. Tell me what you're doing here. Then I'll answer any questions you have.'

He signalled to his bodyguards to remain where they were and advanced, with some effort, fifty yards through the rough grass. He was red in the face by the time he stopped, but decorum prevented him taking off his coat or loosening his tie.

We stood facing each other. A list of questions longer than my battered brain could cope with presented themselves. Not least where he had hidden the Land Rover or similar vehicle he must have used to get up the mountain. Finally, I said, 'You used that poor girl to get at me.'

He pursed his lips and shook his head. 'No. She knew what she was doing.'

I indicated over my shoulder. 'Which is why she is slowly slipping into a coma thinking about her dead boyfriend.'

Together, we looked across the trees to the thinning smoke which marked the funeral pyre. The fire was dying. It seemed as if the entire forest wasn't going to burn after all. 'That wasn't me, Kirby.'

'What was you, then?'

He threw me something that flashed in the last rays of the sun. I caught it cleanly and examined it. A cartridge case, with a big square dent made by a firing pin in it. 'It's from a Sten gun,' I said.

'Yes.' He scratched his cheek, composing his thoughts. 'A few months ago a body was discovered here. In the hut. Not much left of it. One leg was broken, though, the fracture was very clear. The man had also been shot, several times. Followed by what we assumed was a final bullet through the head. But before that last shot, the victim picked up a cartridge case and gripped it hard. There were no other cases around, so they must have cleaned up after themselves but missed that one, the one in his hand.'

The shadows reached us, the sudden chill making me shiver, but I didn't move. 'To prove it wasn't the Germans?' I suggested, holding the case between my thumb and forefinger. 'Different firing pin on an MP38 or 40.' They were the most common machine pistols used by the other side, the kind of weapon that Rosario had liked. 'That was why he gripped it. Post-mortem evidence.'

'Yes.'

'And the bullet in the head?'

'We found that still in the skull. Not a Sten. A pistol, perhaps. We wanted to check.'

'Hold on – tell me why I didn't read about this body.'

'Because the hikers who found the body reported it to the Carabinieri, who told the SISDe, who slapped whatever is the Italian equivalent of a D-notice on it.'

'So Zopatti is one of yours?'

He laughed and his tone was almost horrified. 'Hardly. Let's just say we had certain personal interests which coincided. He'd hit his rubber wall. Like me, he wanted to stir things up, see what bobbed to the surface.'

I heard a noise behind me and turned, but it was only Lindy, coming out into the open and moving into the last patch of shrinking sunlight. It would be dark soon. We had to get away and down the mountain before nightfall.

'So you stole my gun to check the ballistics, to see if it was me who killed this chap.' Then when it turned out not to be, he had given the gun to Lindy to make sure she could get me along to this showdown at the appropriate time. Except the plan had unravelled, as all plans have a tendency to do. 'You thought I'd helped murder him?'

'Yes. It crossed my mind. We needed to flush out whoever had done it, one way or another. I have to admit, you were a candidate.'

I had a cold hate building inside, but letting it rip through me wasn't going to do much good. 'It was Jimmy Morris,' I said. 'The dead man was Jimmy Morris.'

'So you *were* there?'

'No. But no ordinary flyer would think of incriminating his assassins. And no mere dead pilot would bring you out here, Lang – get you to leave your comfy Whitehall desk. It had to be someone you liked.' I took another step forward. 'I've heard the affection in your voice when you talked about Jimmy—'

'Stop it.'

It didn't brook an argument. 'It means he survived the plane crash. Or . . .' I let that tail off.

'He jumped,' he said with a mixture of sadness and irritation. 'The bloody fool jumped. Broke his leg. Crawled to the hut. Waited for help. Someone found him and killed him.'

'Who?' I asked.

'Perhaps someone who didn't want to be replaced as BLO.'

My laughter sounded hard and heartless, but it wasn't meant to be. 'You have to be joking. You think I would kill a man just because you were sending someone to stop Domodossola? That was his brief, wasn't it?'

'Yes.'

'To stop the secession by all means necessary?'

'Yes.'

'Including assassination.'

He took a deep breath. 'We weren't specific. By whatever means Jimmy thought appropriate. If Fausto or any of the others kicked up rough, so be it. We just thought it was an idiot idea. We were right.'

'You were *wrong*. You had to let them make their own mistakes. You made enough in your time. All of us did.'

I was feeling cold now and my face was hurting. Again I had to fight the urge to sink into the grass and curl up. 'So the idea was that I would come blundering in, trying to uncover what had happened to EH-148 . . .'

'Which really *is* still missing. We didn't lie about that. Finding it would have been a bonus.'

'Did you put it to Lindy like that? A bonus? It's more than that for her.'

'We all have our priorities.'

'So I was meant to act like a beater, flushing out anyone who had a guilty secret about the fate of Jimmy Morris.' He gave me his thin smile. Christ, I thought, talk about Machiavellian. But that was Lang: once a conniving, underhand spy . . .

'I rather thought that even if you had nothing to do with it, someone would be worried about you finding the plane, because we'd discover our supernumerary was missing, and his parachute and the canisters perhaps, and we would know that EH-148 made the drop anyway.'

It was my turn to snap. 'They shouldn't have. They shouldn't have done it. They should have just gone home.' I wondered if he knew that there was only one ground flare. Bill Carr would have argued – correctly – that it wasn't enough for a man to make a jump. Jimmy Morris must have ignored him. 'He shouldn't have gone out.'

'Jimmy could be a very persuasive man. Who can be sure? He

may have simply jumped without the pilot's permission. He wasn't the sort of chap who liked to abort a mission. We'll never know.'

'No. But you had to come searching anyway.'

'I did. Call me sentimental.'

I could think of better things to call him. I heard an animal yelp, far away, its plaintive voice hanging in the thickening air. A wild dog, a wolf perhaps. I looked up at the sky. It was darkening, but there were to be no stars tonight. A layer of cloud was sliding in. A storm on its way.

'So someone tried to stop me flying, by planting dead bodies on my plane, complaining to the military, and Zopatti made sure I did get up in the air.'

'That's about the size of it. He's looking for some stolen art, of course, rather than the murderer of an Englishman. But we agreed that the two missions might well intersect at some point. And that you might be of some use to both of us.'

I pointed towards the Beech wreckage once more. 'That smoke also marks the spot where three trucks were burned out sometime in 1944. I think they were taken from the convoy and driven up here. They must have contained Zopatti's missing art. There are bodies in them.'

Behind him, I could see bats darting and swerving as they vacuumed the insects from the dusky sky. 'I will tell him.'

'I'm not your man, Lang. I didn't kill Jimmy. I never even knew he got out of the plane.'

He thought for a few moments before he nodded. 'No. I don't believe you did.' He seemed to shrink a little, his shoulders slouched, and I realised he must have seen sixty pass a while back. Coming up for retirement. I also knew he was doing this off the clock, a personal vendetta to tie up one of his precious loose ends.

'It was a long time ago, Lang. That was yesterday. We're well into a new day, a bright new world, all ballistic missiles and atom bombs. Twenty years. Who'll be interested in our war in five or ten years? Nobody. Our time is past. Let's go home.'

I heard the blades of the helicopter slicing the air. It would do well to go home, too. Darkness, storms, mountains and choppers don't mix. I felt a drop of icy rain on my face.

'I can't leave yet, Kirby. If you didn't kill him, who did? Who else wanted Domodossola so badly?'

I opened my mouth to speak when his chest began to dance, chunks of fabric and sprays of blood flying from it as his knees buckled and he went down.

His bodyguards began to fire and I did what came naturally – I threw myself down and began to crawl.

I pumped my elbows and knees as fast as I could back downhill, aware of the zing overhead of bullets coming from the chopper, but not certain they were meant for me.

'Lindy! Get to the bike.'

The grass around me hummed and thwacked. Those definitely had my initials on them. I risked a glance up and the bubble-fronted Bell was spinning around for another run. 'Lindy!'

'I'm here.' She was already climbing onto the CrossCountry.

'Start it!' I yelled.

As she kicked and the bike caught, I stood and sprinted as best I could, the thick vegetation tugging at my feet, the hiss of rounds driving me on. I reached the treeline and jumped on behind her. '*Go.*'

I half-expected her to stall it, but she found first and accelerated away into the trees, turning us to run parallel with the edge of the meadow. I looked up. The canopy was not as dense as I had hoped; they'd be able to see us. We needed thicker tree cover.

'Go down the hill!' I shouted.

'There are men,' she retorted. 'Moving up towards us.' A series of zips through the air confirmed it. The Bell must have dropped someone down there to sweep up anyone who got out of the field alive.

The clattering from the helicopter was louder now, and the branches above our heads began to rustle as the rotor-wash caught them. My ears hurt from the thrumming air. I looked up, and for a second the machine seemed to fill the sky.

A rattle of machine-gun fire came through the leaves and I heard the sound of metal being punctured and felt the bike almost buckle. Lindy noticed a thin, needle-strewn path off to the left and took it. She squealed as branches whipped into our faces and bodies.

'Want to swap?' I shouted.

'No. I'm OK!'

'Good girl!'

'Don't be patronising!'

'I wasn't!' I felt the bike slide under us and we both steadied and kicked with our feet in unison to keep us upright. My spine began to ache as every stone on the path jarred it. I looked back, wondering what the flapping noise was, and saw the rear tyre was busy ripping itself apart.

As the slapping got worse, I glanced around us. The helicopter was hovering to the south, patrolling downhill, thrown off by Lindy's sudden swerve. To our left, uphill, I could see another factor that might make the Bell keep its distance. A harsh cliff face reared up above the forest in a series of narrow natural steps or terraces, its top almost lost in the mist streaming across it. The storm was rolling over that cliff, and even a chopper jockey would know about the draught that would be carried with it. I also saw something else, although part of me thought I half-imagined it, the way you see faces in the clouds as a child. I looked again, and it was there all right, and it was definitely man-made.

'Turn towards the cliff!' I yelled.

Lindy obediently yanked the bike around and urged it on through the trees, bouncing over fallen branches, all the time the squealing noise from the rear wheel getting worse. Even as I watched it, the last layer of rubber detached itself and spun away.

'Off.'

She did as she was told and I took the handlebars and heaved the CrossCountry up the hill.

'Leave it,' she panted.

'No.'

Our goal was around 200 yards beyond the edge of the trees, sitting in front of the cliff on a pedestal of scree, a single decent stone path leading up to its ruined doorway. I had found one of the chain of forts and lookouts built across Val Grande half a century previously, when the Italians thought the Austrians or Swiss might have territorial ambitions on the region. The structure, snug against the rockface, was well disguised, yet would give its garrison a commanding view over the valley below.

Lindy helped me with the bike as we pushed up towards the decrepit castle, the pebbles and stones skittering under our feet. As I kicked at the gate, crows squawked and took to the air above our heads, outraged at the intrusion. I swore as their vulgar sound swirled across the valley.

Lindy said quietly, 'Now they know where we are.'

'Now they know where we are,' I confirmed.

We managed to manhandle the wrecked bike through the twin wooden doors, and to close them, after a fashion. There was no lock or crossbeam to wedge the gates shut, so I leaned the bike against the gap between the two halves and piled some rocks around the wheels to stop it slipping. I gave the CrossCountry a once-over. The petrol tank hadn't been holed, but the tyre-less rear wheel was badly buckled, and the engine was bleeding oil in several places. We wouldn't be going anywhere on it. Lindy had slid down the inner wall to a crouching position and was sobbing into her folded arms. Looked like I'd be exploring our new home on my own.

The surface of the steps up to the main wall had been badly

crumbled by countless frosts, but they were solid enough to get me to the battlements. I poked my head over the parapet and surveyed the scene below. Low, damp cloud was coming in from each side and I could hear the whine of the Bell's engines, although I could no longer see it. It was landing, probably in the meadow we had just left. They would clean up the mess there, maybe stay the night, and, at some point, come for us.

I checked the magazine of my gun. Six shots left.

I jumped at the touch on my shoulder. It was Lindy, the tears gone, determination in her voice.

'Sorry about that. What do we do now, Skip?'

'We try and stay alive,' I said harshly. I wasn't about to forgive her duplicity that easily.

'Listen, it wasn't all lies, you know. The story of Dad and the plane.'

'I know,' I said, my eyes still on the clearing and the forest beneath us. In my mind, I ran through what had happened in the past few days and weeks. 'What about the little pantomime in the hotel? When you were so pissed you even fancied me? What was that all about, Lindy?'

'I was drunk . . .' she admitted.

'But?'

'Lang told me you'd been honeytrapped by this woman. Is that the word?'

'It'll do.'

'He said your brains were in your balls.'

'And you thought you'd check? See if I'd indulge in some pillow talk?'

'Something like that. I was curious to know . . . ah, forget it. It was a dumb idea.'

'You can say that again.'

'Is it true?' she asked.

'Which bit? My brain being in my balls?'

'That you fell in love. That you compromised your mission?'

'Lang liked to think so. It's not that simple, Lindy. It never is.'

I saw her face crease up and knew she was thinking about Furio. A drizzle hit us, and I took her and hugged her to me. 'What a mess. Come on, let's take a look around.'

She didn't move or say anything. I held her away from me and looked at her smudged face, that healthy glow hidden behind smoke and cuts and blood. I examined the arm, but the wound seemed to have congealed. I licked a finger and ran it down her face. A clean line of skin emerged, pallid but unblemished. Underneath the grime she was in pretty good shape, physically at least.

'You'll live,' I said.

'Will I?'

I didn't need her giving up, I didn't need her even recognising the possibility of death. 'Of course you will. What are you thinking?'

She gave me a wan, tired smile and stared out into the darkness where our opponents were gathering. 'I was thinking . . . have you seen that film *Zulu*?'

Thirty-Four

The fort was even older than I had first thought, probably dating back to the turn of the century, and the weather hadn't been good to it. There was a large courtyard, divided into three separate areas, the central one, where we were, filled with debris from the cliff face above, and colonised by hardy plants used to eking a living from the roughest of grounds. I knew the feeling.

Near the main gateway, I found an old metal chest. It was almost rusted shut, but it opened with a metallic shriek of protest. Inside was a reddish tangle of nuts, bolts and washers, and two corroded screwdrivers. I closed the lid again and tried to drag the box across to help bar the door, but it was too heavy.

'Want a hand?' asked Lindy.

I felt a muscle in my back tense and stood up. 'No. Leave it. Let's see what else we can find.'

At the rear of the fort was the equivalent of the keep, a two-storey bunker with a collapsed slate roof. The structure was big enough to house twenty or thirty men, with a kitchen and what were probably intended as latrines and a washroom, but no plumbing had ever been installed. The forts had never been required, since the Swiss hadn't swarmed over the Alps to ravage and pillage. That wasn't their style.

All I found in the keep, apart from bird and bat droppings, was a lonely bucket, almost rusted through. For no good reason, I brought the pail with me. The way things were going, I might end up having to bucket someone to death.

There was thunder now, away to the west, the rumbles rolling through the valleys towards us; the glow of lightning flicked on the horizon. The air around us was thick and damp. We both finished our brief tour of the main compound and stood shivering.

'What now?' Lindy asked.

I pointed up the steps to the equivalent of the battlements, although the capstones lacked the castellations of olde English models. 'I'll go back up there, keep an eye out. When it gets properly dark, maybe we'll try and find our way down.'

'Is that wise?'

'You're asking *me* about wise?' I shook my head in disbelief. I didn't want to remind her how we had got into this mess. 'None of this is very wise.'

'Who is out there?' she asked.

'I don't know.' That wasn't strictly true. I had a good idea who one or two of them might be. I walked wearily back to the stone steps. Lindy followed and put a hand on my shoulder.

'I'm sorry,' she said.

'What for?'

'All of this. Furio. You. Lang.'

'Don't be sorry for Lang.'

'Why not? If it wasn't for him . . .'

'If it wasn't for him, this would have been a straightforward search for your father.' We had reached the parapet and I lowered my voice. 'But he made sure you saw it as revenge for the plane going down. That was nobody's fault – I see that now. It crashed, for whatever combination of reasons. It happens in war. People die. End of story.'

'And Jimmy Morris?'

271

I paused. That was Lang's real agenda, of course, not Bill or Lindy Carr. 'That's different,' I said. 'That *was* somebody's fault.'

'See?'

'But that wasn't your business; that wasn't your war or your dad's war. That was Lang's. He shouldn't have used you.'

'Or you.'

'Or me.'

When I reached the top of the steps and looked over the parapet I saw the glow in the trees. It was a cigarette. And whoever was at the soggy end of that butt probably knew I could see him in the last of the twilight. I cocked the pistol and the click carried down the scree slopes of the fort to the pines and died in the trees. He heard it, though.

'*Jaaaack.*'

My name made my heart leap in my chest. I swallowed back the bitter taste that comes when you know you have been very foolish. The tone of that voice, the elongated vowel, it took me back twenty years.

Fausto.

'Stay where you are,' I shouted out into the darkness, for want of anything better to say. Like I was in a position to make demands of him.

'*Jaaack.* It's me.'

The rain began in earnest, drumming on the stones around me. 'I know, Fausto. Who else have you got out there? Rosario?'

'Yes. How do you know?'

'I still recognise an MP40 when I hear it.' It was the rate of fire. It was only fifty rounds a minute slower than a Sten, but to the ear it seemed a lot lazier, albeit a damn sight more accurate. The sound of the machine pistol told me that my old friend Rosario, the diminutive jazzman, had been in the chopper. If Fausto said jump, we all asked how high. It had always been the case.

I saw the red tip of the cigarette move between two trees, burning bright as he sucked on it. He was formulating his next move. I had to do the same, to stay one jump ahead of him. *You have the higher ground. Fausto won't like that, will he? He'll try and pull you down.*

Perhaps.

'It's cold up here. Wet. You should come down, Jack. We can go somewhere warm and talk.'

'I was talking to Lang. Look what happened to him.'

A laugh. 'You won't care about that, will you, Jack? You won't hold him against me. You always hated him.'

'Not that much. You're right, though, it's not him I really care about. You killed my friend, Fausto. He was in the Beech. He was just a kid. It was meant to be me, wasn't it?'

'No. No, it wasn't.' It almost sounded genuine.

'Don't give me that crap, you bastard. You didn't know Furio would fly today. Hell, I didn't know till last night.'

I saw the light from the cigarette stop moving and I ducked down, pulling Lindy with me.

'I thought you would be in it, Jack. That's true. But I knew that you wouldn't have crashed, would you? You'd have come out of that with a fright and a ruined plane. Then maybe you'd stop poking around. You may not have been a good partisan, but you were a decent flyer. The boy wasn't good enough, Jack. Tell me I am wrong.'

I didn't answer, because he was right. I'd have recovered from losing an engine, even at that height. Furio didn't have the hours under his belt; he didn't stand a chance.

'Come out, Jack. Let's talk properly. It's been a long time, eh?'

I grabbed Lindy's hand and ran down the steps. I reached the crippled motorcycle and knelt before it, pulling off the tube between petrol filter and tank. The fuel began to spill onto the ground, and I filled up the bucket. I pointed to where Lindy should direct the rest of the flow and she took the line from me.

I tried not to sound breathless when I got back up top with the bucket. I laid it next to me, the fumes stinging my eyes. I said: 'You'll have to pay for Furio.'

'He shouldn't have been up there, Jack.'

I leaned over the wall and thought I saw a movement off to the right. I listened. There were scraping sounds. It was impossible to climb towards the walls without making a noise on the slippery scree, even if you could keep your footing. The figure moved closer, towards the main path that led to the doors of our compound.

'Oh no, Fausto. You let me think I was responsible for that Liberator for too long. I know you didn't light your flares.'

'Ah. She told you that.'

'She told me that.' I had him now, I knew what he'd done. I knew what he was, at last. 'You found Morris and killed him, didn't you? When I heard he had a bullet through his head, I thought of you that night, finishing off the dead of the SS after we had ambushed them. It wasn't a pistol round that they found in his skull, was it? It was a 9mm Labora, through the temple.'

The bullet hit the stonework to my right and whined off into the night, leaving me on the floor, wheezing and panicked.

'I still have the Labora,' came the voice. 'For old times' sake. Don't worry, I wasn't aiming. Not really.'

'Tell me about Riccardo Conti.'

After I said it, I ran down the steps to Lindy and, as we rolled the bike away so the doors could swing freely, I spoke softly, watching her eyes widen in the gloom as I told her what she had to do.

'I don't know if I can,' she began to object.

'For Furio,' I hissed. 'Or he'll never have justice.'

'You want to know about Conti?' came the voice. There was a wistful tone to it as he said: 'You people put so much store by names, identities. You know, for the first six years of my life, I didn't *have* a surname. Imagine that. I was just Cesare the bastard.' Cesare? That was a new one on me. But few of the *gruppi* heads had used their real names back then. 'If you must know, Riccardo Conti was a loyal officer of the Guardia Nazionale Repubblicana by day. By night, he was Fausto, the brave partisan leader, scourge of the Garibaldis and the Nazis.'

I heard the chuckle, and by the time it faded I was back up at the top, hoping my heart wasn't going to burst through my ribs. 'So you managed to get a ride on a convoy carrying stolen art, and in the chaos of the attack you organised, you killed the guards, arranged for the trucks to disappear and came back to the scene as Fausto.'

'Was that so bad?'

'You used some of the loot to buy guns through Nino. And got Nino to fake your death, to stop the OSS and SOE coming after you with their told-you-sos.'

'When it was over, Conti had to be released from his brutal captivity. That bit was easy. A quick shave and a haircut, a smart uniform. We had lost by then. I – he – had the chance to make sure there were no reprisals.'

'Just the odd Communist leader.'

'Just a few token executions. No civilian reprisals. You know how unusual that was? You know how much I worked for that? It could have been another Val Grande massacre.'

I leaned over the wall, saw the bulky figure of inky black, darker than the night, disappearing from view into the archway of the door below.

'Fausto!' I yelled.

'Yes?' came the voice from the treeline.

I loosed off a shot in the general direction of his voice, then screamed: '*Now!*'

Down below, I heard the click of her lighter, the whoosh of petrol igniting, and the crackle as the flames ran under the door to the outside, following the stream Lindy had created.

I heard an exclamation and, as a thin filament of lightning lit the far sky, giving me just enough illumination for an accurate throw, and the big man leaped backwards out of the doorway, I tipped the bucket of petrol down.

Not all of it hit him, but more than half of it went over his head and body. The flames around his feet sucked at the vapour, tendrils of fire sprang upwards and, within a second, his torso was a fiery torch. The screams were louder now, and he was rolling on the ground, trying to extinguish the fire with his hands. They ignited too. The screech of his agony filled my head and I fired two shots at the writhing shape and then a third at the trees.

I ducked back down, pleased that the screams had been silenced, and I heard return rounds hit the other side of the wall, the impact vibrating through the old stone, the air suddenly full of dust. Fine, keep trying to hit me, Fausto.

I heard the door below squeak open and the shuffle of hasty footsteps. Within a few seconds, the gates slammed shut again and the bike was rolled back into place. That was fast, I thought. She could get up some speed when she needed it.

The firing ceased. I tried to close my ears to the hiss and pop of the dying flames outside on the rocky slope.

'You OK?' I shouted down.

Lindy caught her breath before she replied, 'Yes.'

'Got it?'

'Yes.'

I raised my voice. 'Fausto. Now I have an MP40. The odds are getting even.'

I heard Rosario's angry voice across the clearing. 'No – now you have a Sten, you bastard! Not as good!'

I looked down into the courtyard. Lindy bravely held up the machine gun like the trophy it was. It was the unmistakable shape of a Sten. Which meant I must have killed Ragno, the spider boy, the one person in the group who actually liked the weapon. I should have guessed from the size of the figure who'd crept up to the door. I'd assumed it was Rosario with extra padding against the cold, but it was my fat friend Ragno.

He'd come back to help Fausto, his old master, the man who took him and trained him, who gave the boy a chance to fight when everyone else said he was too young. *I would have died for that man*, he had said at the Moto Guzzi factory. Well, now he had.

'*Jaaack.*' It was Fausto again. 'What is this? What have I done to you?'

I checked the Sten. It was a Mark II. There was a full magazine: thirty-two rounds. I flipped the single-shot bolt across. It might jam on full automatic fire. Even if it didn't, I had no desire to empty the whole mag in a few seconds. 'Is there a way to end this then?' I yelled.

'I can get you out of the country, Jack. A safe passage. What happened in Domodossola isn't your business, it never was. You English only thought it should be. Walk away now, Jack. We are even. Furio and Ragno. They cancel each other out.'

'Did Francesca know?'

There was surprise in his voice. 'About what?'

'Any of it. Morris. The money.'

'Why do you care?'

I popped my head up and risked another scan of the approaches, but there was no sign of life. They were staying put for the moment. After all, they didn't know what other surprises we might have up our sleeve. 'Because I do.'

'Morris? No, Francesca knew nothing about that. What do you mean about the money?'

'You didn't trade all the art for guns, Fausto. You kept some to set yourself up as Riccardo Conti, financier, industrialist and charity director. Am I right? Maybe you cut Nino out of it and he came back for his share. Maybe you didn't like him talking to me. Perhaps you knew the SISDe were on to him. Whatever the reason, you killed him and put him in my plane.'

'Nino doesn't count. Furio and Ragno. One each.' Lang? I thought. Morris? Bill Carr? There were too many dead to do any simple sums. 'Did Francesca know?' he continued. 'She's an Italian wife. She knows better than to ask about men's business.' I doubted that, somehow. 'What do you say? You promise to leave Italy, I promise to let you go.'

A squall blew rain into my face and I turned my back on it. Could I trust him? Had I ever been able to trust him? But was this man Fausto or Riccardo Conti? Truth was, they were both killers. The Red Stocking man on the lake – the one that puzzled Zopatti so much – did Conti kill him, too? I'd put money on it. I'd wager that the SOE man was someone else trying to stop the Republic of Domodossola, and had to be eliminated. 'Give me some time to think,' I said. 'The girl is badly burned.'

A silence, then he said: 'Thirty minutes. Before we all freeze to death.'

'OK.'

'*Jaaack.*' Again, the drawn-out vowel.

'Yeah?'

'I know you'll find this hard to believe, but I don't want to have to kill you.'

Lindy wasn't burned, but she was cold, standing in the doorway with the Sten held at waist height, ready to shoot anyone else who tried to enter. I made to give her my jacket to add to her own, but she shook her head.

'You've only got a T-shirt on. You'll catch your death.'

I laughed at that and leaned against her, sheltering her as best I could. I was thankful for the rain. It was masking the sickly smell of burned flesh. At what point had they pulled Ragno in? After he had helped me with the CrossCountry, probably. I didn't think he'd been up to anything at that point. Whenever it happened, Ragno would always follow Fausto blindly. If his old boss told him I had to go, then I had to go. I doubted the spider boy had even asked why.

'You want to tell me who he is?' asked Lindy.

'The dead man?'

She shook her head quickly, as if trying to throw off the image of the incinerated body. 'No. The man trying to kill us. Out there.'

I gave her the short version.

'But you saw a picture of him, Francesca's husband – in the clippings. Why didn't you recognise him?'

'It was the same picture every time. Journalists are either lazy or up against a deadline. They need a photo, they use a library shot. Fausto planted phoney pictures, then became the reclusive, publicity-shy businessman. It looked enough like him to pass as a poor likeness if you actually met him . . .' I felt her start to shiver again. 'Look, I'll go into the other courtyards, see if there is anything else that will keep us dry.' Lightning flashed from over the ridge, and I counted till the next boom of thunder. The storm was coming our way.

The first walled area I tried was mostly covered in a thicket of weeds, and I rummaged through them in vain for any booty. I found what we needed in the final enclosure, long and beautiful and still tangled in its parachute lines, although the canopy had rotted and blown away. For the first time in an age I thanked God profusely. I unclipped the fasteners and prised off the lid. There was a long, soft tearing sound as the two halves parted. I prayed once more, this time that it wasn't a container of replacement boots, bandages, helmets or chocolate bars. I waited until my eyes adjusted to the gloom within and I could make out the boxes. I felt a warm glow of relief. We were in business.

I hurried back to Lindy.

'What is it?' she asked.

'Come with me.'

'What have you found?'

'A present from your father.'

Thirty-Five

Of course I couldn't be certain it was a supply cylinder from Bill Carr's Liberator, but it was a nice thought. It was the right size, eight feet long, but I guessed that scores of them had been dropped in this part of the world in 1944 and 1945. I caught the expression on Lindy's face, though, and realised she was convinced it was from her father's plane. I squeezed her arm.

'Better late than never, eh?' she said. 'Does this mean that he's . . .'

I shook my head. 'Somewhere near? No. It just means he let the cylinders go. He could have crashed miles away.'

The rain was coming down heavily now, plastering her hair to her face. I found a waxed cotton sheet inside the steel tube and wrapped it around her shoulders.

I took out those supplies for which we had no immediate need, such as the dried food rations and cooking utensils, and put them to one side. I began a second pile of useful items, beginning with a first-aid kit and a pack of what were labelled 'energy' bars. Next out was a wooden crate. The planks broke easily, and the raindrops thrummed onto the thick waxed paper within. I tore through it with my fingers and felt steel.

It was another Mark II Sten. Borrowing Lindy's lighter, I read the marking on the top of the magazine housing. STEN MK II LONG BRANCH 1943. That made it Canadian. I did the same with the weapon she had taken from Ragno. There were the same markings. That suggested Fausto and Co had found another cylinder at some point and kept quiet about it. I remembered Ragno at Domodossola being very cagey about where he had acquired his brand new Sten. It made it very likely that my original thought had been right – that this particular cargo had come out of the belly of EH-148.

There was a second Sten and a box of ammunition. I didn't like these crude machine guns as weapons – I preferred my Colt, any sane man would – but in terms of sheer firepower and noise, they made us a small army. Then came a metal case marked *20 × GP Mk 5*, which made us a large army. I lifted it out very gingerly. There was no telling what two decades might do to grenades. It was when I reached the bottom of the tube that I began to feel giddy. I chuckled to myself.

'What is it?'

'Bloody marvellous, that's what it is.'

Not all supply cylinders would have had identical contents, and I was sure that the one where Ragno had found his Sten hadn't contained the six-foot-long crate that occupied the depths of this one. I used the lighter once more to read the crude stampings. *M9A1*. My history of ordnance was rather basic and I muttered to myself.

'What's wrong?' asked Lindy.

'I am wondering if this is magneto or battery operated.'

'Why?'

'If it's battery, it's more than likely useless after all this time. If it's magneto, well, we're in with a chance.'

'What's in it?'

'Give me a hand to lift it out and I'll show you.' I reached in and heaved up one end; she grabbed the other. 'It was named after a musical instrument used by a comedian, I think.'

281

The pair of us manhandled it down to the ground. This crate had been nailed good and tight, so I fetched one of the old screwdrivers from the box of nuts and bolts and began to lever away at the plywood.

We both jumped as a zig-zag of electricity seemed to hug the mountainside, snaking off into the far distance. The clap of thunder immediately boxed our ears. The storm was overhead. It might move along soon, with a bit of luck. I looked at my watch. Eighteen minutes left. Just over a quarter of an hour to learn a set of totally fresh skills. As I pulled the lid off the crating with a squeal of protest from the nails, I tried not to think of old dogs and new tricks. Particularly wet old dogs. I ripped the top from the box, flinging the planks over my shoulders.

'What is it?' repeated Lindy.

'A bazooka.'

I hauled the weapons over to the gateway of the fort and considered what Fausto would do now. It was the same old partisan out there, and he would be running through familiar scenarios. I tried to put myself in his position. We held the high ground, were armed – better than he knew – and he probably didn't have enough men to rush us, not without inviting more casualties.

Who would be left out there? Fausto himself. Rosario. Pavel? Maybe. They weren't good odds. I'd got lucky with Ragno. I just had to hope my luck held. The rain eased, and I caught the sound of a rockfall some way distant. I strained my ears, not sure if I had imagined it.

'Did you hear that?'

Lindy nodded. 'Sounded like stones falling.'

I peered up into the thinning rain, scanning the cliff face, but could see nothing. 'Idiot,' I said to myself.

She lowered her voice, as if we might be overheard. 'What is it?'

We listened intently again to the sounds of the night and the storm. I thought I picked up more movement, but Lindy disagreed. 'And I've got younger ears than you,' she reminded me.

'Maybe. But I didn't imagine the first one.'

'Could be a goat.'

'No.'

'Are you sure?'

I stifled a laugh. 'Of course not.'

I took the bazooka, checked it didn't have one up the spout, and hoisted it onto my shoulder. I held my breath as I pulled the long lever that functioned as a trigger and heard the crackle of an electrical spark in my ear. Magneto, you little beauty, I thought. Maybe we aren't going to die tonight after all.

I summoned Lindy to my side and sheltered us beneath the archway of the gate while I ran through what I thought their strategy would be if we were outflanked from above. I then outlined our response.

'Sounds reasonable,' she said in a tone that suggested it was anything but. I caught her shaking her head in disbelief. I'd been through stuff like this before, so I could believe it was happening. She must have thought she'd be waking up soon, telling Furio over breakfast all about the daft dream she'd had.

'Reasonable? That's the one thing none of this is. You shouldn't be out here, for a start.'

'Hey, as I remember I switched the fan on and helped heave the shit into it. Lang didn't have to bully me, you know. He just told me . . . Well, it doesn't matter now, I guess.'

'You can tell me all about Archibald Lang later,' I said, hoping she wouldn't ask me if there was going to be a later. I opened the soggy cardboard box that held a dozen energy bars, ripped the greaseproof paper off one and bit into it. It was some kind of compressed fruit and cereal, horribly chewy, but as far as I could tell, still edible. I handed Lindy one.

'Christ,' she said as her teeth struggled into the bar. 'You might as well have left the wrapper on.'

'I'll do the chicken chasseur in a while,' I said. 'Right now, it's all we've got.'

A gust of wind moaned through the dilapidated doors and swirled around us. It sounded like the cry of a human being. 'Are you scared?' she asked quietly, as she took another mouthful of the rations.

'Yes.'

'Oh.' She swallowed hard. 'I'm terrified, Jack.'

I reached out and touched her face and could think of nothing to say but, 'So am I.'

She shook her head in disbelief. 'The brave TT rider? Mosquito pilot? Tally-ho and all that? I thought you were never scared, you guys.'

I pulled her close. 'We're always scared,' I admitted. 'Just a little. It's what keeps us alive.' I even half-believed it myself.

Thirty-Six

The voice I had come to hate drifted from the trees, again stretching my name so it sounded like an insult. '*Jaaaaack!*'

I closed my eyes. So he wasn't trying to outflank us personally, someone else was up in those cliffs. Fausto was still in the woods, aiming to keep our attention over there while the others sneaked behind us. At least, that was my best guess.

'Time's up, Jack. Come on out.'

'You know what to do?' I asked. Lindy nodded. 'Sure?'

'I'm sure. We're going to be all right, aren't we?'

'Yes, we are,' I said with all the conviction I could muster.

If a twenty-year-old magneto works; if they don't get you first; if your one good arm is still up to the job.

I'd forgotten what a miserable bastard that little voice could be sometimes.

'Go under the steps, close to the wall,' I breathed. 'Once I fire, then you begin. Just keep going until I tell you to stop. OK?'

'Yes.'

'It's risky. You'll be out in the open.'

'I'll be fine.'

'Arm OK?'

She seemed to grow two inches, irritation in her voice, the

vulnerability gone. 'Stop fussing. Don't worry about me, fly boy,' she said brusquely. 'You just do your part.' She used the oilskin to create a makeshift sack and loaded it with her grenades before taking up her position.

I moved further back into the darkness of the entrance until I hit the remains of the CrossCountry, and I thought for a moment what my father would say if he could see me now. I imagined him shaking his head, rolling up his sleeves, and getting stuck in to help. I wished he was here.

'*Jaack!*'

'*Fausto!*' I yelled back, my voice ringing off the old stone that surrounded me.

While I waited for a reply, I slid a shaped charge into the bazooka, locked it into place and hoisted the tube onto my shoulder once more, pulling it in as snugly as possible. I had no idea how much recoil one of these things had, nor much idea how you ranged them. A bit of on-the-job training was imminent.

'What do you say?' Fausto called out. 'Last chance?'

I whispered to Lindy: 'Your young ears get a direction on his voice?'

'Best I can,' she hissed back from her hiding place.

'More or less straight ahead of you, I think. Can you manage the distance?'

She tutted. 'I told you. I could always bowl my cousins out. Regular Ray Lindwall, me.'

Now probably wasn't the best time to tell her I knew nothing about cricket. I just hoped this Lindwall was good, fast and accurate, because that was what I needed.

I elevated the snout of the bazooka, felt the cold metal against my face, aiming up at the dark slab of granite that loomed over us. The bad weather was rolling away across the plains now, and there was the faintest glimmering of stars, enough for me to make out the jagged line where cliff met sky. However, that was hundreds of feet above me. Too high for them to climb, I suspected. No, they would be moving lower down, along one of the terraces that nature had carved into the cliff face. I would have to wait for them to show themselves.

I raised my voice. 'It's like this, Fausto. You'll have to come and get me.'

'I'm sorry to hear that,' said Fausto loudly. 'You give us no choice then.'

Two muzzle flashes flared simultaneously from above, to my right. The fort filled with the ringing of high velocity rounds hitting the stonework of the parapet, right where they expected me to be crouched. I heard Lindy swear as the fusillade began to move down towards her position beneath the stairs. It was time to find out what twenty years had done to the bazooka.

I swung its flared snout to point at the starbursts of light from the gun barrels, squeezed the trigger, and heard the magneto whirr, imagining the electrical spark travelling down the wires to the shaped charge. Nothing happened.

I pulled the metal level again, twice, harder each time, willing the spark to make contact. There was a hiss as the igniter charge caught and then a terrible roaring in my right ear and I felt a surprisingly small kick against my shoulder. A trail of sparks streaked upwards at a 60-degree angle, then the missile buried itself in the cliff face with a massive thump.

I was already thinking it must be a dud when the night was cut by an orange flash and the detonation came at me like a fist, carrying stones and rocks and dust, the punch throwing me back against the motorbike.

As I untangled myself from the bazooka, Lindy staggered forward into the courtyard and, ignoring the debris raining down around her, threw the first of our grenades in a high arc, over the wall and down towards where we thought Fausto must be. The explosion was a dull, feeble sound compared to the bazooka round, but I knew the effect they could have when you were on the receiving end. She threw four more, then gathered up the oilskin sheet containing the rest and took the steps three at a time up to the parapet.

Sections of the damaged cliff were still falling, debris smacking into the ruined roof of the keep. It was a far larger explosion than I had anticipated. Had I got really lucky and killed or maimed them? Perhaps they were just stunned. I would find out soon enough. I swapped the bazooka for a Sten, and went to join Lindy.

She was kneeling behind the low wall, pulling pin after pin and tossing her grenades down towards the treeline. She was a one-woman barrage, the thump of explosions and the whine of hot metal almost one continuous sound. I watched and waited while she heaved a dozen more before I grabbed her wrist. 'Enough,' I said, as the last one fell well short of the trees. She was getting tired. 'Well done.'

She shook her arm to unlock the tensed muscles, smiled at me, then indicated the cliff. 'That was quite a show. You got them?'

'I don't know. At the very least, it shook them up real bad.' I pointed with the barrel of the Sten. 'And being down under your grenades can't have been much fun.'

'Maybe he's given up and gone home.'

I glanced at the heavens. The light from the stars was glowing stronger now, the night no longer so bible black. I peered over the fort's wall and scanned the forest at the bottom of the rocky slope. It was motionless but for wraiths of smoke. I wondered for a mad, impetuous second whether Lindy was right, and Fausto had got the message not to mess with Jack Kirby. The answer, puncturing our premature self-congratulations, came as slow and laconic as ever.

'*Jaaaack.*'

Thirty-Seven

'Damn,' said Lindy with passion. 'I missed the son of a bitch.'

I shushed her and listened. I could hear him coughing, and when it came again, his voice was weaker than before. 'Jack.'

'How are you, Fausto?'

There was a pause before he answered. 'A little bit knocked about, to tell you the truth, Jack Kirby. You bring an arsenal up the mountain with you?'

'I found a drop canister. From the Liberator.'

I thought I heard him laugh. 'I didn't reckon on that. You always were a lucky bastard.'

'How do you mean?'

He cleared his throat and put some effort back into speaking, so his words carried. 'You survived ditching the Mosquito. You got out of Domodossola alive. I thought it best we just kill you, but the others . . . they said the British would believe Fausto was dead if you told them, if you saw it. I listened to them. Stupid, eh?'

'How many of the others are out there, Fausto?'

'Just me.'

I wasn't going for that. 'Who flew the chopper in, then?'

'Ah, yes. Just me and the helicopter pilot, who is with the helicopter. He's no part of this. Hired hand.'

289

'Then who was on the cliff?'

'Rosario. Pavel. Hey – Jack,' he said, as if the thought had just occurred to him. 'You did what the Germans couldn't. You wiped out Gruppo Fausto. Congratulations.'

'You weren't Gruppo Fausto any more. Just a bunch of men living off Nazi loot with a nasty little secret you didn't want anyone to know. A group who killed anyone who got in your way – even Allies.'

Fausto groaned. 'What kind of Allies were the British?'

'The kind that sent you anti-tank weapons. That was a bazooka I used just then, Fausto. If you hadn't played silly buggers with the plane, Domodossola would have had real firepower.'

'If I hadn't played silly buggers there wouldn't have been a Domodossola.'

Thirty-four days was all you got, I wanted to say, but my teeth were chattering, my bones were aching and I was tired. I couldn't believe we were out here, arguing the toss over events that belonged in the history books.

'What are we going to do?' asked Lindy. 'Shall I get the bazooka? You still have some bombs for it.'

I shook my head. That wasn't how it was going to end.

'*Jaaack.*'

'I'm here.'

'I think you might have killed me, Jack.'

'You're already dead, remember, Fausto?'

'Looks like I can have a second go at it.'

'Better luck this time,' I said.

'I'm hurt, Jack. I think I'm bleeding to death.'

'What crap,' muttered Lindy. 'As if you'd fall for that.' She saw the look in my eye. 'Jack? Just blast the trees with the bazooka. Game, set and matchsticks.' I shook my head.

'I have no gun,' said Fausto. 'My old Labora has packed up on me. Can't even finish myself off now. Unless I club myself to death.'

'I could give him a hand with that,' Lindy suggested.

I was only half-listening to her. I had a fresh concern: if Fausto had pulled in the members of his old partisan group, then perhaps he had brought along his old lieutenant. And we'd been throwing grenades at her. Why hadn't I considered the possibility that Francesca was with him? Because I didn't want it to be true.

I hurried down the steps and from the toolbox scooped up a handful of washers and bolts and pocketed them. Then I picked up the medical bag, checked the contents and added the rusted screwdriver from the scrap metal to it. I slung the kit over my shoulder, along with the Sten, and dragged the bike from the doors to clear my way out.

'What the fucking hell are you doing?' hissed Lindy over my shoulder.

'He's in pain out there.'

'Oh, bollocks to that. He's just been trying to kill us both. Why don't you fire the goddamn bazooka at him and have done with it?'

'No.'

'And if he kills you? What then? What about me?'

There was a screech of metal on stone as I dropped the CrossCountry. A new thought came to me. 'Lindy, I need a favour.'

'What?'

'Your sweater. You got anything underneath?'

'Only underwear.'

'I need the jumper, if you can manage without it for a while.'

'Don't worry, I'll live,' she sneered. As she took off her jacket and stripped off the heavy ribbed sweater, I held her arm and looked at the wound. It was a thin red line, nice and clean. I took the sweater and she replaced her jacket. I took my own jacket off and pulled her jumper over my sodden T-shirt. The sweater was good and heavy and loose, just what I needed.

'Stay here. If there is any shooting, make a run out of the gates and to the right. Downhill. You can pick up the trail back past the meadow. Stay in the forest till dawn—'

'Don't go.'

'I have to.'

'Why?'

'To see if he's telling the truth.'

'About what?'

'Being alone.'

She understood now. 'You think *she's* out there, don't you?' I didn't reply. 'That's why you won't use the bazooka. You think *she's* with him.'

'It didn't even cross my mind until just now. But I hope not.' If Francesca was with him, especially if she was hurt or worse, then I was going to wish it had been me in that plane, not Furio.

'And if she is? If she's chosen Fausto?'

'I have to see. This has to finish face to face, I realise that now. I have ghosts to lay to rest.'

I could tell she was wondering how I could care for a woman who, at best, had lied to me all along. No doubt I'd be asking myself that same question at some point. But I did care. As I turned, Lindy grabbed my bicep. 'He's not some spirit from the past, Jack. Be careful. He's flesh and blood.'

And he's better than you, my inner cynic reminded me. I took her hand off my arm. 'I know.'

The left-hand door's ancient hinges creaked loudly as it swung back and I stepped out into the blue-ish light of a moon struggling from behind the clouds. I looked down at the contorted shape of Ragno, his crisped hands raised to cover his face. I was glad I couldn't see it. I took half a dozen paces beyond the body and stopped. I crouched, considering my options. I was exposed now, right out in the open. If the story of his gun failing was a ruse, there was probably enough starlight for Fausto to drop me where I stood. Then again, Laboras did have a tendency to overheat and malfunction if used on full automatic for any length of time.

To be on the safe side, I had to make sure he let me cross to the forest before he tried anything. If he really was injured, then I had something that could get me close to him.

'Fausto. I've got morphine. It'll help.'

'You are well prepared, Jack. You always carry drugs with you?'

'Surrettes, from the cylinder. I'll come and give them to you. No shooting. Truce.'

'Game of football between the trenches, perhaps?'

'Something like that. I need your word, Fausto.'

I cupped my ear to catch his answer, scattered by the breeze. 'You have my word, Jack. This war is over. Finished.'

Lindy hissed something to me from the battlements behind, but I ignored her. She was probably just trying to supply common-sense, and I had no need of that right now.

I slithered along the sloping path towards the trees. Halfway down, I spotted a clump of larger rocks to the right and headed for them, traversing the scree. I sat down, my back against the largest boulder, shielding me from Fausto. The damp and cold had penetrated even the sweater and I began to shiver. With unsteady hands I took the magazine from the Sten and laid out my motley collection of nuts and bolts and washers on the flat stones beside me. Then I searched the medical bag until I found what I was looking for – a roll of heavy, fabric-backed sticking plaster. I tore some strips off with my teeth and went to work. It was true, I reflected, that Fausto was better than me. At least I recognised that. It might just give me the advantage I needed.

Five minutes later, I reached the edge of the woods and its dense ground-cover of pine needles. I listened for something other than the sound of my breathing and the slow drip of rainwater off the branches. The blackness between the trunks seemed almost solid. 'Fausto?'

There was no reply. I moved along the edge of the wood, past jagged trees which had been split by the grenade blasts, revealing pale innards. The stench of explosives was still heavy. Every few feet I repeated his name. After twenty-five yards I doubled back, not wanting to commit myself to entering the forest until I knew exactly where he was.

'Fausto, if you don't answer, I'm going back up to the fort, along with my morphine.'

'I'm here.'

His voice was loud in my ear, and I turned, bringing up the Sten, but something solid caught me under the chin and lifted me off the ground. I was out cold before I hit the pine needles.

I woke up sitting against a rough trunk on a mostly dry patch of ground, just on the edge of a small clearing. My lower face ached and my head was thumping. I moved my hands and legs to confirm I hadn't been bound or restrained in any way. That was a bonus. I patted the ground around me. The medical bag and Sten were both gone. I touched my jaw, trying to ascertain if anything was broken, but it moved freely, if painfully, in the socket. I could taste blood; my tongue explored my mouth and found a loose tooth.

'You're OK.'

He was standing on the other side of the clearing, his face pale in the new moonlight. His hair was darker than I recalled, there was a trim, neat beard and he seemed more drawn, his cheeks shaded with hollows. The sardonic smile, though, was still unmistakably Fausto's.

'Hello, Jack.'

'You nearly took my head off.'

'I still might.'

'It's been a while, Fausto.'

'Yes, it has. Good morphine, by the way.' He indicated the first-aid kit at his feet. 'Thanks.'

It was as if I'd made him a cup of coffee. He always was very cool, Fausto. And *furbo*, a sly one, I reminded myself.

'You're really hurt?' I asked.

He sounded surprised that I asked, as if it were inconceivable that he would lie. 'One of my legs looks like steak tartare for about half its length. There is metal in there, I can feel it scraping the bone. Or I could before the drugs.'

'And you're alone?'

Fausto smiled. '*She's* not here, if that's what you are thinking.'

He hobbled forward, using the Labora as a walking-stick by pressing the barrel onto the ground and holding the stock. It was just long enough for the job. He held my Sten in his right hand. He must have been telling the truth about his old machine pistol: it had finally let him down. It was an antique, after all, a relic of a war even older than mine. As he moved nearer, I could see that his left trouser leg was torn and jagged, and something that belonged on a butcher's slab was peeking through.

'What happened, Fausto? When did you become a money-grabbing crook?'

He laughed. 'Is that what I am? I fought my war for nine years, Jack. After eight of them I realised that everyone was out for what they could get. Everyone. All had an eye on the world after the war. You British particularly. I helped free Domodossola. After that, Fausto's war was run. Italy was going to be the same old whore, a mess, a *bel casino*,' he said, 'and I was tired, Jack, so tired. It was time to think about myself, maybe for the first time. You know my father gambled away our farm? Then he hanged himself. Then the man he still owed money to took my mother and put me in the home for foundlings. I was three months old. I think I was owed a fresh start.'

I detected something I had never heard from the old Fausto: self-pity. 'Don't give me excuses. You did what you did.'

'Yes. I did what I did.' He let out a long sigh. 'We have business to complete.'

'I thought I had your word about not killing me.'

'Ah. I said that war is over. Finished. A lot of dead men. No more killing over things that are long passed.'

He waited for me to say something, but I knew he'd tell me what was on his mind if I bided my time.

'Francesca, though, Jack. That is not so long past, is it?'

'Is she all right?' I asked, trying to keep the panic from my voice. 'You haven't harmed her?'

'None of your business. She should never have been any of your business.'

'You had her followed,' I said flatly, as it dawned on me that he knew about our night together.

'Not at first. Not when I thought she was on my side, just throwing you the odd bone of work for old times' sake, or swatting you away like a troublesome fly when you came up here poking about. But later, yes, I did have her followed. Right to your bed.'

'So you aren't killing me for Ragno or Rosario, for finding out you killed Jimmy Morris, or about your ruse with Conti and the art treasures that feathered your nest all these years.'

He didn't deny the charges. 'No.'

'You are killing me for screwing your wife?'

'It'll do,' he said bitterly.

I was a bloody fool, not realising that making Fausto a *cornuto*, a cuckold, might be the real motive behind all this slaughter. Men have died for a lot less in Italy. He let the Labora drop, and steadied the barrel of the Sten with his left hand. My mouth went very dry as he pointed it at my chest. 'It's a good reason to kill a man, I think,' he said, the emotion gone now. 'Better than war or politics.'

Fausto made sure the slider through the trigger mechanism was set to single shot, pulled back the bolt, re-aimed the weapon at my heart and squeezed the trigger.

★ ★ ★

Click. You always half-expected a Sten to jam, even on single shot, so Fausto checked the magazine had shells in it and worked to clear the chamber and try again. He knew guns, and he was fast, but that fumble was all the time I needed. I reached up under my jumper and pulled out the pistol that I had taped to my chest in the hope he wouldn't do a thorough pat-down.

I shot him twice with the Colt before he even realised he'd been had. His eyes bulged in shock, his arms flew out wide and Fausto fell back, crashing into the soft carpet of needles.

Who's *furbo* now? I thought.

I crawled over to him, but he was gone already. He looked younger, more like I remembered, as if death had lifted the last two decades from him. I should have felt something, but I didn't. I had a lot of mourning to do, and there wasn't room for a man I had thought dead for twenty years. It had been borrowed time for him, that was all.

I unpeeled his cooling fingers from the Sten gun, pulled out the magazine and fetched the rusted screwdriver from the medical kit. I used it to flick out the steel washer that I had slotted into the face of the breech, the one that had stopped the bolt and its firing pin a precious three millimetres short of the cartridge. I'd known he was better than me, and I had taken a chance on him ending up with my gun. I checked the action on the empty chamber, then replaced the mag. Now I had a working Sten.

The noise behind me made me roll over and aim it, but a familiar voice said, 'Jack?'

I lowered the barrel and looked up at her as she came from the shadows. She had her own machine gun in her hand, pointing at me. It was none too steady.

'Do you mind?' I asked.

She looked down at the weapon. 'Oh, sorry. I thought you might need some help. Looks like I was wrong.' She slung the gun over her shoulder. 'Well done,' she added, without conviction.

I used the Sten to lever myself to my feet, straightened up and set about returning her sweater. 'Don't you ever do what you're told?' I asked.

'Not usually, no,' said Lindy, pulling the jumper down over her head. 'What about you?'

I laughed. I felt twice my age, wet, exhausted and bruised, not to mention surprised to be alive. I'd killed the man who once kept me on as BLO because he thought I was a soft touch. Maybe I had been, back then. Not any more, though.

I looked down at Fausto. His face already seemed waxy, like a shop-window mannequin's. I thought of all the questions I had wanted to ask him. There were lots of answers that had died with Fausto. Zopatti, for one, was going to be mad at me for not bringing him back alive. 'Fuck him,' I said aloud.

'What?' asked Lindy.

'I was just thinking,' I said, 'that I never do what I'm told either. Let's get out of here, eh? I think we've run out of people to kill.'

As I walked away towards the treeline, I stopped and turned once more and looked at Fausto's corpse, a dark stain on the forest floor, a bad man in a good place.

Thirty-Eight

The night had turned bright by the time Lindy and I made it to the helicopter in the meadow, the moon a large crescent behind it, illuminating our way, the clouds dispersed to shadows. The bodies of Lang and the others were still there in the wild grass, more victims of Fausto and his sly machinations.

The nervous chopper pilot, who must have thought World War Three was being rehearsed up the road, didn't need much persuading by two gun-toting maniacs that it was best to get out of there before morning and the police arrived. With the storm passed, there was enough light for him to get us from Val Grande and over the mountains in safety. On the way back, we dropped the Stens into the lake, where they belonged. Somehow, I couldn't bring myself to do the same with the Colt. Not yet.

We landed at a helipad the pilot knew in the grounds of a fancy hotel, and from there we caught a cab to Lindy's lodgings. It was only just after midnight, barely into a new day. Both of us were drained, right down to the marrow. However, united by the nervy satisfaction of surviving the worst day of our lives, we sat and talked, mostly about her father, her future and Furio. She raided the kitchen and we drank strong black coffee and chewed *amaretti* until the first tentative streaks of morning appeared outside her window.

299

Then I kissed her on both cheeks and went back to my own bed, before I passed out on hers. When he saw me walk from the lobby, the taxi driver ostentatiously put a blanket on the back seat of his Alfa, in case any of my grubbiness was contagious. As he drove away after dropping me off, I examined my meagre change and realised he'd charged me some sort of grime supplement. I was too weary to care.

There were two familiar cars parked outside my hotel, one a sleek silver Mercedes, the other a little Alfa sports. Of course. Furio would have been reported overdue after dark. The search planes were probably warming up even now, at first light. So people had come looking for me, too, in case I'd made it back.

As I walked past the Merc I saw that there was someone in the driver's seat. I peered in, then rapped on the glass. The figure sat up and wound down the window. 'Morning,' I said. 'Given the chauffeur the night off?'

Zopatti blinked away the sleep and smoothed the creases from his jacket. 'Yes.'

I indicated the hotel. 'You'd have been more comfortable inside.'

'I didn't want to miss you.'

'You were certain I was coming back?'

'Pretty certain, Mr Kirby. You struck me as the sort who always comes back.' I wasn't sure if he meant like a bad penny, but I let it pass. 'What happened out there?'

'Turn the car engine and the heater on and I'll tell you.'

He obliged and I climbed into the passenger seat. I rotated the dashboard air vents so that the warmth played onto my face and I told him everything, from Furio's crash onwards. All I filleted out was the real reason Fausto wanted me dead. It was best to let Zopatti think this was about ancient history. He listened without interrupting until it came to the part where I shot Fausto.

'You're sure he is dead?'

'Oh yes.'

'Pity.'

'Why?'

'He could fill in some gaps for me.'

'Like what happened to the loot?' I asked.

'Yes. Perhaps the wife . . . ?'

'Francesca? Fausto told me she knew nothing about the robbery, the trucks or the stolen artefacts.'

Zopatti raised a disbelieving eyebrow. 'She was his wife.'

'*Nothing*,' I repeated with some force. 'He was quite adamant.'

Zopatti shrugged to indicate he was prepared to let that go.

'It was all Fausto,' I continued. 'And his alter-ego, Conti. I think he had been fighting too long, and by forty-four he went under. I saw pilots crack in six months. He fought for eight years – Franco and then Mussolini. Maybe after all that, he thought the coffers owed him a little payback.'

'Perhaps. I think it best we leave all such speculation to the professionals. You will repeat all this formally for me?'

'I killed men up there, Dottore,' I reminded him wearily. 'People I thought were my friends.'

'In self-defence. I will send a team to clean it all up this morning. You needn't worry about the police. This is for internal consumption only.'

'Lang?'

'SISDe will get the body back to the UK.'

'And an obituary in the *Telegraph* will say he died peacefully at home, a good and faithful servant to the end.'

'I would imagine so, Mr Kirby. Will you be OK?'

I nodded. The shock of what I had done in those mountains would hit me, but not yet, not until my guard was down. I hoped I was ready for it.

'What good will it do you, Dottore? Knowing what really happened back in forty-four?' I asked.

'Perhaps I just want to prove that no one side had a monopoly on corruption or ruthlessness back then. It's time the scores were evened a little.' He mimed a pair of scales with his hands. 'I'll be in touch, Mr Kirby.'

He turned the car engine off. It was my signal to leave. I held out my hand. 'Call me Jack.'

He took it and smiled. 'I'll be in touch, Jack.'

'And perhaps we can draw a line under all this.'

'A line?' He shook his head sadly. 'It will be a long time before Italy can draw a line under her war. But perhaps, together, we can add a few more dashes to it.'

I got out of the Mercedes and watched him drive away. He was right. The wounds of what had happened twenty years ago were far from healed and still had the capacity for hurt and might even tear a country like Italy apart if they were allowed to. Which meant that Zopatti and I were destined to be trapped in a war that refused to end. I'd been way off the mark when I said to Lang that all interest in it would fizzle out in a few years. I had to come to terms with the fact that, one way or another, I'd be living my conflict until I died. I just wanted to spend those years with someone who understood that.

The sound of my boots on the marble floor disturbed the snoozing night porter, who took my bedraggled appearance in his stride and told me that my friend was waiting in my room. She'd been there since early evening. He hoped that was all right. I told him it was just fine, but I had a sudden attack of nausea in my stomach. Would it be all right?

As I waited for the elevator, I thought about one thing that had emerged from a long night of caffeine with Lindy. In a bizarre way, Bill Car had saved my life and that of his daughter. Twenty years ago, he had come round for a second run in his Liberator and, despite the signals being all wrong, he had ditched the supply canisters in the hope they fell into the right hands. They had, eventually. Without the weapons we discovered in the fort, Fausto would have killed us for certain.

I pulled back the well-oiled gates of the lift and stepped in. Next time I had a drink in my hand, I would raise it to Bill Carr. After all, he was hardly the only one who had pulled crazy stunts during the war. File under 'Reckless Bravery', and God bless him.

I let myself into my darkened room. There was enough light filtering through the curtains for me to make out her shape on the bed, still fully dressed except for her shoes. I called her name and she rolled over and swung her legs onto the carpet and was across in three strides, her arms tight around me, her face buried in my shoulder. 'I heard about the plane. I thought Fausto had killed you. He found out about—'

'I know.' I kept it simple. 'He's dead. I killed him.'

I felt Francesca go rigid for a second, then slump. I carried her to the bed. She was crying, and my heart went out to her as I laid her down. I took a hand, kissed it, muttered an apology, and turned for the door.

She sniffed back her tears. 'Where are you going?'

'To let you grieve for your husband.'

'You idiot. Come here.' She pulled me down next to her and threw an arm across my chest. It was a relief to have her perfume cut through the other odours of that night and I inhaled deeply.

She touched my cheek. Even in the half-light, she could see it was damaged. 'You're burned?'

'Not badly.' Not as much as poor Ragno or Furio.

'We have a lot to talk about,' she said.

'We do.' There was much I wanted to know, but a wave of exhaustion swept over me and I lay back on the bed and closed my eyes. 'But I need to sleep.'

'You need to shower. There is dirt in the cuts.'

'Later.'

'I'm sorry he's dead,' she said quietly.

'I know.' In a strange way, so was I. I wished the story of Gruppo Fausto hadn't ended so ignominiously. I would have preferred my memory of him to end with a crumpled body on a piazza, twenty years ago.

'But I'm more glad you are alive,' she said, and before I could reply, she added: 'You must think me callous, to say that.'

'No. You always were strong, Francesca.'

'Not strong enough when it came to Fausto. Or Riccardo. I couldn't break free when I should have.'

'None of us were strong enough, Francesca.' Ragno, Pavel, Rosario: three others who should have said no, who should have resisted him when he came calling with more demands for old times' sake.

'There you are being reasonable again. I think you are a good man, Jack Kirby.'

I snorted my disbelief at that. 'Rubbish.'

'All this time, you are the only one of us who has been straight and true and honourable. The only one.'

Francesca stood up and rummaged under the bed for her shoes, then slipped them on. There was the rasp of a zipper being done up.

'You're going?'

She nodded. 'I am going, Jack.' The weight of purpose in her voice made me tingle. This was a Francesca I hadn't heard for a long time. 'I shall be away for a few hours and then, when I return, we shall discuss what we are to do.'

'About what?' I fought and lost the desire to yawn.

'About you and me. About us. In the cold light of day. It's better that way. Right now, we might make promises we can't keep.'

I pulled myself up on one elbow. I could feel her slipping away from me. 'I won't change my mind in a few hours,' I said. 'I know what I want to do. I lov—'

She put a finger to my lips. 'We'll see.' She picked up her handbag from the bedside table. 'You'll still be here?'

'You'll be coming back?'

She bent over and kissed my forehead before she tiptoed away and slipped out of the door, closing it softly behind her. I shivered and wondered if I had just committed a terrible mistake by letting her go. Perhaps it was for the best; after all, we carried more baggage than ever before now.

Then I realised she *would* be returning. Francesca was made of tougher stuff than I was. I may have ducked out in the aftermath of 1944, but she had no intention of doing likewise. If there was a way to save us, to reconcile our past and future, she'd find it. At least, that's what I had to cling to for the next few hours.

I stripped off my clothes and wrapped myself in a blanket, slipped the Colt under the pillow and flopped down. I was so tired I felt like I was plunging down a massive chasm, into welcome darkness. As I fell, I recalled the pledge I had made to the memory of Bill Carr, the man who had inadvertently saved my skin. It went like this: no matter what the coming weeks or months held, no matter what happened with Francesca, Jack Kirby still had a Consolidated B-24 Liberator to find.

Acknowledgements

First and foremost, my heartfelt thanks go to Anne Storm, who allowed me to use her father's letter, and her search for him, as the inspiration of this story. Even though she knew I would play fast and loose with it (she had read *Early One Morning*, a previous World War Two novel), she gave me permission to go ahead.

Her father, Bob Millar, was in one of the twenty Liberators (sixteen of 31 Squadron SAAF and four of 34 Squadron SAAF) which took off from Foggia on 12 October 1944 in the late afternoon. Many of the pilots were RAF Flight Sergeants, because some of the SAAF officers were due to attend a party at 34 SAAF. Their mission was to drop supplies to the partisans operating in the Apennine and Maritime mountains of Northern Italy. There were four different drop sites with five planes allotted to each site. Bob was aboard the Liberator KH-158 piloted by Major Urry, SAAF. The crew was composed of five SAAF, two RAF and one RAAF – Flight Officer T. R. Millar, Anne's dad, who, like most of the crew apart from the pilot and second pilot, had flown a mission to Yugoslavia in KH-158 the previous night.

The weather turned nasty in the mountains, with many forced to abandon their mission. However, six planes never made it back. Four went down on the peaks (one plane missed crossing safely by just twenty feet, as related here), one came down near Cantalupa but the sixth, KH-158, went missing and has never to date been located. As no wreckage has been found, Anne now wonders if it went into the sea south of Genoa or even exploded in mid-air. Obviously she would like to hear from anyone who has information. See *http://freepages.genealogy.rootsweb.com/~stormrhb* and click on *The Millar Story*.

Much of the research about the events of 12 October was undertaken by Giuseppe (Beppe) Barbero and others, with Nick and Catherine Madina, in diligent trawls through the Public Records Office (now the National Archives) and Italian and South African sources, and in tracking down survivors and relatives of the various crews. The Madinas, who compiled all the research onto three CD-ROMS, helped Anne develop a detailed picture of the missions.

Lindy Carr and Bill Carr are total fictions, and the character of Lindy is not based on Anne at all, although they do share a certain tenacity: Anne has tracked down surviving family members of the other crew on board her father's plane (plus some crew relatives of the five crashed planes).

Details of the Warsaw run and other missions can be found in *The Men Who Went to Warsaw* by Lawrence Isemonger and *Airlift to Warsaw* by Neil Orpen.

I am indebted to Taigh Ramey of Vintage Aircraft in Stockton, California, who suggested Kirby fly an AT-11 and helped with technical details. A website he runs, *www.twinbeech.com*, tells you all about these remarkable planes. He was also kind enough to read an early draft of the manuscript.

The charming Francesca Lombardi lent me her name and her knowledge of Milan and Italian, for which I am very grateful. Her father Franco makes the best olive oil in the world, incidentally.

The thirty-four days of Domodossola are true but, although I have mentioned real names and some of the political differences (the British and the USA really did advise against the liberation), I have fictionalised the whole episode by inserting Gruppo Fausto into the action. There was no Gruppo Fausto. There were Nello, Fano, Ruggero, Morelli, Mimmo, Piero and Dido groups; there was, I have subsequently discovered, a partisan leader called Fausto, but no resemblance is intended at all. Apologies to such groups and to the Valtoce and Valdossola Formations, the Antonio Di Dio Brigade, 85th Garibaldi Brigade, the Piave division and the other partisan bands, all of whom fought bravely across the whole region for their freedom, and really did set the rest of Italy an example. The fictitious actions of Gruppo Fausto are not meant to impugn them, or their battle, in any way. The whole story is told in the booklet *La Repubblica dell'Ossola* (Grossi), widely available in Domodossola. I would like to thank Rachel Costa of Tuscany and Hither Green for translation and her above-and-beyond research in Italian sources on the subject.

Although the fascist republic at Saló existed, Riccardo Conti is a fiction. There were many fascist officers who worked against the regime from within, and several who really did audaciously switch between a role with the partisans and Mussolini's forces (for instance see p. 225 of Richard Lamb's *War in Italy 1943–45*, Da Capo Press).

As well as the many thousands of men and women in the partisans of all political hues who fought a hard and bitter war against the invaders, there were non-combatant citizens who played their part. Over 12,000 Allied POWs crossed the lines during the chaos of 1943–44; 5,000 of them were helped over the border to Switzerland, sheltered by Italian families along the way and led by brave guides through the mountains to the border. At the end of the war 75,000 'Alexander certificates' were issued as thanks to families who had helped escapers and evaders with food, shelter and clothing. Or, sometimes, just their silence.

The SS 29th 'Italienische' division did exist. It didn't, however, get involved in transporting loot. That part of the story was suggested by an incident related to me by an ex-RAF man, who swore that some French partisans he knew had grown rich attacking German convoys of stolen art and bullion. I could find no corroboration for it, but the idea took hold that there might be other motives at work alongside nationalistic ones. A friend of Anne Storm's, an ex-SOE man called Bill Pickering, has written about the Italian resistance (*The Bandits of Cisterna* by William Pickering and Alan Hart, Pen & Sword Books), and he has stories of in-fighting, murder and banditry among the partisans. Equally, however, there are many tales of bravery and hardship.

The Val Grande is now a national park, and it really is the wildest part of Italy, containing a chain of disused forts from World War One. It isn't quite as remote as I have suggested here, but it is a fascinating part of the country. If you visit the Lake Maggiore region you can do a lot worse than follow Kirby's example and stay at the Hotel Cannero in Cannero Riviera on Lake Maggiore. Maria and her family will take good care of you. I am indebted to Yasmin Sethna for pointing me in their direction.

Mussolini's prison/home, Villa Feltrinelli on Lake Garda, is these days a rather magnificent hotel. My thanks go to its General Manager Markus Odermatt who showed me around and shared its history with me. The tunnels described here as holding the loot did exist, but were mostly used as air-raid shelters. They now house the hotel's generators and heavy machinery.

The ever-helpful Jim Dowdall, a stunt co-ordinator and an ex-movie armourer, came up with Kirby's dodge with the Sten gun and the washer. It does work, but he suggests you don't try it at home.

For the Isle of Man scenes I have to thank Dave Wilson, who introduced me to the writings of Geoff Davison, and Terri and Ray Monks, who moved there from the mainland because of their enthusiasm for the races and to become marshals on the course.

They kindly, and gently, pointed out my errors. Any remaining gaffes are mine and mine alone. Some of the musings on the decline of domestic motorbike manufacturing are based on *Whatever Happened to the British Motorcycle Industry* by Burt Hopwood (Haynes Publishing).

I am grateful to Beth Cort, Bob Millar's widow, of Sydney, Australia, who fed me tea and homemade cakes while I explained how the story had grown from the letter. She was remarkably understanding of my approach, as was Bill Cort, the man she married after the war. After reading the book she wrote to me: 'At least Bob did at least see Ann, when she was three weeks old and we had a week together before he was posted overseas – a day I'll never forget.' Like Ann, she hopes that one day the mystery of KH-158 will be solved.

Thanks also to my agent David Miller, all at Headline (that list gets longer with every book) and, once again, to Susan D'Arcy. Finally, as always, my gratitude to Martin Fletcher, my diligent editor and a proper motorcyclist (a Triumph and Ducati man, now you ask).